John Ward

Experiences of a Diplomatist

John Ward

Experiences of a Diplomatist

ISBN/EAN: 9783337338343

Printed in Europe, USA, Canada, Australia, Japan

Cover: Foto ©Andreas Hilbeck / pixelio.de

More available books at **www.hansebooks.com**

EXPERIENCES OF A DIPLOMATIST,

BEING

RECOLLECTIONS OF GERMANY,

FOUNDED ON DIARIES KEPT DURING THE YEARS

1840 — 1870.

BY

JOHN WARD, C.B.

LATE HER MAJESTY'S MINISTER-RESIDENT TO THE HANSE-TOWNS.

London:

MACMILLAN AND CO.

1872.

OXFORD:

BY T. COMBE, M.A., E. B. GARDNER, AND E. PICKARD HALL

PRINTERS TO THE UNIVERSITY.

PREFACE.

THIS little work is scarcely one of those which require an introduction, for it is no more than a narrative of scenes and events which have passed under my observation in the course of a long residence abroad in an official capacity.

When I retired from active service I soon began to miss the regular occupations to which I had been accustomed, and I bethought myself of the advice given by Horace Walpole to Madame du Deffand, when she complained of *ennui*, not to be always reading, but to amuse herself with writing down the recollections of what she had seen. 'But why be constantly reading? Why not write something? It is more interesting. Write down then what you have seen, and, even if you are not contented with it, it will be pretty sure to amuse somebody else. My friend Mr. Gray says that if any one would only be satisfied with stating exactly what he has seen, without preparation, without ornament, without trying to shine, he would have more readers than the best authors[1].'

I pretend then to no other merit than that of having related faithfully what I have seen and heard. As to my opinions, they may be deemed right or wrong; but none have been expressed without serious reflection, and a deep sense of the duty of speaking plainly where one speaks at all.

[1] Lettres de la Marquise du Deffand. Paris, 1812. Tome ii. p. 300.

If I have not scrupled to censure the violence with which the Prussian government has extinguished the independence of so many German states, I am not blind to the benefits which may eventually accrue to the nation from the establishment of the new Germanic empire under the Prussian lead. Prince Bismarck may be regarded as the instrument of a higher power, whose work, even against his own wishes, must tend to the ultimate realization of national unity, and constitutional liberty, by the German people.

It may appear to some that I have undervalued the importance of the diplomatic profession ; and I have not certainly rated its general utility as very high. But this circumstance does not interfere with my respect for individual members of that profession, many of whom I have learned to know, and entertain towards them feelings of sincere esteem and personal regard.

DOVER, *December* 31*st,* 1871.

CONTENTS.

CHAPTER I.

THE important place occupied by Germany in Europe, and the influence exercised by the Teutonic nation upon the destinies of the world, must always make the state of society in that country interesting to us, and to the people of other states. In their powers of thought and intelligence, the Germans are so superior to other nations, that Englishmen have always something to gain by studying the nature and progress of the German mind. These considerations may perhaps serve to render acceptable the narrative of one who has learned to know the Germans during a thirty years' residence amongst them, and who has had the good fortune to be placed in favourable positions for observing and estimating the feelings and opinions of the nation at large.

Previous to the commencement of my official career, some accidental circumstances gave me an early predilection for foreign society and literature, and led me to devote more attention to continental politics than, I believe, is generally bestowed upon them by my countrymen. When I was a young man in London, qualifying myself for the legal profession, which I soon quitted, I chanced to be thrown a good deal into the company of foreigners, and I formed a friendship with an intelligent German, who not only taught me the language, but introduced me to some of the poets and philosophers of his native country. At this time my father held the office of collector of His Majesty's customs at Dover, and the occasional visits which I paid to the place of his residence suggested naturally enough the thought of making short excursions to the continent. During the years 1826 to 1831 I accomplished regularly autumnal tours in France, Belgium, and Western Germany, and always returned with instruction and delight from the novel scenes which I had witnessed in my foreign travels.

B

1

In the course of one of these excursions I had an interview with Barthold Niebuhr, the historian of Rome, who was then a professor at Bonn on the Rhine, and whose history had been introduced to the English public in an article contributed to the 'Quarterly Review' by my uncle, Thomas Arnold, afterwards head master of Rugby school.   Niebuhr occupied a comfortable house, in the hall of which was a large stuffed wolf, well known to his visitors.   He conversed with me freely about English society and politics, and seemed to be in the English sense a moderate Tory.   He admired Burke, Fox, Pitt, and our great statesmen of former days, and said he was rather puzzled about Lord Palmerston, who seemed to be forsaking his old political friends.   He read our parliamentary debates with interest, and thought that one of the clearest speakers was Mr. Daniel Whittle Harvey.   Niebuhr, who died in 1831, was at the time I saw him about fifty years of age.   His whole life, as well as his published works, shew him to have been a man of high integrity of character ; not free from prejudices, hating injustice, and sympathising warmly with the welfare of the mass of the people in all countries.   He began his career as manager of the Copenhagen Bank, and rose in 1816 to be Prussian minister in Rome, where he devoted himself to literary and antiquarian researches not less than to his diplomatic functions.   As a good patriot he detested the French, and their domination in Germany. His pamphlet written in 1814 in support of the claim made by Prussia after the war to the whole of Saxony[1] is a masterpiece of argument from the specific Prussian point of view, though it did not convince the Vienna congress.   In person Niebuhr was a short, thin man, with mild expressive eyes, unaffected in his manners, and simple in his way of living. Like his father Carsten, the Arabian traveller, he had refused to be ennobled, considering that a title of nobility would be an affront to the race of Holstein peasants from whom he was sprung.   Niebuhr's son Marcus was in the civil service of the Prussian government, and married a daughter of General von Wolzogen, a cousin of the wife of the poet Schiller.   I knew them at Berlin, and often talked with Marcus about his father, and his political views.   Marcus himself was very reactionary, and saw with regret the increasing power of the democracy in the English political system.   He told me that his father's former regard for England had much diminished in his later years, and that he greatly disliked the arrogant

---

[1] 'Preussens Recht gegen den Sächsischen Hof.'   Berlin, 1814.

and uncritical tone of our reviews and newspaper articles. I believe that both Barthold Niebuhr and his son lamented, in common with other German statesmen, the manifestly growing disposition in England towards a French alliance, and our reluctance to continue on an intimate footing with the three Eastern powers, in conjunction with whom we had restored tranquillity to Europe at the close of the revolutionary war.

In the summer of the year 1828 I passed some weeks in Paris, devoting my attention principally to the subject of French industry, of which an exhibition had been held there in the previous year[1]. But I could not avoid noticing the high degree of political discontent which prevailed among the intelligent classes in that metropolis, nor the anxiety with which the adherents of the Bourbons regarded the actual state of things. When I saw King Charles X, accompanied by the Duke and Duchess of Angoulême, in the cathedral of Notre Dame, assisting at high mass on the festival of the Assumption, I felt a presentiment that it might be for the last time, knowing that the Sovereign had no firm hold upon the respect or affection of his people. At the house of the Count de Noé, an old royalist friend of my father, the sentiments I heard were those of unshaken loyalty to the throne, mixed with apprehensions of insecurity, from the restlessness, as it was called, of the movement party. De Noé had seen much of the world, having emigrated to England during the revolution, and held a commission in the English army, in which capacity he formed a part of the expedition from India to Egypt under Sir David Baird, and published a narrative of that expedition in 1825, after his return to his native country. He possessed talents and ingenuity, drew very well, and did much for the revival of the manufacture of painted glass, a good specimen of which, constructed under his superintendence, is to be seen in a window of the Luxemburg palace. A son of Count de Noé, well known under the sobriquet of 'Cham,' is one of the first caricaturists of the day, and has contributed largely to the amusement of the readers of the 'Charivari,' and other journals. His son-in-law, Admiral Manners, lately deceased, was president of the London astronomical society.

I was present at several debates in the chamber of deputies, and among the speakers was much struck by the appearance of General de Lafayette, a dignified old man, with

[1] See 'Foreign Quarterly Review,' No. VI. Art. i. on Arts and Manufactures in France.

hard features and a brown wig, who had lately returned from his second visit to the United States of America, and was reverenced by many as the apostle of freedom in both hemispheres. He was without doubt a noble and generous character, sympathising with the rights and sufferings of humanity in all lands. It was he who presented King Louis-Philippe to the people as 'le meilleur des républics,' and who gave up the citizen-King as soon as he perceived him to be an egotist, and untrue to the principles which had recommended him to the French nation. Lafayette took a deep interest in the fate of Poland, and became president of a society formed in Paris for the relief of the Polish fugitives. The vice-president of the society was his brother-in-law, the Count de Lasteyrie, with whom I was well acquainted. He was an active philanthropist, and at his house I heard animated discussions respecting the improvement of education and the reform of the criminal law. His son, Jules de Lasteyrie, became a leading member of the chamber of deputies, and his relatives, M. d'Assailly, minister of France, and his wife, were much liked at Cassel, where I met them many years afterwards. When I visited Paris in 1831, the citizen-King had not had time to make himself unpopular there, whilst in England people had not yet acquired that confidence in him which gradually increased as it declined in France. Even the English who resided in such numbers in Paris, were generally impressed unfavourably towards the Orleans dynasty, although our ambassador was doing so much to promote a good understanding between the two countries. The hospitalities of the embassy were in those days most liberally distributed by Lord and Lady Granville.

The following letters from Count de Lasteyrie will shew the interest he took in the welfare of the lower orders and in the misfortunes of the Poles :—

[*Translation.*]   'To Mr. Ward.

'*Paris*, April 13, 1832.

'Sir,

'I have received the letter you addressed to me, with the books, and I observe with pleasure your undertaking (the useful-knowledge society) which is carried on in the most philanthropic views, to diffuse instruction among the lower classes. It is in fact the greatest service we can render to them and to the country. Indeed, we have in Paris a beautiful instance of what education can do for the lower orders of society. It is to the systematic instruction we have given in our schools that we owe the order which has reigned among us during the three days of July, when the people were absolutely masters, and could do what they pleased.

' Your political reform is very favourable to educational undertakings, and will doubtless provoke other ameliorations in your country. We have still much to struggle for here in spite of our revolution. For the very same men who governed under Charles X have still the power in their hands, and wish to direct it in ' the same sense. That is what causes great trouble in the country ; but I hope still we shall obtain eventually all that we have a right to claim.

' We are likewise much occupied in forming schools, but the government which is very generous in other matters gives us scarcely anything towards them. I have founded here a book-society to diffuse little books at cost price among the working people, and to found popular libraries, which have been quite wanting here.

' Believe me to be, &c., &c.,
' C. DE LASTEYRIE.'

[*Translation.*] 'To MR. WARD.

'*Paris,* May 7, 1832.

' My dear Sir,

' I profit by an opportunity to acknowledge your letter of the 12th of April, and to recommend to you a Pole who is going to London, viz., Mr. C. E. Wodrinski, a refugee, who was a member of the Polish national committee established at Paris. I hope you will receive him favourably, and give him such information he may want in order to promote the interests of that glorious and unhappy nation.

' I learn with pleasure that you have established a literary Polish association, which is a good thing. But after the misfortunes of Poland, the violation of the most sacred treaties, and the barbarous treatment of the Poles by the Russian tyrant, it was the duty of all the friends of humanity, justice, and liberty, to unite themselves for the support of a nation which the hatred of liberty, and the despotism of all the kings of Europe, have delivered up to the vengeance and fury of a despot who has violated his oaths, and the treaties made by those same kings. The holy alliance continues the impious league which it has formed against the liberty of every people ; and the revolution of July, far from inducing it to renounce its infamous projects, has only inspired it with new fears, and still harsher measures. It has even deemed itself authorised so to act by the perfidy of the French government, which through cowardice has thrown itself into its arms and betrayed the popular cause. This system, as fatal for France as for all nations, has plunged us into a chaos, and a deplorable position, which may one day cost Europe much blood and misery ; for it is impossible that the system they have wished to impose upon us can last, and, as the government wishes to maintain it, that can only end in a lamentable catastrophe. I presume you do not foresee all this in England, since your journals appear very ignorant of all that is passing in France.

'If you could organize a society to give assistance to the poor Poles, and to sustain their cause and nationality in England, as is done by our committee in Paris, you would render a great service to that unfortunate nation, and might influence its future existence. Try if you can excite the humanity of your countrymen in a cause so noble and so just.

'We have formed an association here for the purpose of publishing a journal in the interest of education, which has already a sale of some thousands ; but we find always the same obstacles thrown in the way of popular instruction as during the Bourbon restoration. The government, which promised much at first, has done nothing for us. The men who have seized hold of the government act only in their own interests. The only right left to the people is to pay very heavy taxes for these gentlemen to divide among themselves.

'The Polish society of Paris, of which General Lafayette is president, and myself vice-president, will be very glad to enter into correspondence with your association with the view of rendering services to individuals, as well as to the cause of heroic Poland. When Dr. Bowring, who is now at Lyons, returns to Paris, I shall charge him to take over to the society of useful knowledge the last numbers of my " Journal des connoissances utiles."

'Neither I nor any of my family have been attacked by the *cholera*, except a servant, who is now recovered. I have never been afraid of it, and trust that the temperate way of life I have always followed will preserve me from it. But happily the disorder is diminishing every day.

'I have requested Mr. Wodrinski to hand to you the rules of the literary Lithuanian society just established in Paris.

'May you continue well, and believe in the attachment of, &c., &c. 　　　　　　　　　'C. DE LASTEYRIE.'

Three years afterwards I received from my friend Edward Abdy, since deceased, author of the book on slavery in the United States, and then sojourning in Paris, a letter containing the following remarks on the political state of France :—

[*Extract.*]   ' *Paris*, December 4, 1835.

' Matters are going on quietly here, and not likely to be disturbed. No one knows what the government is about. Perhaps, as the Carlists have rejected its advances, it may seek support and consolation among the opposition. Commerce is flourishing, and people think more of making money than of breaking heads. There seems to be some chance, however remote, for Poland, whose cause is popular not only here and in England, but even in Austria. More extraordinary things have taken place than an union of the latter with the former. I trust, whatever may take place, that the next revolution will be of a moral nature, and that the possessors of power will yield to the resolution of passive resistance and temperate remonstrance what they have hitherto refused to violence and intrigue.

' I wish I could give you facts rather than conjectures, that you might exercise your reasoning powers instead of receiving what the want of them in another may suggest. This country is in a singular state. The king is disliked ; the ministry are distrusted, while the people are calm with a muzzled press and a menacing soldiery. It is the dread of a convulsion, rather than the feeling of contentment, which preserves the balance ; and the nation submits to a nominal oppression in order to escape the horrors of real anarchy. I am inclined to think that commercial ameliorations will lead to political improvement here, and that the various companies and associations which trade and agriculture are creating will produce a more liberal system of administration.'

The Belgian revolution of September, 1830, was characterized in England as a bad imitation of the July movement in Paris. This was a great mistake. The insurrection of the Belgians was a protest against the ill-conceived arrangements of the Vienna congress, whereby an united kingdom was formed out of different nationalities, of opposite religions, and whose interests, in various ways, conflicted with each other. I passed in Brussels a part of the autumn of 1829, and, having had opportunities of mixing with the political leaders, I saw pretty clearly that an attempt would be made before very long to liberate the country from the rule of Holland,

and this opinion I ventured to publish soon afterwards in a London journal[1]. As a place of residence, Brussels made upon me an agreeable impression. It was not then costly, and the society was diversified and easy of access. Among the English families then residing there was that of Lord Blantyre, who was highly respected, and whose death excited much sympathy in his own country. He lived in the *rue royale* fronting the park, and I dined with him in the very room at the window of which he was unfortunately shot by a ball from the Dutch army during the attack upon Brussels in the September following. In the beginning of their revolution the Belgians certainly shewed great energy and courage, and they deserved success, although they were not permitted to retain the whole of Luxemburg, and even the separation of the Belgic provinces from Holland was not finally effected until some years later. Among the revolutionary leaders were some remarkable men with whom I was personally acquainted, and I shall therefore try to sketch their characters briefly in the following pages.

Louis de Potter had one of those ardent minds, which, while sincerely seeking truth, constantly push their own convictions to extremities, and are therefore in political movements usually found impracticable by the men of their party. He was a native of Bruges, and possessed a considerable independent fortune. In his youth he visited Italy, resided a long time in Rome and at Florence, and did not return to Belgium until the year 1817. He first acquired notoriety by several works written in a spirit of hostility to the court of Rome and to the exclusive principles, as he termed them, of the catholic church. These works had, however, little of a theological character, De Potter having had no sort of inclination towards protestantism, but were intended to shew the supposed danger to the world of the undue extension of ecclesiastical power. The most important of them was the life of Scipio de Ricci, Bishop of Pistoja, and introducer of various church-reforms in Tuscany under the government of the Grand-Duke Leopold[2]. It is matter of history that this reforming bishop assembled a synod at Pistoja in 1786, which adopted the famous four articles previously accepted by the assembly of the Gallican clergy in 1682, and thereby disputed the infallibility of the visible head of the christian

---

[1] See 'Foreign Quarterly Review,' No. X. Art. i, on the present state of the Netherlands.

[2] 'Vie et pontifical épiscopal de Scipion de Ricci.' 3 vols. Bruxelles, 1825.

church. He was supported by the Grand-ducal authority of Leopold, and would probably have carried out this and other alterations of the existing religious system, had not the death of the Emperor Joseph II removed his brother Leopold from Tuscany, and placed him on the Imperial throne. The consequence was that Bishop de Ricci was prosecuted and imprisoned, nor did he recover his full liberty until he had recanted his errors by accepting the bull *auctorem fidei* after the return of Pope Pius VII from his captivity in Paris, so that the projected introduction of the Gallican liberties into Tuscany did not take effect. De Potter of course sympathized with the bishop, and his book was evidently written with the view of damaging the Romish church in the eyes of the Belgian people, in which attempt he had little or no success. The doctrine of Papal infallibility does not appear to have had, either then or since, any opponents among either the clergy or people of Belgium, and the archbishop of Mechlin, Mgr. Deschamps, was one of its most zealous defenders at the œcumenical council of 1870.

I first made De Potter's acquaintance in the prison *des petits carmes* at Brussels, where he was undergoing a sentence of imprisonment, together with Edouard Ducpetiaux, for articles written by them in the liberal organ, the 'Courrier des Pays Bas,' against the Dutch government. De Potter had dark hair and eyes, and rather an Italian physiognomy, and his manner of speaking was quick and impetuous. He told me the whole story of the grievances of his country, which had led to the formation of a national association in opposition to the government. The ministers had procured the passing of an exceptional law, authorising them to punish summarily the authors of libels, and it was against this law, and against the banishment of two young Frenchmen, named Bellet and Jador, for satirical verses published in the 'Argus' newspaper, that the strictures of De Potter and Ducpetiaux, for which they were criminally prosecuted, had been directed. An union having been formed between the catholics and liberals in Belgium for the purpose of resisting the systematic oppression of the Dutch government, De Potter wrote vigorously in support of the union, and ceased, or at least suspended, all hostile attacks upon the court of Rome. In April, 1830, he was banished from his country in consequence of an alleged treasonable correspondence carried on from prison with M. Tielemans, an employé in the Foreign Office, and retired to Lausanne. After the accomplishment of the French Revolution in July, he wrote and published a warning letter to the

King of the Netherlands, exhorting him, whilst there was
yet time, to save Belgium from the impending calamity of a
civil war.   The admonition was however unheeded, and in
the September following Brussels was in a state of insurrection.   De Potter soon found his way thither, and was
chosen by acclamation a member of the provisional executive.
On the 10th of November, 1830, he, as President, opened the
national congress of the Belgic provinces, and spoke warmly
in favour of the establishment of a republic.   But the other
members of the temporary government having preferred the
plan of a constitutional monarchy, and tendered their resigna-
tions, De Potter found himself isolated in his views, and
deemed it his duty to relinquish his office, which he did on the
13th of November, and went to Paris, where he chiefly resided during the remainder of his life.

When I revisited Paris in the autumn of 1831, I saw De
Potter several times, and had some interesting conversations
with him.   He had no confidence in the régime of the
citizen-King, and intimated pretty plainly his opinion that
all constitutional monarchies were shams, and that the people
would never be governed for their own benefit except in a
republic.   I urged some objections founded on the abuses
notoriously prevalent in the United States, and I remarked
that in England we enjoyed practically all the advantages of
a republic, only that we had to pay something more for the
King's civil-list.   He said that America was a young country
in its industrial phase, and that the time would come when
public morality would be more firmly established there, and
the value of republican institutions be more clearly discernible.
In England he believed we were ruled by an aristocracy,
which must long be the case, considering the law of primo-
geniture, and the large estates and accumulations of capital
in individual hands.   There was little to be advanced against
this assertion, especially as Lord Grey's reform-bill had not
then been passed.   It must now be admitted that the constitutional government of Louis-Philippe was as great a sham
as that of Charles X.   What is the value of a representative
system in which the members of the legislature are habitually
bribed, by direct or indirect rewards, to vote in a certain way?
The more one reflects upon the differences between particular
forms of government, the less important do such differences
seem when compared with the degree of public virtue existing in the country where this or that constitution is to be
established.   The republicanism of the United States is no
doubt disfigured by political corruption, but is there not in

England a great deal of ministerial jobbing under our constitutional Sovereign? and is there any country in the world where statesmen are so pure that public morality goes before private interests in all political transactions?

In speaking of the alliance between the Belgian catholics and liberals, De Potter described it as a national one, arising out of a common sense of oppression, and thought they would soon separate, as the result has proved. He said the catholic party was, as in Ireland, chiefly led by the clergy, whose influence he regretted, as it seemed to him to raise obstacles in the way of education and other good measures. He did not believe in the divine authority of the catholic church, still less in that of any protestant sect, and spoke much in the sense of the well-known axiom of Napoleon I,—' la religion . vient de Dieu, mais les religions sont les fabrications des hommes.' De Potter was in fact a deist, not disputing the divine government of the world, but hating what he called priestcraft, and the system of religious persecution which was unfortunately too conspicuous in former ages. To my remark that there seemed a great deal of happiness in the catholic life of Belgium, he replied that he did not blame the people, but the hierarchy, which in all countries, whether catholic or protestant, had the same love of domination and was disposed to persecute, when it found opportunities. Look, he said, at your protestant church of England. Has it not been a persecuting church, and does it not debar all non-conformists from participating in the wealth and privileges which itself enjoys? I referred to the law lately passed by the British parliament for the emancipation of the Roman-catholics as a proof of the progress which the principles of religious toleration had made amongst us. He said he rejoiced at it, but much remained to be done in England in that direction, and that the voluntary system, as adopted by the United States, was the only fair and just one in matters of religion. De Potter appeared to me at this period to have a certain bitterness in his expressions, caused, without doubt, by his disappointments, and by the conviction that his political career had for ever closed. I liked him, however, for the candour and openness of his mind. He was a lettered man, and had seen much of the world; and there was far more to be gained by listening to his philosophic censures, than by attending to the frivolous banalities which form so much of the conversation in ordinary society.

But was De Potter a great character? Had he that elevation of soul which distinguishes the hero from the common

herd? Had he that just perception of his own relations to
the Eternal, and to mankind, which imparts to a man some
portion of the divine nature, and enables him to hope and
feel,—' non omnis moriar '? I cannot think so. The religious
element was deficient in him. A nominal catholic, he had
ceased to believe in the spiritual authority of his church; and
from that moment the dogmas of christianity became matters
of indifference to him, and he had no guides beyond his
moral sentiments and the varying considerations of political
expediency. He can therefore hardly be said to have left
behind him the mark of a great man, although he will
long be remembered in Belgian history as an eminent actor in
the scenes which preceded the liberation of the country from
the Hollander's dominion.

De Potter was an enemy to persecution, and it must be
admitted that several Roman pontiffs have laid themselves
open to such a charge[1], and that the duty of tolerating religious dissenters is a doctrine which has only of late years
come to be acted upon in European states. The catholic
church has never admitted that there can be any salvation
out of its own bosom, and, in the times which followed the
reformation, the holy see did certainly encourage the notion
that heresy was to be repressed by the extirpation or punishment of heretics; whilst the same principle was adopted
by those protestant sovereigns who unremittingly persecuted
their catholic subjects. But at the present day the public
voice in all countries is so strongly against any attempts to
force men's belief, that religious persecution may be said to
have almost entirely ceased. The feeling of all good catholics
is that persons of other persuasions are deserving of com-
passion, and of that charity which ought peculiarly to be
extended to those labouring under errors of so serious an
import to themselves. In short, we ought to love our neighbours, whether heretics or not; but not to tolerate heresy in
the sense of giving countenance or approval to it, any more
than we should to vice or crime. This is the language of the
excellent archbishop Deschamps, and probably there is not a
bishop or priest in Belgium who holds contrary sentiments.
The Belgian clergy, whilst adhering steadfastly to their
ecclesiastical duty, are a humane and charitable set of men,
and are valued and loved accordingly by their flocks. De
Potter was well aware of this, and indeed had many personal

---

[1] See De Potter's ' Lettres de Saint Pie V sur les affaires religieuses de son
temps en France.' Bruxelles, 1827.

friends among them, who vigorously supported him during the whole period of his energetic struggle with the Dutch government.

Edouard Ducpetiaux was a man of a different stamp of mind from that I have been describing. At once a political reformer and a pious catholic, he was full of philanthropic zeal for the good of his countrymen and of all mankind. He contributed largely to the 'Courrier des Pays Bas,' the organ of the movement, and when I first saw him, in 1829, he was imprisoned for libel, in company with De Potter. As a lace-manufacturer he was in independent circumstances, and thoroughly free from selfishness and personal ambition. After the establishment of a national government in Belgium, Ducpetiaux was appointed inspector-general of prisons and charitable institutions, the duties of which he executed admirably for many years, and he gave to the world a great variety of works on subjects connected with penal law, pauperism, social improvement, and popular education[1]. He approved of and advocated the discipline of solitary imprisonment, in common with the experienced criminal reformers of other countries, such as Charles Lucas, Julius, Crawford, and Russell. His final retirement from office was caused by a conscientious difference from the legislature upon the question of religious instruction, which only added to the admiration entertained by so many good men of the purity and benevolence of his character. I have received many letters from Ducpetiaux upon the topics which chiefly interested him, and I insert here the two following as characteristic :—

[*Translation.*] 'To MR. WARD.

'*Brussels*, June 18, 1832.

'My dear Sir,

'In availing myself of the departure of Mr. Biernacki for London to recall myself to your remembrance, I am equally pleased to enable you to make the acquaintance of one of the men whom I most esteem and venerate. Mr. Biernacki was minister of finance in Poland during the revolution; being now an exile, he has chosen Brussels for his residence, and is going to pass some days in London, in order to assist at the debates which will probably take place in the house of commons in consequence of the interpellations which will be addressed to your ministers relative to their conduct in the

---

[1] See, for example, 'Des progrès et de l'état actuel de la réforme pénitentiaire.' Bruxelles, 3 vols. 1837.

affairs of Poland.   Your relations with English journals may
perhaps enable you to plead in favour of the sacred cause.
Poland has had her days of mourning, but she has also had
her days of signal triumph ; overpowered an instant by
numbers, abandoned by all Europe, betrayed even by those
whom she had cherished in her bosom and loaded with
benefits, she has yielded without dishonour, but it will be to
rise from her ashes very soon.   Great events are preparing in
Europe ; the volcano roars and shakes itself.   An alliance is
said to be already concluded between Prussia, Austria, Russia,
and Holland against France and Belgium.   Which side will
England take?   Will she unite herself to the thrones of the
holy alliance in order to crush liberalism in Europe, or will
she lay aside for once her ancient prejudices, and make common cause with her brothers in France and Belgium?   Your
journals do not seem to me to insist enough upon the necessity of this new holy alliance to oppose to the old one.   You
have still too much of that old leaven of egotism which made
you isolate your cause from that of the nations which shared
your principles, and which had, like you, hoisted the constitutional flag.   You appear also rather to frown upon Belgium.
What, then, has our poor nation done to you?   Has it not
accepted as King one of the adopted sons of old England?
Has it not even blindly confided itself to the protection and
arbitration of the English government?

'Belgium already owes much to yourself, my dear friend, for
the generous support which you have lent her in some of
your most influential journals.   You will continue to deserve
her gratitude in continuing the work you have undertaken in
this respect.   Mr. Biernacki will tell you as well as I could
what Belgium is worth at this day, and what she has a right
to expect from her neighbours.

'You ought to have received a few weeks since some
pamphlets of my composition, which I sent likewise to Mr.
Bach and Mr. Senior.   They will serve at least to prove to
you that Belgium does not remain behindhand in the movements of civilization.

'Pray do not long delay writing to

'Your devoted

'ED. DUCPETIAUX.'

[*Translation.*]   'To MR. WARD.

'*Brussels*, February 28, 1838.

'My dear Friend,
'I take advantage of M. van de Weyer's departure to

reply to your letter of the 16th of January last, and to send you a report which I have made to the central council of public health on the state of the habitations of our working classes, and the means of ameliorating them. You have probably been making similar researches in your country. Have the goodness to indicate to me the sources from which I could draw to complete my work. We are also occupied in a more general manner with the condition of the labouring classes, and of the children employed in factories. I have the parliamentary report up to 1835. Are there any new documents published since that time?

'You are too indulgent to my own essays. What I have published on penitentiary reform has little value beyond the names of the distinguished men whose authority I have adduced in analysing or reproducing their opinions. I have wished to pay my little debt, and to contribute my portion to the common work, that is all; and I have found my reward in the slow but safe progress which penitentiary reform is making in Belgium. The new central prison at Namur, where condemned women will be subjected to a discipline quite monastic, under the control of nuns, is in the course of construction; and the government will soon present to the chambers a project for the creation of a house of refuge for juvenile offenders, of which I have drawn up the programme. Pray mention this to Messrs. Crawford and Russell, who, by-the-by, have never acknowledged a letter I addressed to them four months ago, with a copy of my work.

'I have just finished a book in two volumes on the state of primary and popular instruction in Belgium, in which I have sketched a complete plan of organization, applicable in some degree to your country also. I shall send you a copy soon, and you will see at least that I am not idle It is only in work that I find relief from the sorrows which have oppressed me, and from the bitter remembrances which often range themselves round me like menacing phantoms.

'I have read with real interest your excellent article in the "Edinburgh Review[1]." Works of this kind have more effect, and consequently more actual value, than isolated publications, which are less circulated, and only get appreciated in the long run. I wish therefore one or other of your reviews could have made mention of my last book. Perhaps you may be able to manage this for me at some leisure moment. You may also render me a very great service in taking notes of

---

[1] No. CXXX. Art. iii. on Prison Discipline.

any works published from time to time in England on prisons,
paupers, schools, and the improvement of the labouring classes,
and directing my bookseller, Mr. Fellowes, to forward them
to me.   What do people say of a book entitled " The miseries
and beauties of Ireland," by Jonathan Binns?

'You lead me to hope that you may come over to Belgium
with Mrs. Ward in the course of the autumn.   I shall make
a point of being at home at the time of your visit, and hope
to serve you as *cicerone* in our little capital, which is every day
more and more embellished.

'Believe me always
'Your devoted Friend,
'ED. DUCPETIAUX.'

As illustrative of the tone of Ducpetiaux's mind, the following
passage from the preface to his book on the penitentiary
system seems also worth quoting :—

[*Translation.*]

'It is to catholicism, I do not hesitate to say, belongs in
our countries the mission of regenerating prisoners ; it is upon
the concurrence and the zeal of the ministers of our church
that must depend the efficacy of penitentiary reform.   Why
indeed should not catholicism do with us what protestantism
operates in England, in Germany, and in the United States?
Is the catholic almoner less beneficent, or less enlightened,
than the reformed chaplain?   Has the remembrance of the
Vincent de Pauls, of the Fenelons, ceased to live in our hearts?
Can we not oppose with pride to the English and American
quakers our brothers and sisters of charity, whose devotion is
without bounds, and whose whole lives are dedicated to the
relief of human miseries?   Do we not already see in Belgium
and France religious women devoting themselves to the care
and instruction of condemned persons of their sex?   And can
we doubt, after that, the possibility of rallying religious men,—
men whose faith and charity do not exhale themselves in vain
words, or sterile demonstrations,—to the holy work of prison-
reform, a work entirely christian and entirely catholic, whose
result ought to be to restore the guilty man to society of which
he has violated the laws, and to God of whom he has misunderstood the commandments?'

Among the men who devoted themselves unceasingly to
the Belgic cause, first in creating, and afterwards in securing,
the independence of their country, there was none more conspicuous than Sylvain van de Weyer, who has lately closed
his long and important diplomatic career.   He began life as

an advocate, and held the office of state-librarian at Brussels, in which capacity he conducted me over the public library in the year 1829. He was a writer in the 'Courrier des Pays Bas,' and one of the counsel who defended De Potter and his friends on the trial which resulted in their being sentenced to banishment in April, 1830. Having, after the revolution, become a member of the provisional government, he was sent to London to sound the dispositions of the British cabinet towards the new state, and received satisfactory assurances from the Duke of Wellington and Lord Aberdeen, who were then in power. He was afterwards president of the diplomatic committee at Brussels, and returned to London with Count Hippolyte Vilain XIV, as commissioners to the London conference on Belgian affairs. In February, 1831, under the Regent, Van de Weyer was foreign minister; and upon the acceptance of the crown by Prince Leopold, he was appointed the King's envoy to the court of St. James's, where he remained for more than forty years, having taken an active part in the long negotiations between the five great powers, Belgium and Holland, which preceded the definitive treaty of peace signed on the 19th of April, 1839.

M. van de Weyer has long been so well known to the fashionable world, that it would be superfluous for me to dwell upon his many agreeable qualities, his wit, his conversational talents, and his oratorical powers, which during the revolutionary crisis he turned to the greatest use. He exerted himself in London, at first with small success, to remove the prejudices of those who fancied the Belgians were discontented without cause, and that they had only obeyed their turbulent and restless spirit in overthrowing the paternal government of the Dutch king [1]. Yet he lived to see a great reaction in English opinion, and to hear praises lavished on all sides upon King Leopold, and wishes universally expressed for the welfare and prosperity of the Belgian kingdom. As a lettered man Van de Weyer mixed much in literary society, and was a good referee on the subject of books. I remember meeting him at a breakfast-party at Mr. Senior's in 1840, when he gave an amusing account of the burning of a book (I think by Froude) which had lately taken place in the university of Oxford, laughing immoderately at the revival of such inquisitorial discipline by the

---

[1] See his clear and convincing 'Letter on the Belgic Revolution, its origin, causes, and consequences.' London, Hansard, 1831. The recent sketch of Van de Weyer's life by Theodore Juste contains many particulars worthy of notice.

protestant zealots of the nineteenth century. In the diplomatic circles I have always heard that Van de Weyer was a popular man, and his fortunate marriage with the daughter of a rich London merchant (Mr. Joshua Bates) enabled him to keep up the representative duties of his mission in a handsome style. When Madame van de Weyer married she was very young, but was notwithstanding acknowledged, in consequence of her husband's long residence in 'London, as the *doyenne* of the ladies of the diplomatic corps.

Jules van Praet, whom I knew both during and after the revolutionary period, rendered great services to King Leopold and to the country in his capacity of cabinet-secretary, and subsequently as minister of the royal household. He was a native of Bruges, and distinguished himself in early life by some valuable works on Flemish history, and on the ancient Flemish constitution[1]. He has since published a series of historical essays on later times. Van Praet had tact in business, and knowledge of the world, and was very valuable to King Leopold in the outset of his reign, when the King had little personal knowledge of the country over which he was called on to rule. The King frequently employed him in confidential missions to London and Paris, making him the instrument of his efforts to obtain more favourable terms for Belgium, before the negotiations were closed by the treaty of peace. Van Praet's historical investigations are well known in Germany, and have formed the basis of further researches in the same direction by learned professors of the German universities.

Among the many foreigners who had been induced by political and other considerations to seek an asylum in the Belgian capital Count John Arrivabene was a man whom one does not easily forget. His estates in Italy having been forfeited, he lived chiefly in the house of his friend the Marquis Arconati, and devoted himself entirely to philanthropic pursuits, in connection with which he occasionally visited England, where he had many acquaintances. He was well versed in political economy, had translated Senior's lectures and Mill's elements, and had published several good essays on economical questions of the day[2]. He had a childlike simplicity of character, and seemed to love everybody with whom

---

[1] Particularly his 'Histoire de la Flandre dépuis le Comte Gui Dampierre, jusqu'aux Ducs de Bourgogne.' 2 vols. Bruxelles, 1828.

[2] See his 'Considérations sur les principaux moyens d'améliorer le sort des classes ouvrières:' Bruxelles, 1832; and his 'Lettre à Monsieur Ducpetiaux sur les colonies agricoles de la Belgique.' Bruxelles, 1833.

he came into contact. As Sydney Smith said of Macintosh, the gall-bladder seemed to be deficient in his organization. Many years afterwards I was rejoiced to hear that he had returned to his native land, and that the sequestration had been removed which so long deprived him of the enjoyment of his large family estates. I have had many interesting conversations with Arrivabene on matters of politics, literature, and social improvement, and for some time kept up a correspondence with him. The subjoined two letters from him are given as characteristic :—

[*Translation.*] 'To Mr. Ward.

'*Château de Gaesback*, October 26, 1830.

'My dear Sir,

'I do not know how your friend could speak of my kindness to him, for I was able to do little, and nothing could excuse me but the extraordinary circumstances in which Brussels was situated when he was in it. When the people of Brussels were fighting against their barbarous oppressors, I was living in this castle a few miles from town. I cannot express to you the interest I took in the struggle. I went into Brussels as long as it was possible to go, and afterwards I went near it to get news. My sorrow was extreme when the news were bad; my happiness extreme too when the news were good; and when I saw the *secours* that the small town of Hal was sending to Brussels, the despair gave place to a great hope, which was realised in the most brilliant manner. The way in which the poor people of Brussels behaved themselves was full of courage and honesty. I was among them in the days of anarchy, when they kept order as well as any government or civic-guard, and I can assure you that they behaved themselves as honourably as possible, and that during the struggle many houses were left open without any protection, and the proprietors on their return found all things in their places. The house of my friend the Marquis Arconati was so for ten days; it was full of precious objects, and nothing was taken.

'I am very little competent to give you an opinion on the state of affairs in this country. It appears to me that the *gouvernement provisoire* behaves well in every respect, but in the military department there is a general complaint of the army not being yet organised. In civil matters it could hardly do better. The law of elections, the law that allows the people to associate together as much as they like, the law that gives to the people the right to elect the parish-officers, appear to me to be excellent, and are very popular. Yesterday the inhabitants of all the parishes of Southern Brabant named the burgomaster and the other officers. I went through many villages, and I observed general satisfaction in the population. There was in the people nothing hostile to the superior classes of society. Where a nobleman was popular he was elected burgomaster of the village. For instance, in this village the Marquis Arconati was elected burgomaster; in another near it the Count Wanderdick. In what relates to the form of the new government I believe the country is more for a constitutional monarchy than for a republic, and in my opinion at this moment the country is right. The difference between the one form of government and the other is nothing, when religious, civil, and political liberties are secured to the nation by the law.

'You will read in the newspapers of political clubs that are spreading themselves through the country, but I think that they are not fit for this quiet and sensible people, and will exercise very little influence on the body of the nation. I hope too that an end will be put to the disorders that have manifested themselves in some places, and which have also been excited by the enemies of liberty. The barricades and the revolution will go the round of the world, but I hope that the great share of liberty which your country already possesses, and the wisdom of parliament and of some of your statesmen, will secure it at all events from any great commotion.

＊　　＊　　＊　　＊　　＊　　＊　　＊

'To write in English is quite a *tour de force* for me. Excuse me therefore if I have given you less information than you wished, and believe me,

'Yours very truly,

'ARRIVABENE.'

[*Translation.*]　　　　'TO MR. WARD.

'*Château de Gaesback*, September 7, 1831.

'My dear Sir,

'Having lost all hope of being able to go to England this year, I replace so far as I can the pleasure of enjoying your company by writing to you. The trouble which you took in procuring me materials to complete my work on the charitable societies of the city of London, good or bad, has borne its fruit. The second volume is finished, and under the press at Lugano. I shall send you a copy of it, as well as of my translation of Mill's elements of political economy.

'I have just been reading again one of your letters in which you congratulate me on the bravery of the Belgians. But how all that has since changed! Nevertheless, the Belgians have not become cowards, but they do not know how either to command or to obey. The lesson has been a terrible one. I hope that aided by the King, who to judge by his conduct is a man of both heart and head, they will soon regain the esteem of other nations.

'You may well suppose how the events of Italy have interested me, in what a state of agitation they have kept me. Unfortunately the result has been bad for the moment, although I am persuaded that Italy is advancing towards a better future. In the meanwhile, our destiny is to suffer. For my part, as if my individual misfortunes did not suffice, it has pleased Providence to send me a new affliction; the Austrians have arrested my younger brother, and God knows what fate awaits him. For all evils the great panacea is work. I am therefore beginning to translate Mr. Senior's lectures. I possess eight of them, and beg you, if he has brought out any others since those published last year, to send them over to me, with any remarkable pamphlets on political economy, finance, or education, and some parliamentary papers. You see that I treat you as an old friend.

   *   *   *   *   *   *   *

'Ever your devoted,

'ARRIVABENE.'

When I revisited Belgium in 1838, I found the country thriving, and the people happy in the enjoyment of their newly-acquired independence. The losses which some had anticipated from the exclusion from the markets of Holland had taken place to a very limited extent. The manufactories of iron, cloth, linen, and cotton were flourishing, and the manufacturers were beginning to find the natural home consumption more beneficial than a forced foreign market, and that they were able to work without the artificial stimulus of the Dutch fund called the 'million of industry.' Foreign commerce was increasing, and a brisk trade was carried on with Holland, notwithstanding the warlike *status* existing for seven years between the two countries. Singularly enough, during the war the Belgians actually supplied the Dutch with arms to be turned against themselves; so superior are considerations of commercial profit to those of national hostility ! The clerical and liberal parties having gained their common object—the independence of their country—were again opposed to each other, and were contending with pretty equal forces for the majority in the legislature. The King was not popular with either party, but shewed the tact and moderation peculiar to him in balancing conflicting claims, and in facilitating the movements of the political machine. In the succeeding year the Belgian question was finally settled, as the phrase went, by the definitive treaty of peace between Belgium and Holland, signed in London on the 19th of April, 1839, and the neutrality of the Belgian territory was placed under the guarantee of the five great European powers. The treaty of peace did no more than justice in recognizing the effects of the revolution which delivered the Belgian people from the oppressive rule of the Dutch king ; but it did much injustice in forcing Belgium to restore to Holland certain parts of the provinces of Luxemburg and Limburg, containing together more than 350,000 inhabitants, against the will, not only of those inhabitants, but of the whole Belgic nation. The Luxemburgers had spontaneously associated themselves with the revolution, and the first wish of their hearts was to continue Belgians for better for worse. The London Conference, however, thought fit to divide that province, and to give half of it to Holland, together with half of Limburg, by way of compensation for the portion of Luxemburg left to Belgium ; and the efforts of M. Dumortier at Brussels[1], and of M. van de Weyer in London, to prevent the partition being made, were of no avail. An article which I contributed to a review[2], criticising the proceedings of the Conference, in regard to Luxemburg and Limburg, excited a momentary attention, but upon the whole the subject attracted little interest in England, and has long since been forgotten by English politicians. I allude to it here as one which had occupied my mind in the early part of life, and to shew that I had looked a little into diplomatic questions, before I had entertained any idea of entering the service of the Foreign-office.

On the return of Lord Durham from Canada in December,

---

[1] See 'La Belgique et les vingt-quatre Articles, par M. B. C. Dumortier, Membre de la Chambre des Représentans.' 4me éd. Bruxelles, 1838.

[2] 'British and Foreign Review,' No. XVIII. Art. vi., on the Territorial Dismemberment of Belgium.

1838, I acted for about four months as his private secretary, and then became official secretary to the New-Zealand colonization company, of which he was governor. Lord Durham, who shewed me much kindness, was a methodical man of business, and the numerous letters and papers which he received were always punctually answered and disposed of. Lord Durham's impetuous character sometimes led him into violent expressions, but he was generous, open, and sincere, beyond most statesmen of his time. He was, in fact, one of those firm and fearless politicians to whom Goethe's lines might so well be applied :

> 'Firm at the helm the steersman stands :
> The wild winds make the ship their sport,
> But cannot shake his manly heart[1].'

Charles Buller, M.P., who had been his official secretary in Canada, was much at Lord Durham's. I need say little here of that amiable and accomplished man, except that I shared the deep regret felt by all who knew him at his untimely death, after a short, though brilliant, parliamentary career. Lord Durham's chief adviser in colonial affairs was Edward Gibbon Wakefield, whom he took out to Canada with him, and continued to consult in regard to New-Zealand, and other public matters which interested him. Wakefield and I were on friendly terms; indeed, he was liked by all who were pursuing the same objects, and came much into contact with him. He was, I admit, rather unscrupulous, and had done things which led many to doubt the integrity of his moral character. But I have since met with so many unscrupulous characters, especially in high places, that I feel it would be unjust to reproach the memory of a man like Wakefield, who was full of philanthropic enthusiasm, and effected a great deal of good in his generation. His well-known book, 'England and America,' published in 1833, is full of original and comprehensive views of the condition of society in both countries, and of the benefits to be derived from systematic colonization.

> [1] 'Er steht mannlich an dem Steuer :
> Mit dem Schiffe spielen Wind und Wellen,
> Wind und Wellen nicht mit seinem Herzen.'

CHAPTER II.

Official Appointment.   King Leopold.   Hamburgh in 1841.   State of
Society.   Sieveking.   Banks.   Von Struve.   Smidt.   Lappenberg.
Frederic William IV.   Tour in Germany.   Cotta.   List.   Von Roenne.
Mission to Berlin.

It was in the beginning of 1841 that I received from Lord
Palmerston, then foreign secretary, the appointment of British
commissioner for the revision of the Stade-tolls, an impost
levied by the crown of Hanover upon ships navigating the
Elbe, and which had become a serious burthen upon the
commerce of all nations.   The exertions of Mr. (now Sir
William) Hutt in parliament had excited a strong feeling
against these tolls, and our government was glad to embrace
an opportunity of getting them abolished, or reduced, through
the instrumentality of a mixed commission.   I accordingly
proceeded to Hamburgh early in that year, in order to meet
the two commissioners named by Hanover, and remained there
until towards the end of it, when the commission was broken
up, on account of our inability to agree upon a basis of reduction.   I, however, thoroughly investigated the question,
and made a full report to Lord Palmerston, which, in fact,
formed the foundation on which our government succeeded in
procuring the abolition of these vexatious tolls at a later
period.   Stopping at Brussels on my way out, I was honoured
(in consequence of an introduction given me by M. van
de Weyer) by King Leopold with an interview of some
length.   He received me after dinner in his cabinet, and,
adverting to the object of my mission, enquired what the
Stade-duties yielded in the whole per annum? how much was
paid on an average by each ship? and whether the money
formed a part of the public revenues of Hanover, or went into
the King's privy purse?   He mentioned that being half an
Englishman, he sympathized very much with the free-trade
policy which our statesmen had of late adopted, and hoped
our corn laws would soon be placed on a more satisfactory
footing.   The King said he was glad to hear that I had at
different times seen something of his dominions, and assured

me that trade and industry were going on very well. He
wished I had time to look a little more at Flemish agriculture, and mentioned the Pays de Waes as a district particularly worthy of a foreigner's observation. In dismissing me
he said, ' You know I am not without difficulties here, but I
take England as my model, and try to get on in a constitutional way.' I could not but be struck with the knowledge which the King displayed of English affairs, and with
the calm and reflective way in which he seemed to consider
everything. He was never popular in England, and our
ministers, especially Lord Palmerston, were believed to be
jealous of the influence which he exercised over their Royal
mistress. Nor can he be said to have been a popular sovereign
in Belgium, although he endeavoured to govern upon strictly
constitutional principles, and certainly worked hard for the
benefit of the country, which advanced and prospered greatly
during his reign, and gradually acquired a high degree of
respect from foreign powers. I have often heard King
Leopold called an egotist, and it is true that he was fond
of money and died very rich. Still it cannot be asserted of
him that he habitually sacrificed the interests of his people to
objects of his own; and with regard to his frugality, it is so
rare a virtue in princes that one is rather disposed to lament
that it should expose them to ridicule or animadversion.

Having arrived at Hamburgh with my wife, we soon made
acquaintance with the leading families, and were hospitably
received. The style of living was much less luxurious than it
is at present, still the dinners were good, and a great deal of
English comfort was perceptible in the houses. All the leading citizens had their country houses, chiefly at Ham and on
the Elbe side, where they regularly spent the summer months;
and the well-kept gardens and pleasure-grounds bore testi-
mony to the wealth as well as the taste of their possessors.
We enjoyed the hospitalities of the Godeffroys at Dockenhude,
the Parishes at Nienstetten, the Mercks at Horn, the Meyers
at Ham, and of several other agreeable houses. But the
foremost man at Hamburgh at this time was undoubtedly the
Syndic Sieveking, of whose civilities and kindness I shall
always entertain a grateful remembrance. On my first visit
to him to present my credentials, he received me in his gown
in the old *Rathhaus* (since destroyed by fire), and after touching upon the business of my commission, he launched out
into a discourse upon the benefits of colonization, praising
especially the operations of the New-Zealand company with
which I had lately been connected. Sieveking resided on his

estate at Ham, where he frequently received the diplomatic corps, and other persons of distinction. I took a house at Ham for the summer months, and had consequently many opportunities of cultivating his society. His intellectual qualities were of a high order, and his vivacity and constant good-humour made him a most agreeable companion. Sieveking was indeed much above the ordinary standard of Hamburgh citizens, and was not sorry to be occasionally removed from home by his diplomatic duties at the Frankfort diet and other places. He had even visited Brazil for the purpose of negotiating a commercial treaty between that empire and the Hanseatic republics. He was one of the three prime favourites of the King of Prussia Frederic William IV, the other two being Radowitz and Bunsen; and it was well known that the four men, with frequent dissimilarity of views, were kindred spirits. I had many interesting conversations with Sieveking on political subjects, and found him impressed with the rottenness of the existing constitutional system of Germany, the improvement of which he feared must be the work of many years. In speaking once of Talleyrand, he said, ' He is one of the many proofs that theology is the best school for diplomacy.' Sieveking was by some considered a pietist, but I never saw a man more free from religious pedantry or affectation. The German pietists are not a very numerous body, and have been a good deal laughed at, especially in Berlin, where they were accused of aspiring to court favour under Frederic William III and his successor. Sieveking, like Frederic William IV and Bunsen, was an enlightened protestant; Radowitz, on the other hand, was a devout catholic. So highly did Sieveking's character stand in the diplomatic circles, that it was at one time in contemplation to refer to the arbitration of the senate of Hamburgh the long-pending dispute between Great Britain and the United States about the Oregon territory, in which case Sieveking, as Syndic for foreign affairs, would in reality have had the decision of the question. He had watched with interest the annually increasing emigration from Germany to transatlantic countries, and being very desirous of establishing a German colony in the Southern hemisphere, he entered into a negotiation through me for the purchase of the Chatham Islands, belonging to the New-Zealand company, but did not succeed in overcoming the objections made by the Colonial-office to the transfer of the sovereignty over those islands to a foreign state. He, however, gave the impulse which led to a considerable emigration from Hamburgh to New-Zealand, as well as to the

British settlements on the Australian continent. Sieveking was an advocate of free trade, and complained much of our navigation laws, which at that time operated injuriously to German commerce, without conferring any substantial benefit upon the British shipping interest, for whose protection they were originally enacted. His death in July, 1847, cast a general gloom over his native city. The Syndic Banks was his successor in the administration of its foreign affairs. Banks was of a germanized English family, and there are in Hamburgh many such families, which, although they retain the English language, have lost the character and feelings of their original nationality. He had previously been employed in diplomatic missions, and was a good practical man of business, but he did not possess the brilliant and versatile talents which distinguished his predecessor.

The Hamburgh diplomatic corps contained at this time one remarkable man,—von Struve, the Russian minister-resident, —who combined with great experience in business a scientific acquaintance with botany and mineralogy, on which he had published several works. Von Struve resided in an old house in a narrow street called the *Caffeemacherei*, which would at present be considered as *mauvais ton*. In fact, few persons of any note now live in the noisy and crowded streets within the city, but prefer the banks of the Alster, or the many pleasant situations on the promenade, formerly the town-wall. Previous to the great fire of 1842, which burnt down two-fifths of the old houses, the architectural character of Hamburgh was very different from what it now is. The new houses are a good deal in the London style, with the advantage of being rather more roomy. The dining-rooms are always on the first floor, an arrangement rendered necessary by the greater severity of the northern winters.

At the house of Sieveking I first met Dr. Smidt, the burgomaster of Bremen, who had acquired a great reputation in Germany for political sagacity, and to whose exertions at the Vienna congress the Hanse-towns were mainly indebted for the retention of their sovereignty as independent states. Smidt had many interesting recollections out of the period of the war with France, especially in 1811, when he went to Paris by command of Napoleon I to give information respecting the local circumstances then unhappily, like Hamburgh, a part of the French empire. Burgomaster Smidt was a tall, thin, old man, and one of the most inveterate smokers that I remember. His long pipe was never laid aside except at meals; yet he lived to an advanced age; and his love for tobacco was not

thought inappropriate in the chief magistrate of a city which
is *par excellence* the tobacco-port of Germany and northern
Europe.

During the summer of 1841 Mrs. Elizabeth Fry, and her
brother Mr. John Joseph Gurney, visited Hamburgh in the
course of a philanthropic tour. The objects of these benevolent
quakers being known, they were induced to give two public
lectures, which were listened to with attention. As neither
of them understood German, the services of translators were
secured, who rendered the English, sentence by sentence, into
German for the benefit of the audience. Mrs. Fry's discourse
on prison discipline was translated by Miss Amelia Sieveking;
and that of Mr. Gurney, chiefly on negro slavery, by Dr.
Ascher. To me these proceedings seemed very tedious, but
the Germans listened to the whole with exemplary patience.
After the lectures Mrs. Fry held a reception in her own apartments, and did the honours very agreeably. In fact there was a
certain courtly manner about both the sister and brother which,
combined with their quaker costume, had an imposing effect.
Mr. Gurney talked a great deal about Mr. Wilberforce; and
Mrs. Fry was warm in her praises of the then Queen of
Denmark, who had invited her to Copenhagen, and whose
letter of invitation she took care to have on the table for the
inspection of her company. These quakers are an amusing
set of people. Narrow-minded and unphilosophical, they have
a certain pretension about them which we should not so easily
excuse if we did not know their real kindness of heart, and
their unvarying readiness to succour the distresses, and assuage
the miseries, of suffering humanity.

Among the literary men of Hamburgh Lappenberg at this time
and for many years afterwards held the first place. After having
studied at Edinburgh, he served for some years as Hamburgh
minister-resident at the Prussian court, which post he subsequently exchanged for the more congenial one of archivist
to the government of his native city. Whilst filling that
office he brought to light many important archives not previously known, such as those of the chapter of the ancient
Hamburgh cathedral, pulled down in 1805; and he published
several learned works on Hanseatic history, and on old Germanic and maritime law. He wrote also two volumes of a
history of England, which were translated in London and
praised by English critics; but not finding time to proceed
with the work it was subsequently continued by Professor
Pauli. Lappenberg had undoubtedly the critical judgment,
and patient industry, which are the indispensable qualifications

of a good historian. He was in easy circumstances, having married in succession two daughters of a rich Altona merchant, and was fond of society. He kept up a correspondence with his Edinburgh friends, paid frequent visits both to North and South Britain, and was conversant with our literature and modes of thinking. When I renewed my acquaintance with Lappenberg some twenty years later, I found him but little altered, and still busily engaged in his antiquarian researches. As an instance of his having imbibed some Scotch prejudices, I remember his vindicating the expulsion of Mr. Turnbull from the post of record-keeper at the Rolls-chapel, which no other German could comprehend or approve; for in that country religious liberty is so well established that no government would permit itself to be deprived of the services of an archivist because he happened to be of a different confession from that of the sovereign. Lappenberg had known at Edinburgh Dugald Stewart, Brougham, Jeffery, Sir John Stuart, the late Vice-Chancellor, and other notabilities, and was fond of relating anecdotes of them to his Hamburgh friends.

The constitution of the republic of Hamburgh was at this period a very exclusive one, for, although the crown was nominally in the senate and burghership, the real power was in the hands of the former body, which elected its own members as vacancies occurred, without in any way consulting the body of citizens. There were twenty-four senators and four burgomasters, chosen out of the leading families of the place, and as those families were generally related to each other, either by blood or marriage, the senate bore the character rather of a private party than of an assembly responsible to public opinion. During the forty-five years which elapsed between 1815 and 1860 there was frequent and repeated agitation in Hamburgh for constitutional reform, and some partial amendments were introduced; but the citizens did not obtain any substantial share of power until the last-mentioned year, when a really representative system was adopted, and took effect on the 1st of January, 1861. According to this new constitution, which still subsists, the number of burgomasters is reduced to two, and that of the senators to eighteen; near relatives are forbidden from sitting together in the senate; the concurrence of the burghership is requisite in the election of senators; and what is still more essential, the burghership is invested with the functions of a representative assembly, and has the power of rejecting proposed laws, and of controlling the public expenditure, as in other constitutional states. Up to 1866 the action of the Hamburgh government was limited by its obligations towards the Germanic body, and subsequently its independence has been still further diminished by having become a member of the North-German confederation; but in respect of all domestic and municipal affairs, it continues unfettered, and in so far retains its character of a sovereign state.

The death of King Frederic William III, which took place in June 1840, after a reign of above forty years, had excited many hopes, both in Prussia and throughout Germany, that his successor would fulfil the promise of a constitution made by the deceased king to his people so long back as the year 1815, on the termination of the great European war. But Frederic William IV soon shewed the country that a real representative system was far from his thoughts. He was not disposed for anything like a charter, or written compact, between him and his subjects, and contented himself with summoning the provincial states of the Prussian monarchy, and granting them some additional powers in the shape of permanent committees to transact business during their vacations, and subsequently of a debating assembly at Berlin, composed of the united committees appointed by the states of the respective provinces. The King, full of love and reverence for the middle ages, and impressed with a deep sense of his own divine mission, did not wish to part with the right of legislation which belonged exclusively to himself, and fancied he was conceding a great deal by permitting the provincial deputies to meet and deliberate in his capital upon such matters as he chose to submit to them. The country, however, thought otherwise. The united committees gave satisfaction neither to the public nor to themselves. The general discontent gradually increased, and the debates of the provincial states became more and more stormy, until in the eighth year of his reign the will of the King was at last modified, and he took a more decided step in a constitutional direction by summoning what was styled the united diet to meet at Berlin in April 1847. This body was composed by an amalgamation of the local diets of the eight Prussian provinces into one body, having so far the attributes of a parliament that no state-laws were thereafter to be contracted, or new taxes introduced without its previous consent. It is from 1847 that the representative system in Prussia may properly be said to date; but during my first residence at Hamburgh constitutional liberty was only in a transition state, and the intentions of the new king were a puzzle even to those who had studied German politics the most assiduously. The Syndic Sieveking indeed predicted that the time would come when Germany would not be behind England in representative institutions; but even his sagacity did not attempt to solve the riddle of the royal mind, nor to guess how soon Prussia would be in the possession of any considerable amount of constitutional freedom.

In the autumn of 1843 I made an excursion through the south of Germany, where the current of life flows so smoothly and calmly, and I was rather captivated by the easy temperaments and kind hearts of the good Würtembergers and Bavarians, though well aware that it was not from them that the political regeneration of the fatherland was in any circumstances to be anticipated. I found Stuttgard excessively hot, owing to its situation in a deep valley surrounded by vine-covered hills, and everybody was rushing away to the neighbouring bath-place of Canstadt for fresher air, and social amusement. I was fortunate enough to see Baron Cotta, the eminent bookseller, and to have some conversation with him upon literary matters. He remarked that the English publishers had a great advantage over those in Germany, from living in a richer country, where capital was abundant, and there were many persons able to purchase books of a costly description. There was more thought, he said, in Germany than in England; consequently German literature, although comprising a great deal of rubbish, was upon the whole superior to that of England, where so much trash appears under the form of sermons and other religious publications, as well as of that inferior class of novels whose manifest tendency is to enfeeble the reader's mind. But, he added, we have too many literary men in Germany; and it would be better for our country if more of our youths devoted themselves, as in England, to trade, and industrial pursuits, or went out as colonists to distant lands. Cotta was undoubtedly the leading publisher in the south, as Brockhaus was in the north, of Germany. The business carried on at Stuttgard and Tübingen was founded by his father, a man of untiring energy, who devoted himself to the good of his native land, not only by his editions of Schiller, Goethe, and other German classics, and his many excellent periodicals, but by his active promotion of steam-navigation, and by his negotiation of the first *Zollverein*-treaty between Prussia, Bavaria, and Würtemberg, which formed the foundation of the present great Customs-Union comprehending the entire surface of Germany, with the exception of the portion of it lying within the Austrian empire. Cotta, the father, established the well-known 'Allgemeine Zeitung' (Universal Gazette) in 1798; a journal which not only became a most valuable property to himself and his son, but maintained its reputation for the greater portion of a century as the best newspaper in Europe. Its articles on the oriental question, and on eastern affairs in general, have long been celebrated for their intimate knowledge of the subject, and although it has at times been considered an organ of the Austrian government, it has never forfeited its character for that impartial treatment of political questions which, upon the whole, creditably distinguishes the newspaper press of Germany.

Baron Cotta having given me an introduction to his chief editor at Augsburgh, Dr. Kolb, I had an interview with him accordingly, and found him in regard to trade a protectionist, although articles in favour of freedom of commerce were occasionally admitted into the paper. He invited me to contribute to the 'Allgemeine Zeitung,' which, however, my other occupations did not admit of. He advised me to see the author of the 'national system of political economy,' Dr. Frederick List, who then resided at Augsburgh, which I did, and found his views to be completely at variance with those of all the distinguished economists of the school of Adam Smith. List was a fat, florid man, possessing a great deal of knowledge which he had picked up by observation both in America and Europe, and full of enthusiasm for schemes of improvement. He reminded me something of Edward Gibbon Wakefield. He was perhaps more than any person the originator of the German railways, and during his residence at Leipsic had advocated the construction of a line of rail to Dresden, at a time when nobody else believed in its practicability. List's mind was, however, more sanguine than logical, and his chief work on national economy is in fact a tissue of fallacies, which were well exposed by the late John Austin in an article on the subject in the 'Edinburgh Review [1].' His pecuniary circumstances were latterly embarrassed, and he died by his own hand during an excursion in the mountains of the Bavarian Tyrol.

A few days agreeably spent at Munich gave me a glimpse of that beautiful capital of Southern Germany, and time to wonder at the genius and energy of King Louis, who had raised out of a dull town of breweries and beershops a magni-

---

[1] No. CLII. Art. viii.

ficent city admired by all Europe for its architectural splendour, and for those spacious museums of painting and sculpture, which have justly conferred upon it the title of the Queen of German art. But not having had time on this occasion to cultivate the acquaintance of either artists or professors, with the exception of my old friend C. F. Neumann, the professor of Chinese in the university, I proceeded across the country by Nuremberg and Leipsic, to Berlin, where I stayed a few days before returning to England. There I found Lord Westmorland occupied with the question of the *Zollverein*-tariff, and engaged in remonstrating with the Prussian government against certain increased rates of duty which had lately been resolved on. I had an opportunity of discussing these matters with one of the best informed Prussian officials, M. von Roenne, who had been envoy at Washington, and afterwards became president of the board of trade at Berlin. He rather leaned to the views of Frederic List, and contended that at all events the German manufacturing interests would for some time to come require protection, and that the time for a considerable reduction of the customs-tariff had not yet arrived. There were, however, some leading official men in Berlin, particularly M. Kühne, director of the customs department, who advocated the policy of free trade, though they admitted the difficulty of converting the protectionists of the southern states, each of which had an equal vote with Prussia in the *Zollverein*-conferences. In an article which I soon afterwards contributed to the 'Edinburgh Review[1],' I endeavoured to explain the commercial policy of Germany to the British public, and to recommend a further adoption of free-trade principles at home and abroad. My journey back to England was diversified only by travelling in the same railway-carriage from Brussels to Ostend with the Earl of Mornington, who then resided in the former city. Provided with a copious luncheon his lordship seemed in a high state of enjoyment, and opened his mind very freely upon men and things at home and abroad. He was a liberal in politics and something more, and gave an account of some communications he had lately been making to Sir Robert Peel on the subject of pauperism, and charitable institutions, in Belgium. Lord Mornington's character was in fact a very common one,— a clever man without moral principle, and it was his former great wealth that gave him the unfortunate notoriety which

---

[1] No. CLIX. Art. iv.

D

does not extend to persons in more humble stations.   In the early part of 1844 I received an appointment as British commissioner for the settlement of the Portendie claims on France, arising out of an illegitimate blockade of a part of the African coast by the ships of that power, and I went out to Berlin, where the mixed-commission was to assemble, the King of Prussia being the arbitrator between the two governments in the disputed questions of international law.

CHAPTER III.

Society of Berlin. Frederic William IV, his court and ministers. Humboldt. Bunsen. Diplomatists: Lord Westmorland, Meyendorff, Wheaton. Professors: Raumer, Ranke, Grimm, Pertz. Lord Palmerston. Sir de Lacy Evans. Political aspect. Religious movement.

BERLIN, the central point of the intelligence of Germany, was undoubtedly during the year I lived there an agreeable place of residence as regarded society, and in the winter season there was scarcely a day when some assembly, ball, or dinner-party was not going on. The Court gave a certain number of fêtes; the Prussian princes, the ministers, and the diplomatic body, entertained pretty liberally; and there were some literary circles frequented by professors and learned men. The scientific societies held frequent meetings, to which strangers had easy access, and the theatres and concerts offered their attractions in the best style. Having been presented at court, I was several times honoured by the notice of the king, Frederic William IV, and could not but be struck by his conversational powers. The first time His Majesty spoke to me was previous to a court dinner, to which I was invited, with my colleague the French commissioner. The King adverted to the commission which had brought me to Berlin, and said he had very good legal advisers, without whom he should hardly have taken upon himself to decide questions of international law. He asked me if I had studied law, and, on my answering affirmatively, said he knew there was a great difference between the legal system of England and that of Germany; that in the former the proceedings were more before the public, but that he had heard that the English judges went rather too much upon the letter of statutes, instead of looking to the general principles of legislation which they had to apply. Speaking of some distinguished person in London, the King said he had a great respect for Lord Aberdeen, then foreign secretary, and supposed I knew Bunsen, then his envoy in London. I answered, 'Yes; everybody in London knows the Chevalier Bunsen, and,' I ventured to add, 'everybody likes him.' The King paused, but soon resumed, 'Madame Bunsen is a very amiable lady, and I daresay is equally liked in London.' I replied, 'Undoubtedly, your Majesty;' and there the conversation, which was in French, terminated. I remember that after dinner the King enquired of M. Engelhardt, the French commissioner, about a Prussian nobleman who had lived much in Paris, and abhorred everything revolutionary, and Engelhardt said that that nobleman had prophesied the restoration of the old Bourbon line within a year or two. 'Yes,' replied the King, 'but did he make that prophecy before or after he went out of his mind?' The nobleman in question was then in a madhouse. On subsequent occasions the King spoke to me in English, enquiring whether I was much in society, whether I went often to the theatre, and how I liked Berlin? On my stating that I enjoyed myself very much in his capital, and had found a great many things to admire, he replied, 'Oh! I am so charmed when a foreigner amuses himself well in Berlin.' The King understood English tolerably well, but now and then made use of an odd expression. In dismissing me he once said, 'Good-bye, my dear!' a phrase which I have also heard him use to others. The King told Lord Westmorland that he was much pleased with Mr. Monckton Milnes (now Lord Houghton), who visited Berlin this winter, and made good use of his observations[1]. Indeed, Frederic William IV was always gratified by the resort of intelligent foreigners to his court. He had undoubtedly great social talents, and, even if born in the middle ranks of life, would have been deemed a first-rate talker. At toasts and after-dinner speeches he was particularly good. His toast to Queen Victoria, when she was his guest at the palace of Brühl, on the Rhine, in August, 1845, was thus reported with applause by the German journals:—'There is a word,' said the King, 'resounding in English and in Prussian hearts, which thirty years ago echoed on the fields of Waterloo from English and Prussian voices, as marking a glorious hard-won deed done as brothers in arms; now it resounds on German ground, in the midst of the blessings of that peace which was the fruit of the great conflict. That word is *Victoria*. Gentlemen, let us drink to Her Majesty the Queen, &c., &c.' It is well known that the sentiment and expression of this

---

[1] See an article on the political state of Prussia, attributed to Mr. Milnes, in the 'Edinburgh Review,' No. CLXVII. Art. viii.

toast were highly gratifying to the King's illustrious guests, and that the Prince-Consort spoke of it afterwards with great admiration.   The King's lively and susceptible temperament was of course derived from his mother, the charming Queen Louisa, whose virtues and sufferings in the cause of her country will never be forgotten in Prussian history.   The calumnies which were so industriously diffused in regard to his habits of life did not rest upon the slightest foundation. The King seldom drank anything stronger than wine and water, and if he was at times in elevated spirits it was certainly not from any cause of that nature, but simply from the effect of society and conversation upon a peculiarly excitable constitution.

The King's affection for the middle ages and the times of chivalry was the result of his education.   He certainly did not inherit it from his father, who, with all his love of dictatorial power, had nothing romantic in his notions, and cared little about historical traditions.   The leading idea of Frederic William IV was that of the continuity of the past with the present; he did not object to the political machine moving forwards, but it must be in such a way as not to break off into a new track—not to violate the memory of what has gone before us.   When he visited Eton college, during his sojourn in England in 1841, he said to the provost, 'This institution has for me an inexpressible charm, for here the old is ever new, and the new never out of harmony with the old.' Accordingly, he believed his hereditary right to be of divine origin, and that whatever concessions he might make to the wishes of his people were to be measured by no other rule than that of his own royal conscience.   This tone of mind he acquired principally from his preceptor Ancillon, who, whilst he imbued his royal pupil with a strong love of the ~~romance~~ and the ~~religion~~ deemed it by no means necessary to impress upon him the supposed advantages of constitutional government.   Frederick Ancillon belonged to a French family of Protestant refugees which had settled at Berlin, and was originally a preacher at the French church, and professor at the military academy in that city.   Having become known by several literary, philosophical, and political works, as well as by the sterling worth of his character, he was selected as tutor to the crown-prince, and held that important charge for some years, after which he was placed in the Prussian foreign-office, and in 1831 became the minister for foreign affairs.   His foreign policy was decidedly pacific, and in domestic affairs he passed for a moderate conservative.   In fact,

his philosophy was one of reconcilement, or what is some
times called the eclectic school.   His latest work, entitled
'Thoughts on Man[1],' and published in 1829, has been very
generally read, and in it are to be found, in the form of
apothegms, his condensed views upon a great variety of subjects.   In order to shew the sort of mind which worked upon
and formed that of the crown-prince, I subjoin a few specimens of the 'Thoughts' referred to :—

'No state can be without religion, nor can religion exist
without the form of a state or of civil government.   The law is
powerless or insufficient to assure order and social well-being
from the moment when the mass of the people are not submitted to the restraints of religion and conscience.   Religion
is insufficient and powerless to prevent or repress all the
crimes which menace social order, if the civil law does not
hold back the arm until religion may have acquired force and
dominion enough to retain the heart, and if the law itself does
not cover religion with its shield against the violence of the
passions.'

'Place religion as little as possible in contact with material
interests, for you make it lose dignity in speaking too much
of its utility.   Do not prefer to present it in its relations with
fortune, well-being, and success of every kind; religion may
in certain circumstances conduce to all that, but even if it
should be good for no material object, it would still be the
most excellent thing to be taught, because it is the life of the
soul.   To endeavour to make it find favour in the eyes of its
enemies by proving its utility, is to make it descend from its
elevation and sublimity, and to degrade heaven without
ennobling the earth.'

'The catholic religion would be inconsistent if it permitted
innovations, or any deviations whatever from its rule.   The
protestant religion would be inconsistent if it sought to make
individual opinions subordinate to symbolical books, or confessions of faith.'

'To say that a religion which is written and committed to
a book will yield to all interpretations, is to say that it has no
determinate sense.   To say that a written religion ought to
become more perfect with the lapse of time, and to advance

---

[1] 'Pensées sur l'homme, ses rapports, et ses intérêts, par Frédéric Ancillon.'   2 vols. Berlin, 1829.

with the human race, is to say that such a religion has no
positive character, and that consequently it does not deserve
the name of a religion.'

'The origin and source of the greater part of the crimes, and
of all the blood, which disgust us throughout the pages of the
Roman history under the Emperors, is the want of an in-
variable order of succession—the absence of legitimacy.
Legitimacy alone prevents revolutions, hinders violent usur-
pations, frustrates culpable hopes, stifles jealousies of sovereign
authority, and thus cuts away the roots of many foul deeds.
To inconstancy it opposes fixity, to the hatred of submission
an order of things which reconciles itself with obedience, because it belongs to the order of nature; to the mistrust of
men, confidence in an innate and hereditary authority; and to
novelty the power of habit.'

'In all the revolutions which have been directed against
legitimate government, the people have begun by being their
instruments, and have ended by becoming their victim. False
liberalism is political atheism; the doctrine of legitimacy
is political theism.'

'In so far as public opinion is sound, ripe, consistent, and
uniform, its decrees are as respectable as they are respected,
and one must be a madman or a criminal to despise them, and
set one's self above them. But *when* and *where* has it such
characters, and how can we be assured of it? As soon as
opinion is divided it begins to be depraved; then corrupt men
oppose the opinion of those who share their faults and vices
to the opinion which condemns them, and learn how to resist
the latter power. In becoming constantly more and more
divided and deteriorated under all sorts of forms, opinion
ceases to be the expression of principles; it does not even
enunciate any decisive manner of seeing and judging; finally,
there is no such thing as opinion at all.'

These extracts will suffice to indicate that the King's preceptor approved of religious establishments, and the principle
of legitimacy, and that he held cheap public opinion as it is
formed and exercised in modern times. In regard to religion,
it would seem that Ancillon's mind, although he had been
a protestant minister, fluctuated between the merits of the
catholic and protestant confessions, and this was probably the
case likewise with his royal pupil. The King admired the

catholic worship, and it was more than once reported that he had become a member of the Roman church. Those rumours were, however, unfounded. He appears to have sympathized with Bunsen, more than any one, in religious sentiments, and views of church reform. Indeed, almost his last act before the stroke of paralysis fell upon his brain, was the reception of the members of the evangelical alliance at Berlin in September, 1857. His Queen, the Princess Elizabeth of Bavaria, was, as is well known, a catholic at the time of her marriage, and subsequently embraced the reformed faith — a circumstance which gave peculiar satisfaction to her devout and narrow-minded father-in-law, Frederic William III.

Frederic William IV was immeasurably superior to his father in talents and accomplishments, but unfortunately laboured under the defect, fatal to one called to rule a nation, of indecision of character. His ministers could not rely upon his consistency in the ordinary affairs of business, and in the great political movement of 1849 his incapacity to take a decided line one way or the other was nearly the ruin of the Prussian state. The great expectations which had been formed of him as crown-prince were in fact disappointed throughout his reign simply because he wanted the power of will.

The Prussian minister for foreign affairs in 1844 was Baron von Bülow, who, with the Baroness, daughter of William von Humboldt, entertained frequently, and kept an agreeable house. In the summer the receptions were at Tegel, a long distance from Berlin, and the roads were so bad that the carriages of the diplomatists and other visitors used frequently to stick fast in the sand in their way to the foreign minister's country seat. Bülow had been for some years Prussian envoy in London, and was a hard worker, but his official duties combined with those of society proved too much for his health, and he died a victim to over-exertion. I had several conversations with him on the commercial relations of Germany to Great Britain, and as to the possibility of a commercial treaty, for which our legislation was not yet ripe. Bülow complained that while we remonstrated against the *Zollverein* tariff, we maintained restrictive duties on corn, timber, and other articles of German produce, and at this time his complaint was well founded, for the abolition of the corn-laws and other protective duties had not yet been effected by Sir Robert Peel, so that we were not in a position to recommend free-trade principles to a foreign government. At the Bülows'

I made the acquaintance of Alexander von Humboldt, then in his seventy-sixth year, but whose extraordinary mind seemed to be still in its youthful vigour. What he said to me related chiefly to English life, and the advantages of our free constitution. He called one day at our residence in the Thiergarten, and left a complimentary note addressed to my wife in scarcely legible handwriting, and not straight on the paper, which we heard was owing to his custom of writing upon his knee. Humboldt was the King's almoner and in high favour with his majesty, who did a great deal through him in the interest of science, and for the protection of scientific men. He enjoyed a high degree of respect and admiration both from the court and the public. One cannot but lament that the indiscreet publication of his letters, after his death, but during the King's life, should have cast a stain upon the memory of the enlightened author of *Cosmos* by laying him open to the charge of habitual insincerity towards the persons among whom he constantly moved. Humboldt despised the court-circle, and therefore did not think himself obliged to give it his real mind. Such, however, is court-life. Did any one ever hear of a royal palace which was believed to be the chosen abode of sincerity and truth?

Eichhorn, the minister for religion and education (*Cultusminister*) had been professor at Göttingen, and was distinguished for his knowledge of German history and law, as his published works sufficiently shew[1]. He was a conscientious administrator, though far from popular, and considered by many as narrow-minded. I occasionally attended his *soirées*, where one had the opportunity of meeting not only official men, but professors, clergymen, medical men, and others of the literary tribe. To mix in such assemblies is of course a great advantage to a stranger desirous of accustoming himself to German sentiments and modes of thought, an acquaintance with the language being presupposed.

The minister of justice was De Savigny, an eminent lawyer, of whose great services to historical jurisprudence it would be presumptuous in me to speak. He had been successively professor at Marburgh and Berlin, and judge of the court of appeal for the Rhenish provinces. His excellent work on the history of the Roman law in the middle ages[2] is well

[1] See his 'Deutsche Staats und Rechtsgeschichte.' 4 vols. third edition, Göttingen, 1822.

[2] 'Geschichte des Römischen Rechts im Mittelalter.' 6 vols. Heidelberg, 1815 to 1831.

known even in England, where lawyers trouble themselves so little about institutes or pandects. Savigny was a large man, with a fine open countenance, and had more dignity about him than belongs in general to German professors. I attended his Saturday *soirées*, but the talk which I had with him ran merely upon ordinary topics. I once had the pleasure at Savigny's of looking upon Bettina (Madame d'Arnim) whose singular character may be partly understood by a perusal of Goethe's correspondence with a child, published in 1835, and of admiring the childlike and enthusiastic expression of her charming features. She was of course a good deal laughed at by the every-day respectabilities of the Berlin court circles.

Whilst I was at Berlin the King sent for the Chevalier Bunsen, then his envoy in London, in order to consult him upon certain political as well as religious questions, and Bunsen came over accordingly in March, and remained there about four months. I had consequently frequent opportunities of seeing that remarkable man, with whom I was already acquainted, and can say with truth that the more I came to know of him the better I liked him. His love of everything good and great, and the high tone of his mind, gave his conversation a perpetual charm[1]; and he was truly benevolent, ever ready to help on deserving persons when it lay in his power. Bunsen was not liked at Berlin, because there were many who envied him the large share which he enjoyed of the royal favour, and others who considered his views both of religion and politics to be wild and unsafe. As I shall have to refer in subsequent pages to public transactions in which he took a leading part, it may suffice to remark here that his favourite scheme of church-reform, as expounded in his ' Church of the Future ' and other works, was to give over to the community (*la commune, die Gemeinde*) the care of their own religious interests, free from state-interference, leaving them to govern themselves ecclesiastically, and to settle everything relating to their own divine service. The application of the voluntary principle to religion has not only many advocates in Germany, but a number of self-constituted free communities (*freie Gemeinde*) are already in existence. The principle has been long in force in the United States of America, and has likewise taken effect in Ireland since the

---

[1] ' Und hinter ihm in wesenlosem Scheine
  Lag, was uns alle bändigt, das Gemeine.'
                                    Goethe on Schiller.

disestablishment of the protestant state-church. The day may possibly come when the same principle may be generally adopted in Germany also. At present three church establishments are recognized by the laws of the Germanic body, viz., the catholic, the lutheran, and the reformed (or calvinistic) confession, the last two being amalgamated in Prussia under the name of the united-evangelical-church. Whether the King went the whole length of Bunsen's views of church-reform does not clearly appear, but it is manifest that he took great interest in them, and placed more confidence in Bunsen's judgment in such matters than in almost any one's. A great deal of light has been thrown upon this subject by the interesting memoirs of Baron von Bunsen, published by his widow in 1868, a work which is admitted by all who knew him to have given a full and faithful account of his long and brilliant public career. The narrative of the Baroness von Bunsen indeed leaves nothing to be desired; and to any one who has mixed much in, or closely observed, the political affairs of Europe during the last fifty years, it conveys the impression of a luminous history of his own times.

In the diplomatic circle the most eminent person was the Russian envoy, Baron de Meyendorff, who exercised great influence, and was ignorant of nothing that was going on. To his exertions was mainly owing the peace concluded between Prussia and Denmark on the 2nd of July, 1850, after the first war on account of Schleswig-Holstein. The Baroness de Meyendorff, an excellent and most charitable lady, was the sister of the Count de Buol-Schönstein, some time Austrian prime-minister, and this connection led the Czar to count upon the alliance of Austria for the Crimean war, in which he was grievously disappointed. The Russian embassy is located in one of the best houses in Berlin, in fact, in a palace in which the Czar takes up his residence during his occasional visits to the Prussian capital. The dinners and other entertainments given by the Meyendorffs were always in the very best style.

Lord Westmorland, the representative of Great Britain, was personally liked at court, and was also popular in general society. His kindness of heart, and amiable disposition, combined with his hospitalities, could not but make him many friends in Berlin. He was a generous patron of artists, his own hobby being music. He had himself composed an opera and various other pieces, some of which were occasionally performed at the public concerts under the trees in the Thiergarten, when he used to attend in person to watch the

performance.   Lord Westmorland's original profession was
the army, for which he was probably better suited than for a
diplomatic career.   He had in fact no statesmanlike qualities,
and understood little of German politics, though he did his
best to maintain the reputation of his country in the circles
in which he moved.   Lady Westmorland was very accomplished, and had adorned her apartments with several good
pictures of her own execution.   There was also much talent
in the younger branches of the Fane family.   An interesting memoir of Julian Fane has lately been published by his
friend Mr. Lytton.

The Sardinian envoy at Berlin was the Count de Rossi,
a tall, fine-looking man, whose chief distinction arose from his
having married the celebrated Henrietta Sonntag.   I used
to meet them at Lord Westmorland's and other houses.
Countess Rossi was then about thirty-six years of age, and
still pretty and engaging.   She never sang in public, but
sometimes allowed her friends to listen to her charming voice
in a private circle.   Count Rossi was unfortunately addicted
to play, and ruined himself by it.   His wife was likewise
fond of cards, and played higher than most ladies.   Some
ten years later she had to pay the penalty of her husband's
gambling propensities by returning to the stage in order
to gain the means of making up his heavy losses.   She died
of cholera at the Havannah during her American tour, and
her remains were brought back for interment in the convent
of Marienstern in Lusatia, where she had received a part
of her education.

Of Mr. Henry Wheaton, then the American minister at
the Prussian court, I saw a good deal, and profited by his
experience and the study he had devoted to international
questions.   He understood the German language, and was
quite *au courant* as to all passing events and political movements.   He had been for some time minister at Copenhagen,
and had published a history of the northmen ; but the works
which gained him the greatest reputation were those on the
principles of international law, and on its history since the
peace of Westphalia[1].   Wheaton, although married, lived as a
bachelor in Berlin, keeping his family in Paris for purposes of
education.   He was recalled from his post rather suddenly in
1846, without either the grant of a pension, or the offer of

---

[1] 'Elements of International Law.'   2 vols., London, 1836.
'Histoire des progrès du droit des gens depuis la paix de Westphalie jusqu'à
nos jours.'   2 vols., Leipzig, 1846.

any other diplomatic office suitable to his long and valuable services. In that country diplomacy appears to be hardly yet recognized as a distinct profession; and the wonder is that, considering the uncertain tenure of the government offices, any men of real ability should be found willing to enter at all into the employment of the state.

I remember talking with Wheaton about the difficulty of finding a *basis* of the law of nations, and he said there never could be any beyond the conventional, each state being at liberty to lay down its own rules of conduct, and to decide whether or not such and such actions were just and reasonable. He has indeed fully explained in his 'Elements' the non-existence of any universal *jus gentium*, and that in point of fact the international law of the civilized christian nations of Europe and America is one thing, and that which governs the intercourse of the mussulman nations with each other, and with the christians, is something quite different. A question of more practical importance is that of the continual validity of treaties under circumstances different from those in which they were contracted; which question was recently raised by Russia in regard to the limitation of her naval force in the Black Sea prescribed by the treaty concluded at Paris in 1856, and was happily set at rest by the resolutions of the London Conference in 1871. Wheaton has not laid down any *dicta* immediately applicable to a case of that kind, but from the tenor of his remarks upon transitory conventions, viz. treaties of cession, boundary, or exchange of territory, it may be inferred that the restriction laid upon Russia in regard to her ships of war in the Black Sea was not one of those which could properly be termed perpetual in their nature, and that the Russian government was therefore fairly entitled to demand its abolition after having submitted to it for a term of fourteen years. It is worth notice that two books by American jurists, viz. Wheaton's 'Elements,' and Kent's 'Commentaries,' have been prescribed by our foreign-office for the examination of candidates for attaché-ships. Both are valuable text-books; but I should say that Heffter's work on the European law of nations[1], of which a French translation exists, is in completeness and lucidity superior to either. Heffter was professor of law in the university of Berlin, and afterwards one of the Prussian judges of appeal.

Among the professors at the university, Frederic de Raumer was perhaps the best known out of Germany. His

---

[1] 'Das Europäische Völkerrecht der Gegenwart.' Berlin, first ed., 1844.

letters from Paris at the time of the revolution of 1830, and
his travels in England and in Italy, are full of interest, and
have doubtless had many more readers than his learned history
of the Hohenstaufen emperors.   Raumer was fond of society,
and was in good circumstances enough to receive much company at his own house.   He has now, I believe, passed his
ninetieth year.   I well remember the favourable reception in
London of his letters on England in 1835.   Everybody was
glad to hear the opinion entertained by an intelligent
foreigner of our manners and institutions, and the praise once
bestowed upon him by Lord John Russell in a parliamentary
speech was by no means undeserved.   Raumer was not free
from the German vanity of affecting to know everybody and
everything ; and he sometimes erred in his judgments, but
was a sincere lover of truth, and travelled in order to refresh
his mind with that sort of knowledge which could not be
obtained from books alone.   In talking with him about
foreign travel, I remarked upon the great number of elderly
persons who annually left England on continental tours.   He
said he thought nothing more natural ; that travelling was
the best specific for giving a zest to life ; and that he himself,
as a teacher of youth, peculiarly felt the want of it in order
to prevent the petrifaction of his ideas, and to vivify his mind
by a succession of new scenes and fresh sensations.

Leopold Ranke, the historian of the Popes, whose critical
acumen is as indisputable as his impartiality,—Dieterici, the
laborious statistician,—Ehrenberg, the naturalist, and dis-
coverer of the organization of *infusoria,*—James and William
Grimm, the Germanists and philologians (*par nobile fratrum*),
—were all at this time distinguished teachers at the university, and I had the advantage of occasional intercourse
with them.   Dr. Pertz, formerly state-archivist at Hanover,
and known to the learned world by his valuable edition of the
‘ Monumenta Germaniæ Historica,’ was director of the royal
library at Berlin, a post for which his extensive knowledge of
books eminently fitted him.   Pertz had formerly been in
Rome for the purpose of assisting his old friend Bunsen in
the collection of materials relative to German history, and
had discovered there important documents, copies of which
now enrich the royal collections at Berlin.   He was a
thorough liberal in a constitutional sense, and well versed in
the intricacies of German politics.   He was very hospitable,
and at his house persons of all ranks and professions were
to be met and conversed with.   Having lost his first wife
(an American lady), he afterwards married the accomplished

daughter of Mr. Leonard Horner, who was for many years resident at Bonn on the Rhine. Pertz had often been in England, and knew how to estimate the English mind and the merits and disadvantages of our institutions.

Lord and Lady Palmerston came to Berlin in the course of a tour in September, 1844. It was Lord Palmerston who gave me my first appointment under the Foreign-office, and I was glad of an opportunity of renewing my acquaintance with a statesman of whom all Europe was constantly talking. He was at this time out of office, Lord Aberdeen being foreign secretary. Lord Westmorland was absent on leave, and the honours of the legation were done by the secretary, Sir George Hamilton. I assisted him in furnishing Lord Palmerston with the *carte du pays*, for his lordship was desirous of information on all matters, political, social, and literary, and took an interest in all that was going on at Berlin. It was the dull season, and many persons of note were out of town, but Lord and Lady Palmerston dined at court, spent a day with the Bülows at Tegel, and attended the *soirées* of some members of the diplomatic corps. I heard that his neighbour at the court-dinner asked Lord Palmerston whether he was aware that he went by the name of Lord Firebrand in Germany? and that he answered in the affirmative with his usual good humour. His lordship told me that he had found the King very lively, and that his majesty had touched upon the subject of the Prussian constitution without seeming to apprehend any danger from the provisional and unsettled state in which the constitutional question at that time stood. I introduced to Lord Palmerston at his desire several literary men, among them Professor Ranke, with whom he had a long conversation on eastern affairs. Ranke, who had travelled in Turkey, and written a book on the Servian revolution of 1807 and the following years[1], considered the Turkish empire as virtually dead, maintaining that the Turk was inalterable in his nature, and that all that foreign powers were doing for the improvement and emancipation of the Christian races could only accelerate the fall of the Ottoman sovereignty. Lord Palmerston did not altogether concur with the professor's view, and endeavoured to explain to him that the situation of the Christians within the Turkish empire had in fact been much ameliorated, and that the Ottoman power, although a falling house, was one which

---

[1] 'Die Serbische Revolution; aus Serbischen Papieren und Mittheilungen, von Leopold Ranke.' Hamburg, 1829.

would still hold together for a great many years. Ranke, however, retorted that England seemed to him rather too careless of the future, and hinted that the longer the eastern question remained unsettled, the more favourable the delay would be to Russian policy and designs. Lord Palmerston took all that he said in very good part, and afterwards addressed to him some compliments on his history of the popes, with which he was acquainted in the English translation. Lord Palmerston was reading as the companion of his tour the journal and correspondence of the first Lord Malmesbury, and he recommended it to me as very instructive. He was much pleased with Alexander von Humboldt, whom he saw several times; also with Cornelius, the chief of German painters, who shewed him the beautiful drawings he had made for the fresco pictures to be placed in the intended Berlin *campo santo*, or royal burying-place adjoining the new cathedral. Both Lord and Lady Palmerston talked very freely about English politics, and criticized the vacillation and temporizing policy of Lord Aberdeen and Sir Robert Peel. In speaking of a late parliamentary debate on the arrest of the British consul Pritchard at Otaheite, he laughed at Peel's complaint of the ' gross outrage and indignity which had been committed,' imitating that minister's slow and solemn manner, and he doubted whether he would succeed in frightening the French government into making any adequate reparation. The secretary of legation having brought to Lady Palmerston some English newspapers, she was rather surprised to find they were tory papers, not having been previously aware that the newspapers supplied by the foreign-office to the British legations abroad were either whig or tory, according to the party of the ministry of the day. A commercial treaty between the *Zollverein* and Belgium having been just concluded, I explained its provisions to Lord Palmerston, as he took much interest in the progress of the *Zollverein*, and indeed in most commercial questions. His presence in Berlin excited general curiosity, although it was well understood that his journey was one of recreation only. He did not even bring his uniform with him, and was obliged to ask the King's special permission to be presented in plain clothes,—a very rare occurrence,— the etiquette of the Prussian court requiring that all presentations to the king and queen, or to other members of the royal family, must be made either in uniform, or old-fashioned court-dress. The latter costume is now rarely used, as almost every man who goes to court is entitled to wear either a civil or military uniform, according to his position in the state-service.

General Sir De Lacy Evans also visited Berlin this autumn, for the purpose of seeing the great reviews which were going on in the neighbourhood. I introduced him to Baron von Bülow and various other persons. Bülow conversed with him about Spain, where the General had so long commanded the British auxiliary legion, and told me afterwards he was much pleased with the General, and his straightforward soldierly bearing. General Evans knew nothing of Germany, but he was very modest, and said how well aware he was of the necessity of living some years in a country in order to understand its social and political relations. Professor Dieterici told him a great deal about the statistics of crime in Prussia, and the general condition of the lower classes, which he took some notes of. He did not seem peculiarly interested about the state of the Prussian army, although he had an opportunity of seeing several military manœuvres. I procured him a horse, which he by no means liked the look of, but happily it did not bring him to any grief, the Berlin hacks being well trained to stand fire. These Prussian manœuvres take place annually, either at Berlin or in one of the provinces. They last several weeks, and there are never fewer troops assembled than an army corps of thirty thousand men. Ten years after this period General Evans had the opportunity of winning fresh laurels by his admirable conduct in the Crimean war. He was a gallant soldier and plain-dealing politician, and the impression which he made upon the persons with whom he came into contact at Berlin was decidedly a favourable one.

In the month of July an attempt was made to assassinate the King, which very much shocked his loyal subjects. The offender was one Tscheck, formerly burgomaster of a small provincial town, who, being disappointed at not obtaining employment in the civil service, revenged himself by shooting twice at the King when entering his carriage in order to proceed on a journey into Silesia. The balls were turned by the King's military cloak, and his fortunate escape called forth addresses of congratulation from all parts of the monarchy, accompanied by wishes for the assassin to be brought to condign punishment, and Tscheck was executed accordingly, glorying in his crime. This lamentable incident had nothing political in it, and the sympathy which it called forth proved the high personal respect entertained by the Prussian people for their sovereign, whatever might be thought of the tone assumed by the government in regard to

E

the important national questions then awaiting their solution. From the commencement of the reign of Frederic William IV, up to the meeting of the united diet in 1847, the constitutional system of Prussia was, as I have already mentioned, in a transition state, and the extent of practical liberty conceded to the people was very limited. The police were omnipotent, public meetings were illegal, and the press was so far from free, that the suppression of Prussian newspapers, and the prohibition of newspapers published in other states, were every-day occurrences. The King cordially supported his Ministers, and gave no signs of his intention to move towards a more liberal *régime*. On the contrary, in a new royal ordinance touching 'the censorship of the press, issued in February, 1843, the King complained of the increasing effrontery of the journals, and of the censors not having fully understood his intentions, and then proceeded :—' What I will not suffer is the dissolution of science and literature into newspaper writing,—the placing the two upon an equality in dignity and pretensions ; the evil of the unlimited diffusion of seductive errors and false theories, touching the most sacred and venerable affairs of society in the most frivolous way and the most fugitive form, among a class of the population to which such forms are more attractive, and newspapers more accessible, than the productions of serious examination and fundamental science can ever be.' This ordinance may serve as an example of the complete adoption by the King of Ancillon's ideas (previously quoted) on public opinion, and of the success of the preceptor in engrafting his own notions of policy and religion, whether right or wrong, upon the impressionable mind of his royal pupil.

The King, who was charmed with Bunsen, seemed at times to assent to his views of what the constitution of the christian church ought to be, but his ministers shewed no disposition to enlarge the religious liberty of the communes, and did its best to maintain the orthodoxy of the Prussian united church, as well as the authority of the Augsburg confession and the symbols of faith. The recent erection of the Jerusalem bishopric, to be filled alternately by a lutheran[1] and an anglican, had drawn attention at Berlin to the supposed advantageous position of the anglican church, and excited the desire of improving the stability of the united church of Prussia, which, as every one knows, was formed by a compulsory fusion of the lutheran and calvinistic confessions, in obedience to the

---

[1] Or rather a member of the Prussian united church.

ordinances of Frederic William III. The government of his successor was now working for a more perfect centralization of the national church, and for the protection of protestant orthodoxy, or what was sometimes called positive christianity. The catholic church, which, since the peace of Westphalia, has stood upon the footing of an established confession in most of the German states, was likewise very favourably treated by Frederic William IV, as it was not from that quarter that any danger of instilling dangerous principles into the minds of the lower orders could be apprehended by the government. Several new monasteries and convents were permitted to be established, and the sisters of mercy received much encouragement and assistance from the court. The ancient orders of the Swan and of St. John, both originally catholic, were revived by the King, with such modifications as made them the appropriate reward of charitable exertions, and of care bestowed in the hospitals upon the sick and wounded.

Towards the end of 1844 a new religious sect sprung up in Germany, under the name of 'German-catholics,' who, without attaching themselves either to the lutheran or calvinistic confessions, separated from the church of Rome, and modified the doctrines of that church so as to suit the taste of the newly-formed community. The immediate cause of the schism was the exhibition of a relic (the holy coat of our blessed Saviour without a seam) in the cathedral of Treves, which drew pilgrims to the spot by countless thousands, and was said to have performed some miraculous cures. Czerski, a parish priest in the province of Posen, first left the Roman church with his entire flock; and then John Ronge, a deprived chaplain living in Silesia, published a violent letter addressed to the Bishop (Arnoldi) of Treves, ridiculing the exposition of the sacred relic, and declaring that the time was come for following Christ after another manner, and for christians to shake off the Papal authority, which was contrary alike to reason and scripture. Ronge was, of course, degraded and excommunicated, but his letter had a great effect upon the public mind, and gave the impulse to the secession of a number of other communities from the catholic church. The Prussian government regarded the movement with abhorrence, as subversive of social order, and the orthodox lutheran clergy joined the catholic hierarchy in condemning it as a scandalous abuse of the liberty of conscience, which tended to extinguish the religious sentiments of a christian nation, and to weaken the respect of the people for what they had been accustomed to consider as inviolable and holy. The schism, however, made some progress, and so-called German-catholic churches were established by the permission of the governments in the principal towns of northern and central Germany. After the events of 1848, however, the zeal of the new sectarians very much abated; several of their churches were discontinued; and the sect itself has fallen into comparative insignificancy in consequence of the more important political movements which have occupied the national mind of Germany since the last-mentioned year.

In rejecting the authority of the church, the German-catholics recognized the liberty of private judgment, whilst they admitted the scriptures to be the only rule of faith. In their articles of religion they further acknowledged the Trinity (' Father, Son, and Holy Ghost ')—' the holy universal church, the communion of the faithful, the forgiveness of sins, and the life everlasting.' They were therefore guilty of the same inconsistency as Luther and the other reformers of the sixteenth century, who, as Hallam has well remarked, acted as if they were infallible, whilst they waged war against that proud word. The church of Ronge, Czerski, and their associates, was either founded upon liberty of conscience, or it was not. If it was, they had no right to require of any christian man to believe in dogmas like that of the Trinity, or in the books of scripture adopted by them. But if the doctrines of religion do indeed depend upon church authority, surely the *dicta* of the greatest historical authority extant, namely, the catholic church, which has survived its divine founder for eighteen hundred years, are entitled to more weight in the mind of any candid man than the crude theological discoveries enunciated by Messrs. Czerski and Ronge. I remember in Dresden the landlord of a large hotel, who was a leading German-catholic, and who used to bore his guests at the *table-d'hôte* with his religious views, to an extent which actually drove from his house several quiet customers who preferred a dinner without polemics at another establishment.

When I was living in Berlin the Prussian government was little disturbed by questions of foreign policy, for the danger of Europe arising from the French intrigues in Egypt with Mahomet Ali had passed over, and Prussia had become a party to the treaty of London, which in the affairs of the east had completely isolated France in her position towards the other European powers. As regarded German politics, Prussia seemed to be content with the dualism of herself and Austria; and the prospect of German unity, though visible to some sanguine minds, was but a distant one, and did not much occupy the minds of the King and his advisers, who were content that Prussia had acquired the rank of the fifth European power, without troubling themselves particularly about the constitutional developement of the German nation, to accomplish which was in fact the chief mission and the indispensable duty of the Prussian crown.

The relations between Great Britain and Prussia were at this period as friendly as possible. The King was pleased with having stood godfather to the Prince of Wales, and his visit to England had left upon his mind agreeable impressions. Lord Westmorland's good humour and hospitalities had their due effect at Berlin, and in London Bunsen had made more friends than any Prussian envoy who was ever remembered there. There was, however, a sort of sparring between the two governments on the subject of the *Zollverein*-tariff, which had caused many fears and apprehensions to spring up among our manufacturers. Our board of trade had suggested that remonstrances should be made at Berlin against certain augmentations of duty which had lately been imposed on manufactured articles, and against the protective principle upon which the tariff in general appeared to have been framed. Baron von Bülow made a strong retort to these remonstrances, and threw in our teeth our restrictive corn-laws, and our differential duties in favour of timber and other articles of colonial produce. The fact was that the Prussian statesmen were favourable to free-trade, and would willingly have adopted a reduced tariff of duties, if they could have secured the assent of the southern states, each of which had an equal vote with Prussia in the affairs of the Customs-union. The South-german states were protectionists, and Prussia preferred going on for a time with such a tariff as they could be brought to agree to, rather than risk the dissolution of the union by insisting upon too great changes in a liberal direction. At the present day all questions of duties and other commercial matters affecting the interests of the *Zollverein* are disposed of openly by a customs-parliament, and no German government has the power of putting its single *veto* upon such measures as have been adopted by the parliament for the general benefit in the manner prescribed by the existing treaties between the states concerned.

On the termination of my mission as commissioner for the Portendic claims, I repaired to London for the purpose of reporting my proceedings to Lord Aberdeen. His lordship wished me to see Mr. Gladstone, then president of the board of trade, and to state to him my impressions in reference to the correspondence with Prussia above referred to on the subject of the customs-tariff. I had an interview, accordingly, with Mr. Gladstone, who said that no one could deprecate more than himself the doing anything to disturb the friendly relations subsisting between our government and that of Prussia, but he seemed rather disappointed that the partial reductions which had already been effected in the British tariff, chiefly at his instance, should have been so little appreciated or followed by Prussia and other foreign states. Two years later Baron von Bülow's arguments entirely lost their force in consequence of the bold and wise commercial legislation of Sir Robert Peel. At this time there were few persons, either in England or Germany, who believed that any such important changes as the abolition of our prohibitory corn-laws were likely to be effected at so early a date. The repeal of the sliding-scale of corn-duties has completely altered the character of the German corn-trade, and has made it a steady mercantile business, instead of a series of merely gambling speculations. I confess that I never held out either to Baron von Bülow, or any other official person in Prussia, the probability of the abolition of our corn-laws, simply because I did not think it would for years to come be in the power of any minister, however able and enlightened, to get such a measure passed, under ordinary circumstances, by the British parliament. But I have since seen so many other things take place which were generally supposed to be impracticable, that I have learned to follow the advice of Shakespeare, and to exercise a little more foresight before deciding on the possibility of future events :

> ' With caution judge of possibility ;
> Things thought unlikely, e'en impossible,
> Experience often shews us to be true ! '

CHAPTER IV.

LEIPSIC, said Goethe, is a little Paris, and educates its own people. Its schools of every description, its university, musical conservatory, and theatre, characterize it not less than its book trade and great fairs. It is the busy centre of the literary intelligence and the mercantile industry of Germany. Leipsic is not, like Dresden, a city to which foreign families resort for purposes of economy, or to dissipate their *ennui*, but is a place where everybody is hard at work, and no companionable idlers are to be found by the lounging rambler. There has long been stationed at Leipsic a consular corps, partly for watching over the commercial interests of their respective nations, and partly for the object of political observation. A British consul had been resident there for some years before my appointment, and the post being vacant, Lord Aberdeen offered it to me in the summer of 1845, with the higher rank of consul-general, and the additional commission to visit from time to time those places in Germany where the *Zollverein*-conferences should be held, and to report specially upon their proceedings. I accordingly settled with my family at Leipsic, regarding the post in the light of a stepping-stone, and hardly supposing that it would be my destiny to remain there during the long period of fifteen years.

The names of some of the most distinguished philosophers and poets are recorded with pride by the annalists of Leipsic. The great Leibnitz, whose glimpses of eternal truth were such as have been enjoyed by few mortal men, was born there. The names of Lessing, and of Goethe, are registered among the former students of the university. Schiller lived for a time at the neighbouring village of Gohlis. Whilst I resided at Leipsic the notabilities were not many, but I had opportunities of intercourse with some eminent persons, who will be mentioned in the sequel. The professors had a circle of their

own, and did not mix much in general society.   The students
who visited us formed an agreeable and refreshing element of
our Leipsic life.   The liveliness of young men is a reviving
cordial for, those who are advancing in years, and are beginning to see things rather in the brown shade of evening than
in the early sunshine of a hopeful existence.

As the German book trade has long centred in Leipsic, the
booksellers here form an important and influential body.
Some of their firms have existed for more than a century.
Mr. George Joachim Göschen, the publisher, and friend of
Wieland, Goethe, and Schiller, was the grandfather of our
present first lord of the admiralty.   Mr. Brockhaus, who has
for some years past been the largest publisher in Germany,
used to give very agreeable evening parties, especially about
the time of the book fair.   Baron Tauchnitz has become
generally known by his cheap editions of the works of British
authors, which have contributed so much towards the diffusion
of the English language and literature in foreign countries.

Soon after my arrival in Saxony an unfortunate incident
occurred, which had its origin in the unpopularity of the
King's ministry, of whom M. von Könneritz was then the
head.   The government had not only discouraged the so-
called German-catholics, but had endeavoured to prevent any
reform movements from going on within the Lutheran church,
and had prohibited the meetings of the new sect of 'protestant
friends.'   A cry of intolerance had been raised, which made it
easy for seditious persons to excite the mob against the King's
brother, Prince John, on the occasion of his visiting Leipsic
for the purpose of reviewing the communal guard.   After
the review a tumultuous mass of people assembled before the
hotel in which the Prince lodged, throwing stones against the
doors and windows, and trying to break into the house, in
order to take vengeance on the royal guest.   A company of
soldiers having been sent for for his protection, they ranged
themselves before the hotel, fired upon the mob, and killed
and wounded several persons.   The Prince escaped with some
difficulty early the next morning.   This deplorable occurrence
excited great indignation at Leipsic, and throughout the
kingdom; and although a strict official investigation at once
took place, it did not altogether allay the bitter feeling
caused by the military having fired upon the people, and it
was several years before Prince John ventured to shew himself
again in Leipsic.   The Prince was known to be a zealous
catholic, and the people had, without the slightest foundation,
been led to believe that it was he who had urged the ministers

to counteract the desired reforms within the sphere of both the protestant and catholic churches. The fact is that, according to the terms of the Saxon constitution, the entire management of the affairs of the protestant churches is entrusted to a council of ministers, and that even the King, so long as he is a catholic, has no power to interfere therein. M. von Könneritz and his colleagues were therefore wholly responsible for the policy they had adopted towards religious dissenters, and the ruffianly attack upon Prince John was thoroughly disgusting to all the respectable inhabitants of Leipsic and Dresden. I was assured by one of the Saxon ministers that the Prince had never meddled with the affairs either of the sect of German-catholics, or of the protestant dissenters, from whose lawless partisans the outrage referred to was supposed to have proceeded.

On new-year's day, 1846, I was presented at the Saxon court. In Dresden, as throughout Germany, new year's-day is a holiday, and after going to church, people pay visits and congratulate their friends. The King and Queen held receptions, both in the morning and in the evening. Between the two assemblies their majesties dined in public, to the great satisfaction of the spectators in the galleries,—a good old custom, since discontinued, which was likewise followed by the court of France before the first revolution. At Dresden the public used also to be admitted to the galleries to see the great court balls given during the winter season.

The King (Frederic Augustus II) was not yet fifty years of age, and had reigned nearly ten, previous to which he had been for several years co-regent with his uncle, King Anthony, who, being unable fully to master the popular agitation for an improved constitution, associated his nephew with himself in the government, as a security to the people that they should obtain something more of a representative system than Saxony had had the good fortune to enjoy. Frederic Augustus had been carefully educated, had travelled much, and combined with a mild disposition an earnestness of character which commanded the respect of those who approached him. His own instincts were essentially conservative, that is, he felt it his duty by all the means in his power to procure the observance of existing laws and international treaties. But he had likewise tact enough to perceive when it was time for the old to give place to the new, and in March, 1848, he recognized the necessity of dismissing the Könneritz administration, and of taking another set of ministers, pledged to act in the sense of the revolutionary movement which in that year so rudely shook the thrones of the German sovereigns. As a catholic, reigning in a protestant state, he was debarred from taking any part in the concerns of the lutheran church, or of the various sectarians who were working to overthrow it. The King was a good portly figure, very fond of shooting, as well as of dancing, in which latter exercise he could hold out longer than almost any one at court. He cultivated botany, and took great pleasure in botanical excursions. It was during one of such tours in the Tyrol, in August, 1854, that he unfortunately lost his life by being thrown from his carriage and kicked by a horse. At the new year's reception the King merely addressed to me a few words of welcome, and made some enquiries about my antecedents, adding that he was glad to have seen something of England during his visit in the previous year.

The Queen, Maria, daughter of Maximilian, king of Bavaria, was taller than any lady in Dresden. She had no children, whilst her twin-sister, the Archduchess Sophia of Austria, was blessed with several. The case was the same with the other two twin-sisters, the Queen (Elizabeth) of Prussia, and the subsequent Queen (Amelia) of Saxony, the former of whom proved childless, while the latter had a numerous family.

There stood upon the bridge across the Elbe, connecting the old with the new part of the city of Dresden, an ancient crucifix, raised upon a mass of artificial rock, which, having been thrown down by the French when they blew up the middle arch of the bridge in 1813, was afterwards replaced by the Emperor Alexander on the bridge being repaired and restored to use. Towards the end of March, 1844, there was a remarkable inundation of the Elbe, and the bridge was so shaken by the violence of the flood that the crucifix fell over into the river and sunk so deeply into its bed, that it was found impossible to recover it. I heard that the royal family were watching the flood from the palace-windows, and saw the crucifix fall, to their great dismay, the Queen Maria exclaiming, 'Oh! that horrid Ronge!' The fact, however, that the crucifix in the place where it stood by no means added to the beauty of the bridge, probably explains why a new crucifix has not since been placed there.

Prince John was favourably known, before his accession to the throne of Saxony, as a man of letters, well versed in history, theology, and German law. As a member of the first chamber of the diet, he frequently took part in the debates, and as one of the committee charged with the examination of the proposed new code of criminal law, he consented to act as *referent*, and his elaborate report materially contributed to the introduction of an improved system of penal legislation. He was in fact, what is so rarely to be found among princes, an accomplished scholar. On the occasion of a visit which Frederic William IV paid to Dresden (I think in 1852) the King of Saxony, and Prince John, received their royal guest from Berlin at the foot of the palace-staircase, who, on catching sight of them, called out to the King,—'But you make too much ceremony with me, you dear little angel!' and then looking towards the Prince,— 'and you too, old schoolmaster!'[1]

Prince John published, under the name of *Philalethes*, a German translation of Dante's 'divine comedy[2]' which is highly appreciated on account of the notes illustrative of early Italian history, and of the many theological points adverted to in the poem. The subjoined extract from his preface to the third volume (the *paradise*) may serve to give a notion of the critical task undertaken by the royal author :—

'Questions will often be found raised by the poet on apparently unimportant points, but always made use of in order to develope grand and important views. In order to make the meaning of such passages clear to the reader, the best way seemed to me to be to cite parallel passages upon such points from the scholastic writers, and to explain their theories in reference to the same. To this end I have frequently made use of Thomas de Aquino. Sometimes I have consulted also Petrus Lombardus, Albertus Magnus, Hugo St. Victor, and the pseudo-areopagites. Now and then I have endeavoured by more prolonged observations to throw light over entire portions of the work.'

'It is, however, undeniable that from the circumstance above-mentioned, the *paradise* has acquired to a certain extent the character of a doctrinal poem, which, with many dry and unequal passages, has still a peculiar sublimity, inasmuch as it takes, as it were, a bird's-eye view of the summits of human knowledge from the height of divine omniscience. This is one of the peculiarities of the middle-age philosophy, on which a word here may not be out of place.'

---

[1] 'Aber Du machst zu viel Umstand mit mir, liebes Engelchen! Und Du auch, alter Schulmeister!'

[2] Dante Alighieri's Göttliche Comödie, metrisch übertragen und mit kritischen und historischen Erläuterungen versehen von Philalethes. New edition. 3 vols. Leipzig, 1866.

'The middle-ages knew of no opposition between philosophy
and theology; they were convinced that truth could be but
one, and in cases of apparent contradiction they placed reason
below revelation.   Hence that faith and constancy to what
they held to be true; that childlike submission to the
authority of Aristotle as readily as to the claims of the holy
scriptures; hence, likewise, on the other hand, that disposition to venture, in aid of revelation, upon questions which
will always remain impenetrable by human understanding,
and are often in themselves subtile and useless.   That the
didactic part of Dante's *paradise* bears such a stamp is undeniable.   Nor shall we, on careful examination, fail to
perceive a certain consistency of plan in the philosophic-
theological passages which might at first seem to have been
by chance admitted into the poem.'

It is indeed no new discovery that the great Italian poet
had nourished his earnest piety by a careful study of Aristotle
and the scholastic philosophers, with whose aid he has shewn
how the earthly part of man, purified by Christianity, returns
to the eternal source of all created things.   The darkness
of hell, the shades of purgatory, and the bright light of
paradise, are all pictured in strict conformity with the
doctrines of the church, and of the philosophical principles
which serve not to controvert but to support those doctrines.
There have not been wanting German critics of Dante and
his poetry, among whom Augustus William Schlegel holds
perhaps the first place; and there are German translations by
Kannegiesser and several others.   But none of them have
furnished the student with more instructive commentaries
than *Philalethes*, or have entered more fully into the spirit of
the 'divine comedy.'

The Princess Amelia, sister of the King, had likewise a
literary turn, and had written several good dramas, which had
a fair success upon the stage.   The King's cousin, the Princess
Augusta, daughter of Frederic Augustus I, was a dignified
old lady, whom I could not look upon without interest, inasmuch as she was one of the three princesses whose names
were submitted to the French council of state, after the
divorce from Josephine, as worthy of the hand of Napoleon I,
the other two being a Russian Grand-Duchess, and the
Austrian Archduchess Maria-Louisa, upon whom the choice
fell.   On my first presentation, I found the Princess Augusta
more disposed to chat than any member of the royal family.
The King and Queen were rather reserved; and I learned from

Mr. Forbes, the British minister, that they were often embarrassed in receiving strangers. Mr. Forbes said that when he first came to Dresden the King and Queen seemed as if they hardly knew what to make of him, but they began to like him as soon as they found he understood his proper distance, and would not take liberties. *That*, he observed, was an important point to be attended to in official life.

The Saxon minister for foreign affairs, M. von Zeschau, was a good financier, and an experienced aud cautious statesman, though not fitted to swim with the current of democratic movement which in fact swept him away two years afterwards, together with the other members of the Könneritz administration. I remember conversing with M. von Zeschau about the rumoured intention of Sir Robert Peel to abolish the English corn-laws, and he said he could hardly comprehend how those laws had so long maintained their place in the statute-book, for they were clearly contrary to the interests of a great manufacturing country. The Saxon population likewise depended in a great degree upon manufactures, and he knew by experience the importance of keeping cheap the necessaries of life. In the ore-mountains (*Erzgebirge*) he said there was a population of hand-loom weavers who had a hard struggle to keep body and soul together, and who would probably have perished but for the cheapness of potatoes and coarse rye-bread. In expressing my satisfaction at hearing the Saxon minister intimate such views, I added the hope that in the councils of the *Zollverein* Saxony would prove the opponent of any new restrictive duties which might be proposed, and he answered that as regarded the *Zollverein*-tariff the Saxon government was, like that of Prussia, the advocate of financial duties only, and that the protective duties comprised in the tariff were entirely the work of the South-German states.

The announcement made by Sir Robert Peel at the opening of the parliamentary session of 1846 that the protective corn-laws were to be gradually abandoned, and the customs duties on timber, and other articles, considerably reduced, excited great interest in Germany. The subjoined letters from Lord Westmorland refer to the commercial policy of our government, and to the change of administration which had nearly taken place when the Queen sent for Lord John Russell in December 1845. Lord Westmorland was a tory, and his proxy in the Lords was held by the Duke of Wellington :—

'*Berlin*, January 8, 1846.

'My dear Mr. Ward,

'Thanks for your good wishes, and I very sincerely return them for yourself, Mrs. Ward, and family.

'There was excitement and alarm here at the prospect of a change of administration in England, and with respect to myself it is impossible to describe all the kindness which was expressed. With regard to the change in the corn-protection I know not what is intended. The Duke of Wellington from the first declared himself as the supporter of Sir Robert Peel, because he considered his government as the first object for the prosperity of the country. I believe Sir Robert Peel to be too good a man to propose anything he thought would be detrimental to the interests of any portion of the population, and too good a financier not to know what would be the operation of any measure he would propose. I have therefore perfect confidence in what is to come. If protection is to be taken in part from agriculture it must be the same for foreign shoes, &c., &c., which the farmer buys, and I can send good boots from here at one dollar per pair. I have forwarded your despatches. The meeting of *Zollverein* deputies will not be at present. Let me know the speculations in your part of the world.

'Yours very truly,
'WESTMORLAND.'

'*Berlin*, February 13, 1846.

'My dear Mr. Ward,

'Your last letter did not reach me till yesterday. I think Sir Robert Peel's measures will have a better effect on the governing powers of this part of the world than you anticipated they will have upon the party of the mercantilists. These people argue that England does all this for her own interest; the reasonable (and I hope the governing) answer "yes," but it is also the interest of every other people who will or can exert themselves.

'As to the people of this country eating all their wheat in the next fifteen or twenty years, I should be of that opinion if they eat wheaten bread, but you know that generally speaking it is not so, and I fear will not become so. I am delighted to see that Sir Robert's measures have not brought down the price of corn, and that the funds have risen. I sent home the convention with Hanover some time ago. Your account of the potato disease will be interesting to our government.

' I had last night an evening party, to which the King and all the royal family came, all *en frac*. An opera of mine, the *Proserpina*, was performed, and I have every reason to be satisfied and delighted with the execution and reception. It was a great compliment on the part of the King. He never before went anywhere dressed as a private gentleman.

' With kind remembrances to Mrs. Ward, believe me,

' Sincerely yours,

' WESTMORLAND.'

The following letter from General Sir De Lacy Evans shews that the carrying of Sir Robert Peel's proposals was anticipated by the liberal party, but not the immediate abolition of the corn-laws, which indeed had been unsuccessfully moved by Mr. Charles Villiers, M.P. Sir De Lacy Evans had lately been returned for Westminster in opposition to the ministerial candidate, Captain Rous.

' TO MR. WARD.

' *London*, April 9, 1846.

' My dear Sir,

' This is the first day of our Easter vacation, and I lose not a moment to avail myself of it, to apologize for my long silence, and to acknowledge with many thanks your very kind and gratifying congratulation on my return for Westminster. You will very justly think I ought to have done this before. But the fact is I have come in suddenly in the midst of sharp contests and of an accumulation of parliamentary business, of which I have rather more than my share, as my colleague does nothing.

' Of the result of the election I had myself no doubt, as I considered that my gallant opponent was in too weak and false a position to be enabled to maintain his ground; and the opinions of the public and the press were certainly flattering to me, and little so to him. The immediate abolition of the corn-laws, I think, is not on the cards. But I hope the measure of Sir R. Peel will be carried; but he has gratuitously interrupted its progress through the Commons by the intro-duction of an Irish coercion bill, the most malapropos and worst in its provisions that could well be devised. It has been almost as bad a selection as to time as that of the unfortunate Poles in respect to their recent insurrection, to which you so justly allude.

' Your observations relative to the surplus wheat of Germany for exportation are highly valuable, and I may perhaps have some opportunity of profiting of them.   I hope you and Mrs. Ward are pleased with Leipsic as a residence, although, of course, in point of society, it must be far inferior to Berlin. But in regard to commerce, I should suppose it must be perhaps the most important post in Germany.   Hoping, should any circumstances bring you and Mrs. Ward to London, we may have the pleasure of seeing you, and with our united respects,

'Believe me, my dear Sir, very truly yours,
'DE LACY EVANS.'

Mr. Wheaton went from Berlin to London in the early part of this year for the purpose of assisting in the then pending negotiation on the Oregon question, to which he alludes in the subjoined letter to me, and mentions also the fact of his recall from his post.   He afterwards spent a day with me at Leipsic, on his way to Paris, which was the last time I ever saw him.   In April 1848, I heard of his death in a deranged state of mind at Roxburg, Massachusetts.   He had been preparing to give a course of lectures on the law of nations in the university of Cambridge, United States.

'*Berlin*, April 29, 1846.
'My dear Mr. Ward,
'I am very much obliged by your kind enquiries.   It is true that I am to have a successor here, for whose arrival I am waiting.   But I do not suppose he will be here before the last day of May, when I shall proceed to Paris.   They are *talking* of another mission for me; there is none vacant at present but Petersburg, for which I have no mind.

'I am sorry I shall not have the pleasure of seeing you in June, as I presume you mean to watch the *Zollverein* congress. I think they will not give you much trouble.   The economists carry the day, and the Prussian board of trade is quite disgusted.   I was delighted with my short visit to London, during which I saw an immense number of persons; was very much fêted, and had every reason to be satisfied with the dispositions of the leading statesmen on both sides.   I believe the two governments are agreed upon the forty-ninth parallel, but the difficulty lies in the question of the navigation of the river and the possession of Vancouver's Island.   I hope these difficulties will be overcome, but the doubt is whether such an arrangement can be made as two-thirds of our senate will ratify.   They are debating as if they were commissioners to negotiate, every man being anxious to appropriate to himself the *glory* of helping or defeating a settlement. It is very much to be regretted that Mr. Pakenham did not send home the proposition made to him by President Polk for discussion. The negotiation would then have been *substantially* transferred to London, and it would have been all settled before this time.

'I will try to take a run some day to Leipzig to see you, as I fear there is little chance of your being here before my departure. I am publishing with Brockhaus a new edition, much enlarged, of my " Histoire du droit des gens." It is the same thing with the American edition in English, published last year at New York.

'With cordial regards to Mrs. Ward,

'I remain, ever truly your faithful Friend,

'H. WHEATON.'

The *Zollverein*-conference sat during this summer at Berlin, and I was there for a few weeks to watch its proceedings. The court was absent. Baron von Bülow was no more, and Baron von Canitz had succeeded him as minister for foreign affairs. M. Kühne, the intelligent director of the customs, invited me to dine with the so-called Spanish club, where a number of official and literary men were assembled. The conversation turned upon Sir Robert Peel's commercial policy, and the question was put to me whether I considered that minister, or Lord John Russell, the greater statesman? I answered that I was a follower of the latter; and that the abolition of the corn-laws was, like catholic emancipation, in reality the work of the whig-party, although Peel had the merit of putting the finishing stone to the work at the last hour. I dwelt also on Lord John Russell's eminent services in the cause of parliamentary reform, which was carried entirely by the firmness of the whig-leaders. The opinion of the club was however against me. Several of the party expressed their warm admiration of Peel, and of his courage in breaking away from his own political friends, M. Kühne declaring ' he is as much greater than Russell in the conceptions of his mind as he is taller in personal stature !'

The question of the right of succession to the duchies of Schleswig, Holstein, and Lauenburg, then held by the crown of Denmark, had begun to excite great interest in Germany, as well as in the Danish dominions. The subject had been discussed in the chambers of most of the German constitutional states, and they had adopted resolutions urging the

federal diet to interfere for the protection of German nationality within the duchies, and for the establishment of the
claim of the Duke of Augustenburg to the crown of the
duchies after the decease of the King (Christian VIII), of his
son then prince royal, and of his brother Prince Ferdinand,
neither of whom had any prospect of leaving issue. The
public excitement was greatly increased by the publication at
Copenhagen on the 8th of July, 1846, of a patent, or open
letter, of the King of Denmark, with the view of preventing
the future disunion of his dominions by combining the succession of the duchies with that of the kingdom. The patent
declared the right of succession in Schleswig and Lauenburg
to be identical with that in Denmark proper, and that although
in certain parts of Holstein the succession might be doubtful,
the King would find the means of overcoming that difficulty
so as to maintain the integrity of the Danish monarchy. The
states of Holstein immediately protested against the tenor of
the royal patent; the Duke of Augustenburg, the Grand-duke
of Oldenburg, and others of the *agnati* interested made haste
to take a similar proceeding in defence of their rights.

The heir-presumptive to the kingdom of Denmark proper
was at that time the Prince Frederic, son of the Landgrave
William of Hesse by the Princess Charlotte, sister of Christian
VIII, and consequently uncle of the Princess of Wales. He
was a widower, having married the Grand-duchess Alexandra
of Russia, who unfortunately died in 1844. His right was
derived from the *lex regia*, or royal law of Denmark, established
by Frederic III on the 14th of November, 1665, in virtue of
the absolute power vested in him by the change effected in the
Danish constitution in the year 1660. The *lex regia* admitted
the succession of females, the descendants of Frederic III, and
of males in heritage through them, but it applied to the kingdom of Denmark only, and was not designed to extend to the
duchies. There were indeed two elderly ladies who stood before
Prince Frederic in the succession, viz., his mother, and his
aunt the Princess Juliana, widow of the Prince William of
Hesse-Philippsthal, but as it was understood that those two
ladies would renounce in his favour, he was generally regarded
as the heir to the Danish crown.

In his capacity of Duke of Holstein and Lauenburg, the
King of Denmark was a member of the Germanic confederation; consequently as to those duchies the question might
have been settled by the Germanic diet to which the ducal
states had appealed for relief against the patent of the 8th of
July. But this was not the case in regard to Schleswig,

where the Germanic diet had no more right to interfere in the matter of the succession than any other foreign power.

The King's *agnati*, who were the heirs male of Christian I, contended that they were entitled to succeed to the entirety of the duchies of Schleswig and Holstein, after the extinction of the royal male line then represented by the King, his son, and brother. Of the *agnati* the first in succession was Christian Duke of Schleswig-Holstein-Sonderburg-Augustenburg, born in 1798, brother of the Queen of Denmark, and father of the present Duke Frederic, and of the Prince Christian now residing in England. In maintaining that no female, or person claiming through a female, could succeed to the ducal crowns, the *agnati* were supported by the opinions of the most eminent German lawyers, and their cause was warmly espoused by the people of both Schleswig and Holstein. The feeling of the states of Holstein was so strong that after having resolved to appeal to the federal diet against the royal patent, all the members except six indignantly quitted the place of assembly, declaring their intention not to appear there again until justice should be done them by the King-duke. The Danish government was in fact unable to substantiate the allegations made in the royal patent, and there could be little doubt that the claims of the Duke of Augustenburg and the other descendants in the male line from Christian I to succeed to the two duchies of Schleswig and Holstein, were well founded in law.

Without entering into any lengthened examination of title, it may suffice to note here that Schleswig and Holstein had for many centuries past been constitutionally united, and that when they elected as their common lord Christian I, king of Denmark, in 1460, he entered into a solemn capitulation, which has been called the magna charta of the duchies, binding himself to the states for the observance, among other articles, of the following points :—

'That Schleswig and Holstein should be for ever united :

'That Christian I was elected not as King of Denmark, but as Lord of the Duchies of Schleswig and Holstein :

'That the rights and liberties of the duchies should remain uninfringed : and

'That the states should be obliged to elect the future Dukes from the male descendants of Christian I or his right heirs ;' which last article was modified in 1616 when the states surrendered the right of election, and the right of the male heirs became absolute in both of the duchies.

The common law of succession had never been altered or

modified in either duchy, although Schleswig belonged in full sovereignty to the King-duke, whereas he held Holstein subject to its federal relations towards the Germanic body. That duchy became an independent state in consequence of the dissolution of the German empire on the 6th of August, 1806, and when it was made a member of the Germanic confederation in 1815 it was of course in the capacity of an independent state, of which the King of Denmark, as Duke of Holstein, happened to be the sovereign. There was no pretence for the assertion that the succession in Schleswig, much less in Holstein, had ever been assimilated to that of the kingdom.

The Danish government, however, in appealing for assistance to Great Britain, France, and Russia, laid stress on guarantees of the succession to the duchies alleged to have been given by the former two powers in 1720, and on certain cessions of right made by the last-mentioned power in 1767 and 1773. The guarantees however related merely to the possession *de facto* of the former ducal-gottorp parts of Schleswig, and had nothing to do with the question of the succession ; nor had the cessions by Russia any further application than to the same ducal-gottorp parts of Schleswig which the King-duke had acquired by treaty, and to the ducal parts of Holstein agreed to be exchanged for Oldenburg and Delmenhorst. From the outset of the dispute Denmark failed to make out any good case for the interference of foreign powers with the duchies' concerns. As regarded the third duchy, viz. Lauenburg, the Danish government failed in shewing that the right of succession had at any time merged in the Danish crown. The *lex regia* had certainly never been introduced into that duchy, which at the peace of 1815 had fallen to the lot of Prussia, and been transferred by her to Denmark in exchange for Swedish Pomerania. Lauenburg was like Holstein an independent state, subject to its obligations towards the Germanic confederation.

Such was the origin of the Schleswig-Holstein question, which for twenty years afterwards kept the Danish monarchy in a state of civil war, and the rest of Europe in constant apprehension and alarm. In August, 1846, I transmitted to the foreign-office a memorial explanatory of the opposite views taken at Copenhagen, and in the duchies, of the law of succession, and concluding in favour of the eventual right of the house of Augustenburg. The only answer I received from Lord Palmerston was a mere acknowledgment of the memorial, and that he had forwarded it to the prince-consort, by whom he believed it would be duly appreciated.

There was one very simple and obvious way of ending the dispute,—I mean by repealing the *lex regia* of 1665,—the effect of which would have been to exclude the female line of heirs from the kingdom, and to open to the Duke of Augustenburg as the first male heir the succession to that as well as to the other parts of the monarchy. But such a plan would by no means have suited the policy of the arrogant ultra-danish party which was predominant at Copenhagen ; nor, so far as I know, was it ever seriously proposed to the Danish government by any foreign power.

Our winter of 1846–7 was passed agreeably in the social pleasures of Leipsic. Among my consular colleagues were two men whose friendship I valued, viz. the Russian Consul-general Baron de Kiel (who had long resided at Naples, and was brother of the superintendent of the Russian artists at Rome), and the Consul-general of Austria M. Hübner, who afterwards as Baron von Hübner filled successively the high posts of Ambassador at the court of France, and at the holy see. Baron von Hübner was of humble origin, and his talents and industry early in life attracted the notice of Prince Metternich, who constantly protected his diplomatic career. The influence of M. Pilat, director of the Austrian foreign-office and editor of the 'Austrian Observer,' whose daughter he married, may also have contributed something towards M. Hübner's rapid advancement. He wrote extremely well, and had a good knowledge of several languages. In conversing with him about European politics I found him impressed with much the same order of ideas as those ascribed to Metternich, and he used to lament that there were so many European nations which were unable to govern themselves, and whose condition was therefore full of danger to the general tranquillity. The policy of Austria at that time was simply conservative. She was struggling to keep her Italian provinces, and to maintain the ascendancy in Germany which belonged to her by the terms of the Germanic constitution. She was of course full of jealousy and suspicion of the designs of Prussia, and seemed to anticipate the attempts subsequently made by the latter power to substitute her own for the Austrian hegemony in the fatherland.

Baron von Hübner was a good catholic, and as such the better qualified to be the biographer of the great and imperious Pope Sixtus V[1], whose name for the few years of his

---

[1] 'Sixte Quint, par M. le Baron de Hübner, ancien Ambassadeur d'Autriche à Paris et à Rome, d'après des correspondances diplomatiques tirées des archives d'état, &c.' 3 vols. Paris, 1870.

reign (1585 to 1590) struck terror into all Europe, and who was the last Roman pontiff that dispensed thrones, and really arbitrated between temporal sovereigns. His life has a peculiar interest for Englishmen, as he was the Pope who urged and subsidised Spain to invade England with her memorable armada. It had already been written by other historians, and Ranke's delineation of his character was deemed particularly successful. But Baron von Hübner's work has the advantage of making us acquainted with many state-papers and documents which had not before been published, and he has also presented us with some original views of the Pope's policy which are well worthy of attention. Sixtus V was a sincere believer in catholic truth, in the infallibility of the church of which he was the supreme head on earth, and in the duty of that head to extirpate heresy by every means at his command. In his reign protestantism was a novelty which few members of the old church thought could be lasting, and many good men were for eradicating it forcibly as a noxious weed. Heresy has, however, thriven in spite of all persecutions, and by its innumerable ramifications has done its best to hinder the unity of the christian world as ' one fold and one shepherd.'

In conversing with M. Hübner upon the case of the republic of Cracow, which had just been annexed to the Austrian empire, he declared himself unable to comprehend how our government could complain of a breach of international engagements by the three powers who were parties to the treaties of the 3rd of May, 1815, which sealed the fate of Poland; inasmuch as those treaties were concluded between Russia, Austria, and Prussia, and neither England nor France was a party to them, or had any real interest in their subject-matter. The extinguishment of the republic had become necessary in consequence of the continual plots and intrigues which were carried on within it, and Austria had accepted the possession of it less in her own interest than for the security of the neighbouring states. I likewise discussed the question with Dr. von der Pfordten, then professor of Roman law in the university, who in 1848 became minister for foreign affairs in Saxony, and subsequently held the same office in Bavaria. The professor concurred in the opinion that the three powers had an undoubted right to destroy a political existence created by them and dependent upon their pleasure. The general act of the Vienna congress, dated the 9th of June, 1815, was, he said, a mere recapitulation of the various treaties concluded between different parties during the sitting of the congress, and was a ratifying or guaranteeing instrument, not a many-headed monster entitled to dictate to Europe, and to over-ride the rights of the different contracting parties. Our government as a merely guaranteeing power had no right to interefere so long as the contracting· powers were agreed, and it seemed as if the legal advisers of the British crown had overlooked this point in the advice which they had given.

M. Brockhaus's paper, the 'Deutsche Allgemeine Zeitung,' took up the question on the same side, and indeed the French and English protest against the annexion found little or no sympathy in the German press. I reported all this to Lord Palmerston, without however anticipating that my observations would influence the policy of Her Majesty's Government. The civil law is so little understood in England that our statesmen are quite unaccustomed to apply its rules to cases of the interpretation of treaties, or other points of international law ; and hence differences with continental governments have arisen, and are likely again to arise. The disposal of the frontier town of Cracow was not under any circumstances worth contending about. The great blunder was made in 1815, when Lord Castlereagh assented to Russia's retaining the sovereignty of the grand-duchy of Warsaw, which the Czar had wrested from the King of Saxony, the ally of Napoleon, during the war. That concession to Russia, though coupled with conditions for a Polish constitution, was in fact the abandonment by England and France of all pretensions to re-establish the Polish nation. The congress of Vienna was *finis Poloniæ*.

Among the Leipsic professors I saw much of Wachsmuth, who filled the chair of history, and whose amiable character rendered him a general favourite. His various works on ancient and modern history can scarcely be unknown to English scholars [1]. At his house I had the pleasure of meeting Godfrey Hermann, the great philologer, then in his seventy-fifth year, but fresh in intellect, and able to continue his lectures on the Greek drama with unabated vigour. He was a short, spare man, fresh-coloured, and of a lively and ardent temperament, which he inherited from his mother, who was of French descent. His habits were active, and he rode a great deal for exercise, contrary to the custom of German professors. We talked of English scholars,

---

[1] Particularly his 'Hellenische Alterthumskunde aus dem Gesichtspunkte des Staats.' 4 vols. Halle, 1830.

most of whom were known to him. With both Porson and Elmsley he had had controversies on subjects of criticism. Upon Gaisford he bestowed much commendation. He said, 'Your English philologers are so fortunate as to be provided with rich prebendaries and dignities in the church. Your church feeds the study of the classical authors who ignored christianity.' I remarked to Hermann that he was himself a doctor of theology, and I presumed had been in some measure occupied with ecclesiastical matters. He answered, 'No, indeed, I care little about them. I have rather accustomed myself to look at religion from the point of view of the ancients, and I do not trouble myself at all about church-affairs.' I asked him whether he thought that for a great commercial country like England the system of classical education followed in our public schools was the most desirable? He said, 'Why not? the ancients are the best humanizers; they inspire youth with brave and noble thoughts. As a nation you are egotistic, and your church is too mercenary to expect much veneration from young men. I should be sorry if the classics should fall into neglect in your academies.' A merchant who was present started some objections, but Professor Wachsmuth supported his colleague's opinion, and thought that the *Realschule*, or non-classical schools, had been carried rather too far in Germany. I walked home with Hermann, and on taking leave of him he said, 'Pray believe that I wish well to old England. I don't forget my English ring.' This ring was a legacy bequeathed to him by Dr. Parr, as the greatest critic of the age, and he wore it with peculiar satisfaction, although he enjoyed decorations conferred upon him by the King of Saxony and other sovereigns.

In declaring his indifference to religious questions, it must not be supposed that Hermann had not really studied them, for he had a strong inclination towards metaphysics, and had made himself so thoroughly master of the philosophy of Kant, as to be able to give two courses of lectures upon it before the Leipsic university. The mind of Hermann was extremely logical, and he felt himself obliged to go to the bottom of every subject into which he commenced an enquiry. He knew how to distinguish between thinking and feeling, between knowing and believing, and he claimed entire freedom from authority in scientific investigations. Those who were best acquainted with him have declared that he appreciated faith in its own sphere, and reverenced what was holy; but that he invariably acted in accordance with his own strong sense of duty, which is in fact the basis of the Kantian philosophy. We are so little accustomed in England to the study of religious philosophy, or indeed of philosophical systems at all, that a mind like that of Godfrey Hermann cannot easily be understood in this country. The English intelligence rarely carries out any principle to its legitimate consequences ; it is governed less by logic than by rhetoric ; and so it happens that so many questions of vital importance are kept floating about in a transition state. Whether Hermann was labouring in the field of language, or of metaphysics, the single object of his research was truth, and the conclusions which he arrived at were adopted by him in the spirit of complete self-denial, and conscientious devotion.

The year 1847 opened with rumours that a better constitution than that of the provincial states was about to be established in Prussia, and on the 3rd of February a royal ordinance actually appeared creating what was called an 'united diet' to be formed by the amalgamation of the eight provincial diets of the monarchy into one legislative body, and to which, as already mentioned, were to be referred for deliberation all new loans, taxes, and imposts, and all new laws affecting the relations of persons and property throughout the kingdom. The King opened the 'united diet' in Berlin on the 11th of April with an extempore speech from the throne, which, as it had not been written out for their perusal, was as great a novelty to his ministers as it was to the assembly. He treated the new legislature as a happy and efficacious medium between the old notion of provincial states and the modern theory of a representative body governing by majorities. 'Prussia,' said the King, 'has become strong by the sword. As in the field, so must the political course of Prussia be guided by one will. No power on earth shall force me to change the natural relations between prince and people into conventional or constitutional ones, nor will I ever consent that between God in heaven and this country, a written paper, like a second providence, shall intrude itself, to govern us by its paragraphs, and substitute them for the old sacred feeling of loyalty.' Proceeding in this style, His Majesty condemned the bad fruits produced by modern liberalism in church and state, declaring emphatically,—'I, and my house, we will serve the Lord!'

It may easily be imagined that the *juste milieu* which Frederic William IV believed himself to have hit upon, satisfied neither the reactionary nor the movement party. An amendment to the address proposed by Count Arnim

was nearly carried against the government, and it soon
became evident that there did not exist either in the united
diet, or out of doors, the expected measure of gratitude and
confidence towards the crown.   The scheme was in fact a
failure, and in less than three years afterwards the King
was forced to eat his own words, and to give to his people
that very 'written piece of paper, with paragraphs, under
the name of a constitution,' against the introduction of which
he had so emphatically protested.

Richard Cobden was making a continental tour this
summer, and was fêted at many places.   At Leipsic there
were no means of getting up a free-trade demonstration, but
at Hamburgh one was prepared on a large scale, and I went
there to take part in the proceedings.   The dinner given
to Cobden was attended by above six hundred persons, M.
Ruperti, president of the Hamburgh board-of-trade, in the
chair.   As all the Hamburgh merchants understood English,
Cobden's speech was perfectly intelligible, and very well
received.   It struck me there were a number of vulgarisms
in it, such as this:—'What, gentlemen, shall I answer to
arguments of such a kind? Why, I will tell the protectionists
that their reasoning is neither fish, nor flesh, nor good red
herring!'   But his eloquence was simple, and at times
felicitous.   Adverting to a tower of about three hundred
feet high which formed a part of the new water-works
erected by the engineer Lindley, Cobden said that at first
he declined the recommendations made to him to mount the
tower for the sake of the view, believing it to be out of his
power in his weak state of health ; but on being further
persuaded he at last resolved to try, and succeeded without
much difficulty in reaching the top.   'So, gentlemen,' he
added, 'it was with the corn-laws. Ten years ago few people
believed that it was possible by any amount of exertion to
obtain their repeal ; but by resolution and perseverance we
accomplished our object, nevertheless.'

The great charm about Cobden was his earnestness of
purpose, and singleness of character.   He was not an accomplished man, and seemed to me to know little about
continental politics.   He talked with me about a pet scheme
which he had of establishing universal peace by means of
treaties between the great powers to which the smaller states
should afterwards be invited to accede.   I reminded him of
the various projects which had been started with a similar
object during the last hundred years, particularly that of
the great German philosopher Kant, all which projects were

open to the objection that any power which felt itself aggrieved might at any time withdraw from the pacific treaty, and thereby provoke the very state of war it was intended to preclude. He still thought however that treaties providing for the settlement of international disputes by arbitration would be a great moral security for universal peace. I hinted to Cobden that the French nation had been and would continue to be the real disturber of European tranquillity, and that there was little danger from any other quarter. In this view he did not seem to concur, attaching a high value to the cordial alliance between France and England, and confiding in the good intentions of the citizen-King who then occupied the French throne.

The death of Felix Mendelssohn, whose spirit departed after a short struggle on the 2nd of November, cast a gloom over Leipsic and the whole musical world. He was in his thirty-ninth year, and had a charming wife, the daughter of a pastor, and a young family. For about twelve years he had been the director of the celebrated Leipsic concerts, which under him had even added to the high reputation they had acquired during the lapse of a century. The Mendelssohns were our near neighbours, and we occasionally met them in society. One could not but be struck with his brilliant talents, his deep feeling, and a certain nobility of character which distinguished him. He was looked up to almost as a father by a number of rising young artists, and was always ready to promote their advancement. I remember hearing him sound the praises of Joachim, then a boy in a jacket, and foretell that he would become the first violinist in Germany,—a prophecy which did not require many years to bring about its accomplishment. The Mendelssohns lived in great intimacy with the Frege family, one member of whom (Livia Frege) interested him much as a *Virtuosin* of the first order.

Felix Mendelssohn was born a Jew, and was converted to the reformed, or calvinistic, confession. His grandfather was the philosopher Moses Mendelssohn, author of ' Phædon,' or discourses on the immortality of the soul; and his father was a wealthy banker at Berlin. He had not therefore to struggle against want, nor did he ever regard his art as a means of subsistence. His genius was precocious. At eight years old he was already a master, and at fifteen he had published the famous quartettes dedicated to Goethe, which still rank among the best of his compositions. The beautiful overture to the ' Midsummer Night's Dream ' was written in his seventeenth year. This and his other two

overtures,—the 'Hebrides' and the 'Fair Melusina,' as well
as his 'Songs without words,' are sufficiently known in
English musical circles.   His opera of the 'Marriage of
Gamacho' was less successful, but his two great oratorios,
'St. Paul,' and 'Elias,' are noble monuments of his splendid
powers.   They are highly scientific, and cannot easily be
comprehended by persons like myself, whose musical sense
has been little cultivated, though their merit has been acknowledged by the most competent judges in and out of
Germany.   Mendelssohn, though not exactly a follower of
Sebastian Bach, was said to have taken some ideas from
that great master, and he rescued Bach's passion-music
from the oblivion in which it had long lain, and brought
it out anew to the delight of the Berlin academy, since
which it has frequently been performed (usually on Good-
Friday) in the churches of Leipsic and other German towns.
Bach has been said sometimes to be an eminently protestant
composer.   At all events, that great master was undoubtedly
a good lutheran, and a pious man.   Whether the composer
of 'St. Paul' has indicated in that oratorio anything of the
spirit of the reformation, is best known to musical critics.
It was Baron von Bunsen's opinion that Mendelssohn alone
was competent to express in measures that great religious
movement.   He however had nothing sectarian in his nature,
and some of his church-music, for instance his 'Tu es Petrus,'
are quite in the spirit of catholic orthodoxy.   Altogether
I cannot but lament that his premature death deprived
me of opportunities of knowing more of the highly-refined
mind of that talented and excellent man.   His musical compositions will long survive him.   His private character may
be in some sort estimated from the collections of his letters
published after his decease by his brother and son[1].

---

[1] 'Reise-Briefe von Felix Mendelssohn-Bartholdy aus den Jahren 1830 bis
1832, herausgegeben von Paul Mendelssohn-Bartholdy.' Leipzig, 1832. 'Briefe
aus den Jahren 1833 bis 1847, von Felix Mendelssohn-Bartholdy, herausgegeben
von Paul Mendelssohn-Bartholdy in Berlin und Dr. Carl Mendelssohn-Bartholdy
in Heidelberg.' Leipzig, 1863.

CHAPTER V.

THE year 1848 opened calmly, and few could have anticipated the revolutionary movement which before its close had rudely shaken so many of the European thrones. In Germany it was the inevitable result of the system of excessive restrictions upon the people which the German sovereigns had followed since the reconstitution of the nation as a federal body at the peace of 1815. The German nation was, to say the least, sufficiently intelligent to govern itself in a constitutional manner, and it felt itself deprived of the requisite degree of constitutional liberty in consequence of the provisions of the so-called final act of the diet, dated the 15th of May, 1820, and founded upon the resolutions passed on the 20th of September in the previous year by the famous ministerial congress at Carlsbad. The nation moreover ardently desired unity,—'*das ganze Deutschland soll es sein!*' and that wish had been effectually frustrated by the tenor of the federal act signed at Vienna on the 8th of June, 1815. The Germanic diet had become a bye-word for its inefficiency, and its incompatibility with public opinion. It was in fact the instrument by which the political system of Prince Metternich was maintained in Germany during a period of three-and-thirty years.

The events of the month of March are known to every one. I venture to insert here a few extracts from my private journal by way of illustration of those exciting times.

1848.—January 11th.—Went to Dresden to a court ball. The King asked me how I liked the Leipsic people? saying they were formerly a contented class, and he wished them still to be so. I answered that the Leipsickers seemed very well off; that there was then no political agitation going on, and all appeared perfectly quiet. 'I hope so,' replied the King; 'I trust we have returned to quiet times.'

January 14th.—Dined at Henry II, Count Reuss's (who resides at Leipsic). Met the four Princesses of Schleswig-Holstein,—fat, fair, and forty,—daughters of the deceased Prince Emilius, and cousins of Duke Christian, the head of the family. The ladies spoke warmly for the cause of the duchies, and against the pretensions of the Danish king to get hold of the succession. One of them asked me if I did not think Lord Palmerston would be disposed to help them. I said I hoped so. Count Reuss observed what a fine fellow Lord Palmerston was, and that he would have been a very handsome man but for the loss of his eye. I protested against this assumption, declaring Lord P. had two as good eyes as anybody present. But Count Reuss persisting, and one of the ladies having heard the same story, it was carried against me, and the party separated, I regret to say, in the firm belief that my official chief was a one-eyed minister.

January 16th.—The hereditary Grand-duke of Oldenburgh, who is studying at the university, and his governor, Colonel Strauss, spent the evening with us. We talked of English history. None of the party admired Queen Elizabeth, and our guests seemed full of sympathy for Mary Stuart, whose cause Schiller has so successfully recommended to Germany in his celebrated tragedy. The young Prince said, 'For my part, I only look at her misfortunes.' Colonel Strauss has made a large collection of the hair of remarkable persons, and considers it as an indication of character. He was surprised to find so many dark-haired persons in England, inasmuch as light hair was one of the characteristics of the Anglo-Saxon race, and there are still many fair-haired persons among the population of the coasts where the Anglo-Saxon invaders chiefly descended.

February 27th.—Sunday. Ball at the Director of the circle, M. de Broizem's. Everybody talking about the rumour of an insurrection in Paris. M. Brockhaus brought the latest newspaper, which was read aloud to the company.

February 28th.—News of Louis-Philippe's abdication. I rejoice at his fall and at that of Guizot, who with all his professions of high moral principles has been the subservient tool of the King's selfish schemes. Thiers would have been a more national minister; he knows France well, and has shewn great skill in managing the Chambers.

February 29th.—The movement in Paris is a revolution.

The Orleans family expelled, a provisional government established, and a republic evidently impending. Accounts very brief and unsatisfactory, the railway between Paris and Brussels being broken up. What will be the consequences in Germany and other parts of Europe, in Italy above all?

March 1st.—The Grand-duke of Oldenburgh, apprehending troubles, has sent for his son from Leipsic, and the ball about to be given by the young prince is therefore postponed.

March 8th.—During the past week great excitement in Saxony, and in all the German states. A general movement demanding of the governments constitutional reforms. Leipsic in a very disturbed state, the King refusing to comply with the universal wish for the removal of the censorship of the press.

March 9th.—The Saxon government gives in with a bad grace, and abolishes the censorship. Read Lamartine's circular on the foreign policy of France. It makes pacific professions, but surely the declaration that France repudiates the treaties of 1815 is full of danger. Yet Guizot said nearly the same thing after the Cracow affair.

March 12th.—Sunday. Had a dinner-party, and everybody talked politics, of which they used to be very shy. There is to be a meeting of patriotic men at Frankfort in order to prepare the way for a German parliament.

March 16th.—Serious riots in Vienna, and continued agitation in those states where the governments have not complied with the popular demands. It looks as if the Germans would be greater gainers than the French by the revolutionary movement.

March 17th.—The new Saxon administration, in which Braun is premier, and Von der Pfordten, late professor at Leipsic, minister for foreign affairs, has begun by granting in a lump the liberty of the press and everything else desired by the people. Leipsic illuminated in consequence. In Vienna the people have succeeded; free press, dismissal of Metternich, and a constitution.

March 20th.—Serious disturbances in Berlin for some days past. A sharp conflict between the soldiery and the people. The King has given in so far as to concede freedom of the press (though less fully than in other states), a change of ministry, and a national guard. But he might have done this earlier instead of waiting till blood had been shed.

March 22nd.—Leipsic illuminated for the second time on account of the military taking the oath to the constitution.

The conflict in Berlin has been very bloody; several hundred lives lost. Public opinion seems more and more in favour of a German parliament. Prussia is the chief difficulty, but the Western states threaten, if she still refuses, to proclaim a federative republic.

March 23rd.—The reformers are sanguine enough to believe that the effect of the Berlin barricades of the 18th and 19th instant will be to annihilate the military system of Prussia, and to lead eventually to a national militia instead of a standing army in all the German states. The quiet times which have existed since I first knew Germany are entirely gone, and political agitation is the order of the day. It must end in democratic institutions, perhaps like those of the United States of America; yet the monarchical principle will not be lightly given up.

March 31st.—The meeting of a self-elected preliminary congress (*Vorparlement*) at Frankfort, in order to organize the intended national parliament, concentrates the public attention. It is to be chosen by the universal suffrage of all male adults of unblemished character. Every one now wears the German colours,—black, red, and gold,—and talks of war as if it were really approaching. But in what shape is it to come? Has France any means of assisting the Prussian Poles in Posen, and the Austrian Poles in Gallicia, both of whom have begun an insurrection? and will she really be disposed to risk a general war for the restoration of the Polish state? or will Russia interpose to prevent the constitutional development of Germany? These and other vague surmises are naturally produced by the critical times in which we are living.

April 1st.—Went to Hanover. The German flag flying everywhere, and nothing but politics talked of. In this little kingdom the agitation has been less violent than elsewhere, and the King will of course concede as little as he can. A national constituent assembly is to be summoned at Frankfort for the first of May,—one member to every 50,000 of the population.

April 5th.—The peasantry have burnt Prince Schönburg's castle at Waldenburg. He had done a great deal for the inhabitants of his territory, but the peasants continued subject to some burthens from which in other parts of Saxony they had been freed. In several parts of Germany the peasantry have risen against the nobility as they did in France before the first revolution; have destroyed the game in the forests; and have committed other acts of hostility against the owners of the large estates. The German peasant (*Bauer*), though not untaught, is an obstinate wrong-headed man, and has shewn himself disposed for mischief since the political movement began.

April 25th.—Received from Bunsen his well-timed pamphlet on the Schleswig-Holstein question. The Germans are clearly in the right, the two duchies being constitutionally inseparable, and the attempt to incorporate Schleswig with Denmark is therefore unjustifiable.

May 2nd.—The Saxon minister of the interior has just published a proclamation, calling upon the inhabitants to extirpate the cock-chafers. The wits say that by cock-chafers the enemies of German unity are really intended.

May 18th.—Constituent assembly opened at Frankfort. The programme is for an unitary constitution with an hereditary emperor.

June 13th.—Slept last night on the Great Winterberg mountain in Saxon Switzerland. Heat 25° R., and so still that we distinctly heard the firing in Prague, caused by the conflict between the troops and the Czech population, who are in an excited state throughout Bohemia.

July 10.—The Archduke John, administrator of the German empire (*Reichsverweser*), came to Leipsic on his way to Frankfort, and was entertained at a public breakfast in a tent. He is sixty-six years of age, a tall figure, with a fine bald forehead, and wore a sky-blue uniform. Before entering the breakfast-tent he stood in the burning sun, with his hat off, to receive presentations, and we all stood round him bareheaded, at the risk of a *coup de soleil*. He said to me, ' I was in England thirty years since. I hope your countrymen are still the friends of Germany.' I answered, ' I was sure that the English Government and people would never forget their old alliance with both Austria and Prussia during the great war.' He then enquired how long I had been at Leipsic, and what was my previous office, and passed on to one of my colleagues.

The election of the Archduke John to the high office of *Reichsverweser* is looked upon as a successful stroke of Austrian policy. His character and abilities quite entitle him to such a distinction. Although his military career was not very fortunate, he did much for improving the organization of the Austrian army, and was long director-general of the engineering and artillery corps, as well as of the engineering-academy at Vienna. He has patronized learning and science; is permanent rector of the university of Inn-

spruck; and has founded. the college at Gratz, named after
him the *Johanneum.*   He possesses a thorough knowledge
of the Tyrol, and of the Carinthian and Styrian alps, and has
encouraged naturalists and artists to extend, by their descrip-
tions, the acquaintance of the public with those mountain-
lands.   The morganatic marriage of the archduke, in 1828, is
said to have been a very happy one.   His wife was the
daughter of a simple postmaster at Meran, and by her excellent conduct has secured universal respect.   The archduke's
favourite country residence is the *Brandhof* in the Styrian
mountains, on the road trodden by thousands of pilgrims
annually on their way to the famous shrine of Maria-Zell.
The wife has been ennobled as Baroness de Brandhof,—the son
as Count de Meran.   It is said that, so long as the archduke
is *Reichsverweser,* his wife will take precedence of all other
ladies in the empire, but I have not heard that the Queen of
Prussia is willing to submit to such a pretension.

July, August.—Spent several weeks at the baths of Kösen,
and saw frequently the reigning Prince (Henry LXVII) and
Princess of Reuss-Schleitz.   The latter is a clever woman, and
interested in politics.   She thought it would be much best for
the petty German princes to be mediatized, but did not like
the thought of its being done violently.   Strong symptoms
of political reaction in Prussia, and doubts whether the army
would acknowledge the *Reichsverweser.*   In Saxony the troops
have acknowledged him at parades ordered for that purpose,
but in Prussia the intended parades have not taken place.

August 24th.—Robert Blum has been at Leipsic, for which
city he is deputy in the Frankfort parliament, and made
several public speeches, vindicating the conduct of himself
and his party.   He is self-educated, having been formerly a
working tinman, and afterwards money-taker at the theatre.
He possesses considerable oratorical talents.

September 18th.—The Frankfort parliament has been very
reluctant to ratify the armistice between Prussia and Denmark
in the Schleswig-Holstein war, signed at Malmo on the 26th
ult., and at first suspended the return of the troops.   It has
at length accepted the armistice by a small majority.   The
impossibility of forcing Prussia to continue the war has led to
this result, for it is clear that the Prussian government was
not authorized to make the terms which it did.

September 20th.—The acceptance of the armistice by the
parliament has caused wider disturbances at Frankfort.   The
mob denounced the majority of the assembly as traitors, and
a serious conflict took place between the people and the

Prussian and Hessian troops. Two of the deputies, Prince Lichnowsky and General Auerswald, have been brutally murdered. The central power is doing its best to suppress the insurrection, but seems to have no easy task.

September 27th.—Visit from Hübner, Austrian consul-general, to take leave. He has been imprisoned for several months of this summer at Milan, where he was sent by Prince Schwarzenberg on a special mission. He speaks with much anxiety about the state of affairs in Hungary.

October 16th.—Vienna has been the scene of another revolutionary movement, caused by the wish of the people to prevent the Austrian troops from being sent against the Hungarians. The minister of war, Latour, and General Bredy have been assassinated. The Emperor has fled from Schönbrunn to Olmütz, and the diet has declared itself permanent.

October 31st.—Inauguration of the rector of the university of Leipsic, who for the first time made his speech in German instead of Latin, and was not accompanied by a royal commissioner.

November 2nd.—The contest in Vienna has at length terminated, the imperial troops under Prince Windischgrätz, Jellachich, and Auersperg, being in possession of the city. A Hungarian army sent to assist the insurgents has been repulsed.

November 10th.—Robert Blum has been shot at Vienna by order of the Austrian commander, for taking part in the insurrection. He undoubtedly risked a great deal in leaving his post at Frankfort to fight in the streets of Vienna against the Austrian government, which was doubtless rejoiced to have an opportunity to get rid of so dangerous an instrument of the revolution. On receipt of the news of Blum's death, the Leipsic mob attacked the Austrian consulate, and tore down the shield with the imperial arms. The acting-consul, M. Grüner, had just time to escape and to deliver his archives to me for safe custody.

The following letter received at this time from the Prussian minister Bunsen, who was working in London with unwearied devotion for the German cause, could not but be gratifying to me:—

> ' 4, *Carlton Terrace, Nov.* 8, 1848.

' MY DEAR MR. WARD,

' I owe you as many apologies as thanks, which is saying a great deal. You have sent me two very kind letters, and you

and Mrs. Ward have been all-kindness to our dear ———.
But in this *deluge* all private correspondence is interrupted.
I now take a quiet moment to express to you all my and my
wife's thanks, and further to say, that it was quite a *refreshment* to me to see you, almost the only English agent, take so
warm and so open a part in our Danish controversy. I can
tell you, that your reports have not been thrown away; that
they have been read with the highest interest in exalted
quarters, and that they have done *much* to counterbalance the
Danish bias in the Government. Will the Danes at last
understand constitutional rights and a *fait accompli*, accomplished by their stubborn love of oppression, for its own sake?
Alas for them! the time is past to govern provinces against
their will; or rather, God be thanked that the time is past!
They now want them to sail under the Danish flag. I know
also that you always have nobly advocated the great German
cause—the cause of the German Fatherland—and also in this
respect your reports have been influential. I will now tell
you very *confidentially*, that Gagern's speech, (on the two
Germanic constitutions, that of the Union or Empire, without
Austria, and that of the Confederation *with* Austria,) has made
an immense effect here on the Government. Cowley behaves
nobly; he has identified himself with Gagern's plan, and is
highly approved here. The view they here take is this:—

'There is imminent danger of European war, by the
almost certain Presidency of Louis Napoléon.

'Germany must therefore be constituted without delay.

'This can only be done, if Austria is given time to reconstruct herself, and retain undivided power over the whole.

'They are most anxious this should be carried into effect.
I am of the same opinion.

'I wish dear *Vetter Michel* was a little more of a quick
politician. He seems not yet to understand it. But he will
by and by.

'Our *Berlin* affairs are deplorable in the eyes of the world.
I, of course, deeply *lament* the prostration of Government, the
inaptitude of the Chamber, the servitude into which Berlin
has fallen; but I am sure it will *come right* without blood,
although not without a contest with the Red Republic. I
agree so far with Pfuel, that it was well to make his peace
with the Chamber first, and then give rope to the Democrats
to hang themselves; but I think he had since excellent opportunities of dissolving the Chamber, or bring them to reason
by exerting the power of Government against the *Wühler*
(agitators) in the streets. Eichmann's proclamation comes

rather late, and coincides ill with Brandenburgh's appointment, which is, of course, a sad mistake, and could not stand.

'I have often spoken to Lord Palmerston about you. First I wanted him to send you to Holstein as Commissioner, but he had fixed his mind on Hodges, whom I, of course, *per-horresco*. I should wonder, if he should not soon see the necessity of sending you to Frankfort or Vienna. I have often told him that the enemy is at *Vienna.* The commercial question must soon be agitated. They have confidence in Duckwitz, but they ought to have a person who would enter more into the detail of the questions, and speak with the influential people in parliament.

'We had hoped to be able to see something of Mrs. Ward, but she did not leave us her direction : we otherwise should have tried to tempt her to spend some days with us in the country. We have taken Totteridge Park, near Barnet, twelve miles from my house, for two years, and my family live there, with the exception of the parliamentary season. Perhaps we may be more fortunate another time.

'I prepare a complete work on the principles according to which the Constitution of the United States ought to be applied to us. Those principles are *not* understood. Everybody thinks he can arrange an Union as he likes. Perhaps you have seen my *second letter*. But I shall soon treat the matter *ex professo*, for the definitive arrangement. Count Donhoff is (or was) on the best terms with Frankfort.

'Believe me, my dear Mr. Ward,

'Ever yours faithfully,

'BUNSEN.'

The disturbed state of Berlin referred to in the above letter was indeed sufficiently alarming. The city was declared in a state of siege. The King had adjourned the Prussian constituent assembly, and ordered the transfer of its sittings from Berlin to Brandenburgh. The assembly having refused to comply with the royal mandate, it was dissolved by force and the president was carried out in his chair by the soldiers into the street. The King's will however finally prevailed, and the assembly met about a fortnight afterwards in Brandenburgh cathedral. The Frankfort parliament protested against the adjournment; and it was observed that, if the King of Prussia had the right to adjourn or remove the assembly which had been summoned in order to frame a constitution for the Prussian monarchy, it would follow that the sovereigns of Germany, acting together, might prorogue *sine die* the

Frankfort parliament, and so make the work of the Germanic constitution impossible. The administration of Count Brandenburgh was very unpopular, and when the King soon afterwards dissolved the assembly at Brandenburgh, and without consulting that body issued a new constitution of his own framing, it must be admitted that the affairs of Prussia had reached a crisis of considerable danger both to the throne and the interests of the country.

The abdication of the Emperor Ferdinand of Austria on the 2nd December in favour of his nephew, Francis Joseph, gave an appearance of renewed vigour to the Austrian empire. The protocol of the abdication was prepared and signed by M. Hübner. But the Hungarians refused to submit to the new *régime*, denouncing as traitors all those who should recognise Francis Joseph as King of Hungary. The policy referred to by Bunsen of Henry von Gagern, who had become imperial minister at Frankfort, was to exclude Austria from the scope of the intended constitution, and to make the rest of Germany a federal state (*Bundesstaat*), with the King of Prussia as Emperor at its head. But opinions were much divided upon the expediency of Gagern's policy, and the party calling itself the great-German (*gross deutsche*) continued to work for the inclusion of the Austro-German provinces within the political limits of the German nation. The idea of uniting within one empire all those who speak the German tongue was a rather too grand one [1], and is even now very far from realization.

At the commencement of 1849 Germany was still without a constitution, and was distracted between the reactionaries and the democrats. France was a republic under the presidency of a Bonaparte; Italy in commotion; the Pope in exile; the Russians on the German frontier and in the Turkish principalities. The difficulties at Frankfort were very great. Austria insisted upon a confederation of states (*Staatenbund*), whilst Gagern would not give up the point of a federal state (*Bundesstaat*). Gagern shewed great tact in carrying a motion in the national parliament for leave to treat with Austria, and many of his supporters thought it possible to arrange a *Bundesstaat* within a *Staatenbund*, so that Austria might belong to the latter only. The Germanic

---

[1] ' So weit die deutsche Zunge klingt
Und Gott im Himmel Lobe singt ! '

—' *Das deutsche Vaterland.*'

constitution was in fact finally settled in the form of a *Bundes-staat* exclusive of Austria, and the negotiation with that power did not end in any practical result. The *Bundesstaat* failed principally on account of the King of Prussia's refusal to accept the imperial crown.

The following letter from Lord Westmorland shews the impression made upon his mind by the then state of things :—

' *Berlin,* January 5, 1849.

' MY DEAR MR. WARD,

' I have received and forwarded the parcels you sent me for the foreign-office. I am glad to have heard of you, and I hope Mrs. Ward and yourself have been well during the last most eventful and disagreeable year, and that a more favourable prospect is opening to us all in the new year, of which I wish you both many happy returns. I learn from all sides that the Saxon elections are as revolutionary as possible, (save Leipsic), a pretty instance of the total unfitness of the constituency to judge of what is required for the good and orderly government of their country. I am not at all assured that the same sort of result may not attend the elections in Prussia. There is, however, in this country the satisfaction of feeling that the army has so completely established its ascendency, that the disgraceful disorders of last summer and autumn cannot be reproduced.

' As to the central-power, I cannot guess how it is to hobble out of its high pretensions and nullity of power. A very wise institution for the whole of Germany might come out of it, but it must be brought about by a great deal of prudence, good sense, and discretion.

' Believe me, very sincerely yours,

' WESTMORLAND.'

Towards the end of February the Saxon ministry of Braun, von der Pfordten, &c. was obliged to resign, being unable to manage the chambers chosen under the law of election introduced by the same ministers. The King determined to try a new administration composed chiefly of official men, the premier being Dr. Held, and the foreign minister the Baron de Beust, who afterwards played so important a part in the affairs of Saxony, the Germanic body, and the Austrian empire. The view taken by Mr. Forbes, then British minister at Dresden, of the position of the Saxon government, will be found in his letter subjoined :—

To Mr. Ward.

'*Dresden*, February 25, 1849.

' My dear Sir,

(After enclosing a document.) 'The secret as to the change of ministers was well kept. It was determined on Monday evening, and Beust arrived on the Wednesday, but going to his mother's, his coming did not transpire. The present ones cannot last. They are, generally speaking, unknown out of the sphere of their *bureaux*, and Tzchirner has already declared the reception they have to expect from the chambers. The person designated for the war-department is Major Rabenhorst of the artillery, now in Frankfort as military commissioner, a man of energy as well as of talent and sense, which latter qualities make people doubt his accepting. Last Sunday Pfordten told me that in the course of the week he intended to declare in the proper quarter that he would no longer form part of a ministry with Oberländer, but feared that he himself would be the victim. I told him then that I hoped such would be the case; that this would separate him in the eyes of the *good* public from one of his colleagues who was a radical, as from the remainder who were honest men but weak. I begged of him to avail of the first opportunity for his declaration, and not to lose sight of the certainty of re-becoming minister with other and stronger colleagues. M. de Carlowitz told a mutual friend that nothing would make him accept office as long as it was considered requisite to remain in the so-called *voies légales*, in other words, that with the present law of elections he feels no good can result, and must have his hands unfettered as to altering it by forcible means. I tell you this in confidence, for I have reason to think he intended it to reach me. The King has been for some time in the greatest spirits without any one being able to guess the reason. He is an excellent man, but not fitted for the place in such stormy times. Georgi was the last who saw him, and remained more than an hour. Of the new ministers I only know Beust and Ehrenstein. The former has talents, and the latter sense and routine; he is married to an Uckermann. That Pfordten must and will come in again cannot be doubtful; but with these chambers no government can stand ; and they are doubly furious because they had reckoned with certainty upon a change of government being in favour of the radical party.

'B. whom I have not seen for forty-eight hours has heard that there are going to be changes amongst *our* foreign ministers. This is probable. Madrid will have to be filled up, and Ponsonby cannot go on for ever; he is going on 79. Stratford Canning is evidently looking out for Vienna, and I did hear that Lord Howden was talked of for Spain. How I wish Lord P. would give me the Rio mission.[1]

'Remember me to Mrs. Ward.

'Very truly yours,

'FRANCIS R. FORBES.'

I went to London in the following month, and had opportunities of conversing with the Chevalier Bunsen, as well as with Baron Stockmar, about German politics. They both told me that our government had decided not to interfere with the question of the constitution, and would recognise the King of Prussia, as Emperor, if he should be duly chosen. This assurance was afterwards confirmed to me by Lord Palmerston himself, who talked to me on the subject at one of Lady Palmerston's assemblies; and, after making enquiries as to the state of public opinion in Germany, assured me that he should see with pleasure the election of the King as Emperor, hoping it would be the means of calming the long-continued agitation, and of settling Germany in a constitutional way. Lord Palmerston did not impose upon me any secrecy in regard to his opinion, but rather seemed to wish that it should be made generally known. It was indeed unfortunate that the King's vacillation, and final refusal of the imperial crown, prevented the realization of the great and admirable constitutional work which had been so carefully drawn up by the German parliament. The best explanation is that the Prussian government did not then consider itself prepared for the war with Austria and her allies which was almost inevitable, and into which it was in fact driven seventeen years later. But it did not count enough upon the goodness of the cause, nor upon the value of the sympathy which it could not fail to secure by following the popular voice in so national a contest.

Whilst I was in London I met at the house of Mr., afterwards Sir, Benjamin Hawes, M.P., one Sunday evening Dr. Wiseman, afterwards cardinal and archbishop of Westminster. Understanding that I resided in Germany, he put some questions to me as to the religious life of that country, and how far the late political movement was attributable to religious differences. I told him that the lutherans, among whom I

[1] Mr. Forbes was some years afterwards appointed minister at Rio Janeiro, but did not proceed thither on account of ill-health.

lived, took their religious duties far more easily than English
protestants; that nobody went to church more than once a week,
and many persons did not go to church more than once in
several weeks. I considered the Germans a religious people,
but they were unwilling to burthen themselves overmuch by
services and forms, and that the learned men looked upon religion chiefly from a philosophical point of view. I added
that orthodox lutheranism was on the decline, and that the
rationalist divines were gaining ground everywhere. Dr.
Wiseman seemed thoroughly to understand German rationalism, and alluded to the difficulties which the orthodox protestants must always have in finding a ποῦ στῶ. He mentioned
Schleiermacher as one of the most consistent protestant theo-
logians. As to the revolutionary movement, I said that its
origin was purely political, and that it received its impulse
from the overthrow of the monarchy in France, but that there
was much religious discontent abroad, especially in Saxony,
where the free communities (*freie Gemeinde*) and the so-called
German-catholics had made rapid progress. I had read
attentively Dr. Wiseman's able lectures on the doctrines of
the catholic church, and would have gladly opened my whole
mind to him, but had no suitable opportunity, nor did I ever
again see him. His name and works enjoy a high reputation
among the roman-catholics of Germany.

On my way back to Leipsic I stopped at Frankfort, and
assisted at the important sitting of the German parliament in
St. Paul's church on the 28th of March, when it was resolved
to offer the imperial dignity to the King of Prussia. The
votes for the motion were 290; the minority of 248 abstained
from voting. Gagern, Radowitz, Mohl, Heckscher, Jahn, and
all the leaders, were of course present. I had brought an
introduction to M. Welcker of Baden, who a few days before
had made a similar motion to offer the title of hereditary
Emperor to the King of Prussia, and had lost it by a majority
of thirty votes. M. Welcker gave me to understand that his
motion was rather a speculation, and was intended to exercise
a sort of moral compulsion upon the King's mind, for his
majesty had already distinctly refused to become Emperor.
Gagern, however, and the other leaders were convinced of the
necessity of submitting to the King a positive resolution of
the assembly, and therefore they persisted in bringing the
question to a second vote. The deputies who declined to vote
either for Welcker's motion, or for that made on the 28th, did
so mostly because they thought the proceeding useless, and
did not believe it possible to obtain the assent of Frederic

William IV. No doubt there were many republicans among the dissentients, but Welcker thought they would have been too glad to hear of the King's acceptance. After the affirmatory vote a deputation of the parliament went to Berlin with the offer of the imperial crown, and the King, as is well known, refused to accept it without the previous consent of the other German sovereigns. Those princes, however, made conditions which would have had the effect of nullifying the proposed Germanic constitution, and so the whole scheme came to nothing, and the work of the Frankfort parliament was virtually brought to an end, though it continued to linger on for some weeks longer. The mission of the assembly was a high and worthy one ; unfortunately its business was not well conducted, and much valuable time was lost in discussing questions of no practical importance. The reformers omitted to strike when the iron was hot. If they had got their constitution ready in the summer of 1848, the force of the national opinion was then strong enough to have secured its adoption, and the assent of Frederic William IV could hardly have been doubtful. They gave another example of Goethe's oft repeated line, ' *Niemand versteht zu rechter Zeit !*'[1] ' No one understands a thing at the right time !'

During the last years of Louis-Philippe's reign the intrigues of the French agents in Greece operated very injuriously to the working of the constitutional system, or of any fair and open government, in that ill-constructed and unfortunate kingdom. There was a French party, a Russian party, and an English party there, the last professing its sole object to be to induce the Greek statesmen to place themselves above considerations of private interest, and to act in the right and Greek sense. Sir Edmund Lyons, then British minister at Athens, did his best, though with no great success, to counteract the national demoralization ; and in pursuance of Lord Palmerston's instructions, I assisted his efforts by a series of articles in a German journal, exposing the abuses of M. Coletti's administration, and the ill effects resulting to the Greek state from the senseless proceedings of the court-camarilla. Sir Edmund Lyons was gratified at finding that any

---

[1] Warum ist Wahrheit fern und weit ?
 Birgt sich hinab in tiefste Gründe ?
 Niemand versteht zu rechter Zeit !—
 Wenn man zu rechter Zeit verstünde,
 So wäre Wahrheit nah und breit,
 Und wäre lieblich und gelinde.—GOETHE.

German journal would speak out so plainly in the matter, inasmuch as the 'Augsburgh Gazette' and other influential papers were among the supporters of King Otho's government. On leaving Athens for a new post at Stockholm, he addressed to me the following letter:—

'*Athens*, March 19, 1849.

'MY DEAR SIR,

'I cannot leave my present post without again begging you to accept my best acknowledgments for the efficient manner in which you have seconded my efforts to arrest the torrent of demoralization which threatens to inundate this poor country, nor without expressing a very sincere hope that my new destination may give me an opportunity of making your personal acquaintance.

'Pray consider me,
'My dear Sir,
'Yours faithfully,
'John Ward, Esq.   'EDMUND LYONS.'

About the middle of April Sir Edmund called upon me at Leipsic in the course of his journey northwards, and we had a long conversation about Greek affairs. He said that after living thirteen years at Athens he could not leave it without some regret, but expressed himself as thoroughly disgusted by the general corruption and mendacity which pervaded all classes of persons in that country, nor did he look to the future of Greece as at all hopeful. He denounced King Otho as *bête*,—a compound of imbecility and wrong-headedness,— the real ruler being the Queen Amelia (an Oldenburgh princess), whose feelings were more Russian than anything else, and who was surrounded by a camarilla working for the private objects of themselves and their friends, without any regard to the real interests of the nation. He described the Queen as a fine, spirited woman, who looked very handsome in her Greek costume, but was very prejudiced and narrow-minded. That she had no children was deeply lamented by herself, and by every one who looked at the importance of the succession being settled. I remarked that Greece had always been under two disadvantages,—first, that the new kingdom was too small; and second, that the Greeks were not fitted for the constitution granted to them, or indeed for any representative constitution. Under an enlightened despotism there would have been a better chance of improving their morals, as well as their physical condition. Sir Edmund admitted there was some truth in my remarks, but said, 'We cannot now go backwards and abrogate the constitution ; there is nothing else to be done than to insist upon its being fully and fairly carried out;' and this has been in fact the consistent language of the British cabinet. At that period the future of the Greek kingdom appeared gloomy enough; but we could not anticipate that it was destined so soon to encounter the attack of a hostile fleet, nor that the Bavarian dynasty was fated in the course of a few years to expulsion from the throne it had so unworthily filled.

The following are continued extracts from my private journal :—

April 28th, 1849.—Of the small German states twenty-eight have given their adhesion to the Frankfort constitution with a Prussian emperor, whilst Prussia herself still holds back. The second Prussian chamber voted acceptance and was in consequence dissolved by the King. The King of Würtemberg was obliged to give in, and proclaim the constitution ; the Kings of Hanover and Saxony have refused, and dissolved their chambers.

May 3rd.—An insurrection in Dresden in consequence of the King's refusal to accept the constitution. A bloody conflict between the Saxon military and the people. The King, Queen, and royal family have fled for safety to the fortress of Königstein on the Elbe.

May 5th.—A provisional government, composed of MM. Tzchirner, Heubner, and Todt, has established itself in Dresden, declaring that the King had abdicated. An insurrectionary movement in Leipsic also, and barricades placed across the principal streets.

May 7th.—Fighting all last night in Leipsic, during which several leading citizens were killed. A scene of devastation this morning, the populace having pulled down the fair-booths to make barricades. The town-council, not knowing whether to recognise the provisional government or not, has placed the town under the protection of the central power at Frankfort.

May 9th.—Dresden, having been bombarded for three days by Prussian troops, has now surrendered, and the King's government has been re-established. The firmness of M. de Beust has contributed very much to this result. The house of the British legation was uninjured, and was filled with valuable articles sent there for safe custody by the inhabitants of Dresden.　Mr. Forbes did not leave the house during the whole time of the bombardment.

May 16th.—Gagern has resigned, and all is in confusion at Frankfort. The Prussian deputies to the parliament have been withdrawn, and the King of Prussia has notified his intention to establish another constitution for Germany, based upon that of Frankfort, but with such amendments as shall have been agreed to by the German governments.

May 31st.—Passing through Magdeburgh on my return from an excursion to the Harz mountains, I learned the publication of the so-called Three Kings' constitution, dated the 26th instant, in which the Kings of Prussia, Saxony, and Hanover offer to the country a new federal constitution, and invite the other German sovereigns to accede thereto.　Talking about this with M. Unruh, late president of the Prussian parliament, and a decided democrat, he laughed at the new scheme as a mere subterfuge, saying that Prussia had been duped by Bavaria, and that there would now probably be three groups in Germany, viz. :—the Three Kings' Alliance,—Austria and Bavaria,—and the Western States.

Found on reaching home that the Frankfort parliament, which has dwindled down to a mere rump, has adjourned to Stuttgardt.　Professor Albrecht, who was one of the committee of jurists charged to prepare the Frankfort constitution, remarked to me how striking had been the fall of that parliament in the national estimation, and how miserably it had managed its affairs.

July 6th.—The hereditary Prince Ernest of Saxe-Altenburgh, who is studying here, and his tutor Baron de Bielefeld, spent the evening with us.　The prince is a young man of twenty-two, amiable and intelligent.　As to German politics, he said his father was an adherent of Prussia, and would be sure to follow the same line.　He was learning English, and said jokingly he would go to England and marry an English wife.　'Why not,' he added, 'the Princess Mary of Cambridge? she will soon be old enough.'　He liked to hear about English society and manners, and asked many questions on the subject.　He had learned mathematics and other things requisite in a military career, but did not know either Latin or Greek.　He enters willingly into our Leipsic society.

[At this time the prince's uncle, Duke Joseph, reigned in Saxe-Altenburgh.　He soon afterwards resigned in favour of his brother, Duke George, who, dying in 1853, the ducal crown devolved upon Prince Ernest, as his elder son.　Duke Joseph left no son, but four daughters, one of whom became

Queen of Hanover, another Grand-duchess of Oldenburgh, and the third a Russian Grand-duchess, under the name of Alexandra-Josephouna, wife of the Grand-duke Constantine.]

August 28th.—This day, being the hundredth anniversary of Goethe's birth, was celebrated as a national festival here, and throughout Germany. An exhibition of autographs, drawings, and other remains of the great poet was publicly made; and a commemoration held in the *aula* of the university, when Professor Jahn delivered a good speech on Goethe's youthful years passed at Leipsic.[1] Saw *Egmont* at the theatre, with a prologue and *tableaux* in honour of the day.

We spent the morning at the village of Schleussig, and there talked to the old postillion Grabel, who conducted Napoleon I during the four days of the battle of Leipsic in 1813. He told us some confused stories of the Emperor's movements, his mind being rather impaired by old age and beer; yet there was a certain historical interest attached to him, and one cannot help liking to see a man who has stood by the side of

> 'The conqueror of thousand thrones,
> Who strewed our earth with hostile bones.'

October 8th.—Lady Jersey, and her pretty daughter Lady Clementina Villiers, came from Vienna, where they had been visiting Prince and Princess Nicholas Esterhazy, the princess being Lady Jersey's daughter. I took them through the fair then going on, and shewed them the picture-gallery. Lady Jersey was very indignant at the conduct of the Hungarian insurgents, and spoke of Louis Bathyani, who was afterwards executed, as well as of General Georgi and Kossuth, in no measured terms. We talked of the lower orders in Austria, whom she thought were the best people in the world, very religious and good church-goers. She said the number of religious sects in England was a great misfortune, and that the English church would have more influence if it was quite independent of the government, and authorized to direct its own affairs. Her ladyship went into a number of shops, and ordered a portfolio of prints and various other articles to be sent her for inspection, but disappointed the tradesmen by buying nothing. The ladies went on next day to Hanover on a visit to their old friend King Ernest Augustus, who is approaching his eightieth year.

October 14th.—Austria and Prussia have agreed upon a

---

[1] This speech has been published in Goethe's '*Briefe an Leipziger Freunde, herausgegeben von Otto Jahn.*' Leipzig, 1849.

political arrangement under the name of an *interim*, to last until May 1st, 1850, transferring the central power to a federal commission, which must lead to the resignation of the Archduke John, as there is nothing left for him as *Reichsverweser* to administer. The opinions of the liberal party are much divided in regard to the 'Three Kings' constitution.' Gagern and other good men are for it, though it is certainly very different from what the nation hoped to obtain through the Frankfort parliament.

November 22nd.—I wrote lately to Bunsen in London, stating my apprehensions that the 'Three Kings' constitution' would not succeed, and that the Kings of Saxony and Hanover, who were really Austrian, would assuredly retire from it. His answer is that he cannot agree with me, and that nothing but the *nucleus* of a German *Bundesstaat* can secure the future, and prevent a second bloody revolution. He adds, ' The Kings of Saxony and Hanover are traitors to the country, and *felones de se* into the bargain. The day of retribution will come. The Germans are lambs, but not asses ! '

December 26th.—Visit from the quakers Josiah and William Forster. These interesting men were travelling to Vienna in the midst of winter for the purpose of soliciting the concurrence of the imperial government in some further measures for the suppression of the slave-trade. I asked one of them his opinion of the utility of the blockading squadron still maintained on the coast of Africa, although it was contended by Mr. Hutt, M.P., and other statesmen, that the operation of the squadron was in reality mischievous. Mr. Forster replied, ' My friend, how canst thou ask me so simple a question ? Dost thou not know that we are against all blockades, and warlike operations of whatever description, both by sea and land ? We are labouring to put an end to slavery by means of moral influence, and believe that so wicked and unchristian a thing cannot last much longer if good men will only unite in raising their voices against its abominations.'

1850. February 10th, Sunday.—Professor Harless and a party dined. He goes to Dresden as upper court-preacher, and will be a loss to this university. He is likewise pastor of St. Nicholas, and an orthodox-lutheran, sticking fast to the Augsburgh confession and concordance book, and is in consequence not on the popular side as regards theology, but is a good preacher and draws hearers to his church. There can be no doubt that rationalism is gaining ground fast against lutheran orthodoxy. How could it be otherwise ? Those

who have rebelled against ecclesiastical authority, merely to
set up a new one of their own, must expect to be subverted in
their turn by the spirit of discord which they have themselves
let loose.

April 29.—The parliament at Erfurt, which had been opened
about a month since by General de Radowitz, and had accepted
the 'Three Kings' constitution,' has been prorogued, with small
prospect of its work being carried into practical effect.

May 19, Whit Sunday.—Took my family to the baths of
Oynhausen, near the Porta Westphalica. The warm salt-
springs, of $26\frac{1}{2}°$ R., are a powerful remedy for many diseases.

Read William de Humboldt's letters to a female friend
(Charlotte Diede), lately published. The parties were old
friends, almost lovers, whilst Humboldt was a student; and
the lady having fallen into distress, renewed the acquaintance.
They preferred venting their thoughts in correspondence to
seeing each other, though nothing would have been easier.
The book is valuable as giving a good insight into Humboldt's private feelings. He was as great in morals and
æsthetics, as his brother Alexander was in the physical
sciences. In one of his letters I note that he praises Bunsen,
and his collection of hymns and prayers, observing, however,
that the latter are inferior to the former. 'The difference,'
he adds, 'lies in the nature of the case. The prayers are
chiefly intended for private devotion. Now, an individual
praying requires no form. He pours himself out more naturally in the thoughts chosen, and connected by himself, before
God, and scarcely requires words. True internal devotion
knows no other prayer than that issuing from itself.' Without questioning the correctness of Humboldt's view of private
prayer, it by no means follows that a liturgy is not desirable
to a public assembly of worshippers. The liturgy of the holy
mass, for instance, is applicable to all the wants of mankind
in mind, body, and estate; and the many fine litanies of the
catholic church are comprehensive and suitable forms of devotion for christians who meet together to pray in common.

The town of Cassel, capital of the former electorate of
Hesse, used to be considered one of the pleasantest residences
in Germany. Situated on a rising ground, it commanded
extensive views over the adjacent country, and its fine park
(the *Augarten*) was an agreeable place of recreation for the
inhabitants. One was struck with a sort of ruin called the
Kattenburg, which was in fact the commencement of a vast

palace undertaken, some fifty years since, by one of the elector's predecessors, but never completed. In the large square known as the Friedrichs-Platz was the palace inhabited by the Elector Frederick-William, who had contracted a morganatic marriage with a lady not born noble, and had successively created her Countess of Schaumburg and Princess of Hanau. He had by her a numerous and handsome family. The elector's country seat at Wilhelmshöhe was deservedly admired for its beautiful gardens, extending to the top of a high hill, on which was a reservoir of water, producing some of the finest fountains and cascades in the world. When the present Emperor of Russia, as a youth, set out on his first European tour, his father, the Emperor Nicholas, is said to have told him, 'There is little to see in Germany, but do not miss the waterworks at Wilhelmshöhe; they are quite as fine as at Versailles.' It will be remembered that Wilhelmshöhe was assigned to the Emperor Louis Napoleon as his place of confinement after his surrender to Prussia at Sedan, and that he was obliged to remain there until the termination of the war.

During the summer of 1850 a conference of deputies from the *Zollverein*-states was held at Cassel, and I was instructed to proceed thither, and watch the proceedings on behalf of Great-Britain. I accordingly went to Cassel early in July, and found there not only the members of the toll-conference, but commissioners from Belgium, Switzerland, and Luxemburgh, having a similar object with myself. The conference was indeed one of unusual importance. Prussia, in order to gratify the South-German governments, had proposed, against the opinions of her own statesmen, increased duties on various branches of foreign manufactures; whilst Austria, who was working for a general customs-union of all the German states with the Austrian empire, considered this toll-conference as standing in the way of her commercial policy, and desired that the intended new duties should not take effect, but that the South-German states should continue discontented with Prussia, and be therefore more disposed to favour the Austrian scheme of a general customs-union in the sense contemplated by the federal act of 1815. The position of the conference was therefore a peculiar one. The southern states were trying to carry the protective duties; Prussia was at least lukewarm in the matter; and the foreign powers, viz. Great Britain, Belgium, and Switzerland, through their commissioners at Cassel, were assisting Austria in her efforts to nullify the business of the conference, and to bring about its dissolution without doing anything. The government of Hesse-Cassel, whilst professing to support the Prussian proposals, really intrigued against them. The prime minister, M. Hassenpflug, and the minister for foreign affairs, M. de Baumbach, were on political grounds strongly anti-Prussian; and I soon found out that in the remonstrances which I made against the new tariff of duties, I had more allies than I at first anticipated. Although the proceedings of the conference were secret, I discovered the means of ascertaining what was going on, and managed to furnish the foreign office from time to time with accurate reports. It is, in fact, never difficult to obtain information from those with whom we sympathize, but where the objects and policy are different, the task of an official agent becomes of course extremely arduous in this respect. After the conference had sat in Cassel for nearly four months, I learned to my surprise that the increased duties proposed by Prussia had been rejected, not by the refusal of electoral Hesse, or of any state in the Austrian interest, such as Hanover or Saxony, but by the single vote of the representative of the duchy of Brunswick! The natural inference was that Prussia did not wish to push the matter further, and that the opposition of Brunswick was merely collusive; for at that period the vote of a single state, however small, sufficed to defeat any changes, whether by way of increase or reduction of the existing tariff, which might have been proposed. The toll-conference finally broke up, and its members returned home early in November, after the occupation of Cassel by a Prussian army corps under General de Tietzen. The Austrian policy therefore prevailed, less by reason of its own strength than because the Prussian government did not think it worth while to raise the tariff in order to please the governments of Bavaria and Würtemberg, which were becoming every day more Austrian, and were, in fact, looking forward to a war with Prussia whenever the proper moment for common action with Austria should arrive.

The dispute between the Elector of Hesse and his subjects, relative to the powers of the representative body, chosen in accordance with the constitution of 1831, which had been going on for some years past, arrived at a crisis whilst I was staying at Cassel. The Elector had changed his ministry in the preceding February, and had appointed as president of the council M. Hassenpflug, formerly president of the court of appeal at Greifswald, in Pomerania,—a man known and disliked for his reactionary politics, and whose private character was anything but unsullied. With him were associated several unimportant persons, viz. M. Lometzsch, as finance-minister, M. von Baumbach, as minister for foreign affairs, and Major de Haynau, nephew of the Austrian general of that name (known at the brewery of Barclay, Perkins & Co.), as minister of war. There is a famous echo at the end of a street in Cassel, and the wits used to divert themselves by calling out the names of the new ministers, to which the echo answered the last syllable, thus,—' Hassenpflug,'—' ugh' ! ' Baumbach,'—' ach' ! ' Haynau'—' au' ! These exclamations of derision will be at once understood by any one familiar with the German language.

M. Hassenpflug did not convoke the Hessian diet till late in the summer, and then laid before them demands for supplies, and for a vote authorizing the levy of the direct and indirect taxes for the current year. The chamber on the 31st of August unanimously required a more full and satisfactory budget, and in the meanwhile refused to vote the direct taxes. The Elector replied on the 2nd of September by dissolving the diet, and on the 5th issued an ordinance to levy the requisite taxes by his own authority, declaring the electorate in a state of siege. That authority, however, was constitutionally null without the assent of the standing committee of the diet, appointed to act in such cases whenever the diet itself might not be sitting. The standing committee refused its concurrence, and on the 10th of September the supreme court of appeal declared the pretension of the Elector, to levy taxes without the diet's consent, to be wholly illegal. The machine of government was brought to a stand-still, and everybody was wondering what would follow, when on the morning of the 13th of September we were astonished by the news that the Elector had bolted in the night, taking with him one of his sons, and his three unpopular ministers, and had proceeded to his *château* at Philippsruh, near Hanau, where his family were residing. M. Hassenpflug and his colleagues took up their quarters at the neighbouring *château* of Wilhelmsbad, and a proclamation was published at Cassel notifying the removal of the seat of government from that town to Wilhelmsbad accordingly. The motives of the change were declared to be the refusal of the officials generally to obey the ordinances of the Elector, and that it was beneath the dignity of the sovereign to remain on the same spot with disobedient servants, who were doing their utmost to frustrate the execution of his will.

It may perhaps be asked, why did not the Elector dismiss from his service those functionaries, whether administrative or legal, who on the occasion referred to, and indeed for a long time past, had been systematically opposing their sovereign's intentions ? The answer is, that he had not the power. In the German states the members of the bureaucracy do not hold their offices at pleasure, but have vested interests in them, and can only be ejected after a legal investigation by which their misconduct shall have been fully proved. The Hessian officials were, to their honour, all ranged on the constitutional side. The President of the Chamber, for instance, M. Nebelthau, who was upper postmaster, was no party to acts of violence, but opposed a passive resistance to all the illegal measures adopted by the Elector at the advice of the Hassenpflug administration. It has been said that the Cassel people made a revolution in their dressing-gowns and slippers. They certainly took no very active measures, much less did they erect barricades, or attempt to expel the Elector by forcible means. Nothing could be more striking than the tranquillity of the town during the days which intervened between the refusal of the supplies by the diet, and the flight of the Elector in the night of the 12th of September. The constitutional cause appeared to triumph, although there was another act of the drama which still remained to be played out.

M. Hassenpflug having appealed for assistance to the Germanic diet at Frankfort, that body soon declared itself against the right of the Hessian diet to refuse the supplies of the Elector, and ordered a federal execution, which, composed of Bavarian troops, entered the Hessian territory on the 1st of November, and occupied the district of Hanau. The Prussian government, unwilling to acknowledge the legal competence of a body which had been dissolved in the previous year, and was not yet re-constituted, answered by ordering the immediate march of a Prussian army corps into the electorate, and I witnessed the entry of General de Tietzen at the head of his brigade into Cassel on the morning of the 2nd of November. They were heartily welcomed by the inhabitants, who however were without the means of ascertaining the King of Prussia's intentions. The danger of a war in Germany appeared imminent, until the retirement of General de Radowitz indicated too plainly that a change had taken place in the policy of Frederic William IV. There was indeed a slight skirmish at Bronnzell, near Fulda, on the 8th of November, between Prussian and federal soldiers; but no actual hostilities followed, and the federal execution was permitted, in conjunction with a Prussian force to continue in the occupation of the electorate for some time longer.

This was one of the results of the famous conferences held at Olmütz on the 28th and 29th of November. Baron de Manteuffel was too happy to be able to break with the revolution, and to unite himself with Austria in the effort to bring back the reactionary system, and to restore the functions of the federal diet. The Prince de Schwarzenberg recognised his own victory, and indulged the hope that the constitutional movement of 1848 had been finally put down, and its work annihilated, by the return of Prussia to Metternich principles and Carlsbad resolutions.

Among the Cassel notabilities M. von Rommel, the state historiographer, archivist, and librarian, held the first place. He had for a time filled a professorial chair at Charkoff, in Russia, and had written a good account of the Caucasian races; but was glad to return to his native land as professor at Marburg, from whence he was promoted to the government offices he then held at Cassel. His great work is the history of Hesse, in twelve bulky volumes, which has its due place in all the public libraries of Germany. I found Rommel in the Hessian question a decided constitutionalist; and in German affairs he lamented the failure of the proposals of the Frankfort parliament. He regarded Hassenpflug as an intruder in the service of the Elector, and regretted the Elector had been led so much astray from the wants and wishes of his people. The Elector, he said, had little of that *bonhomie* which is so natural to German princes. On a late occasion he was waited upon by a deputation to remonstrate against certain taxes, and a brewer having taken upon himself to speak, the Elector abruptly dismissed the remonstrants with the remark,—'A brewer's business is to make beer; government is my affair [1].' How ill the government of the electorate was conducted was proved in the sequel, when it was annexed as a province to the Prussian monarchy.

Louis Spohr, the celebrated composer and violinist, was for many years court music-director (*Capellmeister*) at Cassel, and was highly respected by the inhabitants. I saw him lead the orchestra in the theatre during the performance of his own opera of *Jessonda*, and on other occasions, and I met him several times in private society. He was a tall old man of dignified appearance in a flaxen wig. He sympathized entirely with the constitutional movement, and by no means liked his master, the Elector, who, he said, seemed to wish to spite him, having more than once refused him leave of absence

---

[1] Ein Bierbrauer brauet Bier : Regierung ist meine Sache.

without any good reason. He mentioned that he had visited London thirty years ago, and composed a symphony there. His music to Goethe's *Faust* has always been highly appreciated in Germany, and his oratorios shew his genius to be capable of the most sublime efforts in sacred music. There were several young English musical students at Cassel, to whom Spohr gave lessons and took a kindly interest in their progress.

I saw little of the court, which left Wilhelmshöhe soon after my arrival. The Elector did not even return to keep his birthday on the 20th of August, nor were there any signs of public rejoicings on that day. The small *corps diplomatique* accredited at Cassel began to find their situation rather a dull one. Prussia was represented by the Baron de Thiele, afterwards under-secretary of state for foreign affairs at Berlin, who was attentively watching the popular movements, and in this had the able assistance of M. Delbrück, then the Prussian deputy to the toll-conference. After the Elector, and with him the diplomatic body, had left Cassel, it was M. Delbrück who was charged with the duty of political observation, and who telegraphed to General de Tietzen when the right moment had arrived for a Prussian army to occupy the electorate. The statesmanlike abilities of M. Delbrück could not fail to secure his rapid rise in the service of his country. He now directs the chancery of the German confederation, and in Prince Bismarck's absence acts as chancellor of the federal body.

M. d'Assailly, the French minister at Cassel, took great interest both in the political situation and in the proceedings of the toll-conference; and I made an agreement with him to inform each other mutually of whatever we might ascertain. He talked as if both Austria and Prussia were hostile to France; whereas I argued that the attitude of those powers was merely defensive, and that the recent election of a Bonaparte to the Presidency of the French republic, was a circumstance sufficient in itself to warn other nations to be on their guard. Madame d'Assailly, who was both pretty and *spirituelle*, gave the pleasantest *soirées* in Cassel, and amused herself as well as she could with the local affairs. She laughed at the electoral court, and at the Countess de Schaumburg as a *bonne mère de famille*, who knew nothing of the art of managing society. Madame d'Assailly was the grand-daughter of Général de Lafayette, and great-niece of the philanthropic Count de Lasteyrie, whom I had formerly known. Like a true French woman Madame d'Assailly thought no place comparable to Paris, and was getting rather

tired of her residence at Cassel, when she was placed under
the necessity of removing to Frankfort after the Elector had
fled from his capital in the manner described, and the
diplomatic agents were obliged to follow him.

There was a person in Cassel of whom I shall always retain
an agreeable remembrance, viz. Professor de Müller, who on
account of his close connection with the members of the
diplomatic body went by the name of the *guide diplomatique.*
He was both artist and connoisseur, had some literary reputation, and knew all that was going on in the electoral capital.
He was in the Austrian interest, and though he did not
estimate highly the talents of the Hassenpflug administration,
had little sympathy with the popular, or constitutional cause.
Müller was a convert to the roman-catholic faith, and did
not understand how a painter of religious subjects could be
otherwise. German art he said was essentially catholic, and
such great masters as Cornelius, Hesse, and Overbeck had
shewn what modern genius could accomplish in that direction.
They had realized that harmony between religion and art which
was the great charm of the divine Raphael, and which non-
catholic artists would in vain endeavour to bring into effect.

At their meeting at Olmütz the ministers of Austria and
Prussia had agreed that conferences of all the German
governments should be held at Dresden for the purpose of
revising the Germanic constitution, and of substituting for
the Germanic diet some federal form at once more efficient
and more consonant with the real wants of the nation. The
conferences were accordingly opened in Dresden on the 23rd
of December 1850, and attended by representatives of all the
German governments. Having received instructions from
Lord Palmerston to act as secretary of legation at Dresden
during the conferences (Mr. Barnard being detached at
Coburgh), I went there accordingly, and found a large number
of important and influential personages already assembled.
Austria was represented by the Prince Felix de Schwarzenberg and the Count de Buol-Schauenstein ; Prussia by the
Baron de Manteuffel and the Count d'Alvensleben ; Bavaria
by M. von der Pfordten ; and Saxony by the Baron de Beust.
Among the smaller notabilities were the Burgomaster Smidt
of Bremen, and the Syndic Banks of Hamburgh, with whom
I had frequent opportunities of intercourse. The British
government merely desired to know what was passing, and
did not seek to exercise any influence over the proceedings.
Mr. Forbes's instructions recommended to him 'entire silence'

in regard to the political questions intended to be brought under the deliberation of the congress.

The German public was not from the beginning hopeful of any satisfactory result of deliberations in which the popular element was unrepresented, and they rightly considered the proceedings at Dresden as a continuation of the Carlsbad conferences of 1819. The object of Austria was to perpetuate her own ascendency in Germany, and that of Prussia to check the revolutionary movement and gain time for the furtherance of her own plans. Both powers had actually begun to reduce their armies in consequence of the understanding come to at Olmütz; but the rivalry between the two, which formed the real German difficulty, subsisted as fully as ever; and the Manteuffel administration was in the false position of having submitted to Austrian dictation, instead of securing the support and sympathy of the nation by a bold and straightforward policy which would have given unity to Germany under the lead, or at least the protection, of the Prussian monarch.

Prince Schwarzenberg, formerly in the diplomatic service, had been prime minister of the Austrian empire since October 1848, and it was under his responsibility that the change took place in the person of the sovereign on the 2nd of December, 1848, when the imbecile Ferdinand was induced to abdicate in favour of his nephew, the now reigning Emperor Francis Joseph I. Schwarzenberg's policy for Austria was one of centralization, as he did not believe it possible to hold the empire together upon federal principles. He was a tall, thin man, clear-headed, and agreeable in conversation; but his ideas were bureaucratic, and hardly comprehensive enough for the actual situation. I once sat next him at a dinner-table, and we talked about France and England, whilst the subject of the conferences was naturally avoided. Speaking of the press, and of the greater degree of freedom given to it since the March revolution, he said, 'In England you can afford to let the press entirely loose; but there is an inconsistency in your maintaining a censorship of the theatres. The control of the drama and of the journals is equally a matter of police-regulation, and ought to depend upon the same principles.' Schwarzenberg really wished that the new Austrian monarchy under Francis Joseph should be a constitutional one; and his efforts in this direction would probably have been more successful, if he had not driven too hard his hobby of consolidating the manifold nationalities of Austria under an uniform system of government. His career was closed rather suddenly by death in April 1852.

The Prussian minister-president de Manteuffel was still more a red-tape statesman than Prince de Schwarzenberg, and was brought without much difficulty to concur with the Austrian programme to be submitted to the congress. That programme was to substitute for the smaller assembly of the federal diet, consisting of seventeen members, a new governing body of eleven members, in which Austria and Prussia should each have two votes, and the four kingdoms each one vote. The smaller states were to have curial votes only, viz. Baden and the two Hesses together, the ninth vote ; Holstein, Luxemburgh, Brunswick, Nassau, the two Mecklenburghs, and Oldenburgh, together, the tenth vote ; and all the remaining petty princes and the four free towns, together, the eleventh vote, in the assembly in question. The *plenum*, or general assembly of the federal diet was likewise to be remodelled in so far that Austria and Prussia should each have in it ten votes instead of four, and Bavaria five votes instead of four, so that the total number of votes in that assembly would be raised from sixty-eight to seventynine. The effect of these arrangements would have been to secure to Austria the supremacy in the executive and the federal councils. For the kingdoms of Bavaria, Saxony, Hanover, and Würtemberg were notoriously the allies of Austria ; and by their aid alone, without counting the smaller states in the Austrian interest, the imperial government would have a clear majority of six out of the eleven votes to be assigned to the new executive ; and she could also command a majority in the new general assembly. Such a constitution, combined as it was with a proposed new composition of the federal army, would have deprived the petty states of the small share of power which previously belonged to them, and would have ousted Prussia from her fair influence over the direction of German affairs.

It is indeed inconceivable how Manteuffel should have been so easily induced to fall into the snare. His colleague, Count d'Alvensleben, did all he could to oppose it, but without success, and then deemed it his duty to support his chief, contrary to his own judgment. He was a good Prussian, and a good political observer, but without diplomatic tact or refinement of manners. He was laughed at in Dresden for not washing himself, and it was said one could not shake hands with him without receiving disagreeable impressions. His clever secretary, Count Fleming, ventured to write an anonymous pamphlet against the proceedings of the congress, and by his negotiations with the representatives of the petty states strengthened their objections, and encouraged them to persist in rejecting the Austrian proposals. The petty German governments, in fact, saw their position clearly enough. Baden, the Saxon duchies,.the Mecklenburghs, Oldenburgh, the Anhalt and Reuss principalities, and the Hanse-towns, were decided adherents of Prussia in German affairs, and had no desire to sacrifice their independence to an Austrian hegemony. At the end of two months the conferences were suspended, and it became obvious that there was little chance of the members coming to an agreement. When they met again all were prepared for the alternative of falling back upon the old diet; and after some discussions on commercial policy, and the expediency of admitting the non-German provinces of Austria into the *Zollverein,* the congress separated on the 16th of May, after having resolved that the federal diet should be re-established at Frankfort in the form settled by the acts of 1815 and 1820. At the last sitting the members appeared in uniform, and afterwards went to dine with the King of Saxony, who drank to their health, and bade them farewell. The next day everybody connected with the conferences found it the greatest relief that the business was over, and that they could take leave of their beautiful Dresden, 'the fine lady of Germany,' at that season peculiarly charming with its green gardens, and its blossoming laburnums, lilacs, and cherries.

The period of the sitting of the conferences was one of much social festivity in Dresden. The court gave balls, concerts, and dinners. The court ball on Shrove Tuesday, being also the King's name-day, was very brilliant, and the dancers appeared in fancy costumes. Fêtes were likewise given by Baron de Beust, and the other Saxon ministers, as well as by such members of the diplomatic body as had sufficiently roomy houses. I was rather amused to meet my old friend Professor von der Pfordten as the actor in a new part, viz. that of Bavarian minister-president, and plenipotentiary to the conferences. From his chair of Roman law at Leipsic, he had become a march-minister,—that is a liberal,—at Dresden, and when the liberal cause began to fail he transferred his services to Bavaria, and placed himself at the head of the cabinet as the organ of the reactionary party in that state. He affords an instance shewing how little political consistency was valued by a certain class of German statesmen, and that a learned man and able speaker, as Von der Pfordten certainly was, needed not to trouble himself much about his antecedents if he could make himself useful to a party in power.

The case of Baron de Beust is in some respects the same. His policy as a Saxon minister was strongly conservative. He helped to save the Saxon throne,—exerted himself unremittingly for maintaining the federal diet in its integrity and power,—and took an active part in promoting the war against Prussia in 1866, in which Saxony was Austria's faithful ally. After the termination of that war, Beust became the political leader of Austria, and as the Count de Beust, chancellor of the empire, for some time directed its affairs in the spirit of reform. In many important questions, such as those of the relations with Hungary, and of the modification of the *Concordat* with Rome, Beust has certainly not followed a reactionary tendency, but has shewn a wish to be guided by the temper of his times. If not a great statesman, he is an observant and shrewd one, and has made many friends. His conduct of the Schleswig-Holstein question during several years does him much honour. He consistently worked for the independence of the duchies, and the rights of the house of Augustenburgh ; and although his objects were not attained, his efforts will be gratefully remembered by the inhabitants of the duchies and by the German nation.

At the outset of the conferences the Russian minister in Dresden, M. de Schröder, boasted that he was acquainted with the proposals made by Austria and Prussia, and hinted that his government would be disposed to favour them. No communication on the subject was made on the part of either power to Mr. Forbes, or to myself, and we were left to grope our way to the protocols in the best way we could. I however found no difficulty in obtaining the desired information through the representatives of certain small states who were assured of my sympathy, and Lord Palmerston was constantly furnished with accurate reports of these secret deliberations.

A visit which I paid this spring to Weimar is thus recorded in my journal :—

1851. May 7th.—Excursion with my two boys to Weimar, the so-called ' widowed city of the muses.' To the theatre of classical memory, for Goethe was once its director, and Schiller stage-manager. It is a very plain house, but the scenery excellent. The piece was Gutzkow's *Uriel d'Acosta*, which reminds one of Lessing's *Nathan the Wise*.

May 8th, Whit Sunday.—Many houses decorated with birch-boughs in honour of the season, especially those which contain a bride, that is to say, a woman betrothed. Visited the houses of Goethe and Schiller, and the apartments in the palace called the poets' rooms, the walls being painted with scenes from Schiller, Goethe, Wieland, and Herder; also the Belvidere, and the Mausoleum, where Schiller and Goethe lie entombed on each side of their patron, the Grand-duke Charles Augustus. Called on Mademoiselle de Pögewitsch, sister of Goethe's daughter-in-law, and she shewed us Stieler's picture of the poet, which is considered the best of any. Madame de Goethe with her two sons, Walter, a musician, and Wolfgang, a literary man, had left the place some time since. The family are indeed gone, but the master-spirit has left ample memorials behind him.

May 9th.—To the little university-town of Jena, picturesquely situated in the valley of the Saale. An extensive view from the Fox-tower. The style of living here is simple, and many a poor student gets through his academical course for £50 a year. In the larger universities this cannot be done under £80 or £100 at least.

May 10th.—After going over the ducal library, containing 150,000 volumes, called on Eckermann, and found him engaged in feeding a hawk. He takes much pleasure in animals of all sorts. We talked of Goethe, and he spoke of him with becoming reverence as his benefactor and friend. Eckermann, now sixty years of age, is respected here, and enjoys the title of *Hofrath*, or court-councillor. He was the son of a poor cottager at Winsen on the Luneburgh heath, and continued to educate himself to a point which qualified him to become secretary and amanuensis to Goethe, and afterwards to publish an interesting account of conversations which he had held with the great master during the last ten years of his life [1]. Speaking of Goethe's want of patriotism, Eckermann said it was not exactly so; that the poet loved his country, and rejoiced in its historical reminiscences, its academies and universities, and its numerous capital cities, which he regarded as so many centres of civilization. But he did not feel that hatred of the French nation, or of Napoleon, which impelled others to take up arms to repel the invaders. He was too old to become a combatant in person, and he had not the *élan* which induced others to compose patriotic songs. The truth seems to be that Goethe's feelings were rather cosmopolite, than national. He did not care about politics, and it is related of him that he was very indifferent about the French revolution, and at the time of its outbreak interested himself only in a controversy on a question in natural science then going in the French academy between Cuvier and Geoffroy de St.-Hilaire.

[1] 'Gespräche mit Goethe in den letzen Jahren seines Lebens, 1823—1832, von Johann Peter Eckermann.' 3 Bände. Leipzig, 1836.

But we should not forget how much Goethe's genius did for the instruction and improvement of his countrymen in his own way; and that his works have always been an inexhaustible source of delight to all classes of the German people.

Eckermann mentioned that Goethe had suffered much from the loss of his wife and son, both of whom had injured themselves by intemperate habits. He felt his son's death so deeply that he could not even bring himself to talk of it with his friends; and when the Chancellor de Müller came to condole with him, he immediately changed the subject. Goethe did not much like Müller, considering him rather too officious in his attentions, but Müller has thrown much light upon Goethe's character by the memoir of his career as a statesman and man of business, in which capacities Goethe worked harder than is generally supposed. Goethe's mind, said Eckermann, was a very practical one. Why, indeed, should a poet be less practical in affairs than another man? On the subject of religion, Eckermann admitted that Goethe was no pietist. He never went to church, or troubled himself about church affairs, saying, ' all that sort of thing can go on without me.' Goethe's religion was philosophical, and he was more a pantheist than anything else, understanding by God the great spirit of the universe, whom he constantly venerated. He considered the Bible of divine origin not on account of the proofs usually cited of the authenticity of the sacred writings, but because the divine spirit manifestly pervaded them, in the same way as it influenced the works of Shakespeare, Raphael, and Mozart. Of Christianity Goethe believed ' *descendit cœlo*,' though not indeed in the sense of the church. In one of his conversations he told Eckermann that he thought an immortality might be reserved for minds of a high order, which had done their best to fulfil their mission in this transitory life. Nor was he insensible to the soothing and humanizing effect of religious ordinances upon the inner life of man. In his autobiography he has given us a vivid description of the worship of the roman-catholic church, and has pointed out how the seven sacraments have interwoven themselves with the most solemn passages in human life, and how superior the catholic worship was to that of the protestant confessions, which in his view had not sufficient fulness or consecutiveness in their divine services to enable them to hold a religious community together for any length of time [1].

---

[1] 'Aus meinem Leben. Wahrheit und Dichtung.' Zweiter Theil. Siebentes Buch.

Eckermann had a strong thirst for knowledge, and when in the society of his great master seems now and then to have pushed his enquiries rather too far, forgetting the German proverb that 'providence has taken care not to let the trees grow up into the sky [1].' On such occasions Goethe gently repelled his curiosity with such remarks as these :—

'Man is not born to solve the problem of the world, but to enquire whether the problem approaches, and so to keep himself within the limits of the comprehensible.'

'If we admit that men have free-will there is an end of the omniscience of God; for if the Godhead knows what I shall do, I am forced to act as he knows it. I mention this as a proof how ignorant we are, and that it is not good for us to meddle with divine secrets.'

I took a liking to Eckermann, as a simple-minded man, who loved and sought for the truth, and though not a philosopher, had a good and clear understanding. He owed everything to Goethe, and gratefully acknowledged it. I saw him again two years later, when he dined with me at an hotel in Weimar, but was in ill health and low spirits. He died not long afterwards, having left us in his 'conversations' one of the most interesting and instructive books in any language. It is an excellent supplement to the poet's autobiography, and a proof that Eckermann knew how to 'dwell beside the rose' to an useful purpose.

---

[1] Es ist dafür gesorgt, dass die Bäume nicht in den Himmel wachsen.

CHAPTER VI.

General de Radowitz.   The Zollverein.   Frederic William III.   Lord Truro.
Baron de Martens.   Table-turning.   The Russian War.   Munich.
Industrial Exhibition.   Technical education.   Professor Neumann.
English convents in Bavaria.

THE name of General de Radowitz stands so prominently forward in the years which succeeded the rising of 1848, that it may be worth while to dwell a little upon his characteristics, and to advert to the causes which gave him so great an influence over the mind of King Frederic William IV, as well as over the opinions of the more enlightened classes in Germany. As a soldier, statesman, and author, he deservedly attained a high reputation, and if he had lived until this day he would have seen the chief objects of his national policy realized, by the restoration of the German empire in the form of a federal state, established under the lead of Prussia, with the acquiescence of the German sovereigns.

Joseph de Radowitz was descended from one of those families of poor Hungarian nobility which are common in that country. He was born in 1797 at Blankenburgh in the Harz mountains, where his father then resided, but soon afterwards removed to Altenburgh, and carried on the business of a wine-merchant in the latter town. Joseph's mother was a protestant, and until the age of fourteen he received instruction in a protestant school at Altenburgh. At that period however his father, wishing to preserve to his son the religion of his family, took charge of his education as a catholic, and he was trained in French and Westphalian schools for the military service. He made so good proficiency in mathematics that at the battle of Leipsic he had the command of a Westphalian battery, and was there wounded. Having entered the service of the Elector of Hesse, he became in 1815 teacher of mathematics and military science in the cadets'-school at Cassel, where he found leisure to pursue the study not only of mathematics but of history and philosophy.

What Radowitz learned he learned thoroughly. He was no literary *dilettant*, but pushed his ideas logically to their consequences, and acted accordingly.

Radowitz's functions at Cassel terminated in 1823, in consequence of his having espoused the cause of the Electress in a contest with her husband relative to the position of the mistress of the latter, the Countess de Reichenbach. He then obtained permission to enter the Prussian army, and was appointed by King Frederic William III to be teacher in the Berlin military school, and soon afterwards mathematical tutor of the Prince Albert. This led to an acquaintance and friendship with the crown-prince, afterwards Frederic William IV, who had strong sentiments for poetry, philosophy, and art, and found in Radowitz an æsthetical mind similar to his own. The crown-prince understood the connection between religion and art, and felt the æsthetical beauty of the catholic worship. Radowitz felt this also ; but with him religion was a matter of simple duty ; and through life he never swerved from the rules of his confession, and never permitted himself to doubt a jot or tittle of catholic doctrine. His religion was in fact strictly logical ; it consisted in a manly straightforward adherence to the teaching of his church. He had nothing like pietism about him, and if he was sometimes called ultramontane, it was certainly not from any want of loyalty towards his own sovereign, but from the conviction that implicit obedience was due to the visible head of the Christian church in all spiritual things.

In 1828 Radowitz married the Countess Marie Voss, by whom he had several children. She became a catholic after her marriage. He continued to reside at Berlin till 1836, when he was detached as Prussian military commissioner to the diet at Frankfort. In 1840 and 1841 he went on missions to Vienna and other capitals, for strengthening the military constitution of Germany, and raising the federal contingents. For several years from this time he laboured for the regeneration of the federal body, and especially for establishing freedom of the press, and for the publication of the freedom of the diet. He was unsuccessful, although he had a certain degree of support from the new king, Frederic William IV, who, soon after his accession, signified to Prince Metternich the necessity of following a course different from that which had formerly been followed in German affairs. On the 20th of November, 1847, Radowitz laid before the King a memorial showing that the reform of the Germanic constitution had become indispensable, and he was despatched next day to Vienna to press his

1

views upon the attention of the Austrian cabinet. This date is important to bear in mind, because it shews that the King, on the advice of Radowitz, had decided to take a line on the German question before either the rising in Germany or the disturbances in Berlin had so rudely forced the subject into the foreground of the political situation. After the troubles had begun in March, 1848, Radowitz was again sent to Vienna to propose a congress of the German governments at Frankfort, with a view to federal reform. Metternich suggested Dresden as the place of meeting; but the arrangements were delayed; and the plan of the congress was soon nullified by the German parliament which met at Frankfort as the representative not merely of the governments, but of the nation at large by which it was chosen.

On being elected a member of the Frankfort parliament, Radowitz gave up the offices which he held under the Prussian crown as envoy to Baden, and as major-general in the army, and military commissioner to the federal diet. Having done this in order to relieve his government from the charge of employing 'before March' statesmen, who were excessively unpopular, he took his seat in the assembly and devoted himself with unremitting zeal to the great object of establishing an unitary state instead of the thirty-nine states which then constituted the Germanic body, and of finding a form for an indissoluble connection with Austria, which could not enter the unitary state with either the whole or a part of her multifarious territories. Radowitz belonged to what was called the 'small-German,' in contradistinction from the 'great-German,' party, which vainly hoped to comprise at least the German provinces of Austria within the limits of the united Germany about to be formed; and in this he concurred with Gagern, Bunsen, and many other of the best friends of the fatherland. But the faction with which Radowitz habitually acted in the assembly was a very small one,—so small that on the question of constituting a central executive power it was left in a minority of only thirty-one against five hundred and seventy-seven votes. Radowitz and his friends contended that the central power, desirable as it was, could only be appointed by the German governments, and not by the parliament. In like manner, on the vote of Frederic William IV as Emperor, the Radowitz fraction, although approving the intention, protested that the parliament had no right to vote the imperial crown without the free consent of the German sovereigns.

Radowitz was always listened to, and was considered one of the best speakers in the assembly. A contemporary journalist described him as sitting there like a picture of Velasquez, with an immoveable downcast countenance, and speaking to no one. His *sobriquet* was 'the monk in armour.' Among his best speeches was one on the independence of the church in regard to the state. He advocated the separation of the catholic, as well as the two established evangelical confessions, from all state control; a proposition which has not yet been adopted in Germany, nor is it easy to settle the terms on which churches supported by public funds can be permitted to manage their affairs without any interference on the part of the government.. In the debate on the church question Radowitz admitted that the order of jesuits was no longer a necessity as it had been in the sixteenth century, and that the catholic bishops and clergy were able to do all that was wanted in the interests of religion. The catholic party would not consent to exclude the order from places where it existed, but did not desire its introduction into any German state.

After the King's refusal of the imperial crown the Frankfort parliament began to fall into a state of dissolution, and Radowitz was recalled to Berlin and appointed a lieutenant-general (which carries with it the title of 'excellency'), for the purpose of making a new attempt to settle the German question by a federal constitution emanating from the crown, and to be submitted for approval to another parliament at another place. Saxony and Hanover at first concurred in this attempt, and entered into a treaty with Prussia on the 26th of May, 1849, which for some time was known under the name of the 'Three Kings' alliance.' Some months elapsed in vain endeavours to obtain the adhesion of the South-German states, but a nucleus was formed of the northern and central governments, and although Saxony and Hanover had begun to recede from their engagements, a parliament was actually opened at Erfurt by Radowitz as the royal commissioner on the 20th of February, 1850, which accepted *en bloc* the new constitution as prepared and recommended by the cabinet of Berlin. It was, however, a signal failure. The nation was not disposed to accept it as an equivalent for the real German unity which at Frankfort had seemed so near its accomplishment; Austria and her allies in southern Germany were determined not to concede to Prussia the hegemony of which the new alliance was intended as the foundation; and Hanover and Saxony thought it their interest to go over into the enemy's camp. The danger of a civil war in Germany was becoming daily greater; and when the complications of the Hesse-Cassel question had placed Prussia in a hostile position

towards the confederation, the King sent for Radowitz, made
him president of the council, and authorized him to take immediate steps to provide for the safety of the monarchy. Orders
were issued to make the entire army *mobile*, and preparations
were going on for instant war, when the King's mind veered
suddenly round; and following the counsel of irresponsible
advisers, his majesty decided upon a compromise with Austria,
and the war-note was no longer heard in Berlin. Radowitz
resigned the premiership to Manteuffel, who went to Olmütz,
and in the conferences there, already adverted to, surrendered
the sword of Prussia into Schwarzenberg's hands. By means
of the Dresden conferences, the old federal diet, and with it
the dualism of the two great German powers, was restored,
and the inevitable conflict was postponed for sixteen years.
Radowitz did not live to witness the eventual victory of the
Prussian arms, and the realisation of his wishes for an unitary
German state. He retired to Erfurt, where he occupied
himself chiefly with literary pursuits until his death, on
Christmas-day 1853, leaving behind him a character which
has been a mystery to many, but which I believe to have been
based on the highest principles of honour and truth.

Among the literary productions of Radowitz his ‘Conversations on state and church in the present times’ are the most
remarkable[1]. They were published in 1846 and ran through
several subsequent editions. The leading idea lies in the
questions, how the statesman ought to make the old order of
things give place to the new? how the indispensable regeneration of modern society is to be effected? Admitting that the
old system of government in church and state has become untenable, and that it is time to substitute for it the autonomy
of the individual, the opinions soon began to differ as to the
manner in which individual well-being may be best promoted.
Some consider the general happiness to be *material* only, and
therefore wish for either an absolute monarchy, or an unlimited
representative system. Others prefer carrying the new system
to the utmost length, and desire unconditional individual
liberty, or absolute democracy. In religion, those different
political directions would answer to rationalism on the one
hand, and pantheism on the other. The author introduces
five persons who support their various views in conversation.
Arneburg, a nobleman and an officer in the army, is an orthodox lutheran, a little pietistic, and with strong legitimist
sympathies. Detlev, his brother, is a fiery young democrat,

[1] ‘Gespräche aus der Gegenwart über Staat und Kirche.’ 4te Auflage. Stuttgardt, 1851.

and a pantheist. Crusius, a rich manufacturer, desires liberal progress in both state and church. Oeder is a bureaucrat, devoted to practice and routine in state affairs, and indifferent to religion. Waldheim (*alias* Radowitz) is a catholic, who reveres his church, and in politics defends the historical view of right and abhors revolution. The conversations take us through the field of the great social and religious questions of the day, and of course and by giving to the opinions of Waldheim an easy victory. The author is not less strong in æsthetics than he is in logic, and it is therefore not surprising that his parliamentary speeches should have told powerfully even in the ranks of his political opponents.

In 1851, after Radowitz had retired from public life, and the Dresden conferences were preparing the revival of the old confederation, a second series of the conversations 'in church and state' came forth[1], with this motto, appropriately borrowed from that original French politician, the Count de Montlosier[2]: 'Triste du mal que je prévois, impuissant pour le bien que je desire, je voudrais terminer par un peu de repos une vie que je n'ai point épargnée, mais que je n'ai pu rendre utile. Les temps actuels sont difficiles, je dois dire plus, ils sont impossibles.' In the new series the characters are changed. They consist of Büchner, the burgomaster of a German town; Sielhorst, a physician; Galsdorff, a country gentleman; and Themar, the rector of a gymnasium, to whom Waldheim is adjoined for the purpose of reconciling their diverging views, and of explaining the true position of the fatherland since the failure of the reform movement. In five years, says he, many appearances have changed, but certain elements in religion and political parties have remained the same. He justifies the course taken by Radowitz and his friends in insisting that the unitary state should be formed with the consent of the German governments, and in wishing to ally Austria by treaty with the regenerated fatherland of which she could not form a part. He vindicates likewise the policy of Prussia when she was on the point of waging war against the unconstitutional pretensions of the federal diet. But the author cannot subdue his melancholy feelings that the discord of parties should have stood in the way of the realization of the national wishes, and of securing the permanent well-being of

[1] 'Neue Gespräche aus der Gegenwart über Staat und Kirche.' 2 Theile. Erfurt und Leipzig 1851.

[2] See the 'Mémoires du Comte de Montlosier,' 6 vols. Paris, 1829. Also his essay, 'Des mystères de la vie humaine,' Paris, 1829, to which is prefixed an historical notice of the author's life.

both princes and people. 'There are times,' he exclaims, 'in which the constitution of a nation can neither exist as it is, nor for the present be so altered as to enable it to exist. Those are the times in which the old comes into conflict with the new,—the former state of civil society with another not yet decided, and still far from a decision. Woe to the sovereign, woe to the statesman whose life falls in such times! Whatever he may do, he does it either too late or too soon; he sees the end without being able to attain it!'

The 'new conversations' had interested me not less than the former series, and although my acquaintance with the author was slight, having only once seen him at Frankfort, I took the liberty of writing to him to say how much his works had pleased me, and I added some reflections on the disappointment which the German nation had experienced, with hopes that the day would come when it would enjoy a really constitutional government, and a free press, in the sense desired by all liberal-minded men. The answer of General de Radowitz was as follows:—

[*Translation.*]   To Mr. Ward.

'*Erfurt*, Nov. 4, 1851.

'Your kind letter, respected Consul-General, deserves my cordial thanks. I know how to value the confidence which an honourable man shews towards me, and doubly so in a time in which even old, long preserved, bands have been torn asunder by political and religious divisions. In this more than in anything else lies the misfortune of the present state of Germany,—that the contest is carried on from the narrowest party points of view,—and that the well or ill-being of the fatherland, nay even common justice and truth, are thereby made to fall into the background.

'The book which you are so good as to mention has therefore from the most different quarters experienced misconceptions and attacks. They have neither surprised nor irritated me. Certainly, as you justly observe, the German press in its actual state is a bad middle-thing between freedom and coercion. That such coercion instead of the former active censorship is now exercised in an indirect way, only increases its odious character. But unhappily great and deeply penetrating changes in our political condition must precede before a real and worthy free press can attain permanent life in Germany.

'In expressing the pleasure I feel that a non-German should

have arrived at so correct a knowledge of my country, and hoping to see you if you should travel in this direction, I beg you, respected Consul-General, to receive the assurance of my especial consideration. 'VON RADOWITZ.'

In the course of an excursion which I made into Thuringia in March 1852, I visited General de Radowitz at his house in Erfurt, and was received by him in a friendly manner. He was looking ill, his countenance being of a yellowish hue, and his hair and mustachios being as white as those of an old man of eighty. He was, in fact, suffering both in body and mind, and spoke with despondency of the fate of his country, believing the national cause, which was hopeful three or four years ago, to have been blighted for an indefinite length of time. He said he had been misunderstood and mistrusted by many who had the same national objects at heart, because they wished to proceed in a revolutionary manner, whereas he could not conscientiously violate historical rights. He had sought to regenerate Germany with the consent of the sovereigns, and that consent would have been given if revolutionary elements had not predominated in the Frankfort assembly. Speaking of England, he lamented that neither the English government nor the people had shewn any sympathy with the German cause, and that we did not seem to set much value upon an alliance with a free and united Germany. The convention of Olmütz was notoriously attributable to Russian influence, and in the Schleswig-Holstein question Russia had been working for some time past in a sense hostile to the wishes of the German nation. He (Radowitz) had been much disappointed that England had not supported his policy by declaring against any intervention of Russia in German affairs. Referring to Lord Palmerston, who was then excluded from office on account of the unauthorized approval which he had given to the acts of Louis Napoleon, Radowitz expressed his surprise that so experienced a statesman should have so committed himself, and should have been generally so prepossessed in favour of a French alliance. The consort of your Queen, he added, is a man of great sagacity; there is no one upon whose political judgment she may more safely rely.

We talked of the state of religion in England, and he asked whether Puseyism was making much progress among the members of the established church? I said I thought so, but that the Anglican church was likewise much affected by puritanism, and had within it many differences and shades of opinion. He looked upon the puseyites as religious *dilettanti,* though some of them had proved their sincerity by being reconciled to the roman-catholic communion. English protestantism, he observed, was something very different from German rationalism; he honoured sincere believers, but feared that out of the tents of rationalism nothing good could come. I asked him what he thought of the possibility of an union between the catholic church and the protestant sects, in the sense once contemplated by Leibnitz, but he said he did not see any prospect of such a consummation. A theological professor in Berlin (Marheinike) had once proposed that the question should be settled by making all the men protestants, and all the women catholics; nor was this joke without a meaning, for women had ordinarily more faith than men, only their faith was too much a matter of habit and education, and it was a pleasure to them to have to obey an undeviating rule.

The despondency of Radowitz at this period was, I know, shared by his friend Bunsen, who declared that for a man who had lived sixty years there was nothing left in this world but despair, though in the next generation the good cause might come out victorious. Neither of them lived to witness the great events of 1866 and 1870; but the now united fatherland cannot forget how much it owes to the statesmen who worked at all sacrifices, through evil report and through good report, with their whole hearts and souls, for the national welfare.

Erfurt is an ancient town, formerly more populous than at present, and a portion of its inhabitants are still catholics, and have the use of the cathedral, a fine three-towered gothic structure. The Ursuline convent is likewise a remnant of the catholic times. Radowitz lived in an old-fashioned, comfortable house, in which were some good religious pictures, brought by him, as I understood, from Italy, where he had been in 1824 as the companion of Prince Augustus of Prussia. His work on the 'Iconography of the saints,' and that on the 'Devices and mottoes of the middle ages,' prove the interest he took in everything connected with religious art; and the collection of autographs which he had made was considered one of the finest in Germany. Among his many political pamphlets, his 'Germany and Frederic William IV,' published in 1848, excited general attention, and he was said to have been occupied with a larger work in continuation of it at the time of his decease.

Those who sympathized with the religious sentiments and political views of Radowitz, could not but see in him one of the finest public characters of modern times. He was

surely a liberal in the right sense of the word, desiring the
constitutional freedom of the people without breaking off the
historical traditions derived from the middle ages and the
times of our forefathers. The political career of a nation
cannot indeed too strongly resemble the life of an individual
in the words of the poet :—

> 'The Child is father of the Man;
> And I could wish my days to be
> Bound each to each by natural piety.'

During the summer an important conference of the *Zollverein*-states sat in Berlin for the purpose of considering the
proposal of Austria to form a customs-union with that body,
and I went to Berlin several times to watch the proceedings.
The states in the Austrian interest, which went under the
name of the Darmstadt coalition, considered such an union
desirable, and that it was contemplated by an article of the
federal act which declared that a common system of customs
and commercial regulations should be adopted by all the
German states. But Prussia refused to enter into any negotiation with Austria until the other states had consented to
renew the *Zollverein* itself whose termination was approaching;
and, as she persisted in that refusal, the conferences came
to nothing, and were suspended after several months' sitting.
The object of Prussia was eventually attained, viz. the
renewal of the *Zollverein* without Austria, and a commercial
treaty was entered into between the two bodies which placed
the intercourse between Germany and the Austrian empire on
a more favourable footing for trade than had previously been
the case.

At an interval of leisure I visited the Baltic coast and the
island of Rügen,—the German Isle of Wight,—which contains picturesque scenery and magnificent beech-woods. The
chief proprietor, the Prince of Putberg, had erected a bathing-
establishment, and maintained a theatre for the amusement of the guests. Among several pretty villas at
Heringsdorf, on the Baltic, I found that of an old friend,
Professor Homeyer, one of the judges of the high court of
appeal at Berlin. He was an enlightened conservative, and
while lamenting the failure of the Frankfort constitution,
seemed to regard the restoration of the old diet as the only
thing which remained to be done. We spoke of King

---

[1] Wordsworth, ' Poems on Childhood,' 1804.

Frederic William III, and the titular Bishop Eylert's biography of him, which is full of anecdotes mostly of a flattering kind.   Homeyer admitted that the King was narrow-minded, and something of a tyrant ; but, said he, combined singleness of heart with tenacity of purpose,—both valuable qualities in a sovereign.   The King, he said, was prosaic ; his Queen, Louisa, poetic and imaginative ; and their son, Frederic William IV, took after his mother to a degree which made him inferior to his father as a man of business.   This was doubtless true ; yet there are instances, such as Goethe, which prove that poetic fancy is not always a disqualification from the ability of administering public affairs.   Eylert's book is the work of a thorough courtier.   He has placed the private life of the King and Queen in an amiable and respectable light ; but has not been equally successful in his attempt to vindicate the policy of Prussia towards other states during the French war.   The Prussian government entered alternately into engagements against and with France, which it had no intention of fulfilling, and violated at the first convenient moment.   Its only excuse for such a policy of dissimulation was of course its weakness ; and Prussian statesmen doubtless now look back with shame to the tergiversations of their predecessors in those hard times ; whereas the bishop lavishes praise upon the King for his *finesse*, and gives us to understand that such illusory engagements may very properly be resorted to by a power which has not strength to maintain itself by force of arms against its enemies in war.

Lord and Lady Truro came to see the Leipsic Michaelmas fair, and dined with us.   My friend Mr. Bach, a German lawyer settled in London, was one of the party, and a discussion arose respecting the value of juries in civil cases.   Bach contended they were unnecessary in such cases, and I supported him on the ground that the judge was perfectly competent to decide questions of civil right according to the evidence, and that even in criminal trials the only good reason for submitting facts to a jury was the possibility of the judge being biassed on behalf of the crown.   The ex-chancellor, however, thought otherwise, and hoped trial by jury, as a security for English liberty, would never be given up.   I mentioned to him that jury-trials for criminal offences had of late been introduced into Prussia, and some other German states, but that in Saxony they were at first applied only to offences against the press, and were suspended in consequence of the juries

summoned in all the newspaper prosecutions having given
verdicts against the crown. I explained also that an uniform
criminal code had not yet been established for all the German
states, but that great attention was paid to the subject by the
different governments, and that the new criminal code of
Saxony had been prepared with the utmost care by eminent
jurists. Lord Truro enquired whether the Roman law served
as the basis of decision in cases where the German legislation
might be silent? and Mr. Bach informed him that it did so,
and that England was the only country in which the pandects
and institutes did not require to be studied by practising advocates. He added that the modern philosophy of law was taken
entirely from the principles of the Roman codes, and that some
jurists had maintained that the old common law of Germany
might just as well have been made the basis of legislation in
the German states, but that it was too late to think of that.
Lord Truro said, jestingly, ' You enjoy one great blessing
in Germany; there is no court of chancery;' to which I
assented, explaining that in that country equity and law
meant the same thing, and that the German lawyers did not
understand why the English courts of law should not likewise
administer what was called equity, instead of having distinct
courts guided by different legal principles. Lord and Lady
Truro visited with interest the battlefields round Leipsic,
particularly M. Gerhardt's garden bordering on the Elster,
where the French crossed the river after the battle of the 18th
of October, 1813, and Prince Poniatowsky, and many other
brave soldiers, found a watery grave.

An agreeable addition to the society of Leipsic was made
this winter by the arrival of the Baron Charles de Martens,
nephew of the celebrated statesman and diplomatist, George
Frédéric de Martens, whose voluminous *Recueil de Traités* has
found a place in all the public libraries of Europe. After his
death in 1821 the *Recueil* was continued by M. Frédéric
Murhard, but Charles de Martens proved himself a worthy
successor to his uncle's reputation by his *Guide Diplomatique*,
and by his first and second series of the *Cause célèbres du droit
des gens*. He came to Leipsic in order to superintend the
publication, through Brockhaus's firm, of a new collection of
treaties, excluding the many documents of no general interest
which were accustomed to find their way into Murhard's
Recueil. The Baron Charles, although about eighty years
of age, went by the name of the *young* Martens, to distinguish him from his once famous uncle, and was so lively

and active that few could suppose him to have passed his sixtieth year. He frequented balls and card-parties, and sang with effect a French *chanson*, when he could find a young lady to accompany him on the piano. Charles de Martens was one of those diplomatists of the old school who had been in the service of various sovereigns, and had even held an employment under the goverment of France. His latest post was that of minister-resident of the Grand-duke of Weimar at the Prussian court, from which he had retired on a pension. During the disturbances at Berlin in March, 1848, he did good service to the Prince of Prussia (the present King), by causing a placard to be printed and posted everywhere with the words, 'A prince's property is national property, and ought therefore to be respected.' The Prince of Prussia was at that time so very unpopular as to be obliged to take flight, and repair to England ; and it was feared the mob would break into his palace *unter den Linden* and make havoc of his costly furniture and objects of art. Eventually, however, the palace was respected, and Martens derived much credit from his well-timed advertisement. Martens was a conservative, and had a horror of all revolutionary movements ; but he was nothing of a statesman, and did not care about such questions as national unity, or constitutional reform. He had little confidence in the impulsive nature of the reigning King, and seemed to think that the country was safer under the rule of Frederic William III. He had been well acquainted with the Princess of Liegnitz, the morganatic wife of the last-named sovereign, and praised her uniform discretion and amiable qualities. She was born a Countess de Harrach, and was twenty-four years of age at the time of her marriage, which proved childless, and she soon afterwards gratified the King by abandoning the catholic for the protestant faith. Martens said that, if she had been Queen, the King's behaviour to her could not have been more tender or respectful. He never intruded on her privacy, and paid her formal visits as if she had been a royal personage. Madame de Liegnitz, he added, did not aim at playing the political part of a Madame de Maintenon, or attempt to meddle with state affairs ; but was satisfied with contributing to the King's domestic happiness, and in enjoying the many opportunities of doing good which belonged to the elevated position in which he had placed her. As to Martens, he was a man of sanguine temperament, and had the agreeable quality of generally seeing persons and things *en couleur de rose*. He died some years afterwards at Dresden at a very advanced age.

Table-turning had become the order of the day at Leipsic, and amused us much. A number of persons used to sit round a not too heavy table, form the magnetic chain, and lay their hands on the table ; and in less than an hour it usually began to move ; but it moved much quicker when any one possessed of strong magnetic powers formed a part of the circle. I remember a magnetic young lady of twelve years old, healthy and fresh-looking,—Mdlle. de H.,—who could and did in my presence make a table turn in a minute or two after she had joined the circle which was previously at work upon it. Mdlle. de H. likewise, in conjunction with three gentlemen, by laying hands on an arm-chair upon castors, in which a heavy person was seated, made the chair speedily turn round and round. I have myself in conjunction with two other persons repeatedly turned a small table, a wooden plate laid upon glasses, and other articles. The fact of the table moving was too notorious for any one to dispute, and scarcely any one doubted the existence of the magnetic power which set them in motion. After the tables had had their run for some weeks they became rather a bore, and on the occasion of a christening-party given by the astronomer Dr. d'Arrét, he thought it right to affix to the outside of his door a notice to this effect : ' My respected guests are requested for to-day only to refrain from talking about table-turning,' which was a great relief to more than one of the assembled company.

The fact which I have mentioned of a table being immediately turned by a highly magnetic girl, after several other much stronger but less magnetic persons had been working at it in vain for half an hour, appears to me a sufficient answer to the supposition that the motion is produced by mechanical pressure. The existence of animal magnetism is disputed by no one in Germany. We have all witnessed magnetic sleep ; we know the powers of somnambulists ; and we have well authenticated instances of the extraordinary attraction which certain persons have for others by means of their eyes and their general deportment. We have indisputable evidence of the exercise of witchcraft from the earliest historical times ; and witchcraft, or sorcery, is simply magnetism exercised for bad and unholy purposes. The great interest attached to the existence of magnetic power lies of course in the connection which it appears to open to us between the visible and invisible world ; for

> ' There are more things in heaven and earth, Horatio,
> Than are dreamt of in your philosophy.'

Animal life is a mystery which the researches of physical

science are not permitted to succeed in dispelling. The nervous system is but imperfectly understood; and medical skill can do little for suffering humanity beyond gently assisting the operations of nature. In these circumstances little can be said of animal magnetism but that it is a thing to wonder at, and when used for curative purposes may be not only harmless but beneficial. When employed to deceive, or injure others, or to influence them for bad purposes, it is sorcery, and a wicked and unchristian thing. As such the catholic church has uniformly denounced it, and has cast so severe a censure upon the profane invocation of spirits, that those who pursue the amusement of 'spirit-rapping,' as it is called, may well pause to consider whether this sort of sport, ridiculous as it may appear, does not trench closely on forbidden ground? I have never witnessed 'spirit-rapping,' though I have seen the effects of magnetism; but whether there be anything in it, or not, we ought surely not to look without reverence and awe towards that immaterial world whose existence we believe to be certain, and to which our own spiritual parts are destined sooner or later to belong.

It was the opinion of Goethe that a spiritual immortality was reserved for the minds of superior men who in this life had made the best use of the talents committed to them, although it would not necessarily follow that the personal existence of such men must continue after death. Hegel's philosophy, which exercises so wide an influence in Germany, comprises a similar admission of a spiritual world. Hegel denied a personal God. According to him God was an unconscious power, pervading all personalities, and only becoming conscious in the personality of men. He did not admit that God became man in Christ in any different way from that in which God becomes man in those men who arrive at the possession of mind or spirit (*Geist*). The difference would be only in degree. Christ was a more perfect God-man, yet not an absolutely perfect one. There was, said Hegel, no personal existence of men after death in any other sense than that the spirit (*Geist*) of which superior men enjoyed a portion in their life-time, was in itself immortal. This philosophy has assumed a character of outward, or rationalistic, christianity, and has been adopted by some German clergymen, and a great number of literary men. A village schoolmaster in the neighbourhood of Leipsic once explained to me very clearly in the course of a long walk the leading principles of Hegel's philosophy, and the motives which had induced him to become a *Hegelianer*. Such a system of course differs widely from the orthodox christianity of the catholic church, and of the lutheran and reformed confessions; and I allude to it here merely as shewing that German philosophers, who can hardly be considered as professing the christian religion, still recognise the perpetual existence of a spiritual world; and that, therefore, even according to their views, there may be in magnetism a certain link of connection between what is visible, and what is invisible, which we are unable to comprehend, but whose existence it would be absurd on that account altogether to deny.

The disputes between Russia and the Porte assumed a serious aspect in the early part of this summer, and when the latter refused the Russian ultimatum claiming for the Czar the protectorate of the Greek Christians in European Turkey, and insisting upon immovability of the Greek patriarch and provincial bishops, it was generally believed in Germany that there would be a European war. In July, after the Russian army had crossed the Pruth and occupied the Danubian principalities, the German governments began to consider whether they should be obliged to take part in the war, and the subject was ventilated by the German newspapers. The Saxon court was led to suppose that Prussia would go with Russia in the event of a war, and Baron de Beust, who was then very Russian, appears to have desired to promote that object. The following letter, which I received from Mr. Forbes just before my going over to England on leave of absence, shews that there was some reason for giving credit to the rumour referred to.

To Mr. Ward.

Dresden, August 19th, 1853.

'My dear Sir,

'I am glad for you that you have got a holiday: if there was not that horrid and unjust rule of deducting from our already diminished salaries, I should like to run over to England and Ireland too. My sisters are both absent, the eldest went to Teplitz on the 20th of this month, the other to Baden-Baden, on the 22nd of July.

'I so fully agree in your opinion as to a war with Russia being inevitable, that I wrote it home as my own, ten days ago. I also hear, that there exists a strong feeling in England against Lord Aberdeen personally, for he is looked upon as being the one who has made us truckle to Russia. A person, who pretended to know it (I cannot answer for him), told me that the majority of the cabinet had decided on the fleet entering the Dardanelles, and that on this Lord Aberdeen had tendered his resignation : that the Queen then sent for Palmerston, and closed an hour's argument with the *request* that he would use his influence in bringing round the cabinet : this he did, and Aberdeen remained ; but how the latter must share John Russell's dislike of P—— !

'Did *you* ever hear in Berlin of Prussia having given assurances to Russia, that in case of a war, Prussia would side with her ? It was told me here on high authority (Beust's), and I wrote it home without quoting his name. . . That there is something in it, I am convinced, for it has been stated in Petersburgh too ; but I should like to know whether the King or his brother has not been writing or saying something without the knowledge of the ministers? . . . Beust is so Russian, that even Kuefstein was surprised and displeased at it. He is delighted at having the *police* in his hands (he told me so), but how can any one but an old woman enjoy the sort of dirty gossip it affords? Mercier gave a dinner on the 15th and forgot Falkenstein completely : this is very French : he seems to think of nothing but saving money. I have lately got three despatches, saying that Her Majesty's Government approve of my conduct and language on the eastern question (as reported by me) with Beust. This is satisfactory.

'I see much potatoe blights in the neighbourhood of Dresden. I send you a small parcel directed to my nephew, Wm. Forbes, now in the Guards, &c. &c., and believe me,

'Very truly yours,
'FRANCIS R. FORBES.'

Whilst I was in London I had an interview with Lord Clarendon, then foreign secretary, and he told me there would doubtless be a war between the western powers and Russia, and dwelt on the importance of drawing the public opinion in Germany to the side of the former. On my return to Leipsic I spoke to many persons of the war as a certainty, and endeavoured to explain to them how impossible it was that the unjustifiable acts of Russia could be passed over by the British Government. I was met by the assertion that Germany had a very small interest in the eastern question, and that it was unlikely that either the Austrian or the Prussian governments would be brought to break definitively with their old ally the Czar on account of the Porte. So it in fact turned out; but it should not be supposed that there was not then a strong anti-Russian feeling in Germany, or that Russia was not regarded as an *incubus* pressing upon German liberty, and obstructing, so far as it could, the constitutional development of the nation. The liberal party in Germany had a certain sympathy with the cause of Turkey and the Western powers; but the decision did not rest with the people; and the federal diet, since its restoration, had shewn as little deference as in former times to public opinion. When therefore Louis Napoleon in March 1854 told his Senate that Austria was anti-Russian, that Prussia was friendly to him, and that he was resolved to march to Constantinople with Germany at his back, the French Emperor assuredly reckoned without his host. The diplomacy of the western powers practically failed; and the treaty of the 20th of April proved illusory; for Austria did not become their active ally, and Prussia never departed from her armed neutrality. The Vienna conferences did not help the situation; and the war was waged to its end at the heavy costs of England and France. Whether the objects attained were worth the severe sacrifices which that war involved has now become a question of history. So much is certain, that it originated with Louis Napoleon,—that we in England were led into it by him,—and that he left us in the lurch when it suited his policy to withdraw from the contest. Englishmen in general were vexed and disappointed by the necessity of making peace before Russia had been sufficiently punished and humiliated, while they understood the impossibility of proceeding in the war without allies. The Prussian government applauded its own sagacity in remaining neutral, and I remember an intelligent Prussian, who had no love for Russia, saying to me towards the close of the war: 'England and France cannot justly blame Prussia for refusing to join them, when they themselves have never been in earnest in this contest. You do not mean to reduce Russia to a second-rate power, and you will make peace with her as soon as it may suit your convenience. We have so little to do with the questions which gave rise to the war, that we may well be excused for husbanding our own resources, and preparing for the conflict which Prussia will have to encounter in Germany itself in the course of a few years.' This I believe was the feeling of many liberal Germans, who whilst they feared Russia, likewise feared and hated France, and had no over-weening confidence in the professions of friendship for Germany which had from time to time been made by British statesmen.

In August 1854 I was sent to Munich as British commissioner to the Exhibition of the arts and manufactures of the German states which was held in that capital during the summer. The exhibition had been formally opened previous to my arrival, and the unfortunate appearance of the cholera in Munich had driven most of the Bavarian families into the country. When the existence of the epidemic became known it likewise interfered very much to prevent the expected visitors of the exhibition from coming to Munich, and the city had a dreary aspect, rendered still more melancholy by the number of funerals which were constantly passing through the streets. I however found no difficulty in accomplishing my object, and with the assistance of the president of the commission, Dr. de Fischer, and of the president of the juries, Dr. de Hermann, I was enabled to inspect all the important articles exhibited and to make a full report thereon to Her Majesty's government. Since the last German industrial exhibition which was held at Berlin in 1844 considerable progress had been made in the textile as well as other branches of manufacture, and the German producer began to have more confidence in his own skill, and to be less afraid than formerly of foreign competition. The Austrian empire furnished many interesting specimens of the artistic and technical productions of its capital, and manufacturing towns. Upon the whole the exhibition offered an encouraging picture of the condition of German industry; but in a financial point of view it was a decided failure, inasmuch as the expenditure exceeded the receipts by a sum equivalent to about £120,000 sterling. For this result the cholera was to some extent answerable, although it was from the first doubtful whether the visitors would prove numerous enough to pay for the beautiful glass-palace, and the expenses of management.

There was little to be done at the British legation at this dull season; but an attaché attended daily to issue passports, and answer enquiries. Sir John Milbanke resided at his country-house at Nannhofen, about twenty miles off, where I passed a pleasant Sunday with him. We talked of Lord Durham (Sir John having been secretary at St. Petersburgh whilst Lord Durham was ambassador there), and of his extreme particularity in matters of routine and etiquette. Lord Durham looked himself very closely to the state of his horses and carriages as well as of the harness, and of his servants' liveries. But in Sir John's opinion he was an excellent ambassador, and had a remarkable influence over the mind of the Czar. Speaking of English travellers Sir John mentioned a case which had given some trouble. An English clergyman, having caused letters to be addressed to him at the post-office Munich, called to enquire for them and was told there were none. Going again the next day he received the same answer; when espying his own name written on a letter lying upon the table he called out in German to the official, 'You stupid ass, there lies the letter [1].' The official immediately lodged a complaint with the police, and a prosecution was instituted against the Englishman for defamation. A heavy penalty, or imprisonment, would have been inflicted, but it was mitigated in consequence of the evidence of the offender's daughter, who testified that her father was imperfectly acquainted with the language, and was not aware of the deep insult which the phrase 'dummer Esel' never fails to convey to German ears. Nothing offends a German more than to be called '*dumm*' or stupid. He will bear a great deal good-humouredly, but cannot patiently endure to be set down for a fool.

When I was at Munich King Maximilian II was reigning, who though he had not the genius or energy of his father King Louis, was still a liberal protector of artists and scientific men, and did his best to carry on the work which King Louis had begun. I need not here dwell upon the magnificent public buildings which Munich contains, its collections of ancient art, and the achievements in modern sculpture, castings, pictures, and frescoes, which have been accomplished in it; but it may be as well to say something of the system of technical education which has been for some years past established in Bavaria, and which has done so much for the welfare and improvement of the industrial classes.

The technical branch of the Bavarian educational system dates from the year 1833, when King Louis caused it to be organized in a progressive series of institutions, from the schools of trade and agriculture to the polytechnic, and the technical high-school. In the elementary schools the popular instruction had at the same time a direction given to it corresponding with that of the trade-schools, whereby, and by the formation of drawing schools, an opportunity was afforded to the poorest pupils of laying the foundation of that artistic ability which is always so valuable in the mechanical

---

[1] Du dummer Esel, da liegt der Brief !

and manufacturing career.   For such as might be unable to
attend the trade or the polytechnic schools, separate schools
were opened on Sundays and holidays, where they were
taught drawing and other useful knowledge, and extra
lectures were appointed to be given in the trade schools for
the benefit of apprentices and others, who were not regular
pupils.   In this way technical information has in the course
of the last thirty or forty years been very widely diffused
among the Bavarian population.   The ground-work of the
trade-schools (*Gewerbe-Schule*) is laid in the elementary Latin
and German schools, which all children, whether catholic or
protestant, are obliged to attend ; and in the trade-schools
the pupils are prepared for the higher grade of instruction
given in the polytechnic schools of Munich, Nuremberg, and
Augsburgh.   Superior to these stands the technical high-
school at Munich, where the student may graduate as at an
university ; or, if he prefers it, the university of Munich is
ready to receive him.   I found the latter institution in a
very flourishing state ; it had sixty professors, among them
Thiersch, Liebig, and other eminent men, and above 1700
registered students.   Its library of 160,000 volumes was
valuable, though small in comparison with the royal library,
which contained 800,000 volumes.

For the youth who desires to embrace the career of an
artist the academy of the fine arts offers the requisite means
of completing his education.   It was established on its
present footing by King Louis in 1846, and is at once a
society of artists, and a school of painting and sculpture.   It
is open to foreigners as well as natives.   The celebrated
William de Kaulbach (since called to Berlin) was then its
director, and in his absence the institution was shewn and
explained to me by Professor Schlotthauer.   The instruction
given in the academy was both practical and theoretical, the
latter embracing the history of art, and subsidiary studies.
Historical painting was taught in four separate schools, of
which the most interesting was unquestionably the religious-
romantic, sometimes called the new German, school.   Diligent
and talented pupils who were natives of Bavaria might obtain
small stipends, besides being furnished gratuitously with
models for the cartoons, pictures, or statues which they
might execute within the academy.   The staff of the academy
consisted of five professors besides the director, and the
number of pupils was about two hundred.

In addition to the establishments organized by the government as already mentioned, the inhabitants of Munich had

themselves formed several institutions in furtherance of the same objects, such as the art-union, the trades-union, and the society for the improvement of manufactures, which had had a most useful tendency in consequence of the communications it kept up between the class of artists and that of mechanics. There were, as I was informed, about 800 artists, chiefly Germans, constantly residing at Munich, which thus offered on a smaller scale the same advantages of social intercourse as Rome gives on a larger to artists from all countries. As a school of pure art indeed there is no place out of Italy which holds out so many attractions to the student. He finds in the Glyptothek, the Pinacothek, and the other royal collections, the best opportunities of copying from the antique, as well as of forming his knowledge of the painting and sculpture of more modern times. He sees around him beautiful palaces and churches, whose architecture is only surpassed by their internal decorations. He sees also the statues of Schwanthaler, and the frescoes of Cornelius, Hess, Schnorr, and Kaulbach, revealing a form of art not possessed by the ancients, which the genius of Christianity alone could conceive and accomplish. The new German school of painting may indeed be said to be essentially catholic; and in Munich at least everything breathes the catholic spirit, and there is that perfect harmony between religion and art which in protestant countries must always be so difficult to realize. The artist of merit has likewise the full assurance of royal encouragement and protection, for in this respect the present King Louis II has shewn himself a worthy successor both of his father Maximilian, and of his grandfather Louis I. The memory of Louis I. can indeed not easily be effaced in the capital of which he may be said to have been the creator. The sums which he expended upon buildings and works of art at Munich, including the Glyptothek collection formed by him when crown-prince, and the Walhalla temple on the Danube, amounted, as I heard, to above thirteen million pounds sterling.

The state of practical science in Bavaria was more particularly described in a report on the subject which I made to the secretary of state soon after my return from the Munich exhibition. The continuity of the several schools of technical instruction,—the excellent system of Sunday and holiday schools for drawing and useful objects,—and the advantages offered to students by the large artistical collections of Munich,—were points which seemed well worthy of attention in other countries. It was, moreover, an important fact that in Bavaria, as in other German states, the government possessed the absolute direction and control of all educational institutions, whether in the department of literature, pure science, practical science, or the fine arts. Neither the clergy, nor any corporate bodies, had the right, any more than individuals, to meddle with the system of public education, which it was the business and duty of the government to conduct, and which as I believe it has conducted, in conformity with the moral and physical wants of the Bavarian people.

M. von der Pfordten, the minister for foreign affairs, was residing at his country-house, but he gave me all facilities of obtaining information, and I had some opportunities of conversing with him. He desired me to remark the general well-being and comfort which prevailed in Bavaria, and seemed to think that the people had little to gain from schemes of national unity, or constitutional reform. I could not but admit that the Bavarians took life very easily, and had all the appearance of contentment with the existing order of things At Munich everybody dined at one or two o'clock, and after dinner little or no work was done. People went to the palace-garden to take coffee, and afterwards to the theatre, or they made excursions into the country. Others sat for hours drinking and smoking in the beer-gardens, in fulfilment of the proverb,—'the Bavarian is in the morning a beer barrel, and in the evening a barrel of beer.' The country round Munich, commanding views of the Tyrolian mountains, was really delightful. The clear, green lakes of Stargard and Tegern were chiefly resorted to by the aristocracy, and many elegant villas were ranged along the water-side. At Minterschweige, on the Isar, was a pleasant place of refreshment much frequented by artists, from whence one enjoyed a good view of that deep-rolling river, whose yellowish-green colour is something different from that of any other stream. At Schäftlarm, close to an ancient convent, I found my old friend, Professor C. F. Neumann, residing with his family. Neumann was reputed the first Chinese and Armenian scholar in Germany, and I had been fortunate enough many years ago to procure him a passage to Canton, where he extended his knowledge and brought home a large and valuable library of Chinese books. He was of humble, and jewish, origin, and was a remarkable instance of a man raising himself to eminence by his own laborious exertions. The Bavarian government, not liking his politics, had lately 'quieted' him, as it was called, by obliging him to retire from his professorship on a small pension. Neumann soon afterwards removed to Berlin, and devoted himself to historical studies. His history of the British dominion in India, and his history of the United States of America, were both well received in the literary world, and the latter was, I know, valued by many leading Americans as an impartial and truthful work.

At Nymphenburgh was a large country palace of the king, whose fountains, gardens, and deer-park have long been celebrated. Not far from the palace stood the convent of English ladies (*Kloster der Engländischen Fräulein*), which I had the more curiosity to visit, as it was founded by my pious namesake, Miss Mary de Ward, of the old Yorkshire family of that name long since extinct. The persecutions of the English catholics by Queen Elizabeth led to the establishment of seminaries and convents for their education in various parts of the continent. Among these were the English colleges for priests at Rome, Valladolid, St. Omer, Douay, and Louvain, and the Scotch college for benedictines at Ratisbon. Mary de Ward appears to have been a zealous adherent to the ancient faith, and it was chiefly to her bounty that the several English convents existing in Bavaria owed their existence. She was born the 23rd of January, 1585, at Mollwith Castle, Yorkshire, and was baptized Johanna, but at her own desire received the holier name of Mary at her confirmation. Having in conjunction with other ladies established the convent of St. Omer in the year 1609, she founded a convent in the city of Munich in 1626, with the sanction and encouragement of the then Elector Maximilian-Emanuel, and his wife Elizabeth. The institution occupied for many years the building since used as the police-office, and was afterwards removed to the more tranquil and healthy situation of Nymphenburgh. The lady-superior, Mademoiselle di Graccho, informed me that the sisters were mostly Bavarians, but foreigners were equally admissible with natives, and there was then an English, an Italian, and a French sister in the convent. A candidate for admission must, if not already a catholic, declare her readiness to become so; there is a period of probation in the ordinary dress of the world; then a noviciate of two years; and finally the oath is taken as a nun, and the maiden becomes 'the chaste bride of heaven' for evermore.

The 'English ladies' of Munich were, as I was informed, in very good repute, as well as those of the affiliated convents at Augsburgh, Günzburgh, and Aschaffenburgh, which are colonies from the Munich foundation.   Miss Mary de Ward died in England at the convent of Haworth in 1643.   The effect of the relaxation of those unjust penal laws which formerly prohibited the education of English catholics in their own country has been, that the bounty of that pious lady is now almost entirely enjoyed by foreigners.   Her benevolent purpose is, however, not the less entitled to grateful commendation ; and prayers for the repose of her soul are not wanting, although they are offered up to heaven in a foreign tongue.

During my stay in Nuremberg, I did not fail to mount the *Burg*, that ancient and massive castle from which the royal house of Hohenzollern has sprung, nor to inspect the artistic manufactures, such as the modelling in bronze-casts and the glass-painting, which are so admirably carried on in that venerable city.   Those who wish to know what art was in the middle ages must carefully examine the churches and houses of Nuremberg, which have scarcely at all altered in the course of the last three or four hundred years.   There is an indescribable charm in reverting in this way to the times of our forefathers, in placing ourselves in the same rooms which they occupied, and in revering the same beautiful objects which have already commanded the admiration of successive generations.

CHAPTER VII.

In consequence of his brother's unfortunate death in
August 1854, the Prince John had become King of Saxony,
and his former unpopularity did not interfere with the general
homage which was paid to him by his subjects on his assuming the reins of government. Some weeks after his accession
King John came to Leipsic and held a court at the Blumen-
berg Hotel, which was attended by the civil and military
authorities and the foreign consuls. He said to me after
some unimportant enquiries, ' I honour your country, because
in England the law is respected by all classes of the people.'
The King thought it necessary to make a tour through his
small dominions, and to inspect personally such institutions
and objects as were most worthy attention. He came several
times to Leipsic, and visited the offices of the director of the
circle, the post-office, the military barracks, the principal
manufactories, and the university. At a large brewery he sat
down in the public room, called for a glass of beer and
praised it, conversing familiarly with the manager of the
concern. He went into some of the lecture-rooms of the
university, and listened to the professors who were addressing
the students. The King had a high respect for Dr. Wächter,
professor of law, and taking a seat in his class-room, heard
one of his lectures from beginning to end. Towards the close
of the lecture Wächter said to the students, ' I speak in the
presence of our revered sovereign, who would doubtless have
corrected me if I had fallen into any errors, for His Majesty is
far more competent than I am to lecture to you on the subject
which has to-day occupied us, and I really wish that he had
himself filled my chair,' when the King, looking up, exclaimed,
' No, good Wächter ! we will both for the present remain
what we are[1].' King John would in fact have made a very
good professor either of law, history, or theology. In the
personal inspections which he made in all parts of the country,
it appeared to his ministers that he went rather too much

---

[1] Nein ! lieber Wächter, wir wollen vorläufig bleiben wie wir sind.

into the *minutiæ* of official business, but his motive was the
laudable one of making himself thoroughly acquainted with
the institutions of the country he was called to rule over.

The King's elder sister, the Princess Amelia, was attacked
in her sixtieth year by the formation of a cataract in her
eyes, and passed some months of the winter 1855–56 in
Leipsic, in order to be under the care of the eminent occulist,
Dr. Coccius. The operation was successful, and the princess,
after her restoration to sight, received visitors again and gave
several dinner-parties. At one of these parties, at which
I was present, the conversation turned upon the new tragedy
of the 'fighter of Ravenna,' which had been so successful on
the German stage, on account of the interest of the drama
itself, as well as of its many allusions to the political state of
Germany. The princess commended the piece, saying she
understood it was by Frederic Halm (Count Münch de
Bellinghausen), who was one of the best dramatists of the
modern romantic school. His former plays, particularly the
'son of the wilderness,' had enjoyed a large share of the
favour of the German public. The princess afterwards made
some enquiries of me respecting English literature, with
which she was pretty well acquainted, though she had not
kept her reading up to the publications of the day. She
praised Johanna Baillie, as well as Walter Scott, and found in
Bulwer's works an intimate knowledge of the human mind.
It is remarkable how much Tauchnitz's collection of British
authors has done to promote the reading of English books in
Germany. No German, however wealthy, would think of
giving a guinea and a half for a three-volume novel, but he
is delighted to get two volumes in duodecimo of Bulwer or
Disraeli, at the moderate outlay of a dollar, or three shillings
sterling. The Princess Amelia's recovery was celebrated by
a festive performance, in which her own play of the 'country-
man' (*der Landmann*) was given with a suitable prologue, and
she was to have attended in person, if her physician had not
forbidden such an exertion.

The ducal castle at Altenburgh is one of the finest old
buildings in Germany, and reminds one of Windsor by its
elevated position and its spacious dimensions. In November
1856, we attended a court-ball there for the first time since
the accession of the reigning Duke, and were cordially
welcomed. The Duchess, a princess of Anhalt, was very
pleasing, and as simple in her manners as if she had been a
mere country-gentleman's daughter. There were present the
Duchess-mother (a princess of Mecklenburgh-Schwerin), the

ex-Duke Joseph, and his daughter the Grand-duchess Alexandra, wife of the Russian Grand-duke Constantine, who
shone as the star of the evening in her brilliant toilette, and
her own fascinating beauty.   On being presented to the
Grand-duchess, she referred to the Emperor's coronation at
Moscow in the previous month of July, where she had been
with the rest of the imperial family, and asked me if it had
been much talked about in England? I answered that it
certainly had, and that the fullest details of the ceremony had
been given to the English public through the newspapers.
She then remarked that the special embassy sent over by her
Britannic majesty was a very distinguished one, and she had
heard that not only Lord Granville, but all the members of
his embassy, were persons of importance, and belonged to the
first English families.

Our Prince Alfred, now Duke of Edinburgh, was in
Germany in April 1857, and visited Leipsic, attended by
General Sir Frederic Stovin, and Mr. (now Sir John) Cowell.
I received them on arrival, and the next day accompanied
them to the picture-gallery, and other remarkable objects in
the town.   The great Easter-fair was going on, and the prince
went through every part of it, asking all sorts of questions
about the articles exhibited, where they came from, and for
what countries they were destined? He made a number of
purchases of things which pleased his fancy, usually asking
Sir Frederic Stovin's opinion whether the prices asked were
reasonable? The prince seemed to me very intelligent for
a boy of thirteen, and I never saw any one more desirous of
information upon all topics which were started.   We talked
of the traffic of the fairs, of the university and the manners
of the students, and of the great battle of 1813, the prince
saying he intended to read all about it.   The party proceeded
from Leipsic to Gotha on a visit to the Duke.   It was even
then no secret, that, in pursuance of a family arrangement,
the Prince Alfred had been recognized as his uncle's heir, and
that he would one day be the reigning Duke of Saxe-Coburgh-
Gotha.   His dominions will not be large, but he will have
some 170,000 loyal subjects, and two of the pleasantest little
capitals in Germany.   It is true that since the formation of
the new German confederation, Saxe-Coburgh-Gotha has
ceased to have any voice in the foreign or commercial affairs
of Germany, and that its military contingent merely forms a
portion of the national army under the supreme command of
the Emperor William.   Nevertheless, the position of a petty
German prince is upon the whole an enviable one, and com-

mands at least all the dignity and influence which belong to an English nobleman of the highest rank, who has large estates, and resides upon them.

The political agitation in the duchies of Schleswig and Holstein, and the difficulty of effecting any satisfactory arrangement between them and the Danish crown, had for some years past been a source of anxiety to the British as well as to other European governments. The civil war had terminated, and the authority of the King-duke had been re-established in the duchies in February 1852. The treaty concluded in London on the 8th of May, 1852, had excluded the house of Augustenburgh from the succession to the throne, and given it to the prince Christian of the Glücksburgh line; and the great European powers had solemnly affirmed the integrity of the Danish monarchy. The states of the duchies, however, had never consented to that arrangement, and the hostile attitude of the Danish and German subjects of the King-duke towards each other continued such, that at the beginning of 1857 there was every prospect of a renewal of hostilities, and of the contest eventually leading to an European war. In the April of that year I was entrusted by Her Majesty's government with a confidential mission to the duchies for the purpose of enquiring on the spot into their political condition, and the grievances of which they complained. I was to suggest any practical remedies for those grievances, and to consider in what way a better amalgamation with the kingdom of Denmark than that which then existed could be effected. I accordingly proceeded to Holstein and Schleswig, and remained there long enough to ascertain the state of the country, and the opinions of intelligent and influential men. On my return I made a full, and as I conceive an impartial, report on the subject to the Earl of Clarendon as Secretary of State for foreign affairs.

The struggle going on between the Danish and German parts of the Danish monarchy was essentially one of nationalities, and was only to be set at rest by such an arrangement as should secure to each of the conflicting races the means of social development within its own sphere, free from oppression or molestation by the other race, and at the same time should preserve the Danish monarchy from dismemberment according to the declared intention of the great European powers. The main cause of the civil war was the non-recognition by the Danish government of the historical rights of the duchies, viz. their inseparability, their independence, and the succession to the crown of the male *agnati* of the house of Holstein. The difficulties of the situation in 1857 had been chiefly produced by a *coup d'état* of the Danish government, which had violently established for the entire monarchy on the 2nd of October, 1855, a so-called corporate-constitution (*Gesammt-Verfassung*), the validity of which the duchies of Schleswig and Holstein refused to admit. In the case of Holstein, being a German state, the objections of the inhabitants were supported by Austria and Prussia, and were likewise adopted by the Germanic confederation.

The population of the Danish monarchy (exclusive of its distant islands and colonial possessions) was in round numbers two millions and a half, of which one million and a half belonged to the kingdom, 400,000 to the duchy of Schleswig, and 600,000 to the duchies of Holstein and Lauenburgh. The German duchies, therefore, might be taken to contain two-fifths of the entire population.

Previous to the year 1815, when the territory of Denmark was enlarged by the appendage of Norway, few complaints were heard from the King's German subjects; but when the kingdom was shorn of that appendage, the Danes began to conceive the notion of bringing the concerns of the duchies under their exclusive management. The King was then absolute, and it was not till the 28th of May, 1831, that he issued a law for the erection of provincial states, which were a concession partly to the demand for constitutional reform then prevailing throughout Europe, and partly to the requirements of the Germanic federal constitution as regarded Holstein and Lauenburgh. These provincial states were composed of deputies from the respective classes of the larger and smaller land-owners, the townships, and the clergy, with a property-qualification both for electors, and elected, and were to assemble every two years. They represented the people *curially*, or by classes, so that the states of one province had the same weight as those of another, whether the number of members was greater or less respectively. Their functions, however, were consultative only, and it rested entirely with the King whether he would adopt or reject their advice. This constitution by provincial states, in fact, resembled those which were at first established by most of the German sovereigns in consequence of the provisions of the federal act of 1815.

Such was the constitution of the country down to the time of the issuing of the famous open letter of King Christian VIII dated the 8th of July, 1846, in which the intention was for the first time announced to amalgamate the several parts of the monarchy into one compact Danish state. The states of the duchies protested, and Holstein complained to the Germanic diet, which contented itself with passing a resolution recognizing the rights claimed. Then began the popular demonstrations in the duchies in favour of their nationality, and opposite demonstrations in Denmark in the Danish interest, which lasted until the commencement of the civil war in March 1848.

Christian VII died without effecting any more intimate union between the kingdom and the duchies than that above referred to, which was in fact a mere personal union. Immediately after the accession of King Frederic VII in January 1848, an attempt was made to introduce a new unitary constitution, which was to be submitted to an assembly of notables, but the project failed before the expiration of two months, and the duchies continued separate states. When the civil war had ended, and the time was approaching for the re-investiture of the King-duke with his sovereignty in the duchies, their future constitution naturally became the subject of discussion between Denmark and the German powers. The Danish government in a despatch of the 6th of December, 1851 (addressed to the Danish envoys at Vienna and Berlin for communication to those courts), promised to effect the union of the different parts of the country into one corporate monarchy by legal and constitutional means only, viz. through the consultative provincial states of the duchies of Schleswig and Holstein, as well as the Danish representative diet (established in 1849), and the land-owners of Lauenburgh. This promise was accepted by Austria and Prussia as an engagement satisfactory to them for the fulfilment of an indispensable duty on the part of Denmark.

Accordingly King Frederic, on the 28th of January, 1852, issued a proclamation for uniting the different parts of the monarchy under a common constitution. The existing separate Danish representative system was to be preserved, while the duchies of Schleswig and Holstein were to receive special constitutions respectively, and their independence, as well as that of the duchy of Lauenburgh, was guaranteed. The new common constitution was to be submitted to the provincial states of the duchies for their consideration, and these were to receive such a further development as would give them not only a consultative voice in public affairs, *but the power to resolve.* The King-duke engaged to govern Holstein according to the laws rightfully in force, which should not be altered otherwise than in a constitutional way ; and to the duchy of Schleswig he promised that the new constitution for that duchy should contain all the requisite provisions for securing to the Danish and German nationalities respectively perfectly equal rights and powerful protection. Special ministers were to be appointed for the kingdom, and for each of the duchies, and the domain-lands were to continue to belong to that part of the monarchy in which they respectively lay. The Germanic diet on the 29th of July following recorded its approval of the last-mentioned proclamation, and its hope that the King-duke would not cease to be animated by the same spirit of justice and conciliation in maintaining and developing the institutions legally existing in his German dominions.

The obligations entered into by Frederic VII towards his own subjects and the German powers were thus sufficiently clear. If they had been loyally and faithfully carried out, the people of the duchies would have been satisfied, and would have been content to remain, at least during the King's life-time, under the rule of their Danish sovereign. But there is every reason to believe that these engagements on the part of Denmark were illusory only, and that they were a mere expedient of the Danish ministers to gain time, in order to procure the assistance of the non-german great powers in the work of *danizing* the duchies which it was all along their fixed intention to persevere with. The line of conduct actually pursued by the Danish government will be explained in the sequel.

The Danish ministers having prepared drafts of special constitutions for Schleswig and Holstein, communicated them in 1853 to the provincial states of both duchies, with the injunction that they were not to consider the subject of the general relations between the different parts of the monarchy, but only those paragraphs which related to the future composition of the provincial states, and their competence to regulate the special affairs of each duchy. Six paragraphs of the respective special constitutions, disposing of the general questions which most interested the provincial states, were therefore expressly withdrawn from their consideration. The states of the duchies refused their assent to the projects, and the King-duke was advised to issue (*octroyer*) special constitutions of his own authority, which he did accordingly for Schleswig on the 15th of February, and for Holstein on the 11th of June, 1854. A corporate constitution was likewise issued by the King-duke on the 26th of July, 1854, without having been submitted to the provincial states of either duchy. It provided an imperial council to be partly named by the King-duke and partly elected, by which all the *common, internal,* affairs of the monarchy were to be managed, leaving everything else to the decision of the King-duke and his privy-council. This corporate constitution however never took effect, chiefly owing to the opposition it excited in the Danish part of the monarchy.

The King-duke now took as his prime-minister M. de Schele, who, although a German by birth, was a mere tool of the ultra-Danish party, and under his advice a new corporate constitution was issued on the 2nd of October, 1855, after previous communication with the separate Danish diet, but without having been submitted to the provincial states either of Schleswig or Holstein. It established an imperial council, the mode of election to which was regulated by a separate law. Two separate ordinances determined what were to be the special affairs of the duchies as distinct from those of the monarchy, and a third ordinance regulated the position of the duchy of Lauenburgh. The imperial council was so composed as to give the Danes a large and constant majority in the common legislature. Of the eighty members no less than forty-seven were taken from the kingdom of Denmark, and as at least three Danes would be chosen in the northern parts of Schleswig, the government was thus sure of a majority of fifty against the thirty who were to be taken from the German portion of the monarchy. The electoral law, by providing for the representation of the minority, likewise favoured the Danish element, so far as it existed in the duchies; so that the result of the elections was a legislative body almost entirely attached to the Danish side. The Germans were highly exasperated, and preferred an indictment in the high court of appeal against M. de Schele for having illegally established the constitution of October 1855. The court got rid of the accusation by declaring itself incompetent to deal with the matter, and M. de Schele continued to hold office until the month of April 1857, when his administration was replaced by that of M. Hall.

It was assuredly a great and serious grievance that the King-duke, instead of fulfilling his promises made to the duchies and to the German powers on the 28th of January, 1852, had forced upon the duchies a corporate constitution to which the states had not assented, and which laid their interests at the feet of a perpetually governing Danish majority. The system of treating the duchies as Danish dependencies, instead of states united with Denmark in the person of the King-duke, had in fact caused them to suffer much practical injustice; from which, when I was in the country, they had been wholly unable to obtain redress.

The state taxation throughout the monarchy was very high and unequally divided. The duchies complained particularly of the application of the revenues of the domain lands, contending that they belonged exclusively to the duchy in which they were situated, and ought not to be drawn as a part of the original budget into the common treasury of the entire monarchy for the equal use of Danes and Germans. The domains they alleged offered a fund on which the states of the duchies might lay a per-centage, when extraordinary levies were demanded, and so avoid new taxes upon the inhabitants. The Danes even claimed the right of alienating the ducal domains, which were three times as productive as those of the kingdom; whilst at the same time they were attempting to appropriate to the kingdom alone the capital sum received from foreign powers for the redemption of the Sound-dues, which evidently belonged to the entire monarchy. There were also minor grievances arising out of the introduction of the Danish coinage into the duchies, the operation of the customs-tariff, and the inclusion of the duchies within the Danish instead of the German system of postage. Such annoyances touched the people of Holstein and Schleswig in the ordinary business of their lives; but what they felt much more bitterly was the hostile spirit in which the Danish government of the German parts of the monarchy was invariably carried on. The declared object was Danish ascendency; and, to effect that, the most unscrupulous means were resorted to by the Danish authorities for keeping down and humiliating the German nationality.

Both Holstein and Schleswig were filled with Danish officials. Judges were removed to make room for creatures of the Danish government. The army was composed chiefly of Danes, for few Germans entered it voluntarily, and the German troops were removed into Denmark. The duchies resolutely demanded the exclusion of Danish functionaries, and the employment of native Germans; but so far were their wishes from being complied with that, on the demise of the crown, Ferdinand VII did not even confirm the existing appointments, and hundreds of officials, professors, and clergymen were in this way silently dismissed. Concessions for printing and publishing were withdrawn, and the press of the duchies was generally discouraged and

deprived of free action.   No attempt was made to reconstruct
the monarchy upon a solid basis, although it would not have
been difficult to satisfy the leading men of the duchies, who
were essentially conservative, and did not desire a representative system like that of Denmark, but preferred a constitution by classes; so that the simple re-establishment of
the provincial states would have pleased them better than
the corporate constitution of 1855.

The practical grievances of the duchy of Schleswig were
much the same as those of Holstein, with the addition of that
most serious evil, the forcing of the Danish language upon
the German inhabitants.   Although Schleswig was not, like
Holstein, a German state, yet Austria and Prussia were well
entitled to demand the fulfilment of the promise made by
the King-duke in January 1852, 'that the constitution for
Schleswig should contain the requisite provisions for securing
to the Danish and German nationalities in the said duchy
perfectly equal rights and powerful protection.'   Now, it was
notorious that the Danish rule in Schleswig, since that duchy
was restored to the King-duke, had been partial and oppressive
beyond all measure.   Nearly all the former government *employés* who were natives had been dismissed and replaced by
Danes, and not even the Danish-speaking natives of the
northern parts of the duchy had been allowed to remain
in office.   Further, it was the systematic policy of the
government to force the Danish language upon the German
population of the duchy (forming about two-thirds of the
whole); and not merely in places where the races were mixed,
but in very many parishes where the population was exclusively German, the use of the Danish language in the
churches and schools was compelled by authority.   For
instance, in the district of Angeln alone (called the cradle
of the Anglo-Saxons who invaded Britain) it was within my
knowledge that there were twenty-four parishes with 40,000
German inhabitants upon whom Danish clergymen were
forced, and who were obliged to submit to the exclusive use
of the Danish tongue in their churches and schools.   In such
circumstances it will be easily understood how unreasonable
was the expectation entertained by Denmark that either the
Holsteiners, or the Schleswigers, should accept the corporate
constitution of October 1855, *octroyé* as it was against the
wishes of the provincial states, and in the face of the obligations which bound the King-duke to the Germanic confederation.   The inhabitants of the duchies of all classes, from
the noble land-proprietor down to the peasant and artisan,

felt that the time had arrived for broadly asserting their national rights, and they were much more disposed to prepare for a renewal of the civil war than to entangle themselves in fresh negotiations, still less to enter into any sort of compromise with the Danish cabinet.

These being the embarrassments of the political situation in 1857, I had to consider the somewhat complicated question of the remedies best calculated to put an end to them, and to adjust the conflict of races without endangering the integrity of the Danish monarchy. The difficulty lay chiefly in the excessive self-confidence and boldness of the ultra-Danish party, for although the Danes as a people were inferior (as they well knew) to the Germans both in capacity and education, yet the former had shewn so much energy in their proceedings that they were not likely to part with the power they had *de facto* acquired until some strong external influence should have impressed them with the necessity of adopting a more conciliatory line of policy. Even if the Danish government had conceded to the German powers the convocation of the provincial states of Holstein, that would have been a very small step towards an adjustment, for the states were determined not to assent to the corporate constitution, or to any other based upon analogous principles. The time, therefore, was not inopportune for a mediating power to make a proposition to the contending parties of a more permanent and comprehensive nature; and after having consulted confidentially with some of the leading political men in the duchies, and reflected maturely upon the subject, I submitted to Her Majesty's government the following alternative plans, any one of which, if timely adopted, was calculated to accomplish the object in view.

Plans for the reorganization of the Danish monarchy,

A.—First Alternative.

To allow the duchies of Schleswig and Holstein to return to their ancient and legal *status quo* before the year 1848, viz. to be constitutionally united with each other. They might still retain, in common with the Danish part of the monarchy,

1. The King-duke.
2. Foreign affairs and diplomacy.
3. The fleet.
4. A common army in Danish and German divisions, both under the King-duke as commander-in-chief.

5. The coinage.

6. The customs and postage revenues, but with separate administrations.

Whilst holding so much in common with Denmark, the united duchies would then require their independence to be guaranteed to them by means of the following institutions :—

a. A constitution with class-representation, giving to the states the right not only of consulting, but of resolving, in all matters of legislation.

b. An independent legislature and administration.

c. A separate financial system, subject to the obligation to pay a fixed proportion to the common costs of the civil list, the royal appanages, the diplomacy, the fleet, &c. The public debts and assets of the monarchy to be divided, and the redemption money to be received for the Sound-tolls to be applied towards the liquidation of the public debt. The duchies to have the management and enjoy the revenues of their own domains.

d. Natives of the duchies only to be eligible to offices therein to the exclusion of Danes.

e. A separate German divisional army for the duchies, subject as above stated.

f. Maintenance of the university of Kiel.

g. The seat of the local administration, in whatever form, to be at a place within the duchies. A special minister for the duchies to be fixed at the residence of the King-duke.

This plan of a confederation between the kingdom and the united duchies embraced all (except the particular line of succession to the crown) which the German inhabitants of the duchies at the time desired. It would have required a modification of that part of the understanding between Denmark and the German powers at the close of the war which provided for the constitution of Schleswig as a separate state, though it did not involve the necessity of bringing Schleswig into the Germanic confederation. And upon the whole the plan was neither unreasonable nor unjust towards either of the nationalities whom it was intended to affect.

B.—SECOND ALTERNATIVE.

To divide the duchy of Schleswig according to its nationalities, either by drawing an arbitrary line from a point on the Flensburg-fiord to the river Widau, near Tondern, or by allowing the parishes within a limited range of country to declare, through the votes of their adult male population, whether they would remain Danish or German. The latter mode of division might have been difficult to execute while the Danish *employés* remained in the country, but at all events the line might have been drawn by Danish and German commissioners under the arbitration of a third power.

After such a division the Danish part of Schleswig might be incorporated with the kingdom, and the German part united to Holstein, either by a complete political union (as suggested in the first alternative), or by a union of legislation and administration, but without including it in the Germanic confederation.

The duchy of Holstein and the German part of the duchy of Schleswig would then stand towards the kingdom of Denmark in the same relation as that proposed in the first alternative, viz., they would hold in common as belonging to the entire monarchy the objects specified under A and numbered 1 to 6 inclusive, and would require the same constitutional guarantees for the objects also specified under A and lettered *a* to *g* inclusive.

C.—THIRD ALTERNATIVE.

To establish a confederation of the four states forming the Danish monarchy, viz., Denmark proper, Schleswig, Holstein, and Lauenburgh, each state to be independent within itself, and to retain its actual limits. They would hold in common as belonging to the entire monarchy the same objects, and would require the same constitutional guarantees, as in the second alternative.

Upon the basis of any one of the above three plans, the position of the German duchies towards the other part of the monarchy might have been definitively fixed. The King-duke would then have had to satisfy the following demands of the duchies regarding their respective constitutions and internal affairs :—

1st. A constitution with representation by classes (*Landständische Verfassung*), giving the states the power of resolving (not merely considering) upon all matters of legislation, and establishing, so far as practicable, an uniformity of political rights in all parts of the monarchy.

2nd. The exclusion of Danes from public employments in the duchies, and the appointment of natives only to government offices.

3rd. The revision of all ordinances issued for the duchies since the year 1848 without the consent of the provisional states.

4th. A reciprocity of naturalization in all the three German duchies.

5th. The confirmation and better endowment of the university of Kiel, with the re-establishment of the *biennium*, or two years' course of study for the youth of the duchies.

6th. A general amnesty.

The fulfilment of these latter demands might indeed be expected to follow the recognition of the federal independence of the duchies by the King-duke, but it would have been still more satisfactory to the inhabitants to have them guaranteed if possible by the mediating power or powers which might take an interest in the establishment of a permanent peace.

The principle upon which the three plans suggested as above were made alike to rest was that of a confederation between Denmark and the duchies, as the only form of government suitable to a monarchy composed of two conflicting nationalities, of which neither was strong enough in itself to hold the other in permanent subjection. The argument in favour of a confederation was indeed much stronger here than in the case of Sweden and Norway, where both countries were peopled by the Scandinavian race, yet in that case a federative government had been considered preferable to a corporate monarchy,—the object for which the Danes had for many years been striving in vain. I therefore took the liberty of recommending to Her Majesty's government, that in attempting to reorganize the Danish monarchy the federal principle should at all events be insisted upon ; and I pointed out that if the first alternative should be rendered impossible by the refusal of Denmark to go back to the *status quo ante bellum*, the division of Schleswig, as explained in the second alternative, might then be proposed ; and if that likewise should be rejected, Denmark could have no valid ground of objection to the third alternative of a confederation, consisting of the kingdom and the three duchies as separate and independent states.

After the completion of my report I repaired to London in accordance with Lord Clarendon's instructions for the purpose of conferring personally with his lordship on the matters which had fallen within the range of my enquiries. Lord Clarendon had studied my observations, and had made himself master of the subject, as indeed he always did when the question was of sufficient importance to interest his mind. He had likewise weighed the reports of Mr. (now Sir Andrew) Buchanan, who, like other British ministers at Copenhagen, leaned towards the views of the Danish government, and was by no means favourably disposed towards the Schleswig-Holstein cause. Lord Clarendon asked me a number of questions respecting the political feelings of the Holstein nobility, and of other classes of society in the duchies, and as to the movers of the agitation which had been so long going on in the country against the Danish rule. Of the intentions of Her Majesty's government he said not one word; but dismissed me with commendations of my report, adding, ' I am glad to tell you that the Prince-consort has read it, and is much pleased with it.' A copy of the report was, as I afterwards heard, transmitted to the Danish government, and recommended to its attention as a careful and impartial document. So far as I know, Lord Clarendon never took any further action respecting it, and my suggestions for the reorganization of the Danish monarchy remained a dead letter in the archives of the foreign office.

In the time which elapsed between my visit to the duchies and their final annexion to the Prussian monarchy after the war of 1866, the Schleswig-Holstein question passed through several phases, but nothing occurred to shake the opinion I had formed that, as things stood in 1857, the right way was to re-establish the Danish monarchy upon federal principles. The states of Holstein were assembled by the Danish government in January 1859, for the purpose of deliberating on a new constitution for the entire monarchy, to supersede that of October 1855, which had been abolished so far as it affected Holstein and Lauenburgh. But the states refused to enter into the government proposals, or to accept any constitution not framed upon the basis of a confederation, and which did not give them the power of resolving. They likewise protested against the law of the 31st of July, 1853, founded upon the treaty of London of the previous year, whereby the succession to the throne had been altered without the previous acquiescence of the legal representatives of the duchy. On the 15th of November, 1863, King Frederic VII died. The Duke Frederick of Augustenburgh claimed the ducal crown, and soon afterwards made his appearance at Kiel. Towards the end of the year a federal execution, composed of Saxon and Hanoverian troops, was sent into Holstein; and in the January following Austria and Prussia began a war against Denmark in good earnest. The Austrian forces drove the Danes back from the line of the Dannewerk, and a few weeks later the Prussians stormed the Düppel entrenchments and completed the victory. A conference in London followed, at which a federal union between Denmark and the duchies was proposed by the German powers, and at once rejected by the infatuated Danes. There was therefore no alternative but the cession of the duchies to Austria and Prussia, which was accordingly stipulated by the peace of Vienna. The joint dominion led to some difficulties, and to differences between the two powers concerned. These were terminated by the withdrawal of the Austrian forces in the spring of 1866, and by the war of that summer, one of whose results was that the duchies of Schleswig, Holstein, and Lauenburgh became integral parts of the Prussian dominions.

In the session of 1858 Mr. Wise, M.P., moved for the production of my report on the duchies, and was met with a refusal by Her Majesty's government. Sir Harry Verney, one of the few public men who understood the subject, and sympathized with the grievances of the Schleswig-Holsteiners, made a similar motion in two successive years, and eventually obtained the publication of a portion of the report, omitting, however, all that related to the future reorganization of the Danish monarchy upon federal principles. The omission was unfortunate, because public opinion in England was highly prejudiced against the German demands, and it was desirable to shew that the federal diet asked nothing unreasonable, and that the reconstitution of the Danish states as a federal union was neither an unjust nor impracticable measure. The foreign office might have withheld my report altogether as a confidential document; and I should have preferred its entire suppression to its being presented to parliament in a garbled state. The practice of dressing official despatches and reports, so as to answer the purpose of the department presenting them, has always appeared to me to be an improper one. It is unfair towards the writer, and is calculated to shake the confidence which the legislature ought always to have in the integrity and good faith of an executive department.

The baths of Kösen are pleasantly situated amongst the Thuringian hills, and the saline springs attract many families from Berlin, Dresden, and other German towns. Among the company whom we met there this summer was a Russian landowner, Prince Loof, who cultivated beet-root very largely on his estates near Moscow, and told us much of the flourishing state of the native sugar manufactories; also M. Grimm, Russian councillor of state, with his family. M. Grimm was a German by birth, and had resided long at St. Petersburgh, as the tutor successively of the Grand-duke Constantine and of his son. He has lately given to the world an interesting memoir of the Empress Alexandra, which sets the character and policy of her husband, the Emperor Nicholas, in a more favourable light than it has generally been regarded by Englishmen. In talking with M. Grimm about the Emperor, he always spoke of him as a hero, and as a mirror of honour and truth. The overtures made by Nicholas to England through Sir Hamilton Seymour in 1854 presented, he said, an excellent opportunity of arranging the settlement of the eastern question. They might have been submitted to a conference at which the views of England and other powers could have been stated and calmly weighed; and at all events Europe might have been spared the useless misery of the Crimean war. The conduct of the British government in immediately giving publicity to the Emperor Nicholas's confidential proposals was, in M. Grimm's opinion, quite indefensible. I have frequently heard the same opinion expressed in Germany; and indeed it seems that our government shewed anything but intelligence in its manner of treating the affair from beginning to end. The test of diplomatic skill is to turn an unforeseen incident to the advantage of a permanent peace. A blundering minister will never be at a loss for the means of plunging his country into a war.

A great national festival was celebrated at Weimar on the 3rd of September, 1857, being the centenary jubilee of the birth of Charles Augustus, the brave and patriotic Duke, who loved his country not less than he honoured science and art,—who was the friend of Goethe, the patron of Schiller, Herder, Wieland, Knebel, and Voigt,—who had made his little capital deserve the name given to it of 'the city of the muses;' and, what was better, had governed his little state upon the principles of strict justice and unvarying humanity. Charles Augustus had a firm will, and knew how to exercise it. He was a dynamic man of the right sort. Carefully educated by a highly intellectual mother, he made the campaigns against France in the Prussian army, and after the peace in 1815 he was the first German sovereign to give his subjects a constitution by calling together the states of his duchy. The fifty years' jubilee of his reign was kept on the 3rd of September, 1825, with the heartfelt rejoicings of his people, and his death in 1828 was felt not only by them as a calamity, but deeply affected Goethe and such of his early friends as still survived him. His remains lie in the ducal vault at Weimar, between those of Schiller and Goethe, and on the occasion of this centenary were respectfully visited by thousands. Charles

Augustus was not only a righteous sovereign, but a man of genius who understood the art of awakening the minds of others to the good and the beautiful, and encouraging them to persevere in noble pursuits. When Alexander von Humboldt called him ' the great, humane prince,' it was no flattery, but conveyed a just notion of his fine character.

On the day succeeding Charles Augustus's centenary, the new statues of Goethe and Schiller, erected in an open place in Weimar, were unveiled in the presence of the court and a large assemblage of people. The figure of Schiller is made to stand a little forward, and Goethe's hand is placed at Schiller's back in the manner of encouragement. The houses of the two poets were opened to the public, and thronged with visitors. Mdlle. de Poegewitsch did the honours in Goethe's apartments. His bedroom and study were as he left them, very small and ill-furnished. I was struck with the large collection of majolica ware. Some of the pieces were very fine and costly specimens. Mdlle. de Poegewitsch (who was in full dress in honour of the day) conducted herself admirably, and paid as much attention to the lower classes of people as she did to the more distinguished guests. I was delighted to hear some years afterwards that this excellent lady had been appointed by the King of Prussia to be the abbess of a secularized convent in Schleswig, and that she was living there in an honourable and peaceful retirement. She was for a long time the only representative of the Goethe family to be found at Weimar.

On my way back from Kösen to Leipsic, I stopped a day at Halle in order to witness the manœuvres of a Prussian army corps which was assembled in the fields of Teutchenthal near that city. There were about 25,000 infantry and 5000 cavalry. The King, the Prussian princes, and several reigning dukes were present, as usual, at the September manœuvres. The soil was black, containing an inferior sort of coal, and the clouds of dark dust which arose from time to time during the review were almost impenetrable. We were so dirty on returning from the field that it was with difficulty we could make ourselves presentable enough to dine at the officers' table. The King looked ill, and rode sunk down on his horse as if much fatigued. This was the last appearance of Frederic William IV at any great military manœuvre. A few weeks afterwards he became seriously ill, and his loss of memory, arising from softening of the brain, was such as to make it necessary to establish a regency in the person of the heir-presumptive,—the Prince of Prussia, afterwards King. Frederic

William lingered for about three years in a state of hopeless imbecility, varied by glimpses of consciousness, until death put an end to his sufferings, after a reign which disappointed the expectations of his admirers, and shewed that neither great talents and accomplishments, nor an ardent love of the good and beautiful, furnish an adequate substitute for decision of character, and for that steadiness of conduct, which in a ruler is so essential to the efficiency of his ministers, and to the peace and well-being of all classes of his subjects.

Lord Clarendon, being out of office, made a tour in Germany in the autumn of 1858, and came to Leipsic with his daughter, Lady Constance Villiers, in the early part of October. I shewed them the fair, and what was worth notice in the town, and invited some Germans to meet them at dinner. Lord Clarendon, who understood German pretty well, seemed amused with the conversation, especially with the remarks of one of the party who was very Austrian, and admired the conservative policy of M. de Beust. His lordship made many enquiries respecting the state of public opinion in Germany, and the progress of the national league for the promotion of German unity which had its chief seat at Coburgh, with agencies in different parts of the country. I informed him that the league had acquired considerable influence, that its chief object was to introduce a new Germanic constitution upon the *basis* of that recommended by the Frankfort parliament in 1849, which would of course involve the suppression of the federal diet. Lord Clarendon observed that the suppression of the latter body would be no great misfortune; but that, after what had passed at the Dresden conferences, there seemed no prospect of Austria and Prussia coming to an understanding about a better form of federal government. I said that the nation did not desire a federal government at all, but an unitary state, with a national legislature, and a central executive under the King of Prussia, and that the failure of the constitutional movement of 1848 was to be regretted, inasmuch as it was clear that the formation of an united Germany could not be attended with danger to England, or any other foreign country. Lord Clarendon seemed to believe the idea of an unitary state would one day be realized, but did not see his way (unless a war should arise) to putting an end to the antagonism between Austria and Prussia which, so long as it lasted, formed in fact the German question. Speaking of the Crimean war, I explained that the movement party in Germany had a certain horror and fear of Russia, which was supposed to be hostile to all constitutional development, and had in fact worked against German interests not only in this respect, but in the Danish and other questions. It could not, however, be said that there had been any general feeling in Germany in favour of an alliance with the western powers for the purposes of that war, for Germany had no confidence in such a France as existed under Louis Napoleon ; nor did people believe that either France or England were sufficiently in earnest to prosecute the war long enough to humiliate Russia to any serious extent. Lord Clarendon mentioned that Baron de Bunsen, when Prussian minister in London, had worked very hard to get Prussia into the war, and had at one time led him to believe that she would join the western powers, but the King could not be brought to say the decisive word. Bunsen, he said, was an interesting man, and everybody regretted his leaving London. Among the many visitors, whom he constantly received in his retreat at Heidelberg, had lately been the Duchess of Sutherland with a numerous suite. 'This,' said Lord Clarendon, 'would make a good counterpart to the picture of the Queen of Sheba visiting Solomon!'

Lord Clarendon perfectly understood the system of the *Zollverein* and recognised its commercial utility to Germany, as well as the powerful means which it afforded of effecting the unity of German interests in a material point of view. I reminded him that there were certain articles of English produce and manufacture, such as iron wares and the higher numbers of cotton-twist, which had been unfavourably affected by the existing tariff. But free-trade principles had made great progress in Germany during the last twenty years, and British imports into that country were upon the whole steadily increasing. As to the trade of the Leipsic fairs, I mentioned that large quantities of British manufactures which formerly came to the fairs in transit to the Danubian principalities, and other parts of the east, now found their way directly by sea to Constantinople and Galatz, so that the decrease of the British trade with the fairs did not necessarily prove any diminution in the quantities of British goods annually exported to foreign countries.

During a walk which Lord Clarendon permitted me to take with him before dinner, he referred to some official reports I had made on ecclesiastical affairs, and asked what I thought of the state of religion in the different parts of Germany,— whether the catholics and protestants lived in harmony with each other,—or whether confessional differences led to political animosity to any and what extent ? I endeavoured to explain

to him that the roman-catholics in the southern states, as well
as in several provinces of Prussia, viz. the Rhine, Westphalia,
Silesia, and Posen, were pious people, performing their religious duties regularly, and were strongly attached to their
bishops and clergy; that the catholic population (including
the German provinces of Austria) was still larger than that
of any other confession in Germany, and was likely to remain
so, conversions on either side being very rare. The two
protestant confessions recognised by law were the lutheran,
and the reformed or calvinistic. In the Prussian monarchy
these two confessions had been amalgamated into an 'united
church,' the work of King Frederic William III, who made
for it a new liturgy which, in the words of Henry Heine,
'flew from one church-steeple to another on the wings of the
red-eagle order, fourth class.' Taking the protestants as a
whole, it could not be said that their churches were so well
attended as those of the catholics, and in northern Germany
religious indifference was very prevalent. There were indeed
pietists; orthodox lutherans; and rationalists; but the last
of these were making the greatest progress, and it was
becoming more and more difficult for orthodox protestantism
to maintain its ground. I conceived (and here Lord Clarendon
signified his assent) that it was a great advantage to the
catholic faith to rest upon a basis of church authority which
no other religious sect could ever pretend to. With respect
to religious toleration, Germany, I said, was an example to
most European countries. No man quarrelled with his
neighbour about his religion, and polemics were never introduced into good society. This pacific disposition had partly
arisen from the circumstance that since the peace of Westphalia the three leading confessions, viz. the catholic,—
lutheran,—and reformed,—had been placed on a footing of
political equality in all the German states. But it was likewise the effect of the humane, and philosophical, tone of the
German mind. It was true that in Bavaria, and in the
Austrian dominions, the catholic clergy were very anti-
Prussian, and seemed to wish to maintain a complete separation between northern and southern Germany; indeed the
Prussian government was never able to muster many political
friends in the southern states. The Prussian catholics, however, were good and loyal subjects; and although not without
some grievances to complain of, had never separated their
cause from that of the monarchy. Prussia was not a protestant state any further than that the sovereign happened
to be of that confession. Two-fifths of the population were

catholics, and were in the enjoyment of exactly the same civil rights as belonged to the members of the ' united church,' or of the two evangelical confessions of which that institution had been arbitrarily composed.

One of the ecclesiastical questions on which I had made reports to the foreign office was that of mixed marriages, which had brought the Prussian government into some difficulties in its relation to the Pope, and to its own catholic subjects. A papal brief was publicly notified by the bishop of Treves on the 15th of March, 1853, to the effect that the dispensations for mixed marriages theretofore granted by the bishops were thenceforth (unless in case of urgent necessity) to emanate from the Pope alone, and that an oath was invariably to be required from the protestant party to the marriage to bring up all the children in the catholic religion. Upon these conditions the priest was allowed to assist at the marriage, but not in a catholic church, and without consecration or publication of banns. As these new papal injunctions threw serious impediments in the way of mixed marriages, the protestants generally considered the brief as an act of hostility, and many among the catholics regretted its having been issued. The government complained of the see of Rome having unnecessarily revived a question which had been tacitly allowed to subside, and of which the satisfactory adjustment seemed almost hopeless.

In order to understand the grounds of this complaint it is necessary to remember that, by the old law of Prussia, parties belonging to different confessions could stipulate between themselves before marriage in which religion the children should be brought up. The civil code of 1792 altered this by providing that the children of parents of different confessions should be educated to the age of fourteen by the sons following the father, and the daughters the mother, unless the parents should be agreed on the subject, in which case no one could interfere with that religious training which they might jointly have chosen. A new principle was introduced by a cabinet order issued in 1803 (extended to the Rhenish province in 1825), requiring all the children to be brought up in the religion of the father, unless the parties should be otherwise agreed according to the above-mentioned provision of the civil code of 1792, which remained in force. But the apparent justice of this was often illusory, for King Frederic William III, who had a strong protestant *bias*, visited with his disapprobation those protestant fathers who permitted their children to be educated as catholics, and that disapprobation had the effect of intimidating the numerous civil and military functionaries (almost all protestants) who sought to marry in the catholic provinces where they might be stationed. The clergy of the Rhenish province, in consequence of the cabinet order of 1825, dissuaded the women from marrying protestants; and the Prussian government found it necessary to apply to the Pope for a relaxation of the rule of the church not to consecrate mixed marriages without the engagement of the protestant party for the catholic education of the offspring. The result was a brief of Pius VIII, dated the 25th of March, 1830, which conceded something; for although it enjoined the clergy in the case of a mixed marriage to give a solemn admonition to the catholic party, it did not absolutely insist upon the engagement of the protestant party for the catholic education in the same way that the brief of 1853 appears to have done. The interpretation put by the Prussian cabinet upon the brief of Pius VIII led to the famous contest with the archbishop of Cologne, and to the arrest and imprisonment of that prelate in the year 1837, as well as to the suspension and imprisonment of the archbishop of Posen in 1838. This undetermined state of things went on until the brief of Pius IX in 1853, which simply required the enforcement of the decrees of the council of Trent, so that, as regarded the church, the mixed marriage question was in fact decided, and so it has remained up to this day. It rested of course with the parties to such marriages, whether they would comply or not with the ecclesiastical rules. They might be legally married by a protestant minister either in the Rhenish or any other Prussian province; but as such marriages could not receive the divine blessing through a priest, or be solemnized at all in a catholic church, they would be divested of that sanctity which belonged to a religious sacrament, and it was difficult to conceive how a good catholic could have anything to do with them.

Considering how large a proportion of the population of the Prussian monarchy has always been catholic, it was obviously of great importance to the government to keep on a good footing with the Holy See. The relations with Rome were partially settled by a convention made on the 16th of July, 1821, which determined the mode of electing bishops, and other ecclesiastical functionaries, but left many matters open. The Prussian constitution of 1850 confirmed to the catholic, as well as the protestant church, the enjoyment and management of its property and revenues, subject to the control of the minister for religion and education (*Cultusminister*). Some complaints have been made from time to time in the Prussian diet of undue favour shewn to the protestant united-church in respect of its revenues, and there have been other questions, such as those relating to the order of jesuits, and to the German college in Rome, in which the Prussian government has not quite satisfied its catholic subjects. Even however as matters stand, the catholic church is in an incomparably better position in Prussia than it has been at any time since the reformation in Great Britain or Ireland. The Prussian bishops and superior clergy are paid by the state and recognised by it; the parochial clergy are provided for by endowments in the same way as the protestant ministers, and the law of the land gives to each confession equal rights, over which it is the duty of a ministerial department to watch. The convention with Rome of 1821, though not exactly a *concordat*, has at least been a security that no such misunderstanding with the Holy See could arise in Prussia as that which occurred in England on the establishment of the catholic hierarchy, and led to the ridiculous ecclesiastical-titles act of 1851, lately repealed. I may add, that in those petty German states which were annexed to the Prussian monarchy after the war of 1866, such as Hanover, Hesse-Cassel, and Holstein, the catholic inhabitants have had no reason to be dissatisfied with the change of their masters, and appear to have every confidence that the interests of their church will be duly protected by the Prussian administration.

The contest between the government of Baden and the archbishop of Freiburg, which began in 1854, was likewise of great importance to the church of Rome, for it involved not only particular rights of the church, but the general question of the validity of the canon-law in the grand-duchy of Baden. There was no *concordat* in existence between Baden and the Holy See, but the grand-duchy was one of six states forming the ecclesiastical province of the Upper Rhine, with an archbishop and four bishops, in pursuance of two bulls of the Pope, dated respectively in 1821 and 1827. Although the Grand-duke of Baden accepted and published those bulls, yet he reserved his own supremacy in the affairs of the church, and no agreement was come to with respect to the limits of the ecclesiastical authority. This uncertainty brought on a conflict of jurisdiction between church and state, which finally induced the government to suspend the archbishop from his functions, to commence a legal prosecution against him, and to arrest him in his palace. The archbishop (Hermann de Vicari)—a venerable nonagenarian—firmly opposed the demands of the civil power, and did his best to resist them by excommunicating a number of public functionaries and other persons who were concerned in obstructing the ecclesiastical jurisdiction.

The population of Baden was about a million and a half, of whom two-thirds were catholics. The archbishop complained of the interference of the government in matters purely spiritual,—that it attacked the church's right to teach, and the administration of divine service, and had given over the control of the church in a great measure to temporal officers ; —that it had refused to admit the archbishop's right of presentation to benefices,—and had made the reception of the future clergy in the priests' seminary dependent upon a grand-ducal commissioner instead of the archbishop, who was alone competent to admit candidates to holy orders. How far these complaints were well-founded depended upon the question whether the Grand-duke possessed the right of suspending the canon law in favour of another kind of law established by authority of the civil power ?

The bishops of the upper-Rhenish province protested against the establishment by the state of a new system of ecclesiastical law, and declared their intention to act nevertheless as the canon law prescribed. The Austrian, Prussian, and Bavarian bishops had previously made similar demands upon their governments. The relations between Bavaria and Rome were regulated by a *concordat* dated the 5th of June, 1817, and those between Prussia and Rome by the convention of 1821, already mentioned. The concordat with Austria had not as yet been brought to a conclusion.

It did not appear that the archbishop of Freiburgh had sought to exercise any jurisdiction beyond the spiritual sphere of his church, and it was incontestable that the canon law, which gave to the catholic church the exclusive administration of its own spiritual affairs, had subsisted in Germany for a very early period,—that since the reformation the Westphalian peace of 1648 had guaranteed to the church its former constitution and government,—that a fresh guarantee for the same was given by the imperial recess of 1803, in pursuance of the peace of Luneville,—and, further, that the sixteenth article of the federal act of 1815 had secured to each confession an equality of political rights. Against these considerations was to be set the abstract right of the legislature of Baden to make what laws it pleased for the catholic, as well as the protestant, subjects of the grand-duchy; but no German state possessed the right of setting aside its federal obligations, or of legislating contrary to the principles which

M

were established for the entire Germanic body at the peace of
Westphalia.

The Baden government attempted with little success to
negotiate with the Pope; and the papal brief of the 9th of
January, 1854, continued in force, whereby the Pope commended the conduct of the archbishop, and exhorted him to
persevere in resisting the encroachments made upon the spiritual power, contrary to the canonical statutes and the divine
constitution of the church. An appeal to the Germanic diet
would have been useless, inasmuch as that body had already
decided (in Kettenburgh's case) that it was incompetent to
entertain complaints about religion; thereby leaving the
government of each state the discretion of tolerating particular
churches or not, subject to the rule laid down by the federal act
that differences between the several confessions should make
none in their enjoyment respectively of political rights.

The good old archbishop died before the termination of the
dispute, and his see was kept a long time vacant, which was
rather an advantage to the Baden government. The validity
of the canon law in those German states which have no *concordat* with Rome still remains a mooted point. The church
has of course no means of enforcing it without the consent and
co-operation of the temporal sovereign.

As regarded the Austrian empire, the concessions which it
made to Rome in 1855, during the administration of the
Count de Buol-Schauenstein, were such as entirely recognised
the canon law as the law of the empire in ecclesiastical affairs,
and the independence of the church property from the control
of the state. A *concordat* was signed on the 18th of August,
being the birthday of the young Emperor Francis Joseph; and
the ratifications were exchanged at Vienna on the 25th of
September following,—the day celebrated by the protestants
as the three-hundredth anniversary of the Augsburgh religious
peace of the year 1555. By the provisions of that *concordat*
the church obtained from the Emperor the solemn confirmation
to it of the following rights, which, though not all of them
newly acquired, became thereby indefeasible, viz.

1st. The entire direction of the religious education of the
catholic population of Austria.

2nd. The right of determining all spiritual matters in the
ecclesiastical courts according to the canon law.

3rd. The limitation of the Emperor's right not only to
present to benefices but to nominate bishops.

4th. The exclusive management of the church property,

which was made inalienable; the restitution of the estates of which the church had been deprived; and compensation for tithes abolished by law.

In admitting the great importance of the rights thus formally conceded to the church, we ought of course to bear in mind that the population of the Austrian dominions was pre-eminently catholic, both in numbers, and in attachment to the old faith. The entire population stood at about thirty-six millions, and the catholics numbered twenty-eight millions, or seven-ninths of the whole. The religious instruction of these was confided exclusively to the church of Rome; but the degree of toleration conceded to the protestants remained exactly the same as it was before the *concordat* took effect.. Although it depended upon the pleasure of the sovereign what should be the established religion in any German state, yet the dissentients were protected by the federal act of 1815, which declared that the difference of the established confessions should make none in the enjoyment of civil and political rights [1]. The Austrian protestants were not without a guarantee in this respect, for the young Emperor in his patent of the 31st of December, 1851 (abolishing the revolutionary constitution of the 4th of March, 1849), had proclaimed as follows:

' We expressly declare that we will maintain and protect every church and religious society recognised by law within these dominions (meaning the Lutherans and Calvinists) in the right of the common and public exercise of their religion,—in the independent management of their own affairs,—and in the possession and enjoyment of their establishments, foundations, and funds, destined to the purposes of worship,— subject always to the general laws of the state.'

It seemed, therefore, scarcely possible that the *concordat* could be used as an instrument for injuring, or putting down, the evangelical confessions in the Austrian empire. Even the ninth article, which gave to the catholic church the censorship of books, was not construed as prohibiting the protestants from using any books that might be necessary for their own religious worship and instruction as theretofore.

The conclusion of the *concordat* was not owing to any new or sudden idea of the Austrian prime-minister, Count de Buol-Schauenstein or of any other Austrian statesman. It was the subject of negotiation with Rome in the reign of the Emperor Francis, and when the insurrection of 1848 had been put down, the Prince de Schwarzenberg deemed it necessary

---

[1] Article XVI.

to break off altogether from the theories of those who desired to separate the church from the state, and to deprive the former of its control over the public education. Hence that minister came to an understanding with the catholic bishops, and in the year 1850 actually conceded to the church by imperial ordinances a great part of the rights confirmed to it by the *concordat* of 1855. The Count de Buol merely followed the policy of his predecessor; and those who had watched the march of events in Austria since the insurrection regarded the *concordat* as almost inevitable. The act was unpopular in Germany, and even among the Austrian catholics it had many opponents. It did not and could not affect protestant interests in any way whatever; indeed the arguments used against it from the protestant point of view were directed rather against the catholic religion itself, than against an arrangement which was really an act of peace, tending to promote the united working of church and state for the improvement and well-being of the population.

Austria was not a German power only: she was a consolidation by artificial means of a number of different nations, of which the sole common bond was the catholic religion. The government thought it could not afford to make an enemy of the church, and the *concordat* was the consideration for which the hierarchy was to become the active ally of the state, and to use its mighty influence to support and perpetuate that system of centralization upon which the existence of the reconstituted Austrian empire was believed to depend. The imperial cabinet did not consider itself strong enough to deal with the church at its own discretion, and did not think it wise to adopt the principle established in France and Belgium, where the catholic religion was separated from the state, but protected on account of the considerable portion of the population by whom it was professed.

On these grounds one could hardly have anticipated the disapprobation of the Austrian *concordat* which was expressed by so many persons in northern Germany. The arrangement lasted about twelve years, and in the opinion of some of the most thoughtful men in the empire fulfilled its objects of maintaining the religious influence of the church, and in imparting to the mass of the people a sound and christian education. But after the war of 1866 the new prime minister of the empire, the Baron de Beust, took a different view of the matter, and soon notified the termination of the *concordat* to the Holy See. There were not wanting voices in the Austrian legislature which deprecated the proceeding, and insisted that a subsisting convention between independent sovereigns could not legally or justifiably be terminated otherwise than by mutual consent. Baron de Beust, however, was courting popularity, and he reckoned upon the suppression of the *concordat* as a measure which would attract the applause of the so-called liberal party in Austria, and in most of the German states. The deed was done accordingly. The *concordat* ceased to exist; and the enforcement of the canon law within the Austrian dominions became henceforth dependent upon the will and pleasure of the imperial government.

The great difficulty which the civil government of any state, whether catholic or protestant, must always have in negotiating with the catholic church, is, that the latter claims to be in the possession of objective truth, and is therefore unable to consent to the regulation of such questions as those affecting marriage or education in any other manner than that prescribed by the divine law. Protestant legislators are not encumbered by a similar restraint, for as no protestant church acknowledges the existence of an infallible guide on earth, they may govern their subjects upon principles of expediency, and make such laws as they deem most conducive to the national welfare. M. de Beust was a Lutheran; as a good catholic he could hardly have disturbed the Austrian *concordat*, for the principles which it sanctioned were in conformity with those which the church maintained as an essential part of the Christian religion.

The *Zollverein*-conference sat at Harzburgh in the Harz mountains during the summer of 1859, and that circumstance gave me the opportunity of enjoying for some time the fresh verdure of that beautiful country, which only wants water to make it deserve the name of a miniature Switzerland. The highest point is the Brocken, about 3500 feet above the sea-level, the view from which, when it can be seen, is very extensive, but it is generally obscured by clouds. The inn on the Brocken took fire whilst I was at Harzburgh, and blazed for some hours to the great excitement of the people of the surrounding villages. One of the most interesting towns in the Harz is Goslar, a free imperial city previous to 1803, containing the remains of a cathedral, and the fragment of an imperial palace; also a curious old house in the market-place called the *Kaiserswerth* in which the diet was formerly held. The castle of Quedlinburgh, the former residence of abbesses who were princesses of the empire, with its sculptured church adjoining, and the house in which the poet Klopstock was born, were also well worthy of inspection. Having visited the old town of Halberstadt, and seen its cathedral and other fine churches, I made an excursion to the ancient abbey of Huysberg, about five miles distant. The mountain range called the Huy, little known to travellers, is covered with one of the finest woods in Germany; oak, beech, and maple grow luxuriantly, and are in the best preservation. On the crown of the hill flourished for more than seven hundred years the venerable abbey of Huysberg, which was dissolved in 1804, and the buildings with the surrounding lands were subsequently bestowed by King Frederic William IV upon General de Knesebeck, who had done Prussia good service in the war of liberation. The abbey-church, built in the form of a cross, with three towers, remained intact, and was still used for catholic worship, forming the devotional centre of a number of neighbouring villages which have continued catholic in the midst of the protestant population of this part of the Prussian dominions. A high festival on the Huysberg is that of *Corpus Christi,* when flowers are abundant, and when the procession is made amidst all the magnificence of nature, attracting numerous worshippers from the surrounding country as it had been accustomed to do in the olden times. But the church and its services are all that now remain of the great Benedictine monastery, which is known to have contained a succession of learned and pious monks during many generations.

Whilst I was in the Harz the news arrived of the peace of Villafranca, and everybody was astonished at the sudden termination of the war which had so lately been begun in Italy between France and Austria. What will Louis Napoleon do next? Will he not be encouraged by his success in this short and brilliant campaign to make demands upon other powers? and will Prussia be any longer secure of maintaining her hold of the Rhenish provinces? Such questions were in every one's mouth. There could be no doubt that, if the Italian war had lasted a little longer, Prussia and the Germanic body would have taken part in it. Indeed they seemed bound to do so by their obligations towards Austria as a federal state. The Prussian army was already mobilized, and the side on which it would be ranged was sufficiently obvious. Had it not been for the unexpected Villafranca convention, a war between France and Germany would have been the inevitable result of the Italian campaign. Whether the German armies were at that moment so well prepared as to be equal to the emergency is not so certain. But 'time brings roses.' The lapse of ten years has proved the excellence of the Prussian military system, and has placed the destinies of France at the feet of the Prussian monarch through a series of the most brilliant victories that the history of modern Europe will have to record.

The hundredth anniversary of Schiller's birth was celebrated on the 10th of November, 1859, as a national jubilee in all parts of Germany. At Leipsic the celebration consisted in the performance of one of Schiller's plays in the theatre, with *tableaux* depicting incidents from the poet's life and works, and a suitable prologue. At night there was a festive procession by torch-light through the town, in which the various trade-guilds with their banners and insignia, and the students of the university, mostly in fancy costumes, took part; nor were music and song wanting to the picturesque scene. There never was an author who had a stronger hold on the admiration and affections of his countrymen than Frederic Schiller. He was eminently the poet of the ideal, and his fancy ranging over divine and human things struck the hearts of young and old, and animated them with an enthusiasm for what was good and beautiful in this great world of existence. I hardly remember a more interesting book, or more encouraging to youthful minds, than the life of the poet by Palleske [1]. We learn from it to know the man, as we have recognised the poet in his charming works. There is no fear of Schiller being forgotten by posterity, which, as Goethe has said, is bound to pay to a great man's memory the whole of the debt that is usually awarded to him only in part by his own contemporaries [2].

The sale of ancient manuscripts brought from the east had long been carried on as a trade in Germany, and although many valuable documents had in this way come to light, the business had been discredited through the forgeries of the Greek Simonides, who but for the vigilance of professor Lepsius would have imposed upon the royal library in Berlin a pretended *palimpsest* called the *Uranios*, and manufactured by himself, containing a historical narrative chiefly copied from Bunsen's ancient Egypt. A *palimpsest*, as is well known, is a manuscript whose original text has been washed or scraped away from the parchment on which it was written, and supplied by another writing of more modern date. The monks

---

[1] 'Schiller's Leben und Werke von Emil Palleske.' 2 Bände. Berlin, 1859.
[2] 'So feiert Ihn! Denn was dem Mann das Leben
   Nur halb ertheilt, soll ganz die Nachwelt geben.'
      Goethe, *Epilog zu Schiller's Glocke, am* 10 *Mai* 1815.

used a great many old manuscripts in this way during the middle ages. In March 1860, however, I had the satisfaction of seeing at Leipsic a manuscript of the holy scriptures, which had been brought from the monastery on mount Sinai in the previous year by professor Tischendorf, and whose authenticity had been admitted by the first biblical scholars. It was supposed to date from the fourth century, and was fairly written on parchment of a quarto form, in Greek characters and in four columns. It comprised three hundred and forty-six sheets of parchment, and in addition to twenty-two books of the Old Testament, contained all the books of the New Testament, besides the epistle of St. Barnabas and the first part of the ' shepherd ' of Hermas. The ink was still black and the parchment in very good condition. It had been purchased on behalf of the Russian government by professor Tischendorf, who was partly in the suite of the Russian Grand-duke Constantine during the tour in Syria in the course of which he had the good fortune to make the discovery [1]. The mount Sinai manuscript had some few variations from the received text. The following was pointed out to me. In the first epistle of St. Paul to Timothy, chap. iii. v. 16, instead of Θεὸς ἐφανερώθη ἐν σαρκὶ, it is here written ὀς. Other manuscripts have δ, and so runs the vulgate : ' et manifeste magnum est pietatis sacramentum, *quod* manifestum est in carne,' etc. The difference is curious, and if the christian religion depended upon biblical criticism the above discovery might easily be raised into more importance than it is really worth. The epistle of St. Barnabas however, which forms a part of the manuscript, deserves particular attention on account of the passage which it contains in the original Greek, ' as it is written, many are called but few are chosen.' These words have reference to St. Matthew's gospel, and prove beyond question that in the first quarter of the second century that gospel was not only known but accounted canonical by the church. Previous to this discovery of St. Barnabas's epistle in Greek, a Latin translation of it only was known, and it was doubtful whether the words ' as it is written ' belonged to the original, or had been added by the Latin translator.

Among the noble families of Saxony and the adjacent districts of Prussia, one of the most considerable was that of Hohenthal, whose ancestor, a fortunate merchant, had been wealthy enough to acquire and to bequeath large estates to several distinct lines of his successors. A branch of the family

[1] See his narrative ' Aus dem heiligen Lande, von Constantin Tischendorf.' Leipzig, 1862.

was settled at Dölkau, a few miles distant from Leipsic, and we were indebted to the hospitality of the Count and Countess de Hohenthal for many pleasant days spent in their society, and in that of their agreeable circle. The style of living was that of a rich English country gentleman ; the count had plenty of game, and gave shooting parties in the season, besides many dinners and balls in the course of the year. As a member of the upper house, and one of the King's chamberlains, the count was obliged to be frequently in Berlin ; and as both he and the countess had travelled in Italy and other foreign countries, their interest and sympathy were by no means limited to local, or even to German affairs. I have met at their house a great variety of company from the Grand-duke of Weimar down to the neighbouring land-owners, and I never was in any mansion where a better tone, or more hospitable spirit, uniformly presided over all the arrangements. I take the liberty of mentioning here the Hohenthals of Dölkau as an excellent specimen of a German family in the higher ranks. The last time I was with them was on the occasion of the marriage of one of their daughters to Count Arthur de Strackwitz, in May 1860. The wedding was solemnized in the *château*, in the presence of a circle of relatives and friends, according to the catholic and lutheran rituals successively, after which there was an early dinner, with congratulatory speeches, and much merriment ; and the bridal pair set out under a salute of cannon for their honeymoon excursion just in the same way as would have been done in England. A sister of the bride, the accomplished Countess Ida von Hohenthal, is now well known at the Prussian court as one of the Queen Augusta's ladies of honour.

My Leipsic life closed with the following month of June, when I received through Lord John Russell, then foreign secretary, my appointment as Her Majesty's chargé d'affaires and consul-general at Hamburgh. I had been looking for this promotion, and was of course glad of a better post. Still it was not without regret that I bade farewell to the worthy friends and acquaintances whom I had so long lived among at Leipsic ; and my feelings quite accorded with those expressed in the following lines :

> ' And it is thus, when from some place,
>   As from a long familiar face,
>   Though you may wish the chain to sever,
>   Still you are sad to part for ever [1].'

[1] ' Poems of Many Years,' by R. M. Milnes. London, 1844.

CHAPTER VIII.

Hamburgh in 1860. Syndic Merck. Charles Heine. Bremen. Lubeck.
Predecessors in office. Danish question. Baron Scheel-Plessen.
Stade-tolls. Count Platen. Lord Augustus Loftus. The Zollverein.
Cornelius. Count de Buol-Schauenstein. The Prince-consort. Lord
Russell. Sir Harry Verney. Prussian ministry. Polish insurrection.
Duke of Glücksburgh. Princess of Wales. Ernest Merck. Wiesbaden.
Lord Clarendon. George Bunsen. Countess Hahn-Hahn. Death of
Frederic VII. Christian IX. Lord Wodehouse. Duke Frederic
of Schleswig-Holstein.

On my arrival at Hamburgh I found that the lapse of
twenty years had produced great changes in the place, and in
its society. A large portion of the city had been rebuilt
since the fire of 1842, and its suburbs had been much extended as well as improved. Some of my old friends were no
longer above ground; but as Her Majesty's representative I
was generally welcomed with kindness and cordiality. The
office of minister for foreign affairs was held by the Syndic
Dr. Merck, who, without possessing the versatile talents of
his predecessor Sieveking, was an able man of business,
sincere in his expressions, and straightforward in all his relations. In the Senate were associated with him several
eminent lawyers, such as Dr. Haller and Dr. Frederic Sieveking, and a number of respectable and intelligent merchants.
The leading families, particularly the Schröders, Jenisches,
Godeffroys, Mercks, and Hayns, dispensed their hospitalities
on a handsome scale; and the increase of luxury not only in
the higher, but in the middle ranks of society, was strikingly
perceptible. The literary men were few in number; but the
archivist Dr. Lappenberg still prosecuted his historical studies,
and professor Ægidy successfully excited the public attention
to questions of German politics and international law.

Among the congratulatory letters which reached me on the
occasion of my promotion, I received the following from Lord
Clarendon with peculiar gratification.

'*London,* June 19th, 1860.

'My dear Sir,

'I congratulate you sincerely on your appointment. Lord
John Russell entirely agreed with me that you would be
the right man in the right place at Hamburgh, and I am sure

he was glad when the opportunity arose for giving effect to his convictions.

' I hope that the meeting at Baden which has made such a commotion may not have produced the ill effects that were anticipated from it, though I am rather slow to believe that it will secure the *Einheit* which some of my German friends in this country declare it has done. I wish I could think as they do, for it is the one thing needful at this moment.

' It will be a great satisfaction to me to hear occasionally from you upon German affairs and opinions.

' Believe me, my dear sir,

' Very faithfully yours,

' John Ward, Esq., C.B.'   ' CLARENDON.'

The first dinner-party which I attended was at the country-house at Ottensen of the wealthy Jewish banker, Charles Heine, who carried on business in Hamburgh under the well-known firm of Solomon Heine. Among the company were the French minister, M. Cintrat, and his wife, and M. de Schele, formerly Danish prime-minister, but then residing at Pinneberg, as upper-president in the duchy of Holstein. There was some talk about the late conference of German sovereigns at Baden-Baden, referred to by Lord Clarendon, and opinions were expressed that nothing would come of it; which were so far correct that it merely led to the meeting at Warsaw in the following October of the Emperors of Russia and Austria and the Prince-regent of Prussia, for the purpose of discussing the state of European affairs. Since the victories obtained by the French Emperor in the Italian war, a vague apprehension prevailed in Germany as well as in England, that ulterior designs against the peace of Europe were entertained by that personage ; and neither his letter to Count Persigny, disclaiming hostile designs against England, nor his pacific speech at Lyons had sufficed to dispel the general uneasiness. Madame Heine was a French lady, the niece of M. Fould, sometime French minister of finance, and resided the greater part of the year in Paris. Her marriage with Charles Heine not having been blessed with children, they had adopted a young girl who afterwards became the wife of the Duke d'Elchingen, grandson of the famous Marshal Ney. Charles Heine, having heard that Hanover was likely to receive an indemnity for the surrender of the Stade-tolls, took occasion to offer through me to pay the amount, whatever it might be, if requested to do so by the British government ; but Mr. Gladstone, the then chancellor of the exchequer, eventually preferred another mode of settling the business.

Solomon Heine, the father of Charles, was unbounded in his charities, and, as I heard, was very kind to his nephew Henry Heine the poet, who lived much at Hamburgh previous to 1830, when he went to reside in Paris, and soon afterwards married a French wife,—the good angel of his miserable existence. Henry Heine had not less of political sagacity than of poetical genius. He corresponded from Paris with the Augsburgh ' Allgemeine Zeitung,' and I have heard much praise bestowed upon his letters, which were collected and published at Hamburgh in 1833, under the title of ' Französische Zustände.' It has been said of him that he was a great poet lost for want of faith, for he believed in nothing, and in the absence of a high objective ideal he indulged in eccentricities and frivolities unworthy of his genius. Of satire he was indeed a master; and upon the whole his mind very much resembled that of Voltaire.

Charles Heine died in July, 1865, leaving property to the amount of about two million pounds sterling, which he bequeathed chiefly to his wife, leaving, however, legacies to the hospitals, schools, churches, and charitable institutions of Hamburgh, without reference to their religious denominations. He also forgave his debtors whatever they owed him, an act of generosity the more striking in a banker, who had been in the habit of advancing money to many needy persons.

Having been accredited to the two other Hanse-towns of Bremen and Lubeck as well as to Hamburgh, I proceeded to those places for the purpose of presenting my credentials to their respective Senates. At Bremen I was received by M. Duckwitz, one of the burgomasters, in his capacity of president of the committee for foreign affairs, and was entertained by the Senate at a handsome dinner, at which some famous old Rhenish wine was produced which had lain for many years in the town-cellar. I took occasion to compliment the Hanse-towns upon their steady adherence to free-trade principles, and to express a hope that they would never be led away from their true interests by the clamours of the protectionist party. M. Duckwitz had been minister of commerce for the German empire during the short reign of the Archduke John at Frankfort in 1848, and had rather favoured the notion of establishing a system of navigation-laws for Germany, but as regarded Bremen he was for keeping a free port under all circumstances. It was, in fact, by her liberal commercial system, added to her favourable situation on the river Weser, that Bremen had so long maintained her place as the second German seaport. Bremen peculiarly commands the American trade, and the emigration from Germany to transatlantic countries. Her citizens are a spirited body of men, and have shewn more energy than those of Hamburgh in promoting various measures of political and commercial improvement. Since the erection of the sub-port of Bremerhafen, with its docks and warehouses, at the mouth of the Weser, some forty years since, the Bremen merchants have, in fact, had nothing to fear from Hamburgh competition, as the largest ships can discharge at Bremerhafen with every facility. In a social point of view, Bremen certainly does not stand behind other cities, having a population of eighty-thousand inhabitants. There are fewer millionaires than at Hamburgh, but a great many wealthy citizens. The burgo-master, Dr. Meier, and his brother, M. Henry Meier, the eminent merchant, as well as the literary senator Dr. Gilder-meister, are men of note in Germany, whose talents would be honoured in any community. The fine arts are cultivated in Bremen, and the winter-concerts have long enjoyed a good reputation in the musical world.

The well-known traveller, J. G. Kohl, is a Bremen man, and I was glad to find him, after all his wanderings, established as state-librarian in his native city. Although not a lively writer, there is not one of his books which does not contain valuable information respecting the social and political state of the country described. His tours in Great Britain and Ireland, in Russia, and in the Austrian empire, are full of interesting matter; and his latest work on the country lying in the north of Hanover, between the rivers Weser and the Elbe, gives a curious description of the peasantry and labouring classes of the district, and of their manners and ways of life. This book proves that it is not so much the character of the country, as the mind of the traveller, which is the essential point in the narrative of a tour. One man can amuse us for hours with a 'voyage autour de ma chambre;' another goes from London to Rome and finds all barren. Whether Kohl is traversing the steppes of Russia, or rambling about within sight of the Bremen church-steeples, his observations are equally minute, and he furnishes us with a clear and comprehensive description of men and things. Had he been born an Englishman he would have made an excellent special commissioner for one of our leading journals; as it is, most of his travels have been translated, and English

readers have been enabled to derive from them a great deal
of instruction.

Kohl was a firm believer in the superiority of the Teutonic
race over all others, and in its being the peculiar mission of
Germany to civilize and educate the other nations of the
earth. The Germans were eminently a thinking people. In
what other country was there any speculative philosophy
worthy of the name? We spoke much of these matters, and
he noticed as a remarkable circumstance that the reigning
families of Great Britain as well as of Russia were purely
German. The sovereigns of Denmark and Portugal are
likewise at this time German princes. Without, however,
attaching any importance to the nationality of sovereigns,
there are few who will dispute that a great future lies open
to the intelligence and patience of the German race. Kohl
gave me his treatise on the dependence of the intercourse and
settlement of mankind upon the formation of the soil [1], which
sets in a strong light the influence of localities, and describes
the effects produced by mountains and plains respectively upon
the characters and occupations of the inhabitants. It is of
course interesting to trace the origin of great cities, and to
discover why a commercial emporium has arisen here, and
manufactures have thriven there; why one state has been great
at sea, and another powerful at land. The author explains all
these causes very ingeniously, and inculcates the doctrine of
necessity in so far that Englishmen, Swiss, or Hollanders,
could not possibly have turned out otherwise than what they
are. The theory of dependence upon soil is not novel, but
this treatise has both advanced and explained it with singular
felicity of illustration.

The ancient city of Lubeck has always been considered the
queen of the Hanseatic league, and has about it a certain quiet
dignity which commands the reverence of all who love historical associations. It is still the seat of the high court of
appeal for the three Hanse-towns, and in this way enjoys a
certain primacy among them in a legal sense. The manners
of the senators and leading men are somewhat formal, but
highly refined and courteous. My credentials were received by
the burgomaster, Dr. Roeck, who at an advanced age presided
over the senate with much ability and grace. He had served
in the war against Napoleon I, and in the French language
and literature was quite at home. The most active and in-

---

[1] 'Der Verkehr und die Ansiedelungen der Menschen in ihrer Abhängigkeit
von der Gestaltung der Erdoberfläche,' von J. G. Kohl. Leipzig, 1841.

fluential member of the senate was however Dr. Theodore
Curtius, who then conducted its foreign affairs, and carried on
the diplomatic intercourse with the ministers of foreign
powers.　Dr. Curtius, who is now burgomaster, has taken a
leading part in the formation of the North-German confederation, and in other important political transactions.　His
brother, professor Ernest Curtius, was formerly tutor to the
Crown-prince of Prussia, and is known to the learned world
by his elaborate history of Greece.　The father, Syndic Curtius, was, like the present burgomaster, an eminent statesman
in his day, and managed the foreign affairs of Lubeck for a
long series of years.

The senate gave me a dinner at its country-house called
the *Lachswehr*, which, in a fine summer evening, went off
pleasantly, and enabled me to make acquaintance with some
of the principal citizens.　The usual toasts were drunk and
responded to, not after, but during, the dinner, according to
the German custom.　I did not fail to visit the churches and
other ancient buildings with which Lubeck abounds.　The
cathedral is remarkable for containing the tombs of the old
bishops of Lubeck, and a beautiful altar, erected about the
year 1430, and which has been preserved intact from the
catholic times.　The spacious St. Mary's church (whose spire,
430 feet in height, is visible from the shore of the Baltic)
possesses two valuable pictures by Frederick Overbeck, viz.
Christ's entrance into Jerusalem, and the parting with
our Lord's body after the crucifixion.　The former was
an early production of that great painter, and by no means
free from faults; but the latter has always been deemed a
chef d'œuvre, for not only is the body of the Saviour divinely
modelled, but the surrounding figures of our blessed Lady, of
Mary Magdalen, Joseph of Arimathea, Lazarus, and Nico-
demus, are depicted with an extraordinary conception of the
deep and tranquil grief called forth in those persons by the
sublime occasion.　The subdued evening light cast upon this
precious picture has been greatly admired by German artists,
although, I believe, some objections have been taken to the
colouring by English *connoisseurs*.　There are also two good
cartoons of Overbeck to be seen in the public library, which
contains above fifty thousand books, and is well managed by
the learned Dr. Deecke.　Of the artistic merits of Overbeck,
I need say little here.　He was born at Lubeck in 1789, the
son of a burgomaster, who was also a poet, and spent the
greater part of his long life at Rome, where he became a convert to the catholic faith.　Next to Cornelius he was the

most distinguished painter of the new German religious
school, and has left master-pieces which more than suffice to
ensure him a lasting fame.   The Lubeckers are naturally
proud of him, and it was at the request of a society formed
among the citizens that the great picture in St. Mary's
church was designed and executed in order that a memorial of
him might remain in his native city.   Overbeck died in Rome,
at the age of eighty, about two years ago.   Several members
of his family are still residing at Lubeck, and his nephew fills
the office of secretary to the senate.   He spoke of his uncle with
profound reverence, and was very sensible of the honour he had
reflected from Rome upon his kinsmen in northern Germany.

The British government had long been accustomed to
attach importance to its relations with the Hanse-towns, and
the post of minister-resident at Hamburgh is a very ancient
one.   In the reign of Charles II it was filled for some time by
Sir William Swan.   In 1757 and 1758 it was held by Philip
Stanhope, son of the Earl of Chesterfield, whose published
letters bear witness to the great interest he took in his son's
official conduct and course of life.   Hamburgh at that time, it
was said, 'swarmed with Grafs, Gräfins, Fürsts, Fürstins,
Hochheits, and Durchlauchtigkeits,' and party spirit ran high
in the circle of the foreign ministers.   The minister of France
was M. Champeaux, and that of Prussia M. Hecht, who appears to have kept his colleagues in a state of excitement by
his political 'reveries,' which rarely assumed a substantial existence.   Lord Chesterfield gave his son the sensible advice
that the political differences of the several courts should never
influence the personal behaviour of foreign ministers towards
each other.   Live with your enemies as if they may one day
become your friends, and, *vice versâ*, beware of your friends becoming your foes. Philip Stanhope, like all other diplomatists,
was looking for promotion, and the Munich mission falling
vacant, wrote to his father to ask for it.   Lord Chesterfield's
answer was that Hamburgh was the great *entrepôt* of business,
and Philip could not be spared for such a post as Munich,
which the government had in fact determined to abolish, as
there never could be anything to do there unless a subsidy
should come into question.   Philip might look to some of the
courts in his neighbourhood, perhaps to Berlin.   As we know,
he eventually became British minister at Dresden, and died in
that capacity in 1768.   We learn further from the published
letters that whilst Philip Stanhope was in the diplomatic service he was likewise a member of parliament, and continued to

be so for several years. The government in 1764, wishing to get possession of his seat, asked him to vacate it, which after some negotiation he consented to do upon receiving £1000, being the half of the £2000 which the seat had cost him. Such incidents shew how little diplomacy had then the character of a regular service, and with what convenient simplicity a seat might be long held by a member residing abroad, and then disposed of to a purchaser for a price measured by the supposed length of time which the parliament had to run.

The arrest and imprisonment of our minister, Sir George Rumbold, by the French in 1804, made some sensation at all the European courts. Sir George was carried off from a country-house in Holstein, near to Hamburgh, in which he resided, by a detachment of French troops belonging to the army in the occupation of Hanover. The detachment crossed the Elbe, violating the still neutral territory of the free city of Hamburgh, and the acknowledged rights of the diplomatic representative of a foreign power. Sir George Rumbold was eventually released upon giving his parole not to return to Hamburgh. The French occupation of the Hanse-towns prevented the renewal of our diplomatic relations with them until 1815, when Mr. Alexander Cockburn (the father of the present Lord Chief Justice), who had previously filled the office of *charge d'affaires* and consul-general, was accredited in the capacity of envoy extraordinary and minister plenipotentiary. Elderly persons, still living at Hamburgh, spoke to me of Mr. Cockburn as a man of superior abilities, and pointed out his residence in the Dammthor-Strasse, a handsome old mansion *entre cour et jardin,* which has very lately been pulled down to make room for new houses built in an unsightly modern style. Mr. Cockburn was succeeded by a consul-general, Mr. Mellish; and after him came Mr. Henry Canning, cousin of the great minister, and brother of Lord Stratford de Redcliffe, as consul-general and *charge d'affaires,* who held the post for above fifteen years, and at his death in 1841 left behind him many favourable impressions of his genuine benevolence, kindness, and hospitality. His successor was Colonel Hodges, who had been the British political agent in Servia, and in Egypt, and whom circumstances made it desirable for the government to remove from Alexandria to another post. I was at Hamburgh at the time of Colonel Hodges' nomination, which was mentioned to me by Mr. Richard Parish, the leading British merchant there; and he exclaimed, 'It is a most improper appointment!' In fact, without undervaluing Colonel

N

Hodges' personal qualities, the men of business at Hamburgh soon discovered that he possessed but a slender knowledge either of trade, or German politics, nor did he even acquire the German language during the nineteen years in which he represented British interests at that great commercial port.

The pretty country-house of the late Syndic Sieveking at Ham I was glad to find in the possession of his son Dr. Hermann Sieveking, one of the secretaries of the senate, of whose constant friendship I have many agreeable reminiscences. At a dinner-party at Ham, soon after my arrival, I remember discussing with him and others several German questions, which at that time were likely to be brought into the foreground. Negotiations for a settlement of the Stade-tolls were pending, and the principle of paying Hanover an indemnity was pretty well agreed to by all the powers-interested; but the *ratio* in which Great Britain and Hamburgh respectively should contribute to the indemnity was not easy to determine, for as Hamburgh would be the state most benefited by the abolition of the tolls, Great Britain insisted that she should pay something more than the normal *quota* of the sum to be made up, and this view of the matter was eventually adopted. Then, the differences between the Danish government and the diets of Schleswig and Holstein, were gradually widening. There was no prospect of an agreement with the states of Holstein about their financial budget, and the duchy of Holstein being a member of the Germanic confederation, the question belonged to the federal diet, and might lead before very long to a federal execution. A strong wish prevailed in Germany that the British Government would use its influence with Denmark in order to induce that power not only to fulfil its obligations towards the federal body, but to perform the promises which the King-duke had notoriously made to Austria and Prussia on being re-instated in the sovereignty of the duchies after the civil war. The uneasiness caused by the Danish question was much increased by the fears generally entertained of the designs of the French emperor. If he wished a war with Germany, the complications of that question might at any time serve as an easy pretext. The assistance of Great Britain, if it could be really obtained, would therefore at this time be most valuable to the German powers.

The Baron Charles de Scheel-Plessen, president of the Holstein states, and a large landed proprietor both in Denmark and the duchies, resided at Altona, and I had frequent opportunities of intercourse with him. He had begun to recognise the impossibility of coming to any reasonable arrangement with the cabinet of Copenhagen, and would have been too glad to accept a reorganization of the monarchy upon federal principles, as recommended in my report of 1857. However, the time for this was gradually passing away, and a conflict with the German powers was becoming more probable. Baron de Scheel-Plessen, as president of the states, was the leading man in Holstein, and had actively promoted the resolutions with which the states of that duchy had in successive years denounced and resisted the unjustifiable encroachments of the Danish government upon the rights of the states. As against the Danes, he was true to the cause of the duchies, and an able defender of their constitutional privileges; but, like a few others of the wealthier nobility of the country, he did not relish the idea of the duchies being formed into a small independent state which would give little scope for civil or military employment to the members of noble families, and would, as he thought, rather lower them in the estimation of the world. Accordingly, after the death of King Frederic VII, Baron de Scheel-Plessen did not participate in the public feeling in favour of Duke Frederic of Augustenburgh, and used all the means in his power to counteract and oppose the Duke's legitimate claim to the succession. Such a course could not be otherwise than agreeable to the Prussian government. It fully appreciated the value of Baron Scheel-Plessen's services; and since the duchies have been annexed to the Prussian monarchy, the chief administration of their affairs has been committed to him as upper-president, installed in the castle of Kiel, the ancient seat of the dukes of Schleswig-Holstein, which the people had vainly hoped to see inhabited by the legitimate heir.

Dr. Alfred Rucker, the Hanseatic minister in London, returned this winter to Hamburgh, and was chosen a senator of his native city. He had accomplished the chief object of his mission by inducing the British government to consent to the abolition of the Stade-tolls by way of compensation to the crown of Hanover. A treaty was prepared accordingly, and submitted to a conference of the representatives of the powers interested, which assembled at Hanover in June 1861. I went to Hanover to assist Mr. (now Sir Henry) Howard, who was then British minister there, in the settlement of the business, which was attended with some difficulty in consequence of our government having at a late period of the negotiation required an engagement from Hamburgh not to levy any new tolls in the Elbe in future years. Such an engagement was unnecessary, the obvious policy of the

Hamburgh government being to get rid of tolls rather than to impose them, and Syndic Merck was surprised to be asked to give any pledge on the subject. But after some explanation he was prevailed upon to declare what everybody knew,—that Hamburgh had no intention of imposing new tolls,—and a declaration to that effect was appended to the treaty of abolition, which was thereupon signed and sealed at Hanover by all the ministers concerned. On the 1st of July following the Stade-duties ceased to be levied, and the crown was thus put to my labours for their suppression, which had been going on at intervals for more than twenty years. The merit of having first denounced the grievance in parliament, and forced our government to take steps for its redress, belongs entirely to Sir William Hutt, M.P., but I may without presumption claim the credit of having long since proved the illegality of the Hanoverian exactions, as well as of having at the end contributed to reconcile the differences which threatened to impede the conclusion of the treaty.

I dined with the members of the conference at Count Platen's, the Hanoverian minister for foreign affairs. He mentioned to me the Danish question, saying the King was resolved to do all he could in support of the rights of the duchies, and regretting that the question appeared to be so little understood in England. Count Platen, like the ministers of the other three second-rate kingdoms of Bavaria, Würtemberg, and Saxony, was very anti-Prussian; and when the independence of Hanover was lost in consequence of the war of 1866, he retired into exile with his royal master. After the dinner the conversation happened to turn upon William de Humboldt, and some one remarked that Talleyrand had said of him, ' C'est le sophisme incarné ! ' According to Haym's life of that statesman [1], which I afterwards read, he appears to have been a man of great erudition, powerful understanding, right feeling and taste, but without genius. His mind, dry and clear, was that of a statesman of the first order. He had a strong love of truth, combined with the ability to find sophistical arguments in case of need. He worshipped art in all its forms ; in religion he was a pantheist, like Goethe, keeping aloof from church dogmas and observances. He must have worked immensely at the Vienna congress of 1815, and it was very much owing to his exertions that Prussia was enabled to secure the permanent possession of so many of the territories which reverted to the allies at the close of the war.

---

[1] 'Wilhelm von Humboldt. Lebensbild und Charakteristik von R. Haym.' Berlin, 1856.

Humboldt was specifically Prussian, and except for Prussian objects would have sympathized little with the desire of national unity which has of late years so generally pervaded the German people. As for the ministers of the secondary states, such as Count Platen, their policy was simply *pro domo*,—to maintain their petty sovereignties as long as possible; they considered the idea of national unity to be synonymous with that of the Prussian hegemony in Germany. If the King of Hanover, instead of fighting Prussia in 1866, had consented to enter the North German confederation, he might have saved his crown; but he must have reigned like the King of Saxony, without dignity, and without power to do anything beyond the administration of local affairs.

Lord Augustus Loftus had lately been transferred as British minister (though not yet as ambassador) from Vienna to Berlin. Having made his whole diplomatic career in Germany, he was quite *au courant* with passing events, and well qualified to form a judgment of the line of policy which the Prussian government was likely to pursue towards its rival Austria. I wrote to Lord Augustus congratulating him on his return to Berlin, where he had been so long secretary of legation, and making some remarks on the actual state of the German question. His answer was as follows:—

'*Berlin*, March 3, 1861.

'DEAR MR. WARD,

'I am ashamed when I look at the date of your letter to find it unanswered, but I have really had so much to do of every sort of business, that I have not had a moment to devote to friends.

'I shall always be most happy to be of any use to you here, and shall take care that your correspondence is duly attended to and transmitted. Allow me to thank you very sincerely for your kind offer of reciprocity.

'I am in hope that the Danish Government will be wise enough to take those steps which may be necessary in order to prevent any active interference of the Diet in Holstein. I believe that such an intervention will be congenial to no one, and least of all to those who will have—perhaps unconsciously—provoked it, viz. the Holsteiners themselves.

'The virulence of the Holstein fever has abated here. I believe that, if Denmark will only submit the Budget to the Holstein states about to meet, the difficulties, at least those relating to the financial part of the question, will be arranged.

'The movement in Germany in my opinion is gradually

spreading, and in the late meetings which have taken place I remark a very significant and important feature, viz. a gradual 'rapprochement,' or drawing together of the North and the South, and a fusion of their interests towards one common aim. I have really not had time of late to pursue as carefully as I could wish the progress made in this direction, but still I have perceived in the tone of public opinion that a great progress has been made within the last few months towards the attainment of the object of the *National-Verein* at Coburg.

'If ever you can give me any information I should be extremely obliged, as your opinion on the subject will be of great value to me.

'Believe me
'Yours very truly
'AUGUSTUS LOFTUS.'

In the autumn of this year I was several times at Berlin for the purpose of sounding the Prussian officials in regard to certain desired reductions of customs-duties, and of opening, in conjunction with Lord Augustus Loftus, a negotiation for a commercial treaty between Great Britain and the *Zollverein.* The business lay chiefly in the hands of M. Delbrück, then director in the board of trade, and M. Philipsborn, director of the commercial department in the foreign office. My representations led to some modifications of the existing tariff, but the ground was not yet sufficiently cleared for the commercial treaty, which was not signed until four years afterwards. M. de Clercq, the commissioner of the French government, was at Berlin, negotiating the terms of a treaty of commerce between France and the *Zollverein*, which afterwards took effect. It stipulated for numerous reductions of duties, of which Great Britain afterwards obtained the benefit by being placed on the footing of the most favoured nation. M. de Clercq complained to me of the slowness of the Prussian negotiators, and of the delays arising from their being obliged to consult the other German governments at every important stage. He remarked that a German statesman always said 'no' to a novel proposition, and that the 'no' generally became 'yes' if the negotiator had a good stock of patience, and did not grudge the time to be spent in discussions. This is so far correct that the German mind does not like surprises, and that a modest and respectful demeanour is the surest way of conciliating the German bureaucracy, which is always ready to consider proposals, but will not allow itself to be hurried into a decision.

The great idealist among modern German painters, Cornelius, was living in the *Thiergarten* in a spacious mansion assigned to him by the late King, and was working hard to complete his cartoons for the fresco pictures destined to adorn the *campo santo* of the new Berlin cathedral intended to be raised close to the royal palace.   Cornelius received me in a friendly manner, and shewed me his house and gallery, containing a number of cartoons finished and unfinished, but not his wife, a young Roman girl whom he married when turned seventy, and brought home with him to Berlin.   She was unacquainted with the German language, and did not go into any society. We spoke of Italy.   As a good catholic Cornelius detested the Sardinian government, and wondered that its proceedings should have found so much favour in England.   He said that as a painter he had many adversaries in our country, and that some English artists had intrigued against his reputation in a manner for which he could not account.   However this may have been, there can be no doubt that Cornelius stood long at the head of the religious school of painting in Germany, that his genius has often been ranked with that of Michael Angelo, and that in the opinion of many connoisseurs he approached nearer to Raphael than any artist of the nineteenth century.

After passing the early part of his life in Rome, Cornelius became director of the Düsseldorf academy in 1821, and having spent a few years there was called by King Louis to Munich, where he designed those admirable fresco-paintings in the Glyptothek, the Pinacothek, and the church of St. Louis, which remain among the finest productions of modern ideal art.   In 1841 he was invited to Berlin by Frederic William IV, and there entered upon a new field, viz. the decoration of the intended *campo santo* with a series of appropriate religious pictures, which were to be fifty-five in number and extending over a length of a hundred and eighty feet.   When I visited the painter the series was near its completion, and I believe was just finished at the time of his death.   The general idea to be depicted in these frescoes was taken from a passage in St. Paul's epistle to the Romans: 'The wages of sin is death; but the grace of God is eternal life in Christ our Lord.' With respect to colouring, Cornelius was able to do little himself, and the execution of the frescoes in conformity with his designs was constantly committed to other hands.   This circumstance may detract from his merit in the opinion of those who conceive the gratification of the eye to be the test of a good picture, and therefore lay great stress upon the brightness of the colouring.   No doubt Cornelius would have been a more accomplished artist had he been able to carry out thoroughly his own designs; but the greatness of his genius soars far above all technical deficiencies; and his poetic talent, his depth of sentiment, and the richness of his conception, are beyond all dispute. Whilst at Rome Cornelius became a convert to the catholic faith, and died a devout member of the church which his pencil had done so much to honour, and to adorn.

Count de Buol-Schauenstein, late prime minister of Austria, spent a part of the winter of 1861–2 at Hamburgh, and entered into the society of the place. Dining with me one day, the diary of Frederic de Gentz, edited by Varnhagen, was mentioned, and Count Buol complained of the injustice done to Gentz's memory by such a publication. He said few people of this generation were aware of the great services rendered by Gentz to the cause of order and liberty in Europe. He worked for years, both in negotiation and through the press, for the overthrow of Bonapartism, and as first secretary to the congress of Vienna he materially influenced the arrangements under which Europe was reorganized in 1815. It was true that in some parts of his private journal Gentz spoke slightingly of the statesmen with whom he was associated, but those statesmen all recognised his merits, and Gentz did not seem to have intended that his private thoughts, recorded at the moment, should be given to the world. Dr. Lappenberg, who was present, concurred with this view, and mentioned that Sir James Macintosh had a high opinion of Gentz, and was on terms of friendship with him, continuing to correspond with him from Bombay on European politics. The fact is that Gentz's character was easy to read. He was a man of pleasure, fond of society, and of all sorts of amusements. But he was not the less a statesman, or a philosopher. He perceived that the one thing needful for Austria, and most of the European states, was to get rid of the French domination by putting down Napoleon; and to that object he devoted his energies untiringly during the best years of his life. If he received presents from time to time out of the secret-service money of Great Britain and other states, there is no reason to believe he got more than his services really deserved.

The daughter of Count Buol was married to the Count Gustavus de Blome, who arrived at Hamburgh as Austrian envoy soon after myself. He was the eldest son of the Count Blome, of Salza, a nobleman of large property in Holstein, who had for many years past been an active opponent of the system of government pursued in the duchies by the Danish crown. Previous to his entering the Austrian diplomatic service, Count Gustavus Blome had become a convert to the

catholic faith, and in subsequent years he was a zealous
advocate of the rights of the church in the Austrian empire.
He took great interest in the Danish question, and we used to
communicate to each other mutually such information on the
subject as we were able to obtain.

The untimely death of our excellent Prince-consort made a
painful impression at Hamburgh and throughout Germany.
The official telegram from London reached me in the after-
noon of Sunday the 15th of December, and the next day I
received visits of condolence from my colleagues of the diplomatic body, from the syndic, and several of the senators, and
other leading residents. The British merchants met, and
voted an address of condolence to the Queen, which I had the
honour to forward. These expressions of sorrow were, I
believe, perfectly sincere. The Prince Albert was certainly
not less respected in Germany than he was in England. He
was indeed a very superior man, and perhaps the best part of
his character was that he did not court popularity, but
digested his opinions well, and stated them unreservedly when
occasion required. His speech on the Russian war was a
proof that he did not mind going against the stream in the
interest of truth. It was well known in Germany that the
Prince occupied himself with German affairs, and that he read
all the despatches relating to those affairs which were received
from the Queen's ministers abroad. It was also known that
he desired the reorganization of the Germanic body by constitutional means. Most German statesmen therefore felt that
the Prince-consort's decease had deprived the nation of a
steady friend. They feared particularly that in questions such
as that with Denmark, the Queen's advisers might be induced
to take a part hostile to German interests, for want of some
influential person on the spot who clearly understood the
merits of the case.

The frost set in severely in January 1862, and for several
weeks both the Alster and the Elbe were frozen over, and the
navigation was closed. These hard frosts are considered
healthy, and as all the houses in Hamburgh are fitted with
stoves, and double windows, nobody appears to suffer from the
cold. As little or no business is done during the frosts, the
time is favourable for social festivities. Accordingly Hamburgh
was very gay this winter, and many dinners and balls were
given by the leading families.

A mission from the Jesuits' College at Cologne came in
Lent and excited much attention. The fathers preached a

series of excellent sermons in the catholic church on the
leading points of christian doctrine, which were heard and
praised by many protestants. The Jesuits seem to excel all
other preachers in the logical clearness of their expositions.
They convince the reason even against the will. In listening
to a sermon on marriage by father Zurstrasse, I could not but
reflect upon the facilities which are given to divorces by the
civil authorities in northern Germany, and upon the actual
state of marriage law in England, where a divorce-court sits
daily to do that which the divine founder of our religion
has expressly forbidden. Another Jesuit father, Hergarten,
preached admirably on repentance, and I do not doubt moved
the consciences of many of his hearers. There is no mental
discipline comparable with that of the confessional, nor any
greater relief to the troubled heart than to open it to the man
who is appointed to hear the penitent's tale, and to grant him
absolution. Who amongst us is there that, even without
counting his sins, does not repent of many of the actions of
his past life? ' Ma vie,' said Madame de Savigny, ' est pleine
de repentir.' A lutheran friend observed to me that, considering how much the life of the Hamburghers was devoted
to material objects, the Jesuits' mission could do nothing but
good. The Jesuits are indeed a wonderful body of men, and
far surpass the rest of the catholic clergy in pulpit eloquence.
Father Roh, of Maria Laach, in Baden, is perhaps the most
powerful opponent of infidelity in Germany[1], and when he
preaches on missions, both catholics and protestants flock to
hear his sermons. At Hamburgh he charmed even the men of
business; but with what result I am unable to report.

I visited London for a short time in May. Earl Russell,
who received me in Chesham-place, asked me some questions
about the contest in Hesse-Cassel, and I submitted to him the
reasons why the conduct of the Elector and of the Hassenpflug
administration appeared quite unjustifiable, and that if they
persisted it was not unlikely that the Elector's crown might be
endangered in the struggle. Lord Russell concurred with this
view, and said that, so far as he could judge, the people of
Hesse were demanding nothing beyond their constitutional
rights. The wonder is how M. Hassenpflug managed to
defeat the reasonable wishes of the diet for so long a period of
time, for he had scarcely a friend in the country, and in the
diet could not command a single vote. The difficulties were

---

[1] See ' Die Grundirrthümer unserer Zeit,' von P. Roh, Priester der Gesell-
schaft Jesu. Freiburg im Breisgau, 1869.

at last solved by the war of 1866, when the Elector was made prisoner, and sent to a Prussian fortress, and his dominions were annexed to the Prussian monarchy.

We passed some weeks of the autumn in the pleasant shade of Düsternbrock, near Kiel, where the beech woods run down to the shore, and the bathing is as good as can be expected in a sea like the Baltic, which contains so much less salt either than the North Sea or the Mediterranean. The political troubles have had an unfavourable effect upon the university of Kiel, the number of students having greatly fallen off. The university-library is well stocked, though of late years it has been insufficiently provided with modern books. Professor Forchhammer shewed us the picture-gallery, and the collection of antique costs, both of which are much indebted to his able supervision. As a good commentary I read Stahr's *Torso*[1], a valuable treatise on the chief productions of ancient sculpture. Stahr quotes among other authorities the remarkable æsthetical work of Emilius Braun on the ruins and museums of Rome. He has however done a great deal himself to explain to us the true state of the plastic arts among both the Greeks and Romans, and I do not know that any better book on the subject has appeared since Winckelmann broke ground in the historical exposition of the artistical monuments of the ancient world.

Dr. Nicholas Julius, whom I had long known, died in Hamburgh about this time at an advanced age. He had devoted himself during the greater part of his life to the reform of prisons and penitentiaries, and had been temporarily employed by the Prussian government. Dr. Julius was originally a physician, and served on the medical staff of the Hanseatic legion in 1813 and the two following years of the war against France, after which he devoted himself to philanthropic objects, and travelled a great deal in Great Britain and other countries, with the view of making himself master of the various systems of punishment for crime adopted by the European states. He edited a journal, and lectured in Berlin upon penal and reformatory institutions with much success; but his best work was undoubtedly that on the moral state of North America, published after his return from a visit of two years' duration in the United States[2]. Dr. Julius was a firm

---

[1] 'Torso. Kunst, Künstler, und Kunstwerke der Alten,' von Adolph Stahr. 2 Bde. Braunschweig, 1854.

[2] 'Nord-America's sittlicher Zustand,' von Dr. N. H Julius. 2 Bde. Leipzig, 1839.

adherent of the system of solitary imprisonment as practised at
the eastern penitentiary in Philadelphia, agreeing in this with
the opinions of MM. de Beaumont and de Tocqueville, and
of Mr. William Crawford, the British commissioner, who had
shortly before been sent out to inspect the American penitentiaries, and had made an official report in a similar sense.   I
had often talked with Dr. Julius on these subjects, and had
found him deeply impressed with the necessity of isolating
convicts from the society of others, and not less so with the
importance of founding reformatory discipline upon the *basis*
of religious sentiments.   In what way he considered religious
instruction ought to be given. may be inferred from the fact
that he was a convert to the catholic church.   Out of a small
property which he left at his decease he bequeathed an endowment in aid of the catholic mission at Hamburgh, to enable a
priest to travel to the neighbouring towns and villages where
churches or chapels had not yet been provided.

In the early part of September I heard from the Prussian
minister, Baron de Richthofen, that his government was
uneasy about the passing of the military budget through the
house of deputies, and that there were apprehensions in Berlin
of a political crisis.   Such a crisis arrived accordingly towards
the end of the month, when the house deducted a sum of
between six and seven million dollars, or about a million
pounds sterling, from the government estimates for the army.
The consequence was the resignation of the von der Heydt
ministry, and the nomination of M. de Bismarck-Schönhausen
to be president of a new administration which he was com-
missioned to form.   M. de Bismarck was known to be a
thorough conservative, '*Kein Fortschrittsmann, sondern ein
Feudal.*'   His mission was understood to be to keep the army
on its actual footing notwithstanding the vote of the house of
deputies, and in this King William cordially supported him.
There was much murmuring in Prussia, and the conduct of the
liberal deputies in the Prussian lower house excited very
general sympathy and approval throughout Germany.   The
people saw no prospect of war, and therefore no necessity for
so large an army as that actually maintained.   The new
minister-president was of a different opinion, and certainly
the wars in which Prussia was engaged in the following ten
years, and their brilliant results, have more than justified his
political sagacity.   There is no saying more true than that the
military budget of a state ought to depend upon its foreign
policy.   The liberal opposition in Prussia were guided by the
most conscientious motives, inasmuch as they expected neither

a war with Denmark, nor with Austria, much less that sanguinary conflict with France which has so lately astonished and terrified Europe. But it would seem as if M. de Bismarck and his political friends were not without presentiments of coming events, and, as things have turned out, it was at any rate a piece of good fortune for the Prussian monarchy that the economical vote of the opposition in September 1862 was not permitted to take effect.

Our gracious Queen visited this autumn the Duke of Saxe-Coburgh, and was attended by Earl Russell, as secretary of state for foreign affairs. His lordship whilst at Gotha, with characteristic candour and love of truth, took some trouble to investigate the merits of the Schleswig-Holstein question, and his views were published in a despatch which seemed to modify considerably the previous Danish bearings of the British cabinet. It led to no practical result; but the favourable impression which it made upon the friends of the duchies will be understood by the following letter from Sir Harry Verney, M.P. :—

'*Claydon House, Bucks*, Nov. 6, 1862.

'MY DEAR SIR,

' I dare say that you were not so unprepared as I was for the announcement in the *Times* about a fortnight since that Lord Russell took a view of the Schleswig-Denmark case different from that which the British government had been supposed to hold up to that time. I need not say how extremely pleased I was with the information. Lord Russell is a just and truth-loving man. I suspect that he had never investigated the subject thoroughly until this visit which he made to Germany, and as soon as the truth flashed on his mind, he wrote his despatch in the sense which he then, for the first time, became convinced was consistent with justice. If that is so, I cannot absolve Lord Russell for not having learnt the truth long before. He might have done so, for instance, from you ; and I am sure that he must know how entirely he may confide in your information and opinion. But really our ministers have such abundance and such variety of work, and are necessarily so obliged to consult each other's views and wishes, and are sometimes so compromised, that I am far more inclined to admire and approve Lord Russell's bold conduct in this matter, which I believe that he adopted as soon as he ascertained on which side was truth and justice, than to find fault with him for not having learnt it earlier. I expect that there will be a hot debate on the subject as soon as our Parliament meets, and

I venture to ask you to give me any further information, or to tell me where I can procure it, that may be of use in the discussion.

'When I had the pleasure of seeing you in May, I think you said that you might perhaps return to England towards the close of the year; and I venture to say to you that, if you do come, it will be particularly agreeable to Lady Verney and me to welcome you here.

'The *Times* says that the present is a most inopportune occasion for taking a part displeasing to the Danes. The contrary appears to me to be true. The Danes must know that at this time we desire to act towards them in a most friendly spirit, and to do anything that may be in our power to promote the welfare of the Danish monarchy; they must feel that nothing but an impartial love of justice actuates Lord Russell, and therefore it may be hoped that they will be inclined to review and reconsider the whole matter. I am convinced that the views shadowed out in the short paragraph as being Lord Russell's, at Gotha, afford the only solution to the whole question. The different nations of Germany never can quietly acquiesce in a portion of the German people, though not German subjects, being oppressed by the Danes. The inhabitants of every state in Germany would rise and expel any government that would consent to such pusillanimous conduct; but Lord Russell's opinion may lead to some compromise by which the just claims of all parts of the Danish monarchy may be considered, and peace and contentment once more restored.

'Some people have expected an autumnal Session, to vote money for the distress in the cotton districts, but as it has not been announced yet, I think it improbable.

'I am, my dear Sir,

'Yours very faithfully,

'John Ward, Esq., C.B.'   'HARRY VERNEY.

On Sunday the 30th of November, Prince Christian of Holstein-Glucksburgh, with his daughter the Princess Alexandra, the affianced bride of the Prince of Wales, came to Hamburgh on their return from England, attended by General and Madame d'Oxholm. I waited upon them and was favourably received. The Princess, who was on the point of attaining her nineteenth year, struck every one who saw her, not only as pretty, but as having remarkably pleasing manners. She expressed great gratification with the visit she had been paying to her future country. It is well known that the children of Prince and Princess Christian, now King and Queen of Denmark, were very simply though carefully brought up, that they were a happy and united family, and that the household of Prince Christian differed little from that of an ordinary country gentleman. Previous to the year 1850, Prince Christian could not of course entertain any thought or suspicion that his destiny would one day call him to fill the Danish throne, nor was his way of living at all arranged upon such a supposition.

The cause of the Poles has never excited much sympathy in Germany, still there was a feeling of disgust with the continued brutality of the Russian government which led to the unfortunate insurrection of Poland in the beginning of the year 1863. Notwithstanding the professions of conciliation made by the present Emperor, the conscription made in Poland for the Russian army was an act of cruel violence, which deprived the Poles of every hope of generous or compassionate treatment by their ruthless masters. The men were seized in their beds at midnight, and taken away from their families to remote stations in Russia, never to return until their old age, or perhaps not at all. As the insurrection proceeded, the insurgents became more and more desperate and reckless; and the combined remonstrances of England, France, and Austria, only served to delude them, for they indulged one vain hope that Europe could be brought actually to take up arms in their behalf. Russia, however, even refused to grant an armistice at the request of the three powers; and the provisional government continued for some months its hopeless struggle, proclaiming its intention to fight to the last for an independent Poland as before its partition. The Polish government certainly was not wanting in courage or talent, but without foreign aid it had not the means of effecting the liberation of the country. One of my colleagues in the Hamburgh diplomatic circle remarked to me that before Russia had definitively answered the remonstrances of the three powers, a leading member of the British cabinet had publicly declared in parliament, 'we shall not go to war.' Therefore, he added, Russia had nothing to fear from rejecting the proffered mediation. Whatever might have been the policy of the British government, it was surely unnecessary to inform Russia that the mediation would not in any case be followed up by measures of coercion on the part of the allies.

The Duke Charles of Holstein-Glucksburgh called upon me in the early part of February, and told me of the approaching marriage of his niece the Princess Alexandra, and that she would pass through Hamburgh on her way to London. The Duke, who is the head of the Glucksburgh family, had been rather a popular man in the duchies, having usually resided in the winter in the castle of Kiel, and in the summer on his estate in Schleswig. He married the Princess Wilhelmina, daughter of Frederic VI, King of Denmark, but has had no children, on which account he was passed over by the European powers when they took upon themselves to settle the succession to the Danish monarchy. Duke Charles spoke to me with disapprobation of the continued efforts of the Danish government to draw Schleswig into the monarchy, and of the pertinacity with which the remonstrances of the Holstein states had been rejected at Copenhagen. He feared there was now no alternative but a federal execution, unless the cabinet of Great Britain could influence that of Denmark to submit to the just demands of the German powers. I agreed with the Duke that this was highly desirable, but feared that Lord Russell was not prepared to exercise the requisite degree of pressure upon the Danish government.

The Princess Alexandra, accompanied by her parents, brothers, and sisters, as well as by Duke Charles, Prince Frederic of Hesse, General Oxholm, Mr. (now Sir Augustus) Paget, and a numerous suite, reached Hamburgh late in the evening of the 27th of February. I received them on arrival, and presented to the Princess the syndic, Dr. Merck, who brought her an address of congratulation on the part of the senate, also several members of the diplomatic corps who were desirous to pay their compliments upon the occasion. The houses round the Alster, as well as the environs of the city through which the procession passed from Altona, were brilliantly illuminated; and an immense concourse of people stationed themselves before the hotel, greeting the distinguished guests from time to time with vociferous cheers. In the course of the evening the Princess and her father appeared at the window, to the great gratification of the assembled multitude. The next morning the Princess and her party pursued their journey to England by way of Hanover, and I took leave of them at the Grasbrook ferry, being the limits of my official district. All those at Hamburgh who were introduced to the Princess expressed themselves as delighted with her appearance, as well as with her affable and pleasing deportment.

The 18th of March was kept as a public holiday in order to commemorate the expulsion of the French from Hamburgh fifty years ago. There was a great procession of the guilds through the streets in the day-time, and in the evening much eating and drinking, and an illumination. The French minister, M. Cintrat, refused to illuminate, but was not subjected to any attack or insult on that account. As the French returned again to Hamburgh after evacuating it, the jubilee of this day seemed rather premature. The right jubilee was the anniversary of the battle of Leipsic, which, on the 18th of October following, was celebrated here and throughout Germany for the fiftieth and last time. The movement party however had ceased to take much interest in that festival, thinking that the disunited and degraded state of Germany in a political sense formed a sad commentary upon such celebrations.

The death of Baron Ernest de Merck was universally deplored at Hamburgh, which lost in him one of its most enterprising and intelligent citizens, who had not only the will but the means of doing a great deal of good. Ernest Merck was a son of the former senator Merck (a man of mark in his day), and brother of the syndic. He succeeded his father in mercantile business, but his mind ranged far beyond the counting-house, and he was for a short time finance-minister of the German empire under the provisional rule of the Archduke John. During the panic which made such havoc among the Hamburgh merchants in 1857, he prevailed upon the Austrian government to make the city a large loan in silver, which tended materially to the re-establishment of commercial credit. He was much engaged with railways and other undertakings in the Austrian empire, and was made an Austrian baron, in spite of the reluctance with which the republic of Hamburgh permits its citizens to accept either titles of nobility or decorations from foreign powers. He was the chief promoter of the Hamburgh agricultural exhibition of 1863, as well as of the zoological gardens, in which a monument has since been erected to his memory. Ernest Merck was a remarkably fat man, and like most fat people very good-natured, His familiar figure will long be remembered on the Hamburgh exchange, as well as in Baden-Baden, where he possessed a villa, and resided with his family during a part of the year.

The German bathing-places are annually frequented by so many families that it is necessary to know them in order to form a complete acquaintance with German life. We spent some months of the summer at Wiesbaden, whose pleasant situation amidst vine-covered fields and gardens at the foot of the

Taunus mountains, would alone be very attractive even without the recommendation of its curative springs. The Greek church on the Neroberg, with its gilt cupola, is a striking and beautiful object in itself, and has an important meaning, as covering the remains of the late Duchess of Nassau, who was a Russian princess and therefore of the Greek confession. There was much good company, both British and foreign, this season in Wiesbaden. I found my old friend M. de Rönne residing there, he having retired from office after having filled some distinguished posts, the last of which was that of president of the Prussian board of trade. Rönne was a liberal, and did not like the position in which the Bismarck administration had placed itself in regard to the Prussian diet. He was likewise a Holsteiner by birth, and wished for nothing better than a war between Prussia and Denmark on behalf of the duchies. We spoke of the approaching congress of German sovereigns at Frankfort, and concurred in the opinion that nothing would come of it. The whole value of the meeting lay in the possibility of a conference with Prussia upon the German question. But it was already known that the King of Prussia had declined the invitation, and would not appear at Frankfort. The congress was therefore little more than a friendly meeting of the Emperor of Austria and his allies, who partook of some sumptuous dinners, and other festivities, and returned to their homes not at all wiser than when they left them.

Lord Clarendon came to Wiesbaden for the benefit of his health. He continued to take a great interest in German politics, and seemed to think the democratic party in Prussia had gone rather too far in endeavouring to cut down the military budget. The King, he observed, possessed the power under the federal act, of taking at all events the financial budget of the previous year. Lord Clarendon was not surprised by the refusal of Prussia to take part in the impending congress of sovereigns, for, he said, its real object was obviously to prevent Prussia from assuming the lead, which belonged to her, in German affairs. He afterwards went to Frankfort, and was received by the Emperor of Austria, and other high personages, who were aware of the influence which he still exercised in England on questions of foreign politics. I mentioned to Lord Clarendon that there would surely be a federal execution in Holstein, and probably a war between the two great German powers and Denmark, on account of the duchies; and I then sounded him as to his view of the treaty of London which guaranteed the succession of the duchies to Prince

Christian, observing that German lawyers did not consider it valid for want of the assent of the states of the duchies, as well of the *agnati* who were next entitled. Lord Clarendon merely said it would be time enough to consider that question when the treaty should be disputed ; but that he could not blame the federal diet for ordering an execution, and hoped the Danes would be reasonable enough to comply in time with their legal obligations. He did not at this time seem to be- lieve that Prussia and Austria had serious intentions of com- mencing hostilities against Denmark, although there were many persons in Germany by whom such a war was already looked on as inevitable. It will be remembered that the claim of the Duke of Augustenburgh to reign in Schleswig-Holstein had not yet been formally advanced, consequently the ques- tion of the succession may have appeared to Lord Clarendon of less moment than it actually was.

A bathing-place is the world in miniature. No sooner have we made some agreeable acquaintances than it is time to take leave of them, perhaps never to meet again. In the words of the poet,

> 'To come together, to part ;
> Welcome and farewell,
> Is the lot of life.'[1]

We left Wiesbaden with regret, and returned by way of Treves, one of the most interesting of German cities. The Moselle on which it stands flows between hills of red sand- stone, thickly covered with vines and woods. The Roman remains comprise the *basilica*, the baths, the amphitheatre, and the *porta nigra*, perhaps the most perfect building existing out of Rome itself, and still in use as one of the city gates. The Roman monument at Igel, a short distance out of the city, is likewise a remarkable structure, and in good preservation. When the state of the water allows, the voyage by steamer down the Moselle from Treves to Coblentz is worth under- taking on account of the picturesque river-scenery, smaller indeed than that of the Rhine, but not less beautiful in its peculiar way.

We visited at Bonn the Baroness de Bunsen, and looked with respect on the house in which her distinguished husband had lived for some short time, and had breathed his last. In this spacious mansion, whose garden runs down to the Rhine

---

[1] 'Zusammen zu kommen, zu scheiden ;
Willkommen, und Lebewohl,
Ist das Lebens Loos !'

and commands a view of the seven hills, Madame de Bunsen
was living with several of her children, and no less than ten
grandchildren, and was preparing those memoirs of her accomplished husband which have since charmed the world.
George de Bunsen happened to be at Bonn, which town he
has for some years represented in the Prussian house of deputies.   He was a liberal in the best sense of the word, desirous
that the political machine should not move otherwise than in
a constitutional way, but was deeply sensible of the national
honour, and thoroughly attached to the monarchy and to his
sovereign.   He complained of the narrow view which the
British government had been accustomed to take of the
Schleswig-Holstein question.   Because the independence of the
little kingdom of Denmark (the dot above the i) in its actual
dimensions was taken for granted as a necessity to the political equilibrium of Europe, therefore a million of people in-
habiting the duchies were to be kept in bondage, and to lose
not only their constitutional rights, but even the use of their
language, and the exercise of their religion.   Your government, said George de Bunsen, seems to have lost its habitual
foresight in regard to Danish affairs.   It is our mission and
duty to deliver the Schleswig-Holsteiners from their oppressors, and that we shall do this eventually you may regard as
certain.   Why not then tell the Danes the truth, and exhort
them to comply with the demands of the German powers,
whilst there is yet time to arrange differences without kind-
ling a war in the north of Europe?   It is indeed singular how
completely our leading statesmen seemed to be blinded in regard to the Danish resistance, and its inevitable results; nor
was there in parliament, so far as I know, a single man, except Sir Harry Verney, who either cared for the complaints of
the duchies, or had taken the trouble to investigate the merits
of their case.

From Bonn we proceeded to Cologne and surveyed the
magnificent cathedral with more leisure than usually falls to
the lot of a passing traveller.   During the thirty-five years
that I have known and admired this noble structure its progress towards completion has been really wonderful.   The
large grants made to the building-fund by successive Prussian
kings, added to the collections made by the association called
the *Dombau-Verein* throughout Germany, and in all parts of
Europe, have furthered the work so well that there is every
reason to hope the cathedral will stand in a finished state before the eyes of many of the present generation.   Whenever that
great event shall take place, the memory of Sulpice Boisserée

will deserve to be especially honoured, for he was the architect and friend of art, who, when the church resembled a ruin, first made a design of it as if it were completed according to the original plan, and who more than any other man gave the impulse which is gradually leading to its perfect restoration.

Countess Hahn-Hahn's new novel of 'The two sisters' was much talked of at Wiesbaden. It had of course a strong note of catholicity; but it inculcated duties and principles which are equally binding upon members of other confessions. Richenza, the protestant sister, is an intelligent and sentimental girl, belonging to a noble family, who falls in love with and marries a poor painter, near to whom she used to sit copying in the Dresden gallery. The marriage leads to misery; the children turn out badly; and Richenza becomes an habitual gambler at the play-tables of Baden-Baden, losing in her destitution all sense of propriety and self-respect. Euphrosyne, the other sister, marries a worthy catholic gentleman, becomes herself a convert, and goes to live at an old country-house, formerly a monastery, in which the family chaplain, a model for priests, had once been a monk. Her husband's father, the owner of the property, had likewise been a monk in the same confraternity, and by means of falsehood and fraud, had not only promoted the dissolution of the monastery, but obtained the transfer of its landed property to himself. On this account the old sinner, as well as his children and grandchildren, are represented as lying under God's displeasure, and suffering the temporal punishment due to the ancestor's misdeeds. Euphrosyne's husband, as well as his nephew, become incapacitated by nervous diseases, and she loses two blooming boys, retaining, however, a pious daughter, who sacrifices herself by marrying the invalid nephew from a pure sense of duty. Euphrosyne and her daughter are models of catholic piety, charming us by their constant self-denial, and by their hearty, though somewhat austere, devotion to the discipline of the church. The history of the family's sufferings in consequence of the divine displeasure is perhaps carried rather too far, although it cannot be denied that there are penalties inflicted upon sinful actions in this world as well as in the next, and that human nature is so constituted that a father's misdeeds are visited both morally and physically upon his innocent children. Upon the whole, the tendency of the novel appeared to me unobjectionable. The advantages of union in families, and of establishing in them a system of fixed rules of action, is sufficiently apparent. The fluctuating and loose characters of those persons in the story who do not act upon religious principles are very well drawn.   Richenza, for instance, was a nominal lutheran, and, not believing in her own church, shaped her conduct entirely according to her own inclinations.   But Euphrosyne had chosen a better part, and had built her faith upon a rock which was not to be shaken by the concurrence of new religious systems, or by the varying opinions of the sophists of the day.

The energy of mind and love of truth displayed by the Countess Hahn-Hahn in her numerous works deserve our admiration, although, as she herself tells us, she is not exactly *eine schöne Seele* (a beautiful soul) in a theological sense.   Her life appears to have been an unhappy one, except the incident of her conversion, which she attributes to St. Augustine's confessions, but Bishop Keteler probably had some share in it. After her conversion she disowned her former writings as unworthy of her, and with reason, for she was no longer the same person.   A biographical sketch of Countess Hahn-Hahn was published in 1869 by her friend *Marie Hélène* (Madame le Maître).   Why this was done in her lifetime I have not been able to ascertain.

In consequence of the rather sudden death of Frederic VII King of Denmark on the 15th of November, the Danish question passed into a new phase.   The King, a weak-minded, selfish, man, who cared for little beyond his personal comforts and enjoyments, had been made a tool of by the ultra-Danish party, and was held in very little respect by the inhabitants of the duchies.   His morganatic wife, the Countess Danner, formerly named Rasmus, and not of noble birth, exercised anything but a good influence over him.   She was in fact not more refined than the King himself, and she led him to think ill of his German subjects, by representing them as a body of agitators disaffected towards the monarchy.   Indeed, she threw her weight entirely into the scale of the Danish ministers, and never took any pains to urge the King to conciliate the goodwill of the German parts of his dominions.   Frederic VII was not malevolent, as the Elector of Hesse is said to have been, towards his subjects; but he was stupid and obstinate, and in fact the last man who could be expected to take any personal trouble in reorganizing the monarchy, or in placing the conflicting nationalities upon a fair and equal footing in regard to each other.

Previous to the King's death a plan of a common constitution for Denmark and Schleswig had been prepared, with the view of realizing the long cherished wishes of the so-called Eider-Danes to incorporate that duchy with the kingdom, so that the river Eider would become the frontier of Denmark; and the duchy of Holstein, though still a Danish possession, would be left to settle its constitution with the Germanic confederation. The King having died whilst this new constitution was waiting for his assent, the duty devolved upon his successor, Christian IX, to decide whether he would give effect to it or not. He ought, of course, not to have done so, because Schleswig and Holstein were already constitutionally united, and the royal word had long since been passed that Schleswig should never be incorporated with the kingdom. But the Copenhagen mob insisted in a violent and tumultuous manner that the new King should forthwith assent to the proposed law; and Christian IX deemed it expedient to yield to the wishes of the Eider-Danish party, though he could hardly be ignorant that by so doing he broke the faith of his royal predecessors towards the duchies, and gave the German powers a just and legitimate cause for commencing a war.

Whilst the new King at Copenhagen was thus doing his best to provoke a war, people in Germany were excited by a proclamation of the hereditary Prince Frederic of Augustenburgh, eldest son of Duke Christian, dated from his seat at Dolzig in Lusatia, and claiming the sovereignty of the duchies, as the legitimate heir of Frederic VII, in consequence of the renunciation of his father, made and published some years since. Prince Frederic, therefore, assumed the title of Duke of Schleswig-Holstein, and his claim was at once joyfully recognised in the duchies, and hailed with approbation by public opinion in most parts of Germany. The German nation desired nothing better than to see the duchies effectually separated from Denmark by becoming an independent state, and the Duke Frederic was believed to possess not only an hereditary title to the ducal crown, but all the personal qualities which would make his accession a fortunate circumstance for the interest of the inhabitants. He was closely connected with the courts of England and Prussia through his wife, (a princess of Hohenlohe-Langenburgh and niece of Queen Victoria,) and their union had already been blessed with several children.

The best German lawyers were clearly of opinion that after the extinction of the elder Danish line, which took place on the decease of Frederic VII, the next line in succession to the crown of the duchies was that of Augustenburgh, after which stood the lines of Glücksburgh, and of Oldenburgh. I have

read a great deal relating to this subject, and believe Duke
Frederic's claim to have been perfectly well founded in law.
There was, however, a question whether the previous renunciation of Duke Christian barred the rights of his son, or
others of his family ?   Duke Christian, having taken an active
part in the first civil war against Denmark, was banished from
the country, and had his large estates forfeited, subject to a
pecuniary indemnity equivalent to about £400,000 sterling.
In consideration of that compensation, which he received, the
old Duke was obliged to engage, for himself and his heirs, not
to make any further claims hostile to the Danish crown, and
he never did so.   But were the rights of the young Duke, his
son, barred by that engagement ?   I conceive not; for he was
no party to it though of age at the time, nor was his consent
even asked by the Danish government.   In what country has
it been considered that a reigning sovereign can exclude his
heir-apparent from the succession without the latter's express
consent ?   The case of the duchies was that of an independent
sovereignty, and when Duke Christian resigned his right to
the crown, it descended as a matter of course to his eldest son.
The circumstance that the old Duke was obliged to make a
forced sale of his lands, and was paid a certain sum for them,
could not possibly have affected Duke Frederic's right to the
crown, founded both upon the established law of the country,
and upon the general wishes of its population.

Lord Wodehouse (now Earl of Kimberley) came to Hamburgh
in the middle of December on his way to Copenhagen.   His
mission was ostensibly to congratulate King Christian on his
accession ; but he had likewise instructions to endeavour to
mediate, and I am sure that he did his best to prevent the
war, which was evidently impending.   He was very desirous
of information respecting Danish affairs, and seemed to hope
that it might yet be possible for Denmark to avert the wrath
of the German powers.   I told Lord Wodehouse that I did not
believe in the possibility of an arrangement so long as the
joint-constitution for Denmark and Schleswig remained in
force; that Germany could never permit the incorporation of
Schleswig with the kingdom, considering that the two duchies
had an ancient constitutional right to be united with each
other.   Lord Wodehouse observed that Schleswig did not
belong to Germany, and that there were differences of nationality within the duchy itself which made a solution
difficult.   In fact, the Danes had gone so far that it had
become very difficult either for Lord Wodehouse, or for any

negotiator, however able, to mediate successfully at Copenhagen, and his lordship's mission had therefore no other result than to prove the goodwill entertained by our government towards the Danish King. The right time for the British cabinet to have made an earnest remonstrance, was when the project of law for the incorporation of Schleswig was still before the Danish diet, and had not received the royal assent. Frederic VII was then alive, and there was really more chance of inducing him to stop the progress of the measure, than of making Christian IX 'revocare gradum' by repudiating a law to which he had so lately given his solemn assent, and thereby purchased the confidence and support of the Eider-Danish party.

Before the close of the year 1863, the long threatened federal execution had entered Holstein. The troops were chiefly Saxon and Hanoverian, under the command of General de Hake, a gallant Saxon officer, with whom I was well acquainted at Leipsic, and who took up his quarters in the house of Baron Scheel-Plessen at Altona. The civil commissioners who had the conduct of the execution were M. de Könneritz from Dresden, and M. Nieper from Hanover. Their first act was to dismiss the Danish upper president de Schele, and to replace him by a German official; and a number of other Danish officials were likewise at once removed from their posts. The people witnessed these proceedings with satisfaction, and looked upon the commissioners in the light of their liberators from the Danish yoke. They now considered themselves at liberty to avow their wishes in favour of the succession of the Prince Frederic of Augustenburgh. A large public meeting was held in Altona at which the Prince was proclaimed by acclamation Duke of Schleswig-Holstein, the speakers declaring that the duchies would never give their allegiance to any other sovereign. Similar meetings were also held at Kiel, Neumünster, Glückstadt, and all the market-towns in the country; no one doubted the Duke's legitimate right; and the pastors enforced it from their pulpits as a divine ordinance to be respected by their flocks. In the midst of these demonstrations, the news reached Hamburgh that Duke Frederic himself had suddenly and privately arrived at Kiel, and was engaged, with the aid of his adviser, State-councillor Francke, in planning measures for obtaining possession of the throne of the duchies, which, so far as depended upon the popular voice, seemed already to have been given to him by universal consent.

CHAPTER IX.

Hamburgh continued. The federal commissioners. Field-marshal Wrangel. The war in Schleswig. Duke Frederic. British policy. M. de Koudri-affsky. Denmark loses the Duchies. Baron de Gerolt. The Zollverein. Archbishop of Cologne. Berlin in 1865. King William. Queen Augusta. Prince Bismarck. Treaty with Austria. Dobberan. Dr. Lappenberg. Dr. Schleiden. The Augustenburgh family. Lord Palmerston. Made minister-resident. Mdlle. Tietjens. Lord Napier.

THE presence of the federal commissioners in Altona tended to excite much speculation and discussion at Hamburgh as to the probable results of the execution. M. de Könneritz, like his political chief, Baron de Beust, was a steadfast adherent of the rights of the confederation, and looked with favour upon the claim of Duke Frederic, which indeed was affirmed by the majority of the states represented in the Germanic diet. I had many conversations with M. de Könneritz on the political situation, and he explained very clearly the competence of the diet to reorganize Holstein, and to give that duchy a limited independence, subject to the federal laws. He did not admit the application to the duchies of the London treaty of the 8th of May 1852, inasmuch as the states had never been consulted, or given their assent to it. He did not conceal his apprehensions that it was the intention of the Prussian government eventually to annex Schleswig and Holstein to the Prussian monarchy, and he saw no remedy for this but the firm determination of Austria, in concert with the secondary German kingdoms, to give the duchies the sovereign of their choice, so soon as the Danes should have been expelled from the country. Both M. de Könneritz and his colleague M. Nieper saw plainly enough the object at which the Prussian policy was aiming, but they did not seem to be aware of the great military superiority which Prussia was about to display, and which gave her the hegemony of Germany after the short and successful campaign of 1866.

It was in the last days of January 1864, in the midst of a severe frost, that the real war against Denmark began, and the Austrian and Prussian armies marched through Hamburgh and Lubeck on their way into Schleswig. The two great

German powers had a good *casum belli* in consequence of the breach of the guarantees given to them by the Danish King on being re-invested with the possession of the duchies after the close of the civil war, which guarantees were recapitulated in the royal proclamation issued on the 28th of January 1852 ; and they had now decided to enforce their right by arms, independently of the federal execution, which continued in possession of Holstein. The Austrian forces were under the command of Field-marshal de Gablentz ; the Prussians under that of Field-marshal de Wrangel, who was accompanied by the King's brother Prince Albert, and other distinguished officers. They all attended a ball given by M. Theodore Schmidt, a merchant in Hamburgh. Prince Albert, to whom I was presented, seemed fully cognizant of the political events which had led to the war then beginning, and said to me, ' If we (the Prussians) deserve any blame, it is for permitting so long a time to elapse before redressing the grievances of the duchies, but now you will see we shall do it in earnest.' Field-marshal de Wrangel, then approaching to his eightieth birthday, was very loquacious, and said some odd things, particularly to the ladies. After asking me about my former career, he congratulated me on being fixed at Hamburgh, a place he should like much to live at on account of its hospitality and good dinners. He amused the burgomasters by addressing them as ' your eminence,' a title belonging to cardinals only, which Wrangel had confused with that of ' your magnificence,' —the proper appellation of a Hanseatic burgomaster. It was understood that Wrangel had been placed at the head of the army on account of his name, which sounded well with the soldiers, and that he was in reality quite *effete*. He had however an excellent staff, and the business was done for him so effectually, that nobody grudged the old soldier the honour of the victory, and on his return to Berlin he enjoyed the applause of the street population to his heart's content.

In less than a week the Austrian army had driven the Danes back from their line of the *Dannewerk*, and forced them to retreat to the island of Alsen where they had strong fortifications. The Austrians fought most gallantly ; the Croatians seized the Danes by the throat, and, as the latter declared, were like so many devils. It was agreed that the Prussian army should undertake the task of pursuing the Danes, and of taking their entrenchments at Düppel, which protected the island of Alsen, separated from the heights of Düppel by a narrow channel only. The Prussian camp was therefore established at Düppel, and they waited patiently there for more than

two months without doing anything. At length however the
propitious day arrived ; the storm began ; the Prussians rushed
upon the enemy ; and in a few hours had taken the whole of
the Danish entrenchments. On the 18th of April I was at a
dinner given in Hamburgh by General de Hake, when the
news arrived to the great joy of the assembled company, composed chiefly of persons belonging to the duchies, or interested
in their fate. It was felt that the Danish government had
become powerless, and that, without foreign assistance, was no
longer in a position to continue the struggle.

But were there any, and which, foreign powers, disposed to
enter into a war with Germany in defence of the Danish pretensions? This would soon be seen from the deliberations of
the diplomatic conference on the Danish question which had
been summoned to meet in London, and was about to assemble.
The Germanic confederation was represented in the conference
by the Baron de Beust, who although he was said not to have
enchanted Lord Palmerston, acted undoubtedly in accordance
with the national sentiment of Germany by refusing to accede
to the proposed division of Schleswig. The German powers
however made Denmark the offer of reorganizing the monarchy upon federal principles, so as to give the duchies a
constitutional autonomy under the Danish King. Strange to
relate, this concession, which held out to Denmark the last
chance of saving the duchies, was obstinately refused. The
members of the conference then began to perceive the inutility
of their further labours, and the assembly broke up towards the
end of June. The consequence was the renewal of the war.

Previous to the opening of the London conference, it was
rumoured in Germany upon some authority that our gracious
Queen had expressed a strong disinclination to a war with
Prussia in support of the Danish pretensions, to which it was
well known the Prince-consort had in his lifetime never given
any countenance or approval. Many leading members of the
liberal party were likewise of opinion that the circumstances
were not such as to justify a departure from the policy of peace
and non-intervention which they held ought to be the standing
rule of Great Britain in her foreign relations. In a letter
which I received from Mr. (now the right hon^{ble}. William
Forster, M.P., dated the 30th of March 1864, after expressing
his concurrence in my general views of the Schleswig-Holstein
question, he adds :
    ' I hope you are aware of the extent to which your report of

1857 on this question is considered an authority in the house. Had the war feeling, too rife in the country, shewn itself in strong anti-German speeches in the house, I was prepared to say what I could for peace; but the Commons have been very creditably quiet, and though we must expect some debates after the recess, I hope now that the effect of the conference must be to keep us off from active intervention, very doubtful as it must be whether it will lead to a real settlement.'

The Crown-prince of Prussia returned from the campaign in Schleswig about the middle of May, and the Crown-princess came to meet him at Hamburgh. She was full of enthusiasm for the German cause, and drove through the streets in an open carriage, arrayed in the Schleswig-Holstein colours, viz. a pink gown, a white bonnet, and a sky-blue parasol. The Duke Frederic of Augustenburgh, who was residing at Kiel, came up to see his royal cousins, and honoured me likewise with a visit. He spoke of his indisputable rights, and his intention to persevere to the utmost in his claim, but seemed to have little confidence in the rectitude of the Prussian government, although the King had always been his friend. The Duke has a handsome, grave, Holsteinish physiognomy. His character is serious, combined with a certain dignity, which struck and pleased the people of the duchies. It has been said that he was wanting in energy, and that he ought to have risked a *coup d'état* on his arrival in Holstein, by summoning the states to meet him, in order that they might at once recognise him as their lawful sovereign. No doubt the states were disposed to offer him their allegiance; but the duchy was in the occupation of federal troops; and even if the federal commissioners had permitted such a proceeding, the Prussians would assuredly have expelled the assumed sovereign from the duchy when the war began a few weeks afterwards. His advisers considered it of great importance that he should remain at Kiel, in readiness to take advantage of any favourable circumstances which might arise out of the impending conflict between Denmark and the German powers. On Whit-sunday the 15th of May the Duke made a public entry into Altona, and was received at the town-gates by the authorities and a large mass of people, in a festive manner. The next day he drove through the villages on the Elbe-side to Blankenese, and was greeted by the inhabitants with many demonstrations of attachment and respect. He continued to live chiefly at his villa at Düsternbrock near Kiel until the spring of 1866, when the retirement of the

Austrian forces made the duchy no longer a secure place of residence for the legitimate claimant of the crown.

Previous to and during the London conferences much anxiety prevailed in Germany to ascertain the line of policy which the British cabinet really meant to follow in regard to Danish affairs. Lord Russell seemed to have changed his tone, and had sent strong remonstrances to the German powers; in fact, our government had got into an undignified habit of scolding about the Danish question, which might, or might not, have a serious meaning. M. de Koudriaffsky, the Russian *chargé d'affaires* at Hamburgh, was specially instructed to watch the progress of events in the duchies; and knowing that I was in communication with many Schleswig-Holsteiners, called upon me frequently to make enquiries, and to sound me as to the disposition of Her Majesty's government to go to war in defence of the integrity of the Danish monarchy. I said I was left altogether without official instructions upon the latter point, but my own opinion was that Great Britain would never go to war in such a cause, and that I had letters from parliamentary friends in London, who described public feeling as being very much against it. 'What!' said M. de Koudriaffsky, 'will your government not fulfil its guarantee of the succession contained in the treaty of London?' The validity of that treaty, I answered, had been much doubted; nor could any guarantee affect the rights of third persons who were not parties to it. Besides, we did not yet know whether Russia and France were prepared to engage in a war with Germany, and those powers had at least as much interest as Great Britain had in the question at issue. My belief, as a private individual, was that we should let Germany settle the Danish question in its own way; and that belief I took no pains to conceal from any of the foreign ministers at Hamburgh, or from Baron Scheel-Plessen, M. de Könneritz, or any one else who asked me what I thought about it. I had not been officially instructed to hint at the possibility of a war, and I considered the Danes had no valid claim to our material co-operation. The parliamentary debates a few weeks later put an end to all mystery on the subject. The war had its partisans both in parliament and in the cabinet; but public opinion was upon the whole so strongly pronounced against it as to render it impossible. I have since observed that, in his late interesting sketch of our foreign policy[1], Lord Russell

---

[1] 'History of Ten Years of Foreign Policy. By John, Earl Russell.' London: 1871.

mentions as the chief reason for not going to war the non-concurrence of France. It was indeed a strong reason; but even if the French Emperor had been disposed to draw the sword, the objections to the validity of the treaty still remained, and I cannot conceive how a British minister could think himself justified in enforcing a law of succession which had never been either submitted to the legislature, or adopted by the people, of the country designed to be thus summarily disposed of.

When the Danes found that Great Britain had decided to remain neutral in the war, and that they could not secure the alliance of either France or Russia, they perceived the hopelessness of carrying on the contest any longer with the superior forces of the German powers. Their infatuated leaders had committed the folly of rejecting the overture of a federal reorganization made to them by the representatives of Germany at the late conferences in London. This was the very plan which I had recommended to Lord Clarendon in my report of 1857, and the reasons for its adoption were even more cogent for the Danish interests in 1864. The integrity of the Danish monarchy might have been preserved by a federal union resembling that of Sweden and Norway, and in some respects similar to that which has since been established between Hungary and the Austrian states. But Prussia counted upon the Danish obstinacy holding out to the last, and expected therefore that the proposal of a confederation would come to nothing. By accepting it the Danes would in fact have defeated the policy of Prussia, and at the same time closed the door to the Augustenburgh claim. As it was, Denmark had no other course left than to negotiate for peace, the preliminaries of which were signed at Vienna in the month of August following. She surrendered the three duchies of Schleswig, Holstein, and Lauenburgh, to Austria and Prussia as victors in the war, to be held and disposed of according to their joint will and pleasure. This joint sovereignty led to serious differences between the two great German powers, and became the proximate cause of the memorable war in Germany of 1866. For some time there was a *condominium* of the three duchies, which did not work well. Then Prussia took Lauenburgh to herself, paying Austria an indemnity; and it was agreed that she should rule in the duchy of Schleswig, leaving to Austria the government of Holstein. But this arrangement also was not destined to be permanent; the mutual jealousies and disputes gradually increased, and in the spring of 1866 it became evident that the Prussian govern-

ment had set its mind upon the possession not only of
Schleswig, but of both duchies.   It did not suit the views of
the Vienna cabinet to go into a war in this part of Germany,
and the Austrian brigade was therefore ordered to quit
Holstein, leaving the sole occupation of that duchy to the
Prussian forces.   During the period of their occupation, the
Austrians governed the country with humanity and discretion ;
the officers as well as soldiers made themselves liked, and the
people witnessed their departure with many expressions of
unaffected regret.

In September 1864 I was again in Berlin for the purpose of
ascertaining the disposition of the Prussian government in regard to the customs-tariff.   Some few modifications favourable to British interests had been made, and Great Britain
would at all events participate in the concessions made to
France under the commercial treaty with the latter power.
But Great Britain, having already reduced her own customs-
tariff within the smallest possible dimensions, had no equiva-
lents to give Prussia for any important reductions in favour
of her manufactures ; and all that we could reasonably expect
was to be placed on the footing of the most favoured nation
with respect to our trade with Germany.   Sir Andrew Buchanan, who was packing up for his new post at St. Petersburgh, had already communicated to the Prussian cabinet the
wishes of our government, and I did my best to support them
at the board of trade in Berlin.

I was so fortunate as to meet at Berlin my friend Baron de
Gerolt, the Prussian envoy at Washington, who had just returned home on leave of absence.   We talked of the civil war
in America, which Baron Gerolt had always foretold would
end in the discomfiture of the Southern states and the re-
establishment of the North-American union.   Having resided
twenty years at Washington his sympathies were entirely with
the North, and he knew the strength and resources of the republic so well as never to have doubted an instant of its eventual victory over the insurgents.   When he arrived in Berlin
a hint was given him that the King, as well as the princes,
had wished success to the cause of the Southern states, and
would have gladly seen a federal government erected under
Jefferson Davis, believing the men of the South to be more of
gentlemen, more conservative, and altogether better allies,
than the yankees of New England and Massachusetts.   But
Baron Gerolt was not deterred by such considerations from

speaking his mind freely both to the King and to the court and official circles in Berlin; and the result shewed that the judgment which he had formed was the correct one. I confess that my own sympathies, like those of most Englishmen, were in the outset of the contest on the side of the South. We saw in the proceedings of the United States legislature an infringement of the constitutional rights of the southern members of the union, and we did not sufficiently calculate upon the vast power of the republic, or upon the firm determination of its leading statesmen. Baron Gerolt had been on friendly terms with several successive presidents and secretaries of state, and described his post as an agreeable one on the whole, though he had had a great deal of trouble with questions of naturalization. Such questions are now happily set at rest, both for Germany and England, by the respective conventions which have applied to their subjects domiciled in the United States the laws of the country, according to which they are American citizens. Baron Gerolt had occupied his mind with geology and other branches of natural science, and kept up a correspondence with learned men in Germany, which was doubtless not less interesting than his official despatches. He had likewise studied the question of an international coinage, and made some valuable reports on the American monetary system. The retirement of Baron Gerolt, which took place very lately, was, as I understood, much regretted at Washington, where he was dean of the diplomatic corps, and generally respected.

The British chambers of commerce had for some time past been filled with apprehensions of the injurious effects of foreign tariffs, and according to evidence given in the last session before a committee of the house of commons, an opinion prevailed that enough had not been done by Her Majesty's government to induce foreign states to modify their restrictive duties and imitate the free-trade policy of Great Britain. In these circumstances Lord Russell desired me to repair to London, where I received instructions to visit the leading chambers of commerce in Great Britain, and to explain to them fully the system of the *Zollverein*, and its bearings upon British commercial interests. I proceeded accordingly to the north, and during the month of October attended sittings of the chambers at Leeds, Bradford, Newcastle-upon-Tyne, Manchester, Sheffield, Birmingham, and other commercial towns. My statements and explanations were well received by those bodies, and I was struck not only by the intelligence they displayed, but by the patience and calmness with which they

P

listened to my account of the difficulties which had impeded the progress of free-trade principles in the German states. Lord Russell communicated to me the satisfaction of Her Majesty's government with my proceedings, and when I took leave of him at the foreign office he said, 'I can tell you a good piece of news. I have just received information that the definitive peace between the German powers and Denmark was signed yesterday' (October 30th). On my return to Hamburgh I found the city full of Austrian and Prussian troops on their way back from Schleswig, and the federal troops were likewise very soon afterwards withdrawn from Holstein, so that at the close of the year the *status belli* in the duchies might be said to have ceased, whilst the jealousies between the two victorious German powers were beginning to take root.

The thousand years' commemoration of the death of St. Anschar, the patron saint of Hamburgh and Bremen, by whom christianity was introduced into northern Germany, was celebrated on the 3rd of February, 1865, by the catholics of these parts, with much devotion. The bishop of Osnabrück (Paul Melchers) came to Hamburgh to solemnize a pontifical mass on the occasion, after which he addressed the congregation from the altar on the life of St. Anschar, his merits, and works. The bishop with some of his clergy afterwards dined with me, and pleased the company by his simple manners as well as by the hilarity of his conversation. Speaking of the general tone of Hamburgh society, he said that so much luxury combined with the universal addiction to the pursuit of wealth were circumstances not very favourable to christian life, but he acknowledged the benevolent spirit which prevailed, and how much the citizens were constantly doing for the poor and for suffering humanity. Referring to the late conversion of an amiable and accomplished lady (the wife of the Russian minister), he said it should teach catholics to be instant in prayer for their protestant friends, who wanted God's grace in order to enable them to perceive the truth. How many hearts had been turned by an illness, or some unexpected incident of apparently small importance! The bishop recommended a book lately published by the bishop of Padderborn as likely to strike the attention of protestant readers who possessed candid and enquiring minds[1]. He was going the next day into Denmark in the midst of severe cold, but did not at all mind it, being used to travel a

---

[1] 'Ein bischöfliches Wort an die Protestanten Deutschlands,' von Dr. Conrad Martin, Bischof von Paderborn. 2 Bände. Paderborn, 1864.

great deal both in winter and summer. The career of bishop Melchers has been a distinguished one. Having originally studied law, he entered the judicial department of the Prussian service, and left it on account of the superior attractions which theology held out to him. After filling some subordinate clerical offices he became bishop of Osnabrück, to which the northern catholic mission was attached, and after the lapse of a few years he was promoted to the highest ecclesiastical dignity in Germany, viz. that of archbishop of Cologne. The archiepiscopal see was kept vacant for about a twelvemonth in consequence of the chapter wishing to elect bishop Keteler of Mayence, who was not entirely acceptable to his Prussian majesty. Eventually three names were submitted by the King to the Pope, and of these the holy father preconised bishop Melchers of Osnabrück to the archbishoprick in question. The choice was in all respects a fortunate one. The temper of bishop Melchers was mild and conciliatory, and he had tact enough to recognise the necessity of keeping on a good footing with the civil power. That did not of course imply that he would ever deviate from the strict line of his spiritual duty, or abate one jot or tittle from the rules of the canon law which it was his mission to enforce. But he had not the polemic inclinations of the bishop of Mayence, who has always been ready to break a lance in controversy, and represents the church militant more eminently than any other German prelate. It would be presumption in me to praise the great talents and energy of bishop Keteler ; no one can read his works, whether theological or political, without admiration[1]. His piety is fervent, and his eloquence irresistible. With all these qualities it is not difficult to understand why the Prussian bureaucracy should be a little afraid of him, and the King should have been advised to prefer a smoother kind of man to fill the first ecclesiastical dignity in his dominions. Hitherto the new archbishop of Cologne has been winning golden opinions in the Rhenish province. His duties, as I have heard, are very arduous, and his emoluments do not exceed a modest sum, equivalent to about two thousand pounds sterling per annum.

In the œcumenical council of 1870 most of the German bishops, and among them the archbishop of Cologne, and the bishop of Mayence, voted against the expediency of propounding any new decree with respect to the infallibility of the head of the church. They considered it so settled a point that the vicar

---

[1] See, for instance, the sermon ' Warum liebt der Katholik seine Kirche ?' von Wilhelm Emmanuel, Bischof von Mainz. Mainz : Kirkheim, 1863.

of Christ, speaking *ex cathedrá*, was free from error, as to render it useless and inopportune to raise a question which, with the exception of the Gallican church, was not disputed by orthodox catholics. They foresaw the agitation which would arise in Germany in consequence of the publication of a new catholic dogma, as it would appear to many persons, and therefore they counselled the holy father *quieta non movere,*— to let the matter rest as it was. But since the decree was adopted by the council, and officially published, no German bishop has for an instant doubted that it became his duty to act upon it, and to enforce its observance upon all those to whom the ecclesiastical jurisdiction extended. Hence the contest which has arisen with the professors of catholic theology in several of the German universities. The men of learning have been disposed to set up their own infallibility against that of the Pope, and have not been wanting in followers who even threaten to separate themselves from the hierarchy, and to form new religious communities. In other countries no such effect seems to have been produced by the new decree, which has been received by many catholics with indifference, and by still more in a spirit of pious submission to the teaching of the church of which they are members.

The interpellation made by Sir Harry Verney in the house of commons on the 7th of April was gratefully acknowledged by the Schleswig-Holsteiners, who will not easily forget the repeated exertions of the honourable baronet to promote the cause of their independence under their own duke. From the following letter it would appear that there was at this time in our parliament a general feeling of displeasure at the prospect of the duchies becoming appendages of the Prussian monarchy.

'32 *South Street, Park Lane,*
'April 20, 1865.

'My dear Mr. Ward,
'I am much gratified to learn, by your letter of the 12th, that what I said in the house of commons on the 7th gave any encouragement or comfort to the inhabitants of the duchies, or to any of them; but I would not on any account let them be deceived in the matter, I do not think it did them any good *here.* There was no one member in the house who in the slightest degree sympathised in my views; and the few who knew or cared anything about it thought that Sir F. Goldschmidt's reply to me was perfectly true,—that I, and the few M.P.'s who thought as I did, were to blame for

assisting M. de Bismarck and the Prussians for carrying out, as they would say, the views of ambition which alone induced them to engage in the Schleswig-Holstein cause. I had a conversation a few days since with the French ambassador. His opinion is, I gathered, that M. de Bismarck will be allowed to do just what he likes, that Austria will not interfere, and that without her the smaller states are powerless. Of course the French ambassador holds language which has been well considered and determined beforehand, and with a definite object,—probably that of encouraging Prussia to unjust and overbearing conduct, thus affording to Louis Napoleon the excuse or reason for taking the Rhine provinces, or whatever he can obtain, some day, as compensation to France for the augmented territory and power of Prussia. Unless there is some active stir against Prussia in Germany itself, I do not see what will prevent M. de Bismarck carrying out his views. I have always believed the King to be an honourable man and friend of the Duke of Augustenburg, and also the Crown-Prince ; but whether their influence will restrain the ambitious minister, and whether the Prussian chambers can, and indeed will, oppose him in this matter, is all unknown here, at least beyond ministerial circles.

'If you should think that anything said in the house of commons can be of any use in preserving for the Schleswig-Holsteiners their legitimate rights, I shall be very happy to endeavour to help them; but I cannot say that what has passed has been of the slightest use here. I never expected that it would, but I did hope that we might have got up something of a debate which would elicit strong opinions against the ambitious course pursued by Prussia.

'I entirely concur with you that by failing to support the side of justice and morality, we lose prestige and influence. But I must also add that nearly all the M.P.'s are convinced that the cause of justice and morality was that of Denmark as against the duchies, so that though they do not like Prussia, they are not inclined to the side of the Schleswig-Holsteiners.

'So, in my opinion, there is a bad look-out for our friends in the duchies. I should like to hear that the liberal party, not only through Germany, but in Prussia, took a strong part in favour of the Duke of Augustenburg. I believe that would bind the inhabitants to German interests more than anything else ; and I feel quite as anxious for a Germany united on all great German questions, internal and external, as for an united Italy.

'If the duchies fall under the domination of Prussia, I do not think that I shall visit them. I could do no one any good, and it would be painful to me to see it. If they were free, under their own duke, I should much like to pass a week or two there.

'I am very faithfully yours,
'HARRY VERNEY.'

The negotiation of our commercial treaty with the *Zollverein* called me again to Berlin in the early part of February. It was the season of festivities in the Prussian capital. The court, the princes, the ministers of state, and the diplomatic body, were giving balls or receptions every evening, and I had therefore opportunities of renewing my acquaintance with Berlin society. Lord Napier, who had for some months been installed in the British embassy, dispensed his hospitalities liberally, and had established his influence in the court circles. He took me at once to M. de Bismarck at his official residence in the Wilhelmstrasse, and I was welcomed by that minister with cordiality. M. de Bismarck said he readily acceded to the proposal of making a treaty of commerce with us, not only on account of the thing itself, but because it would be a means of perpetuating the friendship which happily subsisted between the two countries. For settling the details of the arrangement he referred me to M. Philipsborn, of the commercial department in the foreign-office, and to M. Delbrück, the director in the board of trade, remarking that, as he understood, Great Britain would be entitled even without the treaty to claim the benefit of the reductions of duties lately made in favour of France, as those reductions were likewise applicable to all states which had placed German commerce on the most favoured footing within their territories. Lord Napier having alluded to the possibility of the Hanse-towns acceding to the *Zollverein,* M. de Bismarck asked me what I thought of the state of feeling at Hamburgh in regard to such an accession? I answered that the chief difficulty would always be about the free-port. The leading Hamburgh merchants considered it essential to their interests to maintain complete freedom of importation and exportation within the city itself, the more so as large quantities of goods were imported as materials for manufactures, and worked up or improved on the spot for re-exportation. A good warehousing system might perhaps eventually answer the same purpose, but Hamburgh had no such warehouses as were used at British ports under the bonding system, and their construction would require a long time and a heavy outlay. M. de Bismarck then enquired whether Great Britain had any treaty of reciprocity with the Hanse-towns? I explained that we had an old treaty of navigation, but none of commercial reciprocity; that some preliminary discussions with a view to a treaty of commerce had taken place, although our government was not anxious on the subject, since free-trade was already in effect established in the Hanseatic ports, the greater number of goods being free of import-duties, and the rest being taxed at the low rate of a quarter per cent *ad valorem.* Here the conversation terminated. It was the only one which I had with M. de Bismarck in relation to our treaty. I saw him however several times afterwards, when he talked about matters unconnected with business.

As British plenipotentiary it was requisite that I should solicit an audience of the King, which was at once granted, and I went accordingly in uniform to the private palace *unter den Linden,* where his majesty lived when Prince of Prussia, and has continued to reside since his accession to the throne, the spacious royal palace being only made use of for state-balls, and other festivities on a large scale. King William was alone in his cabinet, and received me graciously. After expressing his satisfaction with the occasion which had brought me to Berlin, his majesty enquired how long I had been in the diplomatic service, and what posts I had held previous to that of Hamburgh? Understanding that I had been twenty-five years in Germany, he said, ' then by this time you ought to know something of our affairs; it is not always easy for foreigners to understand us.' The King then asked me how I liked Hamburgh, saying there were many friendly people there, and mentioned the names of some leading families. ' I shall never forget,' he added, ' my visit to Hamburgh in 1848, in order to embark there for England. The then Prussian minister, de Hänlein, was very attentive to me, and so were also several of the citizens.' On my saying I remembered M. de Hänlein when I was residing in Hamburgh in 1841, the King remarked, ' then I hope you dined with him, for he gave excessively good dinners. That however is no uncommon thing in Hamburgh; they keep good cooks and know how to give entertainments. Whom do you suppose,' said the King, ' to be the richest man in Hamburgh?' I replied, M. Charles Heine, the banker; but that M. John Henry Schröder, M. Gottlieb Jenisch, and several others, were known to be very wealthy, and it was difficult for a foreigner like myself to form a correct judgment of people's property. ' Oh!' said the King,

' I only mean with reference to common report.'   After some
further remarks about Hamburgh affairs, the conversation
(which was in German) ended, and the King dismissed me.
He was writing when I entered, and he then stood up and
remained standing during the interview, resting now and then
against the edge of a table.   Nothing was said about England
or English concerns, which I presume were reserved for the
ambassador.   King William, who was at this time in his
sixty-eighth year, struck me as looking hale and hearty, and
had so much elasticity about him that he might easily have
passed for being ten years younger than he actually was.

King William (now the German Emperor) has always been
more of a soldier than anything else.   He entered the army
young, served in the war against France, and with his father
Frederic William III, and the allied armies, marched into and
occupied Paris in 1814.   During the succeeding twenty years
of his father's reign his occupations were chiefly military, and
in 1840, when he became prince of Prussia, and heir-presumptive to the crown, his ardour for parades and manœuvres did
not relax, and he was regarded as one thoroughly acquainted
with the Prussian army, its discipline and condition.   His
character resembled that of his father.   Rather narrow-minded,
he had strong conservative instincts, and did not like the
notion of change either in civil or military affairs.   He was in
fact far less enlightened than his brother Frederic William IV ;
had read much less, and took comparatively little interest in
works of literature and art.   He was, however, clear and
straightforward in matters of business, and there seemed
nothing to prevent his making a good king of Prussia, at least
as good as his father, if his destiny should hereafter call him
to the throne.

The constitutional movement which prevailed more or less
in Prussia from the accession of Frederic William IV down to
the insurrection of 1848, was anything but agreeable to the
sentiments of the Prince.   He considered the best rule was
that of the sovereign, who had always the means of ascertaining
the wishes of his subjects through the annual assemblies of the
provincial states, and was disposed to accede to them whenever
it could reasonably be done.   But like the conservative party
in general the Prince was opposed to the introduction into
Prussia of a representative system like that established in
England and other constitutional countries.   Accordingly,
when the French revolution of 1848 had led to a rising of the
people in all the German states, and the inhabitants of Berlin

were fighting under barricades in order to compel the King to secure to them their liberties, the Prince of Prussia could have no sympathy with such proceedings, and his advice to the King would naturally be to concede nothing to the violence of the democrats, but to put down the insurrection by force of arms.

The King, after much wavering, declined to order the troops to fire upon the insurgents, and an arrangement was made with them to discontinue fighting, upon His Majesty's assurance that the troops should be withdrawn. The promise of a representative constitution to be settled by a national assembly followed, and in so far the revolutionary movement produced its fruits. But the people had set their mark upon the heir-presumptive, and reviled him bitterly upon the supposition that he was the irreconcilable enemy of the national cause. The Prince found himself obliged to retire to his villa near Potsdam, and to fly from thence to Hamburgh, where he embarked for England in a private manner. The Berlin mob heard with joy of his departure, and required all his tradesmen, who had inscribed his name or arms over their shops, to remove them immediately. A riotous assemblage appeared before the Prince's palace *unter den Linden*, making hostile demonstations and forcing the sentinels (taken from the civic guard) to quit their posts. But when a train of professors and students, headed by the rector, marched across from the university in order to protect the palace from violence, a workman stepped forward and chalked on its wall the words 'national property,' which gave occasion to Baron de Martens's placard intimating that the property of the nation ought, as such, to be respected by every honest citizen. Another working man mounted the balcony and fixed in it a tri-coloured flag, which remained there during the whole of the following summer. By these means the palace was saved, under the guise of national ownership, from destruction or damage, and time was gained by the government until the popular fury had abated, and the Prince was enabled to return with his family, and re-occupy the mansion without opposition.

The mob desired to turn the Prince of Prussia's residence into either a house of parliament, or an infirmary for invalid workmen. A commission for petitions, composed of three self-elected *chevaliers d'industrie*, took possession of it, installed itself in the Prince's apartments, and continued for some time to do all sorts of absurdities, without Count Arnim's government feeling strong enough to put an end to the farce. The so-called commissioners were however at length dislodged and thrown into prison. The recall of the Prince from London was officially announced, much to the dissatisfaction of the people of Berlin, who fancied that by his flight he had abandoned his right of succession. The Prince however returned, and on the 8th of June made his appearance in the national assembly, in uniform, to take his seat as deputy for the district of Wirsitz, by which he had in the meanwhile been elected. In the speech which he delivered on the occasion, the Prince declared his intention to observe the constitution, simply because it was the form of government prescribed by the King, and concluded with the motto of the reactionary party, ' For God, the King, and the Fatherland ! ' The speech was received with hisses, and the Prince retired from the assembly in disgust, never again to enter it. The blame of this unlucky incident was considered to rest chiefly with the prime-minister (then M. de Camphausen), who ought to have advised the Prince either to express himself with more tact, or to keep away from the assembly. But the revolutionary spirit was gradually cooling, both at Berlin, and in other parts of Germany, and by the end of the summer, the Prince was fully reinstated in his position, and residing again in his palace, as if he had merely left it on an excursion of pleasure.

During the nine years which intervened between the revolutionary crisis and his appointment to the regency in 1857, the Prince of Prussia moved and spoke so cautiously, that it was easy to perceive how much he had benefited by the lessons of experience. Having solemnly recognized the constitution of the 31st of January 1850, and taken his seat in the Prussian house of lords as a prince of the blood, he abstained from all reactionary attempts, and never lent himself to the designs of those who were trying to obstruct the policy of his brother's government. Indeed for some time before the King's illness began, it was believed by many that the heir-presumptive had become a liberal. Certain it is that he had acquired the good will of the liberal leaders, and that his palace was thronged with many guests belonging to the movement party, who were looked upon with little favour in court circles. The Count de Schwerin had become the confidential friend of both the Prince and Princess of Prussia, and a certain jealousy was observable in the King's palace of what was going on in the palace *unter den Linden.* So far as the Prince was concerned he had no talent for intrigue, and I have been assured by those who knew him that he was incapable of any underhand action against the King's wishes, and that he came to the regency pure in heart and actuated by the single motive of the national good.

The present Empress-Queen, when Princess of Prussia, shewed much talent for society, and liked to fill her saloons with persons of any importance, political or otherwise, so that she easily got the reputation of coquetting with the liberal party, and her conduct was upon the whole not agreeable to the Queen Elizabeth (now Queen-dowager), so that no love was lost between the two royal ladies. The Queen-dowager, as every one knows, is a most amiable and excellent person, but is less clever, either in conversation or observation, than the Queen Augusta, who is well fitted, both by her intelligence, and her charming appearance, to preside over a great court. When I was presented to her in February 1865, I could not but be struck by a certain personal fascination about her, which left its impression, although in the few questions which Her Majesty addressed to me, she said nothing out of the ordinary routine. I heard at Berlin that Queen Augusta was very charitable, and that she took a strong interest in the management of the many benevolent institutions which were under her especial patronage.

There are some who remember the visit of the Princess of Prussia to England in 1848,—what activity she shewed in inspecting many objects of interest, in company with the chevalier and madame Bunsen, and how much she pleased our court, and all who came into contact with her, by her fascinating ways. In a letter I received from Mr. Monckton Milnes (now Lord Houghton), dated Broadlands, September 20th 1846, I find the following passage:

'We had early in August, not a report, but a certain intimation in London, that the Prussian constitution was proclaimed at last. Little immediate good as I expected from it, I rejoiced it was out, and believed it must be left to mould itself according to the times and people; but now there seems no more chance of it than ever. In the meantime the Princess of Prussia is delighting everybody here who comes within her range by her beautiful manners, and tact of conversation.'

Among several pleasant dinner-parties to which I was invited in Berlin, I remember one at M. de Bismarck's, where I met the French ambassador M. Benedetti, and several of the corps diplomatique, also the minister of commerce, Count d'Itzenplitz, and other official persons. Count d'Itzenplitz, by whom I sat, spoke of our treaty as not really essential, but said that it gave them pleasure to gratify our government in the matter. He complained of the slow progress of the negotiations then pending for a commercial treaty between the

Zollverein and Austria, for which the Austrian privy-councillor M. de Hock had been for some time in Berlin. The Austrians, he said, were proverbially slow in business, but he had little doubt the affair would end satisfactorily, as it afterwards did. The Austrian policy of forming a customs'-union between the empire and the *Zollverein* had long since been shewn to be quite impracticable. After dinner M. de Bismarck took me round his suite of apartments, and shewed me some family portraits and other pictures. He spoke of English country life, which he said must be a most agreeable thing, and that he himself was fond of the country, and regretted that his official duties prevented him from spending more time upon his estates. He enquired how I liked Berlin, and said that the Prussian capital was really well off for good society. The court was very hospitable (as indeed I had experienced), and a man need never to be at a loss how to spend his evening. ' I have had a glimpse of London,' added M. de Bismarck ; ' your nobility are said to be rather exclusive, but London in the season must be very enjoyable.' He then reverted to Hamburgh, saying it was quite the metropolis of north-western Germany, and had wonderfully increased in wealth and population. To this I of course assented, observing that Hamburgh had become quite a centre of attraction to the land-owners and farmers of Mecklenburgh, Holstein, and Hanover, and that its annual horse-races were inferior to none in Germany. I also mentioned the successful agricultural exhibition of 1863, as an instance that Hamburgh was not less favourably situated in an agricultural than in a commercial point of view.

Although my personal acquaintance with M. de Bismarck (since raised successively to the rank of Count and Prince) was but slight, I have sufficiently followed his political career to be able to estimate his great ability as a statesman, and to appreciate the eminent services he has rendered to his country in a specific Prussian point of view. The Bismarck policy has aimed steadily at two objects,—the maintenance of the royal power, and the aggrandizement of the monarchy,—and in both of them, even before the war with France, it was attended with signal success, and its author had, more than any man in the country, acquired the right to say, ' *civis Borussianus sum !* '

Otto de Bismarck was born at Schönhausen in the old mark of Brandenburgh, in 1815, and was educated at a gymnasium, after which he studied law at the universities of Göttingen and Berlin[1]. Having entered the Prussian civil service, he rose to

---

[1] For an account of his family and early years see Hesekiel, " Das Buch von Grafen Bismarck," Elberfeld, 1868 (translated by Mackenzie, London, 1870).

be a referendary ; but in 1838 was called away by his military duties, which he went through in the chasseur-guards. He studied agriculture at Greifswald, and in 1839 took the management of the family estates in Pomerania, where he is said to have suffered from *ennui*, and disgust of life. At his father's death the two sons divided the property, and Schön-hausen with Kniephof fell to Otto's share. Although he went by the name of ' mad Bismarck ' in consequence of his pranks, that sobriquet did not prevent him from marrying, in 1847, an accomplished lady, Mademoiselle Johanna de Puttkammer, with whom he lived for some time at Schönhausen, and had three children. Some years afterwards he transferred his country residence to Varzin in Pomerania, an estate which he purchased, having taken a fancy to it from its being near the birthplace of his wife.

In 1847 M. de Bismarck became a member of the Prussian united-diet, and soon began to distinguish himself as a leader of the party of *Junkers*, or young noblemen attached to the conservative cause. His policy at this time was simply a defence of the King's sovereignty against the encroachments of the movement party. In the debate in the united-diet of the 3rd of April 1848, upon the address thanking the King for the constitution promised by him in consequence of the Berlin barricades of the previous month, M. de Bismarck opposed the address on account of the satisfaction it expressed with the course which events had taken, declaring that the new constitution could be accepted only as an inevitable necessity, and that tranquillity and order ought at any rate to be first re-established. In all his speeches his love for the Prussian army was perceptible; nor was he ashamed of being one of the *Junkers ;* on the contrary, he gloried in that appellation. As a member of the Erfurt parliament in 1850, he spoke against the proposed constitution of the new union as humiliating to Prussia ; and on this point he was an opponent of the views of General de Radowitz, because he believed that so long as Austria was hostile to the scheme, an effective union of the German states was impossible without a previous war. Rado-witz was in fact much too sanguine ; and as is well known, the Erfurt constitution proved a failure, nor was it possible even to lay a foundation for German unity until after the war of 1866, when the north-German confederation was called into life. That union will remain a proof of M. de Bismarck's steady devotion to Prussian interests. After waiting sixteen years he accomplished by force what the best German patriots, such as Gagern, Radowitz, Bunsen, and Stockmar, had in vain tried to bring about by negotiation, viz. an union of German states under Prussia to the exclusion of Austria, who was thereby obliged to give up her political influence in Germany, and to retire within the range of her own empire.

At the time of M. de Bismarck's appointment to be Prussian envoy to the Frankfort diet in 1851, the policy he had to carry out was that of antagonism to the Austrian cabinet, which, under Prince Schwarzenberg, and after him under Count Buol-Schaunstein, was working in concert with the secondary German states for the repression of Prussian ambition, and at least for keeping things in Germany upon the footing on which they had been re-established by the revival of the old confederation. M. de Bismarck followed his main object unremittingly for eight years, occupying himself also with incidental questions, such as that of the new constitution of the *Zollverein* after 1865, with a customs'-parliament, which he held to be indispensable. He likewise assisted the Duke of Augustenburgh in effecting a settlement of his pecuniary claims upon the Danish government. In 1859 he was sent as envoy to St. Petersburgh, from whence he wrote to a friend that the position of Prussia in the federal diet was becoming untenable,—that the defect must be headed *ferro et igni*,—and the mere abolition of the Germanic confederation was a desirable thing. Whilst at St. Petersburgh he received an intimation that it was King William's intention to nominate him to the premiership, but the appointment was postponed, and he went for a few months as envoy to Paris. In September 1862, however, the difficulties of M. von der Heydt's administration became so serious that the King found a change of policy to be unavoidable. M. de Bismarck was recalled to Berlin, named minister-president, and charged with a new administration, the task of which could not be an easy one, the house of deputies having just cut down the military budget by a sum of nearly seven million dollars, or about a million sterling.

The new premier began by withdrawing the unpopular budget for 1863, and went on for some time without any budget at all, by which was understood simply that he contented himself with an estimate equal to that of the previous year. On the 29th of September he delivered the memorable speech which has been so much criticized, declaring that political circumstances had made it necessary for Prussia to consolidate her power, and that the great questions of the day were not to be decided by talking and voting as in 1848, *but by iron and blood.* As minister during the campaign in Denmark in 1864 M. de Bismarck is entitled to share in the honour of the Prussian victory; and he conducted the subsequent negotiations with Austria until the *condominium* in the duchies was put an end to by the convention signed with Count Gustavus de Blome at Gastein on the 14th of August, 1865. In the following month he was created a count, having already received the order of the black eagle, the highest which the King of Prussia had it in his power to bestow. The war with Austria in 1866 was his act, and it is characteristic of him that he began it by ordering the Prussian columns to move twenty-four hours sooner than had been originally intended. His sovereign, whom he led reluctantly into the war, on its termination made him chancellor of the north-German confederation, (his own political creation), and a major-general in the army. Between that period, and the breaking out of the war with France in 1870, he enjoyed three or four years of comparative repose; but his great personal exertions had somewhat impaired his health, and during six months of the year 1868 he was detained by illness in his country-house at Varzin.

That Prince Bismarck is an able statesman in a specifically Prussian sense is generally admitted, nor can it be denied that his career has been thoroughly honest and straight-forward. He began his political life as a *Feudal*, and he has consistently upheld the feudalist banner inscribed, 'For God, the King, and the Fatherland!' The national armies, under his direction, have been covered with glory in three victorious campaigns; and something of a foundation has been laid for that German unity which is the chief object of the national wishes and prayers. But a great deal remains to be done in Germany before those wishes can be fully realized, and the fatherland be blessed with a really free and constitutional system of government.

When the territorial limits of the German states were settled at the Vienna congress in 1815, Prussia was left in the possession of such extensive dominions as to encourage the ambition of her rulers to acquire the hegemony of the newly-constituted confederation. For some years indeed Austria and Prussia went hand in hand, contenting themselves with taking measures to check popular movements, whilst Austria having the perpetual presidency of the federal diet was enabled to exercise a paramount influence over the deliberations of that body. But, after the popular rising of the year 1848, the political face of Germany was changed; and, although Frederic William IV

did not venture to accept the imperial crown at the hands of
the Frankfort parliament, Prussian statesmen perceived the
expediency of making use of the demand for national unity,
and made unsuccessful attempts to form a nucleus of states
depending upon, and directed by, the Prussian crown. The
rivalry between Austria and Prussia then became more obvious and striking; it was more than a dualism; it was an
antagonism which divided Germany into two hostile camps,
and which M. de Bismarck, as well as other less sagacious
persons, soon foresaw must lead to a war. But, in 1850,
Prussia not feeling herself strong enough to encounter her ad-
versary, the crisis passed over, and as the result of the Dresden conferences, the old federal diet was restored to life, and
the Austrian influence was again in the ascendant. Austria
had, as before, not only the presidency of, but the majority of
votes in the diet, so that she possessed, as in the time of
Prince Metternich, the legal means of directing the foreign
and domestic affairs of Germany. The four kingdoms, viz.
Bavaria, Würtemberg, Saxony, and Hanover, were her sted-
fast allies; and they agreed that the ambition of Prussia
threatened them with danger, and was at all events to be kept
down. It was indeed not unknown to Austria and her allies,
that the federal diet was excessively unpopular, and that its
proceedings were considered by thinking men a very inade-
quate expression of the national will. A congress of sovereigns
was therefore summoned at Frankfort in 1863, at which the
Emperor Francis-Joseph appeared, surrounded by the other
German sovereigns, with the exception of the King of Prussia,
and a plan of federal reform was propounded, which like that
of the old diet, would have continued to secure to Austria
the majority of votes in the assembly. The refusal of Prussia
to concur with any such scheme indicated clearly enough that
the dualistic government of Germany was approaching its
end. The Austrian party had succeeded in preventing Prussia
from forming an alliance with other German states, but it had
not succeeded in establishing any satisfactory form of federal
government for the whole of Germany. M. de Bismarck
therefore began to prepare for war, for which a pretext was
soon found in consequence of the line taken by the federal
diet in regard to the Schleswig-Holstein succession, and of
the differences with Austria arising out of the joint conquest
of the duchies, which purported to have been settled by the
treaty of Gastein.

In refusing submission to the federal diet the conduct of
Prussia was of course not legally justifiable. She had no

right to take forcible possession of either Hanover, Hesse, Holstein, or the free city of Frankfort, or to compel by menaces the accession of other states to the north-German confederation. The Bismarck policy in Germany was in fact revolutionary, and was founded upon the assumed necessity of taking up arms, in order that the Prussian monarchy might not be crushed by Austria and the states of the Austrian coalition. The result proved that, with her well-disciplined army, and needle-guns, Prussia had no reason to be afraid of any European power, and people began to find there was within that kingdom a master-spirit, equal alike to the exigencies of war or peace, who brought back to remembrance the vigorous and unscrupulous doings of a Frederic the Great.

Hitherto the people of Germany have gained little by the brilliant victories of the Prussian armies. The principles of the Frankfort constitution of 1849 have not yet been established, and securities for personal liberty are yet wanting in all the German states. There is indeed a German parliament; but the local diets are suffered to co-exist, and every petty sovereign is suffered to send and receive diplomatic representatives. The press is not free, and public meetings for the redress of grievances are still forbidden. In fact the measure of constitutional freedom existing in Germany is very incomplete, and there is no reason for believing that Prince Bismarck has any particular desire to promote its extension. The liberal members of the national parliament, however, console themselves with the reflection that a foundation has been laid upon which a solid edifice of German unity and constitutional liberty will be one day erected. They may not be wrong in indulging such hopes, but will assuredly have to exercise much patience before they witness their accomplishment. Prince Bismarck cares little about constitutional development, whilst he cares a great deal about a large and effective federal army, and insists upon the maintenance of such an army by the states of the confederation.

Our commercial treaty with the *Zollverein* was signed at the foreign office at Berlin on the 30th of May. No presents or orders were exchanged or offered on the occasion. On account of the great number of decorations enjoyed by M. de Bismarck and the other Prussian plenipotentiaries, it was proposed by them to omit in the treaty all notice of decorations on both sides, which we agreed to, Lord Napier observing with a smile that the omission was rather hard upon us, as he and I possessed only one order each. A supplemental

treaty of navigation with Prussia was afterwards concluded at
Gastein on the 16th of August, to remain in force for twelve
years, being the same term as that stipulated in the treaty of
commerce.   By these conventions our trade was placed upon
the footing of the most favoured nation in the ports of the
Zollverein, and a concession was made to us, which was regarded at the time of much importance, to the effect that
British trade-marks should enjoy in the German states exactly the same legal protection as those belonging to native
subjects.

Whilst our negotiation was going on at Berlin, overtures
were likewise made to Austria to enter into a commercial
treaty with Great Britain, which, in the outset, were attended
with the greatest difficulties, but in the autumn of the same
year resulted in a convention which placed our trade on the
footing of the most favoured nation in the Austrian dominions,
and thereby secured to us the benefit of the reduction of
duties recently conceded by Austria to France.   This was the
work of Mr. (now Sir William) Hutt, M.P., then vice-president of the board of trade, who went himself to Vienna as
the first British member of the mixed commission of preliminary enquiry, and by the influence which he judiciously
exercised with Count Mensdorff overcame the obstacles perti-
naciously raised by the protectionist party.   The language of
our chief commissioner to the Austrian minister was this :—
' England does not ask for favours of any kind, and will make
no bargain.   Frame for yourselves and in your own interests
a good financial and commercial tariff, and you will meet all
the requirements of England.   France will demand reductions
of duties on certain articles of her produce which may or
may not coincide with the well-being of your own affairs.   We
favour trade, but no particular section of our industry, and
except to secure such things as most-favoured-nation treatment we do not want any treaty.'   The object sought by
Great Britain was thus wisely and clearly explained to the
imperial government.   The impediments and chicaneries
which had to be vanquished will be understood by a perusal
of the two following letters with which I was favoured by Sir
William Hutt.

' Vienna, June 1, 1865.

'My dear Ward,

' Your letters, always welcome, came to me when I was in
the agony of a crisis which I will explain to you.

'Commercial reform is making proselytes here, and generally, without the commission, affairs were going well. Not so in the commission itself. De Kalchberg, who put the Austrian part of it together, merely asked a few men, generally unfit for it, to act on the commission, without making any condition with them that they should attend to its duties. The consequence was that some never attended the sittings at all, some came in a very disloyal spirit, and four resigned their places on frivolous pretences. Then the president kept no order, never carried out the votes of the commission, and had no protocols. After many vain attempts to put a little order into this confusion, I saw that the whole thing was in a state of collapse, and that it never would be productive of any good. Accordingly I went to Count Mensdorff and apprised him of my conviction, and of the necessity of a complete reconstruction of the international commission, and of giving it a new basis of operation; I added that as I was not sent to Vienna *pour jour une comédie*. Unless my views in all these respects were adopted and acted on I should request to be recalled. Of course there was a great ferment, but it has ended in the capitulation of the government. I am to have, I believe, all I asked for, and a treaty into the bargain. The treaty will consist of most-favoured-nation engagement, reduction of various duties, a maximum duty for the tariff, which will greatly simplify the *enquête*, and other stipulations for facilitating it. I learn these facts unofficially, but I believe they are real ones. This is the courier day, and I have been writing all the morning the explanation and defence of my conduct to the foreign office. I know all the horror such proceedings will excite there, having been undertaken and carried out without orders from home, but I really had no choice in the matter. If I had referred home, I should have lost the opportunity.

'You will understand from all this that at present everything is in the way of dislocation,—perhaps myself included.

'Yours very truly,
'WILLIAM HUTT.'

'*Paris*, July 2, 1865.

'My dear Ward,

'I am here on my way home for a couple of months. The commission is adjourned, as you will have heard, and as I will explain to you. I go to be re-elected and to look after the election of others in my neighbourhood. I have no opposition.

'Well, now for Vienna. When I last wrote to you I was in the ferment of a crisis; I found that de Kalchberg was only trifling with us, and that the hope he had dangled before the British government of arriving by the *enquête* at a commercial treaty with us, he never designed to fulfil. His was the de Hoch policy, though he pretended something else. I saw this, in the course of time, but saw also that in following up his crooked purpose, Kalchberg had unconsciously committed the Austrian government to more than he was aware of. So I immediately broke up the commission and declared to Count Mensdorff, whom I had partly converted and whose goodwill towards me I had secured, that I should at once return to England, unless the imperial government would re-construct the Austrian commission as I pointed out and give it a definite and practical programme. He admitted the fairness of my demand, and finally it has been arranged that I am to have my own way, that every protectionist in the cabinet is to be turned out of it, and that in their stead men of real ability and knowledge, approved by me (it is ridiculous, but the fact amounts to this), are to be appointed. This settled, we have adjourned to let our purpose as to ministerial changes be accomplished. I have received for this decided and un-authorized proceeding the warm approval from home. But what I did not expect has also occurred: I had been compelled to say rough things to the imperial government; Count Mensdorff has sent a complimentary despatch to the British government on the conduct of the chief commissioner, with the thanks of the cabinet. On the 1st of September we are to begin matters in earnest. Two things only can now prevent success to the entire satisfaction of the free-traders: · Mensdorff, the prime minister, may be overpowered; and the French may step in before our *enquête* is concluded, and thus the special alterations in the tariff of Austria, bargained for by France, may be given us, with the most-favoured-nation engagement, as the only possible provisions of our treaty; which, however, in itself will be no unimportant gain.

'Such are the facts. They surprise me when I contemplate them. You will see that I had a good deal to do with the dislocation of the Vienna cabinet, which has created surprise. I do not enter into the Hungary question. I do not quite understand what is intended. I hope it is more than a spasmodic effort, and part of a well-considered policy.

'Yours very truly,
'WILLIAM HUTT.'

Dobberan is one of the liveliest of the sea-bathing places on the Baltic, and is much frequented by the Mecklenburgh country gentlemen with their families. We passed some weeks of the summer of 1865 at the *Heilige-Damm,* an assemblage of from fifteen to twenty houses between the beech-wood and the sea, distant four English miles from the town of Dobberan. The Grand-duke of Mecklenburgh, who usually makes it his summer residence, was absent this season on account of the recent loss of his wife ; but the Grand-duchess dowager (sister of the King of Prussia) was there, as well as Prince Hugh Windischgrätz, whose first wife was a sister of the Grand-duke, and who was rather a favourite of the *Heilige-Damm* society. The amusements consisted of the theatre and the gaming-tables at Dobberan, and there were horse-races, at which good running was to be seen. The Mecklenburgh breed of horses has long been famous, and the equipages of the land-owners shew what handsome cattle they are able to turn out. All the arrangements at Dobberan were under the direction of the Grand-ducal intendant, the Baron de Suchow, whose polite attentions to the guests were generally acknowledged.

The novel of this season was decidedly Freytag's ' Lost Manuscript[1],' his best since ' Debit and Credit,' which had a still greater run. The search after the missing manuscript, and the discussions relating to it, give the author an opportunity to draw the characters and describe the manners of the German professors, which he does remarkably well. There is also a good deal about court ways, and the petty German princes are exhibited not altogether in an unamiable light, but in a manner which does not increase our respect for either the dignity or utility of such personages. Freytag's novels are rather long and heavy, though they contain some excellent pictures of social life in Germany.

When I went to reside at Hamburgh I expected more visits from passing travellers than I eventually received. English tourists now use the direct steamers to the Elbe comparatively little, preferring the routes by Ostend or Antwerp, which enable them to enter Germany by way of the Rhenish province. Now and then, however, an intelligent traveller used to turn up, and this year we were gratified by a visit from Mr. E. A. Freeman, the learned author of the history of the Norman conquest in England, who took great interest in

[1] ' Die verlorene Handschrift. Roman in fünf Büchern, von Gustav Freytag.' 3 Bände. Leipzig, 1864.

the subject of the Hanseatic league and the past and present
condition of the Hanseatic cities.   We discussed the questions
of the probable annexation of those cities to the Prussian
monarchy, or of their inclusion within the limits of the
Zollverein, and we agreed that such changes might be convenient and beneficial to Germany, but that it was not so
clear they were desirable in the interest of the Hanse-towns
themselves.   Subsequent experience has shewn that Hamburgh
and Bremen have had to submit to very heavy annual pay-
ments for the conservation of their free ports, whilst Lubeck
has entirely lost that privilege, and been reduced to the same
footing as the Prussian Baltic ports.   It is possible certainly
that some political advantages may accrue to the Hanse-
towns from their having become members of the new German
confederation, but such advantages belong rather to the future
than to the actual order of things.

Mr. Freeman was acquainted with the works of our distinguished Hamburgh archivist, Dr. Lappenberg, and was
desirous of conferring with him, but he was absent at Munich,
having promised his assistance to an undertaking which
created much interest in the German literary world, and in
particular among historical scholars.   King Maximilian of
Bavaria had called into life a historical commission, designed
chiefly for the collecting and editing of the early historical
monuments, such as chronicles, songs, &c., extant in the
archives of the several cities in Germany, above all of his own
dominions, which include, in Franconia and elsewhere, so
many ancient free imperial towns.   Professors Cornelius,
Döllinger, and others, formed a committee for the arrangement
and distribution of the work ; and in this committee Lappenberg, as the literary representative of the Hanse-towns, had an
honoured place.   He either prepared or edited a Hanseatic
contribution to an undertaking which, when completed, will
rival the publications of the old English record commission,
the interruption of which Lappenberg, among others, deeply
regretted.   Dr. Lappenberg died in the following November, at
the age of seventy-one, very highly and generally respected in
his native city.   I had long been in the habit of friendly intercourse with him, and had found him a high-minded, straightforward gentleman in all his relations.   His Edinburgh
education had given him advantages possessed by few German
professors.   It had made him more a man of the world, and
had induced him to take an unusual interest, as a foreigner,
in English affairs.   It had likewise instilled into him some
Scotch prejudices.   I remember his arguing that Mr. Turn-

bull, as a catholic, was an improper person to be employed as keeper of the records at the Rolls-chapel, and that he rather rejoiced when Mr. Turnbull was forced to retire from the office, for which he admitted him to be otherwise well qualified. The fact is that Lappenberg had a great deal of the old ' no popery' feeling about him. He feared and disliked the catholic church, and spoke with still more contempt of the romanizing protestants, who he said had broken with the reformation without having the courage to go back to the old faith. Lappenberg left behind him a considerable property, and always lived in very good style. His sons continue to reside at Hamburgh.

Among the many pleasant diplomatic dinners which I have enjoyed at Syndic Merck's elegant villa at Blankenese, I remember one about this time, when I met Dr. Rudolphus Schleiden, who then held the post of Hanseatic minister-resident in London. There was much talk about the late treaty of Gastein, and of the new position of the duchies in consequence of the arrangements made there by the two great German powers. Dr. Schleiden considered it an unsatisfactory one, and thought the states ought to have been consulted in regard to the succession, and the future permanent settlement of the country. He hoped that Austria and her allies would still prove strong enough to protect the rights of the house of Augustenburgh, but seemed to fear that the ambition of Prussia might induce that power to try a *coup d'état* in order to get possession of both duchies for herself. Syndic Merck said he saw a war looming in the distance, and did not believe the Gastein arrangements would be of long duration. An opinion lately given by the Prussian crown-syndics was referred to, who had maintained that King Christian IX had as good a title to the duchies as to the rest of his dominions, and that he was in a condition to make a legal cession of them to Austria and Prussia by the treaty of peace. Dr. Schleiden said that this opinion was laughed at by the best German lawyers, who all agreed that the succession to the duchies passed to the Augustenburgh male line after the extinction of the royal line of Denmark with Frederic VII. The Prussian law-officers had probably not been uninfluenced by the wish to promote the Prussian policy, for it was evident that a cession by the King of Denmark of a right he never possessed was null and void. Whether Austria and Prussia had a title by conquest was another question ; but even if they had it was their moral duty to restore the territory to its legitimate sovereign. Reference was made to a claim lately made to the duchies by the Grand-duke of Oldenburgh, but nobody believed in it, and the Grand-duke had never had any kind of support from the Schleswig-Holsteiners themselves.

· I cannot mention Dr. Schleiden's name without a tribute of respect to the high character for political integrity which that eminent person has long borne in Germany. A native of the duchies, and in the employ of the former Danish government, he was banished with many other good patriots at the termination of the first civil war, and after a time entered the diplomatic service of the Hanseatic cities. For several years he was *chargé d'affaires* at Washington, and on the retirement of Dr. Rücker, became minister-resident in London, where his talents and exertions were duly appreciated by the Hanseatic governments. When the Hanse-towns joined the north-German confederation, after the war of 1866, Dr. Schleiden very gallantly threw up his post on the ground that he could not be the useful servant of states which had surrendered their independence into the hands of a greater power; and returning to Germany he became a member of the national parliament as representative for the town of Altona, in which capacity he has not ceased to watch over the interests of the duchies, and to labour with disinterested devotion for the good of the fatherland. As he did not choose to belong to the so-called national liberal party,— the habitual supporters of the Bismarck policy,—Dr. Schleiden has never been a favourite in the court and official circles of the Prussian capital.

The Augustenburgh family resided at Nienstetten on the Elbe side during the summer and autumn of 1865, and we had frequent opportunities of intercourse with them. Duke Christian, the father, gave up his own villa to his son, Duke Frederic, and lived in an adjacent house with his duchess, who was in infirm health, and his three daughters, the princesses Augusta, Amelia, and Henrietta. The Duke Frederic, who had with him his wife, the Duchess Adelaide, niece of our gracious sovereign Queen Victoria, and three .beautiful children, entertained company at the villa, and was on a friendly footing with his neighbours, particularly with M. Cæsar Godeffroy of Dockenhude. That gentleman, who is one of the Hamburgh merchant princes, and lives in a very handsome style, had always been a supporter of the national cause in the duchies, and was on intimate terms both with Duke Christian and his son the present duke. The princesses enjoyed their proximity to Flottbeck-park, the seat of Madame Jenisch, famous for its fine old trees, and for a conservatory

and flower-garden which would not suffer by comparison
with those of any English mansion.

Christian, Duke of Schleswig-Holstein-Sonderburgh-Augus-
tenburgh (born 1798 and died 1869), was the lord of a fief in
the duchy of Schleswig, extending over some twenty English
square miles, and including fourteen thousand inhabitants, in
which the chief seat was the ancient castle of Augustenburgh,
now a Prussian barrack, in the island of Alsen.   Early in life
he was fond of horses, and in order to encourage horse-breeding,
took great pains to establish races at several places in Holstein and Schleswig.   He likewise gave a prize annually until
his death for competition at the horse-races of Hamburgh.
He became a member of the assembly of the states in 1836,
when he shewed much public spirit, particularly in endeavouring to reform the taxation of the duchies, by substituting an
income-tax for the customs and personal imposts.   In the civil
war against Denmark he put himself at the head of the popular
cause, and asserted his right of succession to the ducal crown
after the extinction of the royal Danish line then represented
by Christian VIII.   The result of the war was the banishment
of the Duke from the country, and the sequestration of his
estates, for which (as previously mentioned) a pecuniary indemnity was guaranteed to him, and which he eventually received.
After this the Duke lived chiefly at Gotha, and at Primkenau
in Silesia, where he had purchased an estate.   He latterly
began to re-invest money in the duchies, and purchased the
fine property of Gravenstein near Flensburgh in Schleswig, on
which stands an enormous mansion used by the Prussians as a
hospital during the campaign of 1864.   The Duke had some
Danish blood in his veins, his mother having been the
daughter of King Frederic VII.   He married Louisa Countess
of Daneskiold-Samsœe, who died two years before him.   That
lady not being of royal descent, it was pretended by the
Duke's political adversaries that the marriage excluded him
from the right of succession.   The question was however investigated by competent lawyers, who reported that there was
nothing to be found in the laws of the duchies which debarred
the issue of such a marriage as that contracted by Duke
Christian with the lady referred to.

Duke Christian and his duchess Louisa had five children,
viz. Duke Frederic, born in 1829, who, in consequence of his
father's renunciation, acquired the right to succeed to the
ducal crown ; Prince Christian, the fortunate husband of our
Princess Helena, born in 1831 ; and the three amiable and
accomplished princesses already noticed, who have never

married, although report says that opportunities have not been wanting, but the aspirants were not of the rank deemed essential by the head of the family. Duke Christian bequeathed his property both real and personal at his death to his eldest son, subject to a moderate provision for his younger children.

The Duke's only brother Frederic, commonly called the Prince of Augustenburgh-Nöer from the name of his estate, was born in 1800, and was likewise a member of the assembly of the Schleswig states, where in most questions he took the popular side. He also consistently maintained the rights of succession vested in the family, although, unless the two sons of Duke Christian should be excluded, he had not himself any chance of wearing the crown. The Prince of Nöer married the Countess Henrietta of Daneskiold-Samsœe, sister of his brother's wife, and had by her a son, Prince Frederic, born in 1830, who has resided some time in London, and is known as an oriental scholar to the learned world. In 1864 the Emperor of Austria legalized Prince Frederic the father's assumed title, by creating him in due form Prince of Nöer; and having become a widower, he married secondly Miss Lee, an American lady, and died not long afterwards. The orientalist has therefore succeeded to the title of Prince of Nöer, and represents the younger branch of the Augustenburgh family.

In several conversations which I had with Duke Frederic on the position of affairs in the duchies, he told me he intended to persevere with his claim so long as the people of the country wished to have him, and remarked upon the injustice of not assembling the states and consulting them previous to a definitive settlement. Almost all the landed-proprietors and former members of the Schleswig and Holstein diets had declared themselves individually in his (the Duke's) favour, and it was well known that Austria, as well as the secondary German states, were satisfied with the validity of his hereditary title. The difficulty was created by Prussia alone, and the situation, notwithstanding the Gastein arrangements, looked far from promising. I asked the Duke how it was that the negotiation which he had entered into some months since with M. de Bismarck had so completely failed, and enquired whether it was too late to endeavour to find a solution of the difficulties which had impeded an understanding with the Prussian government? He said it was hopeless; for the Prussian ministers were predetermined not to concede his claim; and, if the objections respecting the allegiance of the military could have been got over, the Prussians would have invented others rather than come to an arrangement with him. The King of Prussia had always been his friend, and would gladly have seen him installed as reigning duke ; but Count Bismarck and the Berlin officials had other views, and had intimated plainly enough their wishes to turn Holstein and Schleswig into Prussian provinces. Berlin however was not yet Germany, and it remained to be seen whether a cause which had the warm and decided support of the German nation would not in the end prove triumphant ? The Duke's assertion of the ambitious spirit which animated the Prussian bureaucracy was, I believe, perfectly correct. When I was last in Berlin I had talked to several leading official men about the duchies, and found them all impressed with the conviction that no time ought to be lost in annexing the country to the Prussian monarchy.

At a dinner-party at Duke Frederic's at Nienstetten, the recent death of Lord Palmerston, and the probable effect of that event upon the foreign policy of Great Britain, formed the subject of discussion. The Duke said Lord Palmerston was a great minister in so far that he knew England well, and understood how to act in accordance with the national opinion, but that he had always had a strong leaning towards the Danes and the Danish cause. Senator Godeffroy, who was present, referred to a proposal made by Lord Palmerston some years ago for the division of Schleswig, and remarked that the Danes had by this time discovered their error in not accepting it, as well as in refusing the offer made to them at the London conference to re-constitute the monarchy upon federal principles. The Danes appeared to the senator to have been an impracticable set of people throughout the whole affair. I concurred with this view, and regretted that Lord Palmerston had not thought it right to exercise a little more compulsion upon the Danish cabinet, in order to make them comply with the demands of the German powers. I added that Lord Palmerston's decease was not likely to bring about any material change in British foreign policy, and that the new premier, Lord Russell, was distinguished for his love of justice, and his sympathy with the constitutional rights of other nations. For myself, I could not but regret Lord Palmerston's loss. He gave me my first appointment under the foreign-office, and was uniformly kind to me in after years. I suppose no minister ever made more personal friends. He had great administrative abilities, and the power of easily mastering political questions. His name was long a bugbear to foreign governments, which erroneously supposed him to be much more of an agitator on the continent than he really was. Nor was he ever an active reformer of domestic abuses until public opinion began to set strongly against their continuance. The office of a minister in these days has been described by an intelligent German professor to be ' to prepare an easy birth for the future, and a decent grave for the past.' In this sense Lord Palmerston played his part well. He excited no popular movement, but held himself ready to give effect to the national wishes at the right time, and when the country had become ripe for the introduction of a new order of things.

Lord Russell did not leave the foreign-office without acknowledging the services I had rendered in respect of the commercial treaty; and in consideration of them I was raised to the rank of minister-resident. This circumstance gave much gratification to the Hanseatic governments, as fifty years had elapsed since a British minister had been accredited to them in the person of Mr. Alexander Cockburn at the peace of 1815. I proceeded to Lubeck and Bremen, to deliver my credentials, and was invited to complimentary dinners at which the health of my august sovereign was drunk with every demonstration of respect and attachment. I found that at both places an uneasy feeling was prevalent in consequence of the differences between Austria and Prussia, which were regarded as anything but settled by the treaty of Gastein. The King of Prussia had lately visited Ratzeburgh, the chief town of the duchy of Lauenburgh, in order to receive the homage of the states of that duchy, which had been given up to Prussia upon payment of an indemnity to Austria for her share of the joint dominion; and a deputation had been sent from Lubeck to Ratzeburgh to congratulate the King on becoming so near a neighbour of the free city. I asked the senator Dr. Curtius, who was one of the deputation, whether he did not think the proximity of so ambitious a power might under certain circumstances prove dangerous to Lubeck? He replied, ' Perhaps so; but we must always behave to so inevitable a neighbour as if he were in reality our best friend.' Before the lapse of a year the independent sovereignty of Lubeck had ceased to exist, and its territory was included within the limits of the north-German confederation.

Madlle. Tietjens, who was accustomed to pay Hamburgh an annual visit, came there in the early part of this winter, and gave us an opportunity of hearing her still powerful voice, both in the theatre and in the concert-room. This great artist was born at Altona in a humble station of life, and by her extraordinary talents has raised herself, as is well known, to the first rank among the *prima donnas* of the European opera. Her portly figure conveys the impression of friendliness, and she combines amiability of manners with a most benevolent heart. She has always been very kind to her poor relations, and on this occasion was accompanied by her sister, who like herself began life in a humble way. We met Madlle. Tietjens at the house of M. Hayn, one of the leading senators, where she was treated with the respectful attention which her splendid talents deserve. She was said to have realized a considerable fortune, and the chief object of her annual visits to Hamburgh was understood to be to look after her pecuniary affairs, and to invest money through the medium of a mercantile friend who acts as her trustee, and has always given her judicious advice. She was expected to retire to Germany after the conclusion of her theatrical career.

The Hamburgh opera is not upon the whole in a flourishing condition. The theatre is a spacious building, and the orchestra a good one, but the attractions of the performers are not in general sufficient to fill the house, and it is only when stars like Tietjens, Lucca, Artot, Wächtel, or Niemann appear, that there is a great demand for places, although on such occasions the prices of admission are doubled and trebled. The citizens of Hamburgh will not go to the opera-house unless there is something good to be seen and heard ; the consequence is that the manager is always in difficulties, and the management continually changing hands. The senate grants no subvention either to the opera-house, or any other theatre,—contrary to the customs of the German kings and princes, who invariably subsidize a court-theatre in their respective capitals, whether large or small. The Duke of Saxe-Coburgh, for instance, is a liberal patron of the theatres at Coburgh and Gotha, although the wealth and population to be found in his dominions are very inferior to those existing in the Hamburgh territory. The result of the Hamburgh theatre being neglected by the state is that a number of small places of amusement have sprung up where theatrical performances of a low kind are given, rather to the detriment of the public morality and taste. I do not of course include among such establishments the Thalia theatre, which, although on a small scale, has deservedly earned a high reputation for its acting in tragedy, comedy, and farce, and where the regular drama has been successfully represented from the days of

Lessing and Klopstock down to the present time. Up to a late date the opera-house was limited to musical, and the Thalia to dramatic pieces, but those restrictions are now removed, and performances of whatever character may be given at either theatre. There are likewise winter concerts at Hamburgh, which are well attended, and where the best instrumental and vocal music is made accessible to the amateurs of the art.

Lord Napier, after having held the Berlin embassy for about fifteen months, retired at the close of this year, and went into another branch of the public service, having been appointed Governor of Madras. His lordship had shewn much diplomatic ability, had acquired the confidence of the King, and stood well with Count Bismarck and the other members of the Prussian cabinet. His resignation was therefore to be regretted; the more so as the motive was understood to be the inadequacy of the ambassador's salary, which at that time was only £6,000, but has since been raised to £7,000 per annum. Previous to his leaving Berlin, Lord Napier wrote me a kind farewell letter, which I here subjoin.

‘ *Berlin*, December 20th, 1865.

‘ My dear Sir,

‘ First let me congratulate you on your well-earned elevation to the rank of minister, which must have been pleasing to yourself and to all your friends and colleagues.

‘ I have lost no time in making the proper application to the Foreign Department, and I have sent in copies of your letter and the Dundee Memorial.

‘ Yes, we are on the eve of starting for a far country and a very novel kind of employment. The place was offered to me two months before Lord Palmerston's death, and had nothing to do with ministerial changes. I was chiefly influenced in accepting it by pecuniary considerations, yet I confess the business, and the change of life and scene, have also their charms.

‘ Good bye; I wish you every prosperity, and believe me

‘ Very truly yours

‘ NAPIER.’

‘ John Ward, Esq., C.B.’

CHAPTER X.

DURING the first months of the year 1866, the differences between Austria and Prussia seemed to be continually increasing, and in Hamburgh the opinion prevailed that Prussia would attempt a *coup d'état* or some act of violence for the purpose of appropriating both Schleswig and Holstein to herself. This was evidently the wish of the Prussian feudals and officials, but the King was believed to entertain scruples both as to the general policy of a war with Austria and in respect of the rights of the Augustenburgh family. Austria continued to make great military preparations, and the common notion of the strength of the Austrian army was such that few persons out of Berlin supposed Prussia to be capable of making head against the combined forces of the confederation. Some feeble attempts at mediation were made by neutral powers, and a congress at Paris was projected, but came to nothing. For several months the German newspapers spoke of the crisis of civil war, as if a crisis were a progression of events instead of being their culminating point. The crisis of a disease is its turning-point for better or worse, and the political differences in Germany did not reach such a point until the early part of the month of June, when the war actually began. The Prussian cabinet had decided upon seizing Holstein, and every one was anxious to see whether Austria would permit it, as she had the power of re-inforcing her brigade in Holstein by sending fresh troops thither through the territory of Hanover, her faithful ally. She did not however take that course, and as soon as a Prussian force passed from Schleswig into the north of Holstein, field-marshal de Gablentz withdrew his brigade to Altona, and from thence marched immediately southwards, leaving the Prussians in quiet possession of both of the duchies.

Our government had in the meanwhile made some changes in the British diplomatic posts in Germany, the motives of which excited more speculation in that country than they probably deserved. Lord Augustus Loftus, who had the first claim to an embassy, was promoted to be ambassador at Berlin, and Sir Henry Howard, our envoy at Hanover, replaced him at Munich. The mission at Hanover was given to Sir Charles Wyke, whose whole official life had been passed in Mexico and South America, and he held it for the few months which intervened until the annexation of the former kingdom of Hanover to the Prussian monarchy. An opinion prevailed that Sir Henry Howard, who had formerly been secretary of legation at Berlin, and had acquired experience in German affairs, was destined for the Berlin embassy, and certainly there was no diplomatist in our service who was more generally liked, or had superior qualifications for the dignity of an ambassador. I have, however, no reason to believe that Sir Henry was dissatisfied with the post actually assigned to him at Munich.

The federal diet having now determined upon a war against Prussia, the Prussian government cut the knot of its relations with the other states by formally retiring from the confederation. On the 14th of June, General de Manteuffel was inspecting troops at Wandsbeck and the parts of Holstein adjacent to Hamburgh; and on the 15th a Prussian army crossed the Elbe into the Hanoverian territory, and occupied Harburgh. We in Hamburgh were surrounded on all sides by the Prussian forces, and news arrived that they were occupying not only Hanover, but Saxony and Hesse. Austria and her allies were said to be concentrating their forces near Frankfort-on-the-Main, from whence a line of conjunction would be made with the Austrian armies already in Bohemia, but we learned nothing certain of the confederate movements. On Sunday the 17th I visited the Prussian war-steamer *Arminius*, then lying in the Elbe, in company with the Prussian minister. Baron de Richthofen, who gave me some details of the fighting in Hanover, but knew nothing yet of what was passing in southern Germany. He told me that he felt confident of procuring the accession of Hamburgh to the newly proposed north-German confederation.

The plan of a new federal constitution was communicated by Prussia to the smaller states of northern and central Germany at the outset of the war. Lubeck and Bremen acceded to it without much difficulty, but the senate of

Hamburgh shewed more reluctance, and the Syndic Merck stoutly opposed it as long as he was able. The Prussian government, however, threatening to abolish the Senate and to take possession of the city, all further resistance on the part of Hamburgh became hopeless. The Senate had the fate of Frankfort before its eyes,—a city which had been guilty of no crime beyond that of adherence to its federal engagements, and had been treated with a degree of harshness well calculated to terrify the other free cities of Germany into a speedy acceptance of the conditions of the new constitution.

In such circumstances the Austrian minister to the Hanse-towns, Baron de Lederer, had no other alternative than to retire from his post, and indeed he had some apprehensions lest he might not be able to escape from a city so completely surrounded by the enemy's forces. I took charge of the interests of Austrian subjects with Lord Clarendon's approval, and continued to act as Austrian minister for about a twelve-month. The charge gave me some little additional work, but I accepted it with pleasure, in order to shew disapproval of the violence with which Prussia was suppressing the rights of the Schleswig-Holsteiners, and of the small German states. It is possible that much good may ultimately arise out of these compulsory arrangements; still the acts of Prussia were re-volutionary; and I saw no reason why the British repre-sentative in the Hanseatic cities should display any sympathy with the power which had forcibly deprived them of their independence, and had put an end to an order of things which was working well for British interests, and indeed for those of the whole commercial world.

In the midst of these troubles Prince Christian of Schleswig-Holstein came to Hamburgh in order to embark for England, where his marriage with the Princess Helena was about to be solemnized. The prince, as well as his sister the Princess Amelia, honoured me with his company at dinner, and I invited a small party to meet him. There was much talk about the war, the results of which it was not yet possible to foresee. The Austrians had defeated the Italian army at Custozza, and the Prussian victories in Bohemia had not yet been gained. The cause of the duchies was therefore not hopeless, and many persons still indulged in the agreeable vision of their independence under Duke Frederic. Prince Christian, who was little disposed to enter into politics, embarked the next morning with his aide-de-camp, Count Ranzau. I took leave of them on board the *Helicon* war steamer, which was

R

waiting in the Elbe to convey them to England. The heat was above 25° Reaumur.

Within a few days afterwards the news of the Prussian successes came upon us, and after the brilliant victories of Nachod, and Sadowa, the fate of the campaign was evidently decided. The intelligence of the cession of Venetia by Austria to the French Emperor, and of the latter personage having been requested to mediate a peace, was unwelcome to the Hamburgh exchange, because it seemed to admit the dangerous principle of the French right to interfere in German affairs. The prospect of a peace was however satisfactory, and after the Prussian forces had twice defeated the Bavarians in their own territory, an armistice was agreed upon, which led to the conclusion of a definitive treaty of peace at Prague on the 23rd of August. Austria not only ceded Venetia, but consented to be thenceforth entirely excluded from the Germanic body, and to pay Prussia a large pecuniary indemnity. The intrigues of the French government procured the insertion of a clause recognising the right of Prussia to both Schleswig and Holstein, with the reservation that the inhabitants of the northern districts of Schleswig should be re-united to Denmark if they should freely express their desire to that effect. This clause has been supposed to have been intended to serve as a pretext for a future war between the allies of Denmark and the German powers. After the formal cession of both duchies to Prussia and Austria by the King of Denmark in 1864, it was absurd to suppose that Germany would give back to the Danes any considerable portion of Schleswig, much less the districts of Alsen and Düppel, which had been so gallantly wrested from the Danes by the Prussian arms. The clause, moreover, was difficult to carry out on account of its ambiguity. Nobody knew what were meant by the 'northern districts' of Schleswig, or how many of the inhabitants were to be included in the permission which the treaty purported to have in view.

The Austrian army in Holstein had made itself liked by the people of the duchy, and the officers stationed at Altona and Kiel were gladly received into the society of those places. The Austrians have a certain *bonhomie* about them which usually makes them friends wherever they go. General de Kalik, who commanded the garrison of Altona, was detained there by illness when the Austrian army quitted Holstein, and died in the month of July following, leaving a young widow, who was inconsolable for her heavy loss. The inhabitants vied with each other in offers of assistance to her, and demonstrations of respect. The funeral was attended by the local authorities, by several members of the diplomatic body, and many leading citizens both of Hamburgh and Altona. I followed it, in my capacity of Austrian minister, as chief mourner, though I had no personal acquaintance with General de Kalik, and had, in fact, never seen him. I felt myself in a singular position; but I found that my presence was expected; and the gratitude of the afflicted lady more than repaid me for such small services as I was able to render her.

Ostend, as a sea-bathing place, is very much frequented by German families. The extensive sands make the bathing safe and pleasant at all times of tide, and the large concourse of persons male and female who assemble together in the water is an amusing spectacle. We spent some weeks of this summer there, and found the long journey from Hamburgh well repaid. Among the guests were the King and Queen of the Belgians, the Queen of Würtemberg, and General Prim with his family. The Queen of Würtemberg, whose noble physiognomy and commanding figure reminded one of her father, the Emperor Nicholas, was in ill health, and very pale and emaciated. She had apartments in the house of her physician, Dr. Verhaege, the learned author of several treatises on the curative influence of the sea, its phosphorescence, and other qualities. He considered that the benefit derived from sea-water arose chiefly from its electricity, and that on that account it was more desirable to bathe in the waves than in still water. Queen Olga did not, of course, mix in the general society of the place, but had a private room reserved for her in the large glass-house on the dyke, which served as the *Kursaal.* General Prim was surrounded by a number of Spanish gentlemen, with whom he held daily consultations, and was doubtless preparing the plans which ended in the expulsion of the Bourbon dynasty from Spain. The general had a swarthy, soldierlike look, with a pensive expression of countenance. He was rather intimate with Prince Couza, the ex-hospodar of Wallachia, and the two might be seen daily pacing the dyke together in conversation. One of the most influential persons in Ostend was the burgomaster, M. van Iseghem, who knew all that was passing, and was ever ready to assist strangers with information and advice. The king was said to place much confidence in him.

An excursion to the ancient city of Bruges could not but suggest some thoughts on the mutability of human greatness. From being the commercial *entrepôt* of the Hanseatic league, and the centre of the Netherland's cloth trade, it has dwindled down into an ordinary provincial town, though still including within its walls spacious palaces, and magnificent churches— the monuments of its ancient grandeur. It was under the dukes of Burgundy that Bruges appears to have reached the summit of its splendour. It then commanded the trade of northern Europe, and counted 200,000 inhabitants. In the year 1486 the traffic was such that a hundred and fifty foreign ships used to pass up the canal from Ostend in a single day, and arrive at Bruges to discharge their cargoes. At the same period there were consuls resident in Bruges of no less than seventeen foreign nations. Of the many churches we visited, the cathedral of the Holy Saviour, the chapel of the holy blood, and the church of Our Lady, in which are preserved the inimit- able marble group of the Virgin and Child, the work of Michael Angelo, and the beautifully sculptured tombs of Charles the Bold, duke of Burgundy, and his daughter, the Princess Mary. Among the charitable institutions existing in Bruges, there is one of peculiar interest to English catholics, viz. the orphanage of St. George, founded by Mr. Arthur Robinson and his sister, who have not spared expense in the erection and maintenance of their philanthropic establishment, and have devoted them- selves to its superintendence with a rare and truly christian zeal for the welfare and improvement of the destitute inmates.

Stopping for some hours at Hanover on my return to Hamburgh, I found the city occupied by a Prussian garrison, and a Prussian civil commissioner for the government of the newly acquired province domiciliated in the house formerly tenanted by the British legation. The kingdom of Hanover, so long allied to Great Britain by personal unity of the sovereign, and by family ties, had been for ever suppressed, and the king was an exile in the Austrian dominions. The indemnity promised to King George by the Prussian govern- ment was ultimately fixed at sixteen million dollars, or about £2,400,000 sterling, exclusively of his property in England. The King of Prussia, having already appropriated Schleswig- Holstein, had formally announced to the two houses of the Prussian legislature, the further annexion to the monarchy of the territories of Hanover, Hesse-Cassel, Nassau, and Frankfort. Saxony had been spared at the special intercession of the Austrian emperor, but upon the condition of her acceding to the North German confederation ; and the aged King John was permitted to return to Dresden, not indeed as an inde- pendent sovereign, but with some outward show of royalty, and with the general respect and sympathy which could not be refused to his dignity of character, and the honourable fulfilment of his federal obligations.

Count Bismarck returned to Berlin after a long absence towards the close of the year, and arrangements were then made for the settlement of the constitution of the new confederation by means of a German parliament, which was elected in February 1867, and met soon afterwards. This parliament, which was in fact a constituent assembly, sat in Berlin, and discussed, paragraph by paragraph, the project of a federal constitution for the states concerned, as submitted to it by the Prussian government. The project was adopted with little opposition on the 16th of April, and took effect as law in the Hanse-towns, and most other states, on the 1st of July following. I proceed to recapitulate its leading enactments.

The North-German confederation, thus constituted, was composed of twenty-one northern and central German states, in addition to the Prussian monarchy. There was to be a common *indigenat* for all the states, so that the natural-born subject of any one of them became *ipso facto* naturalized in all the others, and was to enjoy equal rights throughout the territory of the union. After this important alteration, it was declared that certain affairs, particularly specified, should be deemed federal, and should be regulated by common legislation only. These were—

1. Matters relating to settlement and citizenship, the removal from state to state, passports and police jurisdiction, insurance and emigration.

2. Customs and commercial legislation, and federal taxation.

3. Weights, measures, coinage, and paper currency.

4. Banks and banking.

5. Patents for inventions.

6. Protection of literary property.

7. Common protection of German commerce in foreign countries, and of German ships and their flag at sea, with common consular representation.

8. Railways, roads, and canals.

9. River navigation, and river tolls.

10. Posts and telegraphs.

11. Mutual execution of judicial sentences.

12. Mutual attestation of public documents.

13. Common legislation and procedure in matters of penal, and of commercial, law.

14. The federal army and navy.

15. Medical and veterinary police.

Such were to be the objects of federal legislation, and the legislature was to consist of a federal council (*Bundesrath*), and an imperial parliament (*Reichstag*), presided over by the King of Prussia, as the central executive authority.

The federal council was to comprise forty-three votes, of which seventeen were assigned to Prussia. Resolutions might be passed by a simple majority, and if the votes were equal, Prussia, as president, had the casting-vote. The president had the sole right of making war or peace, of concluding treaties with foreign powers, and of sending and receiving diplomatic agents ; but all treaties concerning federal objects would require the subsequent assent, both of the council and of the parliament. The summoning and closing of both these bodies belonged to the president, who was to name a federal chancellor to conduct the business; an office which was, of course, conferred upon Count Bismarck. The parliament was to be elected by universal suffrage of the adult male population, and by secret voting. The federal territory was divided into electoral districts of about 100,000 souls ; so that the number of members elected to the parliament was rather less than three hundred. They were to serve three years, and were not entitled to remuneration. The parliament, like the council, might resolve by a simple majority ; but, in case of any alteration of the constitution, it must be agreed to by two-thirds of the votes of the latter body.

The constitution then proceeded to lay down certain principles of legislation, applicable to the various federal matters above particularized. The military budget was voted for four years and a half; viz. until the 31st December, 1871. Every able-bodied man must serve in the army for seven years, from the end of his twentieth to the beginning of his twenty-eighth year ; of which three years under colours, and three years in the reserve, after which he was to belong for five years more to the national militia (*Landwehr*). The strength of the army on the peace footing was to be taken at one per cent. of the population, which would give a federal force of about 300,000 men. The annual cost of each soldier was reckoned at two hundred and twenty-five dollars, or £33 15s. sterling; and each state was bound to pay over to the King of Prussia, as federal commander-in-chief, a sum equivalent to that cost multiplied by the number of soldiers which such state was liable to furnish. The federal forces were placed at the entire disposition, and under the sole command, of His Prussian Majesty, as commander-in-chief, whether in peace or war.

Subject to the modifications made in consequence of the accession of the southern states, at the close of 1870, the constitution thus introduced has remained in force. It consolidated the military power of Prussia as the head of the union, and established national unity in a number of matters affecting the social intercourse of the people, and their material well-being. But it did little or nothing for securing the liberty of the subject in Germany ; it did not guarantee either a free press, or the right of public meetings ; it did not proclaim the equality of all classes of society before the law ; in short, it made no mention of those important constitutional principles which were enunciated in the 'fundamental rights' (*Grundrechte*) of the German people, adopted by the Frankfort national assembly, and published by the Archduke John as *Reichsverweser*, on the 27th of December, 1848. The new constitution permitted the continuance of the local legislatures, or diets, of all the separate states ; and it also permitted the separate governments to send and receive diplomatic agents at their discretion. The centralization, therefore, which was aimed at by patriotic men in 1848 and 1849, was very far from being completed, and the North-German union was regarded by the liberal party rather as a *basis* capable of further extension, than as an actual realization of the long-cherished wants and wishes of the German nation.

The party of Austria and the secondary states, mortified and indignant at their defeat, exclaimed against the violation by Prussia of international law and federal engagements, and denounced Count Bismarck's policy as altogether revolutionary and unjustifiable. Among the many treatises and pamphlets on this subject, which issued from the press, Bishop Keteler's work on Germany since the war of 1866 excited much attention. The bishop pointed out the great evils which must result to society from the utter disregard of the principles of justice and morality by the Prussian government. Its partisans, said he, sought to vindicate all sorts of wickedness, because such acts were alleged to be in the future interest of Germany. To defend them, we ought to be prepared to defend likewise the crimes of the first French revolution, and of all the other revolutions which have since disturbed the peace of society, and retarded its progress in virtue and happiness.

It will be the office of future historians to pass judgment on Count Bismarck's public acts, and to decide whether the circumstances in which his country were placed were such as to justify the apparent violations of public morality with which he is chargeable. It may be true that Prussia found herself cramped and inconvenienced by being subject to the laws of the old Germanic confederation; but she voluntarily entered into that confederation in 1815, and renewed her engagements after the Dresden conferences of 1851. The motives which influenced the Berlin cabinet were specifically Prussian, and its policy was directed to the exclusion of the Austrian hegemony from the Germanic body. This was forcibly accomplished, and the power of Prussia immeasurably raised, by her victorious campaign of 1866. Still the moral question has not been satisfactorily solved. Is a state at liberty to withdraw from international treaties, when such treaties are found inconvenient to her own ambition? The same question has recently been raised by Russia, in a case of less importance certainly, but calculated to excite alarm in the minds of those who had been accustomed to regard treaties as sacred and inviolable compacts between civilised states. Are we approaching a time when might will be generally acknowledged to go before right, and when mankind will be content to secure their peace by the same means as the creatures of flood and field alluded to by the poet?

> ' For why ? because the good old rule
> Sufficeth them, the simple plan.
> That they should take who have the power,
> And they should keep who can [1].'

The present German confederation, even since its extension to the southern states, as Count Bismarck's creation, bears, of course, a specifically Prussian mark, and is too limited in its provisions to satisfy the nation for any length of time. Of this the various sections of the liberal party are fully aware, and it will rest with them to impress upon their federal head the necessity of enlarging and improving the work which has been begun. Frederic William IV did not dare either to accept the imperial title, or the Frankfort constitution of 1849. His successor has become German Emperor with the unanimous assent of the German people; and it would seem to be now his mission to put the nation into full possession of the political liberties for which it has so many years been struggling, and which its intelligence thoroughly qualifies it to enjoy and to exercise.

Baron de Richthofen, the Prussian envoy to the Hanse-towns, having procured their formal accession to the new confederation, was transferred to Stockholm. He was an amiable and conciliatory man, but it was presumed at Berlin

---

[1] ' Rob Roy's Grave.' Wordsworth's poetical works, vol. iii. p. 127.

that another person would be more agreeable to the Hanseatic governments than one who had been made the instrument of requiring them to surrender their independence. In the month of May, M. de Richthofen received his friends for the last time, on the evening before his daughter's marriage, called in Germany the *Polter-Abend*, which is usually the scene of much merriment, and is sometimes diversified by *tableaux vivans* and theatrical performances. The Germans always enjoy such festivals, and the ladies like to be invited to inspect the bride's *trousseau*, and admire the wedding presents which she is pretty sure of receiving. The next day I attended the wedding of the Spanish consul, which was celebrated by a great dinner, on the day of the ceremony, at the house of the bride's father, a merchant in Hamburgh. Toasts were drunk, and speeches delivered, pretty much as in England. The marriage being a mixed one, both the catholic and the protestant pastors were invited to the dinner, and entered heartily into the hilarity of the festival.

The Frisian islands, on the west coast of Schleswig, being included within the limits of the duchy, became Prussian with the rest of the Schleswig territory. The principal islands are Föhr, and Sylt, which are much frequented for the purpose of sea-bathing. Having visited Sylt, and some other parts of Schleswig, in the summer of this year, I subjoin a few extracts from my travelling journal:—

August 8th.—To Husum, and dined. Thence by steamer through the group of the north-Frisian islands to Föhr, and on to Sylt. At Wyk on Föhr there are good hotels and lodging-houses; but the bathing establishment has the disadvantage of not facing the German Ocean, as it does at Sylt. We reached the point of Nörse on Sylt at 10 p.m., and after a rough drive in the bright moonlight, reached our lodgings at Westerland about midnight. The village of Westerland lies on the west side of the island, and near it is the bathing place on the ocean, where there is usually a swelling surf.

August 9th.—Surveyed the country, which consists of heath and sand, without any trees. There is nothing but sea between us and the coast of the English county of Durham in the same latitude. To the light-house, and the red cliff. Rye, barley and oats are grown here, but no wheat. The houses are small, and all built alike. The peasantry, or small proprietors, are said to be well off, and there are scarcely any paupers. In the winter season a great deal of wool is knit into stockings, and other garments, which are exported for sale in Germany.

August 12th.—The devastation made by the successive inroads of the sea upon the Frisian islands is very remarkable. Three hundred years ago the group contained double the surface of land which now belongs to it; for instance, on Hornum peninsula, which forms the southern part of Sylt, I saw a village called Rantum, consisting of six houses only. The ancient church and village of Rantum were situated several English miles west of the actual coast, and were swallowed up more than two centuries since; another church and houses were built, further east, on a part of the coast now covered by downs, or sand-hills, and this second Rantum was gradually smothered by sand, and disappeared in the beginning of this century. The present miserable village of that name lies on a grassy plain, a little to the south-east of the spot where the church of the second Rantum formerly stood. In all probability, the whole of the long tongue of land called Hornum is destined to be swamped by the violence of the sea. There is an old geographical description of Schleswig and Holstein, by Caspar Danckwerth, burgomaster of Husum,[1] in which a great deal of information on the past state of the north-Frisian islands is to be found; and their history has been brought, with much industry, down to the present time, by a resident in Sylt, Mr. C. P. Hansen.[2]

August 13th.—To Keitum, the capital of the island, a small town, lying on its eastern coast. Visited Mr. Hansen, who has a sort of museum of curiosities, and is much occupied with antiquarian researches. He told us that, according to his estimation, the north-Frisian islands, before the great flood of 1634, comprised a surface of 100,000 demaths (the demath being equal to 180 square roods), and that the group now scarcely comprises 50,000 demaths. The island of North-strand contained, before that flood, 40,000 demaths of land, and now only 6000. Whilst the islands had thus suffered, the mainland on the opposite coast of Schleswig had gained something from the sea, for the marshy districts of Tondern, Eider-stedt, &c., comprise 30,000 demaths more land than in 1634. Mr. Hansen thought that the inroads of the sea upon the western coast of the island were likely to go on, and that Wester-

---

[1] 'Neue Landesbeschreibung der zweii Herzogthümer Schleswick und Holstein,' von Iohanne Mejero chorographice elaborirt, durch Casparum Danckwerth D. zusammen getragen und verfertigt: in folio. Husum, 1652.
[2] 'Das Schleswig'sche Wattenmeer und die friesischen Inseln,' von C. P. Hansen auf Sylt. 8vo. Glogau, 1865.

land and its bathing station might not be very long in safety; but that at Keitum and the eastern coast, the sea appeared to be rather receding, so that eventually the island would gain on the one side what it might lose on the other.

August 15th. – The group of islands of which Sylt is the largest is sometimes called the north-Frisian outland (*Utland*), and the sea in which it lies the *Wattenmeer*,—a term scarcely translatable, but the *Watten* mean the tracts of sand and mud emerging at low water. The group contains a series of islets named the *Hallige*, mere patches of land in the midst of the water, covered with green grass washed by every tide, and inhabited by a few families who dwell in houses raised on hillocks of turf, or supported by piles of wood driven into the wet soil. A recent storm had swept away the entire crop of hay from one of these *Hallige*, and a piteous appeal for assistance was made by the pastor on behalf of the inhabitants, who had thus lost the whole of their year's harvest, and would be forced to sell their cattle to provide themselves with subsistence. These pastors on the *Hallige* were, as I was informed, young lutheran ministers, who were expected to serve an apprenticeship in these desolate places before they were promoted to more remunerative livings upon the mainland.

August 18th, Sunday.—Drove to List, a Danish village on the northern point of the island, from whence there is a fine view over the Ellenbogen to the island of Rom. The road lay mostly along the shore, and I never saw so many sea-fowl. Passed the Vogel-koje, the property of a company, where wild ducks of various sorts are decoyed, and preserved for eventual sale. It is the only spot on Sylt where a few trees have been reared, and they do not appear to thrive.

List was a little Danish colony on which the Danish government had bestowed some care, for they had erected a church and school-house, and eleven children were in the course of being *danized*, when the operation was interrupted by the restoration of this part of the island, after the war, to the duchy of Schleswig to which it properly belonged. We found the Danish schoolmaster superseded by a German, and the German language restored to official and clerical use. The arrangement by which the northern portion of Sylt, a part of Föhr, and the whole of the little island of Amrum, were treated as Danish *enclaves* belonging to Jutland, was very properly put an end to when the whole of both duchies was ceded by Denmark to Austria and Prussia in 1864.

August 27th.—By steamer from Monckmarsh across the smooth Frisian sea to Hoyer, and thence to Tondern and

Flensburgh, the largest town, next to Altona, of both the duchies. The *Fiord*, or harbour, resembles that of Kiel; but the country is more beautiful, and the rising ground on which the houses and gardens are seen from the water reminded me of my native port of Cowes in the Isle of Wight. There is here a Danish church, and a considerable Danish population, which occupies the north part of the town, leaving to the Germans the southern side. The Danes proved the strongest at the first election to the German parliament, and they will doubtless carry their candidates at the second election now approaching.

August 28th.—We took the steamer which runs down the Fiord from Flensburgh to Sonderburgh on the island of Alsen. Passed the castle of Glücksburgh, the ancient residence of the Dukes of Schleswig-Holstein-Sonderburgh-Glücksburgh, a plain old building looking very white in the gleams of sunshine. The Glücksburgh line is the second in legitimate succession to the crown of the duchies after that of Augustenburgh, and its present head is the Duke Charles already mentioned, whose younger brother Prince Christian has been King of Denmark since 1863. We had a good view from the sea of the battle-field of April 1864; but having landed at Sonderburgh, we crossed over to Düppel, examined the remaining entrenchments, and surveyed the surrounding country. The spot will long be memorable in Prussian annals, and I cannot suppose Count Bismarck to be the man to give it up in order to satisfy the Danish interpretation of the ambiguous clause in the treaty of peace.

August 30th.—To Schleswig and Kiel on our way back to Hamburgh. At the former town saw the castle of Gottorp, once the residence of the Dukes of Schleswig-Holstein, of the Gottorp line. It has a spacious park and gardens, and is now used by the Prussians for barracks and government offices. This has been the fate of more than one royal and ducal mansion within the duchies. The cathedral has a beautiful altar-screen, richly carved by Bruggemann. In the ducal vault we saw the coffin of the lately deceased Duchess Louisa, mother of the Glücksburgh princes, and grandmother of our Princess of Wales. In the deep harbour of Kiel, the Prussian fleet was lying at anchor, but the interest of the inhabitants was absorbed in the election to the German parliament which had just taken place. Kiel had shewn itself to be anti-Prussian; and indeed of the whole number of deputies chosen in the two duchies, there was scarcely one who could be considered a supporter of Count Bismarck's administration. Two

Danish deputies were elected in the northern districts. The rest were good Germans; but they felt disappointed at not having recovered their independence, or their legitimate duke; and had not yet reconciled themselves to their country having been transferred from one master to another without its wishes and feelings being asked or consulted, through the medium of the states, or in any other manner.

I met at Sylt Professor Hallier of Jena, whose entomological researches, and discoveries as to the nature of cholera, and the causes of its propagation, have gained him some celebrity. The conversations which I have had with him and other scientific men suggest some reflections on a subject of the utmost importance to the present and future interests of the whole human race.

There is a philosophical school in Germany composed of naturalists, chemists, and metaphysicians, whose members agree in explaining everything in nature upon atheistical principles. According to them matter is eternal, and the world goes on of necessity without the intervention of any supernatural being. Power is inseparable from matter, and the energy which maintains the world and everything in it is derived from the substance of which the universe is composed. There is no matter without power, nor any power independent of matter. Thought is a power of the brain; there is no soul without a body, and consequently no future state of existence for men. As a good compendium of the atheistical doctrines in question I may refer to the little work of Dr. Büchner, entitled, 'Power and Matter [1],' which quotes the opinions of a number of eminent writers of the day against theism, and in contradiction to the notion of the world having been created out of nothing by an Almighty hand. I subjoin a few instances:

'Power is not a God thrusting itself against anything; it is not a substance separated from a material foundation   It is the quality inseparable from matter, residing in it from all eternity. A power not bound to matter, but hovering freely over it, is quite a vain idea. Nitrogen, carbon, hydrogen, oxygen, sulphur, and phosphorus, have had their peculiar qualities in them from all eternity.'—*Moleschott.*

'If we go to the bottom of the question we must admit that there is no such thing as either power or matter. Both are

---

[1] 'Kraft und Stoff,' von Dr. Louis Büchner in Darmstadt. Dritte Auflage. Frankfort a. M. 1856.

abstractions, taken from different points of view, of things as they are. They complete and presuppose each other. Isolated, they have no real existence. . . . . . Matter is not like a carriage of which the horses can at some times be put to, and at others unharnessed. A bit of iron is, and certainly remains, the same thing, whether in a meteoric stone it makes the tour of the world, or in the wheel of a steam-carriage glides along the rails, or in the blood-cells runs through the sleep of the poet. These qualities are from eternity; they are not to be parted with; not transferable.'—*Dübois-Reymond.*

'No power can arise out of nothing.'—*Liebig.*

'There is nothing in the world which authorises us to pre-suppose the existence of powers in themselves, without bodies from which they spring, and upon which they work.'—*Cotta.*

'Electrical and magnetical appearances arise, like light and warmth, according to our experience, out of the reciprocal relations of bodies, molecules, and atoms. . . . . . An absolute nothing cannot be thought of.'—*Czolbe.*

'Nobody has ever ventured to maintain that the power of secretion could exist separately from the glands, or that of contracting apart from the muscular fibres. The absurdity of such an idea is so striking that it cannot for a moment be thought of in connection with the organs mentioned.'—*Vogt.*

'Through a knowledge of the working of nature's unchange-able laws will the soul be set at rest, and in harmony with the whole of nature, and be purified from that superstitious fear which arises from the supposition that powers out of the order of reason might interfere with the eternal progress of nature.'—*Oerstedt.*

'The earth, as a material existence, is in fact without end; only the changes which it has experienced may be in some measure determined by periods of time that have their ends. . . . . All that may be said of the destruction of the world is about as vague as the myths about its beginning which have been invented by the childish imagination of the early nations; the earth and the world are eternal, for that quality belongs to the very existence of matter. But the world is not un-changeable; and, therefore, because it appears changeable, the short-sighted view of men, who are not enlightened by scientific enquiries, has deemed it also finite and transitory.'—*Burmeister.*

'Physical science has calculated, that as a time once existed when the earth was without organic life, so also in a future lying immeasurably distant from us a time must and will come in which the existing stock of natural powers will be exhausted, and therewith all that lives on earth must return to death and night. Against such facts, in what light must appear all those high-trotting declamations, unworthy of any rational man, about the general purposes of the world being developed in the creation of mankind, about God becoming man in history, about the history of mankind as the self-revelation of the absolute, the eternity of consciousness, the freedom of the will, and the like? What is the whole life and struggling of men individually, or together, in the face of this eternal, inexorable, irresistible, partly casual, partly necessary, course of nature? The short play of a one-day-fly hovering over the sea of eternity and of a world without end.' —*Helmholtz.*

'The external and superhuman God is nothing else than the external and supernatural self,—the subjective being of men released from its bonds, and placed above its objective being.'—*L. Feuerbach.*

'If philosophy means to be the science of actual things, it can only go the way of the knowledge of nature, and seek in experience the objects of its enquiry and ascertainment. It will then become natural science both in contents and method, and will be distinguished by its objects from the philosophical schools which pursue transcendental objects, viz., the investigation of the plan of the world, or the discovery of the absolute; whilst the true enquiry into nature follows concrete ends, and considers as its chief mission the ascertainment of the essence of the individual. For the example of all times has taught it how fruitless were the efforts of former ages to find the universal,—how hopeless is the way to the absolute.'—*Virchow.*

I have thought it worth while to give these extracts as a key to the atheistic doctrines which are prevalent among a large class of German philosophers. There is another set of learned men who have adopted a modification of atheism called pantheism, regarding God as the soul of the world, which pervades and animates it in the same way as the mind vivifies the human body. Goethe was a pantheist; so was Lord Byron; and indeed the pantheistic view is altogether rather a poetical one, and not capable of being so clearly expounded as the purely atheistic system above referred to. Polytheism, or the worship of the personified attributes of the deity as so many distinct divinities, is still less susceptible of reduction to any philosophical form. There are really at bottom only two systems, viz., theism, and atheism, between which we have to make our election, and to put our belief into practical shape accordingly.

The existence of a God,— that is, a God out of nature,— cannot, as it would seem, be proved by any process of metaphysical enquiry, or logical demonstration. The greatest of moral philosophers, Emanuel Kant, has declared that he could come to no other conclusion. Dr. J. H. Newman has informed us in his *Apologia* that, although the being of a God was as certain to him as the certainty of his own existence, when he tried to put the grounds of that certainty into logical shape, he had found a difficulty in doing so to his own satisfaction. The case is that the certainty of a supernatural God can only be derived from personal faith, or consciousness. ' C'est le sentiment,' said Madame de Staël, ' qui fait pencher la balance.' And Pascal, that great master of both logic and mathematics, expressed the idea still more clearly in this sentence; ' Les verités divines sont au dessus de la nature. Dieu seul peut les mettre dans l'âme.'

This is not the place for theological disquisitions, but it may be useful to point out how little the tenets of the German atheists can be shaken by such works as those which abound in England on the wisdom and goodness of the Creator, and on the ingenious designs manifested in the construction of the universe. The Bridgwater treatises, for example, involve a *petitio principii*. They assume that which is required to be proved, viz., the existence of a supernatural being before matter, time, or space, who out of nothing created all things. The German materialists declare themselves unable to conceive how, when, and where such a being could exist. *Ex nihilo nil fit.* To myself, as a sincere catholic, the prevalence of infidelity in Germany has often suggested painful thoughts, and the progress of what is called rationalistic christianity can only appear in the light of infidelity under another form.

I am continually reminded of a remark of Alexis de Touqueville that we are approaching a time when, in respect of religion, there will be only two classes of persons in civilized Europe,—roman-catholics and infidels. In northern Germany more particularly, the established protestant churches, which are well intended institutions without any logical *basis*, are gradually losing their hold upon the national belief; and no one who knows the real state of men's minds could venture to assign to any of the evangelical communities the prospect of a long-continued existence. The catholic church stands upon other ground. It is the greatest historical authority on record, and claims the prerogative of an unerring judgment to be exercised for the preservation of religion in the world, and for the correction of the errors arising out of the unbounded liberty of human thought. If its influence is unable to supply an antidote to the arguments of the German materialists, the prospects of mankind are gloomy enough; for what other power is capable of relieving society from the mass of evil and corruption which constantly oppresses it, and of raising it up to the level of purity and virtue?

The year 1868 was a quiet one in Germany. The North German confederation was firmly established; and by means of a new commercial union between that body and the South German states, an extended *Zollverein* was founded comprising the whole of Germany, with the exception of the Austrian dominions. Hamburgh and Bremen reserved their free ports, upon payment of an annual equivalent for the customs duties which would otherwise have been collected in them. The French diplomatic agents at Berlin and other German capitals watched with jealousy and suspicion the constitution of the Prussian power. They threw out hints of dissatisfaction prevailing in the newly conquered provinces, of anti-Prussian movements in the south, and of the actual situation not having the character of permanence or durability in the eyes of the great European powers. M. Cintrat, who had been for many years the French minister to the Hanse-towns, was re-called, and replaced by M. Rothan, a man of a more active turn of mind, and who had already, in subordinate situations, acquired much experience in German affairs. The ambassador at Berlin, M. Benedetti, was understood to place great reliance in the judgment and abilities of M. Rothan; and the reports of the latter, although dated from Hamburgh, embraced the condition of other German states, and were doubtless designed to instruct the French government as to what would be the feelings of the German people in the event of a future war with their trans-rhenan neighbours.

It was generally known that the Emperor Louis-Napoleon was dissatisfied at France having derived no actual benefit from the Austrian-Prussian war of 1866,—that the emperor laid great stress upon the Main-line fixed as the boundary between northern and southern Germany by the treaty of peace, —and that he was not likely to consent to any further exten-sion of the territory of the north-German confederation. It was notorious, in short, that France desired a divided Germany, and that the establishment of the Prussian hegemony in so many of the smaller German states was highly dis-tasteful to her. The Prussian statesmen were well aware of having an enemy near them, though they could not tell what incidents might arise to provoke a conflict, or how soon a spark might fall upon the mass of combustible matter which had been gradually accumulating.

The sad results of the French intervention in Mexico, and especially the barbarous murder of the Emperor Maximilian, had made a deep impression in Germany, and the young and chivalrous Austrian prince was considered, whether rightly or wrongly, a martyr to the treacherous policy of the ruler of France. I allude to the circumstance here merely as adding to the disgust in which the imperial government of France was at this time held by the thinking part of the German nation. In the best circles of Hamburgh society the fate of the innocent Maximilian excited universal sympathy. The journals written by him of his travels as Austrian archduke had been published, and read with interest. They make one admire his noble and religious character, and his love for everything good and beautiful. His description of works of art, and of natural scenery, in transatlantic countries, and in Spain and other parts of Europe, are not ineffective, and prove that he possessed a cultivated taste. Of all the members of the imperial family, Maximilian passed for the cleverest, and the most accomplished. He had it in his power to save his life by timely flight, but as a true *chevalier sans tache* he preferred sacrificing it at the age of thirty-five rather than that the slightest stain upon either his personal, or political, honour should be attached to his memory.

During this summer I obtained three months leave of absence (the longest I had ever had since I entered the public service), and went to England. Returning by way of Paris, which I had not seen for many years, I was struck with the new streets and boulevards, which gave a new face to the city, as well as with the increase of luxury, and the enhanced cost of purchasable articles. The international exhibition of the previous year was still much talked about; of war with Germany, neither in the journals, nor, so far as I could learn, in general society, was a syllable breathed. Among the new French books, I met with the charming *Récit d'une sœur*, by Mrs. Augustus Craven, which has deservedly acquired so great a reputation throughout Europe. Albert de la Ferronays, whose life was so short, must have been truly happy in such a wife as his Alexandrina. Born and educated as a protestant, the daughter of Count Daniel Alopeus, Russian envoy in Berlin, she declared that any one of three events would make her a catholic—the death of her husband, that of her mother (a protestant), or the approach of her own dissolution. The first happened, and, as it impended, she threw off all scruples, and had the supreme consolation of communicating with her husband on his death-bed, in the sacrament of the altar. She did not long survive him. Her mother married a second time the Prince Lapuchin, a Russian nobleman, residing in the Ukraine. Mrs. Craven has since published a novel called *Anne Severin*, which has had some success. It concludes with the prayer ' that it may please God to unite in the same faith ' all those who are already united in the same charity, and the ' same hope ! '

When I got back to Hamburgh, I found people occupied with the recent visit of the King of Prussia, who had been spending a couple of days among the citizens, and had said many courteous and agreeable things to them. The object of the visit was, of course, conciliatory, having been occasioned by the entrance of Hamburgh into the sphere of the North German union. In the following November, Madame Jenny Lind-Goldsmid came for some weeks, with her husband, who is a native of the city. I met them at the Swedish minister, M. Sterky's, and found them much anglicized by their long residence in England. Jenny Lind has become a grave person, very philanthropic, and ever ready to contribute, either by money or personal exertions, towards undertakings for improving the condition of the people. She does not affect to have preserved her voice ; but she is still able, at times, to give evidence of the powers of a great *virtuosa*. M. Goldsmid is an intelligent little man, and those who know them best say he has made her a very good husband ; and that her property has not only been taken care of, but improved by his management. I reminded Madame Goldsmid of her first appearance at the Berlin opera-house, in 1844, in Meyerbeer's new opera of ' the camp in Silesia.' ' Yes,' she said, ' that was in the fresh days of my youth ; I had then seen but little of the world.' The opera, which was a successful and popular one, was composed to celebrate the opening of the new house, after the destruction by fire of the old one, built in the reign of Frederick the Great. ' The camp in Silesia ' contains, of course, military scenes ; and in one scene the flute of the great king is heard in an adjoining room, the court-etiquette not permitting royal personages to be represented bodily upon any stage. The Swedish nightingale, in her *début*, charmed and astonished the Berlin world. Lord Westmorland was one of her warmest admirers, which soon gave rise to a rumour that she was engaged to be married to Julian Fane, who was then an *attaché* to his father's legation. The truth was that Mr. Fane had scarcely spoken to her, and that she was betrothed to a Swedish pastor; but circumstances led to that engagement being subsequently broken off.

The new year found Dr. Schleiden installed at Altona, as one of the senators of that town, as well as being its representative in the German parliament. The appointment was indicative of anything but a specifically Prussian feeling among the leading men of Altona, who were, in fact, members of the Augustenburgh family. Dr. Schleiden had already done the town some service by procuring a modification of the payment required by the Prussian government, as the condition of permitting the continuance of the free-port which Altona, like Hamburgh, had hitherto enjoyed. The two towns really adjoin each other, like London and Westminster, so that it became necessary to place the relation of Altona to the *Zollverein* upon the same footing as that of Hamburgh. In both cases the merchants complained of the hardship of having to buy a privilege, which, in conformity with long-established usage, they fancied themselves entitled to exercise gratuitously in the interest of the commerce of all nations.

The house of John Henry Schröder & Co. is one of the greatest mercantile firms in the world. Its chief seat is at Hamburgh, with branches in London, New York, Havannah, and other places. The head of the house, M. John Henry Schröder, who had been the architect of his own fortune, was a hale and hearty octogenarian, possessed of great wealth, and generally respected. He celebrated about this time the fifty years' jubilee of his Hamburgh citizenship, and received the congratulations of the principal inhabitants. The Senate voted him a gold medal, and presented it to him with a formal address. The King of Prussia, having been informed of the approaching jubilee, resolved to elevate M. Schröder to the rank of a baron, and the patent of nobility duly reached him on the day of the festival. To many of his friends, it was a matter of surprise that M. Schröder should have condescended to accept such a title; he stood so high in the commercial world, and his property was so considerable, that such a title could add nothing to his position in public estimation; and he seemed rather to let himself down by taking a title which is very widely distributed in Germany, and is held by a great many *nobodies*, who have done nothing for their country, and are altogether useless, except to themselves. This was believed to be M. Schröder's own feeling,—the more so as he had no particular attachment to Prussia, but was rather opposed to the ambitious policy of the Prussian cabinet. He excused himself, however, on account of the wishes of his sons, and became a Prussian baron, though he did not at all change his manner of life, but continued to appear in his counting-house, and to pay the same attention to business as before he was ennobled.

The Prince and Princess of Wales spent a day at Hamburgh on their return from a visit of some weeks to Copenhagen. I met their royal highnesses at Lübeck, and accompanied them to Hamburgh, where apartments had been taken for them at the Victoria Hotel. I had the honour of joining the royal dinner party in the evening, which consisted of the princess's uncles and aunts, viz. Duke Charles of Holstein-Glücksburgh, and his Duchess (daughter of Frederick VI), Prince Julius, and the Princess Louisa, abbess of Itzehoe, besides the gentlemen and ladies of the royal suite. The Prince of Wales seemed well informed of all that was going on in Germany, and constantly received telegrams containing information. His sympathies were, not unnaturally, Danish; whilst those of the Glücksburgh family were generally on the German side of the question. The Prince and Princess of Wales went on the next day to Berlin, *en route* for Egypt. The Honble Mrs. Grey, who was in attendance on the Princess, published an agreeable narrative of the tour, which I have since read with interest.

The death of the senator, Dr. Alfred Rücker, formerly Hanseatic minister-resident in London, at an early age, was a serious loss to Hamburgh. Having been for some weeks in the south of France for the recovery of his health, he was on his way back to his native city, and died suddenly in a railway carriage of an affection of the heart. Dr. Rücker had paid great attention to foreign affairs, was the pupil and friend of the Syndic Merck, and, if his life had been spared, would probably have succeeded the syndic in the foreign department of the Hamburgh government. Dr. Rücker's habits of industry, and his calm and equable temper, fitted him peculiarly for the diplomatic career, but he preferred the ordinary work of a senator at home. He was in affluent circumstances, and was entitled to expect a very large reversionary property, under the will of his uncle, the late Senator Jenisch. Everything favoured the supposition that he would become a leading man, in both the business and the society of Hamburgh, when his health unhappily began to break down. His young and lively widow, the daughter of M. d'Araujo, Brazilian envoy at Paris, survived him scarcely two years, and died at Rome. When M. and Mme. Rücker resided officially in London, they were favourites, as I have heard, at our court, and had conciliated the friendship of many distinguished persons in London society.

Until this summer I had not seen the British possession of Heligoland, although the governor, Colonel Maxse, who was now and then at Hamburgh, had frequently invited me to pay him a visit. The island has been called a German Margate anchored out at sea; and indeed it is a favourite bathing-place of the citizens of Hamburgh and Bremen, as well as of some persons of a higher class from the interior of Germany. After a voyage of about six hours, the steamer anchored under the red-sandstone cliffs of the island, which rising out of the blue sea had a striking and picturesque appearance. According to the verse of the poet the red border, white sand, and green fields of this outlier of the north-Frisian islands, correspond with the national colours of the duchy of Schleswig, to which it geographically belongs.

> Roth ist der Rand,
> Weiss ist der Sand,
> Grün ist das Land,—
> Die sind die Farben von Heiligeland!

On landing I found much more life and bustle in the lower town than I was prepared to expect; a great many shops, and a crowd of boatmen and fishermen standing together in the street like a flock of sea-gulls. A long flight of stairs leads to the upper town where the governor resides, and where the church, the school, the battery, and the light-house stand. At the government house a liberal and elegant hospitality was exercised by Colonel Maxse and his accomplished wife. In their society I met Prince Edward of Saxe-Weimar, M. Dingelstadt, imperial theatre-intendant at Vienna, Count Hartig, late Austrian envoy at Hesse-Cassel, and others whose conversation on literature and politics was full of interest. A German theatre, generously supported by the governor, was to be opened in a day or two. One evening we rowed round the island with a so-called corso-party of boats. The cliffs and grottoes were illuminated with torches, and the red-sandstone lighted up had a beautiful effect. There were also fireworks and bengal-lights, to the great delight of the German spectators, who are perfect children in regard to such exhibitions.

The sand-island on which the bathing establishment is placed is distant an English mile and a half from the main island, and the bathers are conveyed across the channel in boats. The two islands are said to have been separated by a strong north-west wind in the year 1720. The sand-island is in fact little more than a *Watte*, and is liable to be swamped any day by a violent storm. In the main island some parts of the red-sandstone cliffs have been gradually broken off, and the pillars and grottoes give evidence of the soil having crumbled away to some extent, and fallen into the sea. But this process of decay goes on very gradually, and there is no reason to believe that any immediate danger threatens the stability of the red-sandstone formations, which rise to the average height of two hundred and twenty feet above the surrounding sea.

The actual Heligoland is said to be the remnant of a much larger island which existed in former times. In Caspar Danckwerth's geography, already quoted, are to be found maps of its supposed extent in the year 800, 1300, and 1649 respectively, on which the names of various churches and villages are particularly marked. The subject has since been discussed by M. von der Decken in his description of the island, published in 1826,[1] and some other authorities in proof of its assumed ancient dimensions have been cited by him; but the question is involved in much obscurity, and Dr. Lappenberg, who likewise investigated it,[2] arrived at the conclusion that the main island was never much larger than it is at present.

The inhabitants are Frisians of the same race as the people of Sylt and Föhr, and the other islands composing the north-Frisian group on the west coast of Schleswig before adverted to. They are a part of the German nation, and their language differs little from that spoken in the duchies, or elsewhere in the northern parts of Germany. The normal population of Heligoland is about two thousand five hundred souls. They are lutherans, and have their church and school, the latter containing some two hundred and fifty children, or a tenth of the population. There are no very rich people among them. A man worth 100,000 marks courant, or £6000 sterling, is

[1] 'Untersuchungen über die Insel Helgoland oder Heiligeland, und ihre Bewohner,' von F. von der Decken. Hannover, 1826.
[2] 'Ueber den ehemaligen Umfang und die Geschichte Helgolands.' Hamburg, 1831.

considered wealthy according to the local scale. The bathing season is of course the harvest time for the letting of lodgings, and the employment of labour. If the fashion should change, and deprive the Heligolanders of that resource, they would have to depend upon fishing and piloting, which would yield but a scanty subsistence to the present population.

The ancient constitution of the island, founded upon charters granted and confirmed respectively by its former sovereigns, the Dukes of Schleswig-Holstein and the Kings of Denmark, gave to the Heligolanders the management of their own communal affairs, and provided that they should not be taxed without their own consent. Certain officers, called *Rathsherrn, Quartiersleute,* and *Aelteste,* had the disposal and control of the revenue and expenditure, in the manner prescribed by the established laws. When the island was seized by Great Britain during the war of 1807, and formally ceded by the Danish governor, the enjoyment of their existing rights and privileges was guaranteed to the inhabitants on the part of the British government, and they seem to have continued to exercise the same for a considerable period of time afterwards. Indeed, even without such a guarantee, the British crown was bound by the rules of international law to maintain the fundamental laws of the ceded possession as it found them; for the cession of the sovereignty could not transfer more power over the subjects than was possessed by the former ruler, the King of Denmark. However, a few years ago our colonial department deemed it expedient to advise the crown to grant to this little nest of fishermen and publicans a representative constitution, which was published accordingly on the 7th of January, 1864. The inhabitants remonstrated against the proceeding, and demanded of the British government the restoration of their ancient rights. After a trial of about four years, the new colonial legislature proved unmanageable; it refused to vote the requisite taxes, and the constitutional machine came to a stand-still. It was therefore abolished by an order in council dated the 29th of February 1868, and the British crown assumed to itself the sole legislative and executive power over the island and its inhabitants. The governor became, in consequence, the absolute ruler, subject to the instructions issued to him by the colonial-office. Whether the crown has acted according to strictly legal principles, in thus superseding the ancient rights of the islanders, is a question not entirely free from doubt; the answer depends upon a careful historical investigation of the former legal *status*, and I do not know whether it has ever been made.

This remark is by no means intended to imply that the paternal rule of Governor Maxse has not been a good one, or that he has not done much for the benefit of the islanders, and for the reform of some disgraceful abuses which had tended to give them a bad name in the civilised world. The old strand-laws have been abolished, which sanctioned a system of licensed plunder of the cargoes of wrecked vessels not tolerated on any part of the German coasts. The public gaming-tables have been suppressed after the termination of their existing contracts, which expire with the year 1871. The revenue of the island has been augmented by a property-tax, and by customs duties on spirits, wine, and beer ; and more than half of the public debt has been paid off, although the operation of clearing off incumbrances may probably be interfered with by the cessation of the revenue accruing to the government from the play-tables. Education has been made compulsory, and the school is conducted in a manner suitable to the real wants of the population. The lutheran church is protected, and no attempt is ever made to anglicanize the children, or anyone else. A theatre is maintained in the summer season, and everything done to make the island an attractive sojourn to visitors from the continent. In fact, I saw everywhere signs of Governor Maxse's active exertions for the improvement of the place, and he has, undeniably, been an excellent administrator. Order is maintained by a British coastguard force of five men, whose chief acts as a police-magistrate, and by the occasional inspection of a ship of war. The islanders declare this police-force to be unnecessary, as there is scarcely an instance of a crime committed in the course of the year, and thefts and other offences against property are entirely unknown.

The Heligolanders complain that England will neither let them govern themselves, nor do anything on her part to help them on. A pier, or breakwater, for example, is an urgent necessity for the protection of shipping, and a telegraphic communication between the island and both England and Germany is much to be desired ; yet the mother-country has hitherto been indifferent to both of those wants, and lets the islanders jog on, without any hope of a material amelioration of their actual condition. There is a national feeling in Germany for acquiring, if possible, the possession of this Frisian fragment of the fatherland, which would at all events be useful as a naval station, in the event of Germany being again at war with France, or with any other power. The time will probably come when a negotiation with England will be opened by Prussia or the German confederation, for the acquisition of the island against a fair equivalent, and we shall then have to consider whether the possession of this little bit of Germany has any, and what, permanent value to British interests. The only case in which I can imagine such a possession to be of importance to us, is that of our being at war with Germany herself; and such a contingency is surely too absurd to be seriously entertained by any reflecting man. No one who knows anything of German affairs can imagine the possibility of the statesmen of that country provoking a war with Great Britain; and, if it should ever come, the fault and the responsibility will be exclusively our own. We may safely venture to give up Heligoland to Prussia, or the Germanic body, if the islanders desire it; though, at present, there is no evidence at all that they wish to change masters. I believe them to be indifferent under which king they live, provided their ruler will lay out some money on them, and not tax them too heavily. They do not much like the colonial-office; but they do not know to what ills they might fly if they should ever be placed at the tender mercies of the Prussian bureaucracy.

With respect to the allegation that if we were to part with Heligoland at all it should be to Denmark, as the power from which we wrested it in war, it would seem scarcely necessary to explain that the island belonged to the duchy of Schleswig, in the same way as Sylt, or Föhr, or the rest of the north-Frisian group, and that it was in his capacity of Duke of Schleswig that the Danish King was its sovereign, up to its cession in 1807. It follows that Prussia, having succeeded by conquest, and the consent of Austria, to the entire duchy of Schleswig, is now the only power whose application could be listened to, if she should ask for the restoration to her, or to the confederation, of this detached remnant of German territory.

We spent the remainder of the summer at Düsternbrock near Kiel, the Duke of Augustenburgh having kindly permitted me to occupy his villa, for which he had no longer occasion. The Prussian fleet lay in our sight, consisting of three large iron-clad war steamers, besides gun-boats, and several old sailing ships, Kiel being now the principal station of the German navy[1]. The new steam frigate, 'König Wilhelm,' had cost the government £600,000, including the guns, which were furnished by Krupp's well-known factory at Essen in Westphalia. The beautiful situation of Düsternbrock, already

---

[1] In the German navy are now 7 iron-clad steamers, with 77 guns and 4800 horse-power.

noticed, attracts many summer visitors, but the best society is to be found among the professors of the neighbouring university of Kiel. Professor Forchhammer combines social talents, with extensive historical and philological learning. His work on ancient Troy has long been well known and appreciated by antiquarian scholars. He was preparing for the general meeting of German philologers, to be held this year at Kiel, and over which he had been invited to preside. The professor, like most of his colleagues, was a good patriot, and had done a good deal in former years for the Schleswig-Holstein cause; he was employed for some months in England, in 1864, on business connected with the proceedings of the London conference. I talked much with him of the actual state of public opinion in Holstein, and he considered it was still anti-Prussian, as proved by the choice of the deputies made at the last election of the German parliament. He had himself been elected deputy for the Pinneberg district in the Prussian diet. He thought that things were settling down, and there would be no factious opposition to the Prussian administration, for people were sufficiently disposed to submit to inevitable necessity. In some things, however, the Prussians had shewn little respect for the feelings of the inhabitants. It would have been easy, for instance, to fix the naval arsenal on the other side of Kiel, instead of disturbing the tranquillity of the Düsternbrock villas, and of the bathing establishment, by the noise and concourse of the workmen, and of the crews of the ships of war. A large naval store-house, erected immediately in front of the duke's villa, almost deprived it of a view of the sea. I conversed also on these subjects with professor Rathjen, the director of the university library, and found that he entirely concurred with professor Forchhammer's views. The librarian is a great authority on the history and literature of the duchies, and has likewise worked hard in his time for their liberation. Another distinguished Schleswig-Holsteiner was the state councillor Francke, who, after many years of banishment, had returned to his native land, and was then residing at Düsternbrock, but was in ill health, and died the following year. Francke, who was an able administrator, had been in the service of the Duke of Saxe-Coburgh, and would doubtless have been Duke Frederic's prime minister, if the latter had had the good fortune to establish *de facto* his right to the ducal crown.

The Grand-duke of Oldenburgh possesses a large *enclave*, situated locally within the duchy of Holstein, and resides for a part of the year at his castle of Eutin, standing on a lake,

and surrounded with spacious gardens. The town of Eutin
was the abode of Voss, the best German translator of Homer,
whose work has the reputation of being more *homeric* than
that of Pope, or any other modern translator. It was likewise the birth-place of the great composer, Karl Maria von
Weber. There are several large lakes in this part of Holstein,
particularly that surrounding the castle and town of Plön.
At Preetz there is an old secularized convent, to which the
lands in the district, called the Probstei, continue to belong.
The produce of the district is exported from the little port of
Laboe, lying near the entrance of the bay of Kiel. During
my excursions in these parts I heard sad complaints of the
foot and mouth disease, from which the cattle were then
grievously suffering; the loss to the dairy farms was very
serious. Holstein is a great grazing country, and the farms
(*Meiereien*) are mostly on a large scale, and well kept. The
landed proprietors, who have considerable estates, are able to
divide their properties, and let off their farms to responsible
tenants, pretty much as in England. Some few farm their
own estates; and there are also peasantry, or small holders, in
certain districts; but upon the whole, the position of the
landed aristocracy, and its relations to the cultivators of the
soil, in Schleswig and Holstein, very nearly resemble those
existing in Great Britain.

The horticultural exhibition held this autumn at Hamburgh
was supplied with choice flowers and fruit from Germany, and
other European countries, and attracted strangers from all
parts. The British government deemed it of sufficient
importance to send out a commissioner, in the person of
Mr. Berkeley, a distinguished botanist, and referee of the
London horticultural society. A silver cup given by our
gracious Queen as a prize for the best grapes, was won by a
Liverpool gardener. The undertaking more than repaid its
expenses, and its success was in a great degree owing to the
artistical beauty of the garden itself, which was tastefully
laid out on an unequal soil on the bank of the Elbe, near the
city and the port. The Syndic Merck, who presided over the
exhibition, had exerted himself very much in its formation,
and hospitably entertained the foreign commissioners, and
others concerned, at his villa at Blankenese. The wits on
the Hamburgh exchange observed that, since the political
changes of 1866, the syndic had lost many of his diplomatic
customers, and had found it advisable to strike into a new line
of business.

After the retirement of Dr. Schleiden from the Hanseatic mission in London, in 1866, it was filled for about two years by Dr. Frederic Geffchen, a very able man, who had been some time minister-resident at Berlin, and, among other services, had been instrumental in negotiating a treaty of commerce and navigation between the Hanse-towns and France. But the Hanseatic burgherships began to grudge the expense of a standing mission, and the result was that Dr. Geffchen was recalled, and is now employed in the home service of his native city, being one of the syndics of the Hamburgh senate. The talents of Dr. Geffchen are such as to make him a valuable servant of any government. He has a peculiar power of influencing the press, and the many articles contributed by him to the *Hamburger Correspondent* have proved his statesmanlike qualities, and his accurate knowledge of most political questions of the day.

The cessation of the Hanseatic mission in London, and the desire manifested by the House of Commons for further retrenchments in diplomatic expenditure, may have suggested to the foreign-office the expediency of suppressing the British mission to the Hanse-towns, which had existed in one shape or another for two or three centuries, and had at times shewn itself to be of great value to British interests. Early in the year 1870 I received a private intimation that the suppression was intended, and soon after an official notification to prepare for my recall. Lord Clarendon's despatch to me, dated 1st of February, ran to this effect :

'The arrangement under which the Hanseatic states have taken their place among the members of the North-German confederation, renders it unnecessary to retain the post of minister-resident and consul-general at Hamburgh, and Her Majesty's government have therefore decided that on the 1st of July next that appointment shall cease, and British interests at Hamburgh be confided to Her Majesty's consul.'
'In now instructing you to make this arrangement known to the governments of the Hanse-towns, I have the pleasure to convey to you Her Majesty's approval of the manner in which you have discharged the duties entrusted to you ; and I must at the same time state that Her Majesty's government regret the necessity which will thus deprive the public of the benefit of your services.'

As this communication was not accompanied by the offer of any other official employment, I had of course no other alternative than to retire on a pension. The government of Hamburgh, as well as those of the two other Hanse-towns, saw the approaching termination of their diplomatic relations to Great Britain with extreme regret, but as they had taken the initiative in the matter, it was out of their power to make any well-founded remonstrance against the step in contemplation by the foreign office. They therefore contented themselves with expressions of regret towards myself, and the leading citizens of Hamburgh who had welcomed me on my arrival now vied with each other in hospitable demonstrations on the occasion of my intended departure. At the farewell dinner to which Syndic Merck had the kindness to invite me at Blank- enese, I could not but be sensible how much I was honoured by the friendship of the excellent men who surrounded me, and how many happy days I had enjoyed during the ten years of my residence among them. I did not exactly wish to close my life at Hamburgh, but I felt deeply grateful for the testimonies of respect and goodwill which had been so constantly and liberally bestowed upon me by the Hamburgh citizens.

The last token of esteem which I received previous to my return home was that of a gold medal voted to me by the Senate in token of the approval of my public conduct as Her Majesty's representative. Having communicated this pro- ceeding to the secretary of state for foreign affairs, and solicited leave to accept the medal, I received from Lord Granville the following official answer:

> *Foreign-Office,* July 12, 1870.
>
> ' Sir,
>
> ' I have received your despatch of the 1st instant, marked " separate," enclosing a copy of a letter addressed to you by Syndic Merck on the occasion of your recall, stating that the Senate of Hamburgh have voted to you an honorary gold medal in testimony of the respect entertained for you by that body, and by the citizens of Hamburgh generally.
>
> 'Having laid your despatch before the Queen I have received Her Majesty's commands to express her satisfaction at your receiving this mark of the esteem of the government and people of Hamburgh, and to convey to you her permission to accept the medal.
>
> ' I am, with great truth and regard, &c.,
>
> ' GRANVILLE.
>
> 'To JOHN WARD, ESQ., C.B.'

I had scarcely been a week in England before general alarm
was excited by the warlike declarations of the French ministers against Prussia, and it soon became evident that the
incident of the candidature of a prince of Hohenzollern for the
Spanish throne was about to kindle a war between France and
Germany. That there were many persons in Germany who
considered such a war inevitable I have already stated; but
no one expected it was coming so soon, and even Count Bismarck must have been startled by the rapidity with which the
eventful crisis was hurried on. After the King had dismissed
the French ambassador at Ems, his majesty is said to have
turned to his prime minister, and asked 'Well, what is now
to be done?' Count Bismarck answered 'We play again at
six-and-sixty' (*Wir spielen wieder sechs und sechzig*), alluding
to a game at cards of that name, and meaning that the campaign of 1866 was then to be repeated. M. Rothan, the
French minister at Hamburgh, was certainly not one of those
who anticipated so early a war, for he had recently taken a
house and brought his furniture and pictures from Paris at a
heavy expense. The French government had not deemed the
formation of the North-German confederation a sufficient
reason for withdrawing its diplomatic representative from the
Hanse-towns; and the ministers of Russia, of Sweden, and of
Prussia herself, still continued to reside at Hamburgh. With
the exception of the Austrian envoy, Count Guido Thun,
I was the only member of the diplomatic body who had been
recalled from Hamburgh in consequence of the altered political situation.

The early and brilliant success of the Prussian arms was
scarcely believed in at the opening of the war. It was supposed that the French might win a battle or two in the outset,
but of the final result of the campaign neither the statesmen
nor the people of Germany were for a moment doubtful. The
nation was resolved to put forth its strength, and to shrink
from no sacrifices for the deliverance of the fatherland from
this new and wanton aggression by its ancient enemy. The
war entailed great sufferings upon Germany,—sufferings
which no amount of pecuniary indemnity could entirely heal.
In respect of money it was from the beginning freely contributed by all those who had anything to give. The subscrip-
tions of the Hamburgh merchants, for instance, to the voluntary
loan solicited by the central government were on a generous
and even magnificent scale. The firm of John Henry
Schröder & Co. alone subscribed 500,000 marks courant, or
about £60,000 sterling, nor was there one of the old-

established houses which did not likewise subscribe liberally according to its means.

This is not the place for discussing the merits of the war itself, or for enquiring whether it might not have been prevented by a strong word spoken in due season to France by the neutral powers? So far as England was concerned the principle of neutrality was of course the only right one to follow; but an impression has been left on the German mind that British neutrality was not altogether real, and that it was made to work for the benefit of the French, who were permitted to receive from us a supply of arms, cartridges, and coals, which ought to have been declared contraband of war. It certainly does appear that the rules of international law prohibit a neutral state from furnishing a belligerent with arms and ammunition to be made use of against an enemy in the cause of a war which is being actually waged; nor is there any tangible distinction between the case of the exportation of arms, and that of the arming or equipping vessels, or the enlisting soldiers, within the neutral territory. The principles recently agreed upon as the basis of settling our disputes with the United States of America relative to the *Alabama* and other transactions are equally applicable to cases of the supply of arms, and munitions of war. The law of nations on the subject seems too clear to admit of a doubt. Vattel has told us that the impartiality which a neutral nation is bound to observe between belligerent parties in time of war, consists of two points, viz. ‘First. To give no assistance where there is no previous stipulation to give it; nor voluntarily to furnish troops, arms, ammunition, or anything of direct use in war. I say, to give no assistance; not to give assistance equally, for it would be absurd that a state should assist two enemies at the same time. And besides it would be impossible to do it with equality; the same things, the same number of troops, the same quantity of arms, of munitions, &c., furnished in different circumstances form no longer equivalent succours. Secondly. In whatever does not relate to the war, a neutral nation will not refuse to one of the parties by reason of his present quarrel that which it grants to the other. . . . . If it were to refuse anything to one of the parties merely because he makes war upon the other, and in order to favour the latter, that would be to maintain no longer a strict neutrality[1].’

---

[1] Vattel, ‘Droit des Gens.’ Paris, 1835. Liv. iii. ch. 7, § 104. (Conduite que doit tenir un peuple neutre).

If Vattel is right, it follows that we were not justifiable in supplying France with arms or ammunition, merely because we furnished, or were ready to furnish them, to Prussia also. It should also be observed that the defects of its municipal laws can never form a sufficient excuse for a state's non-compliance with its international duties towards other powers. The difficulties which the British government may have had in prohibiting the equipment of armed cruisers, like the *Alabama*, or in preventing the supply of guns to the French army by the Birmingham manufacturers, did not, according to the law of nations, constitute any valid reason for Great Britain having thus succoured one of the belligerent parties who were respectively engaged in an actual war.

Whilst Paris was still under siege, and the conclusion of the war was yet uncertain, a most important event for Germany occurred, viz. the completion of the empire, which took place on the 31st of December, 1870, by the accession of the South-German states to the North-German confederation. King William became in consequence German Emperor, and the Prussian hegemony was extended over the lands south of the Maine, and comprised a population of forty-one millions of souls including Alsace and Lorraine, being the entire fatherland, with the exception of the German provinces of the Austrian empire. I have already explained the original constitution of the North-German confederation, which came into operation on the 1st of July, 1867, and whose legislature was composed of a federal council of forty-three members, and an imperial parliament of two hundred and ninety-seven deputies. The victorious progress of the Prussian King had determined the waverers in the south to accede to the union. First came Baden and the southern portion of Hesse-Darmstadt, by a convention signed on the 15th of November, 1870. The treaty with Bavaria was concluded on the 23rd, and that with Würtemberg on the 25th of the same month, and they severally took effect at the close of the year, just before the assumption of the imperial crown by the King of Prussia.

Baden and Hesse adopted the federal constitution with very few alterations. It was however stipulated that the president should in no case declare war without the consent of the federal council, and that any changes in the constitution should require a majority in the council of three-fourths instead of two-thirds. The number of votes in the council was increased from forty-three to forty-eight, and the number of deputies in the parliament from two hundred and ninety-seven to three hundred and seventeen. Baden reserved to herself the taxes to be raised on brandy and beer.

By the treaty with Würtemberg the votes in the council were raised to fifty-two, and the deputies in the parliament increased to the number of three hundred and thirty-four. Würtemberg reserved the taxes on brandy and beer, and also the regulation of her own posts and telegraphs. The military relations of Würtemberg to the confederation were settled by a separate convention bearing the same date, in such a way that the Würtemberg army was to form a compact corps as a part of the federal army, and under the supreme direction of the president of the confederation.

The accession of Bavaria was not so easily effected. By the treaty with that state the votes in the federal council were finally raised to the number of fifty-eight, and the deputies in the parliament to the number of three hundred and eighty-two. In submitting to the federal laws respecting changes of residence (*Freizügigkeit*), the Bavarian government reserved to itself the right of separate legislation in matters of domicile and settlement (*Heimaths- und Niederlassungsrecht*), of the enjoyment of political rights and of marriage, and of regulating the laws of assurance and mortgage as affecting landed property. It further reserved the administration of its own railways, posts, and telegraphs, subject to the control of the confederation in so far as the general interests might be concerned, and to the normal principles which the confederation might prescribe for railways to be used in the federal defences. A committee of the federal council was to be appointed for foreign affairs, consisting of Bavaria, Saxony, and Würtemberg, with Bavaria as president. At those foreign courts where there were Bavarian envoys, they were to represent the federal body in case of the absence of the federal envoy; and at the courts where Bavaria might keep envoys, the federal envoy should not be charged with affairs exclusively Bavarian. In the absence of Prussia, Bavaria was to have the presidency in the federal council. The taxation of Bavarian brandy and beer was reserved to her. The costs of the Bavarian army were to be borne by that state as a corps belonging to the federal army, and such army-corps to be regulated in time of peace by the Bavarian government. The Bavarian fortresses were to continue her own, subject however to federal supervision. Lastly came the important stipulation that in the federal council fourteen adverse votes should suffice for the rejecting of any measure affecting the constitution, so that the provision previously agreed to with Baden and Hesse for a majority of three-fourths of the council fell to the ground, and it has become in the power of Bavaria, in conjunction with the other southern states, to defeat any amendment whatever which may in future be proposed of the federal constitution.

In diplomatic intercourse it may thus happen that the Bavarian envoy may be called upon to represent the German Emperor, but this is a matter of no moment to foreign courts. It will also be remembered that by the terms of the constitution established on the 1st of July, 1867, no German state was deprived of the right of sending and receiving separate diplomatic agents, nor have the southern states lost that right in consequence of their accession to the confederation by the conventions of November above cited. Upon the whole, Bavaria has driven a hard bargain with the northern states, and it has excited some surprise that Prince Bismarck should have deemed it necessary to concede to her so many exceptions from the general principles of the federal legislature.

How far it is worth while for Great Britain, under existing circumstances, to maintain diplomatic relations with any of the petty states of Germany is a question upon which a difference of opinion appears to prevail in official and parliamentary circles. The foreign-office has just suppressed the missions at Stuttgart and Munich, and has established *chargés d'affaires* at those capitals in addition to the *chargés d'affaires* already resident at Dresden, Darmstadt, and Coburgh, on the ground that these small states possess a certain influence with the federal government, and that valuable information is often to be picked up in the streets of the little capitals of Germany. Now I will not dispute that the services of an intelligent and judicious agent may be useful to his government anywhere, even at Coburgh; but I think it a mistaken policy to accredit diplomatic agents at all to states which are politically effete, having surrendered their independent sovereignty into the hands of a superior power. The Kings of Saxony, Bavaria, and Würtemberg have lost the right of deciding upon peace or war, or upon any question of foreign policy,—they have no longer the chief command of their own armies,—and, as they are members of the *Zollverein*, they are unable to legislate separately in matters of commerce, or customs-duties. They are, in fact, pretty much in the situation of a dethroned Indian *rajah*, living in their ancient palaces, with a certain external splendour, but non-entities as regards either the great interests of their fatherland, or its relations to foreign powers.   If the necessities of British subjects, or of British trade, require our government to keep agents of its own in the dominions of these mediatized sovereigns, such agents should clearly not be above the rank of consuls.   It is not our business to gratify the vanity of effete kings and grand dukes by pretending to cultivate their political friendship and alliance ' Le jeu ne vaut pas la chandelle.'   A good consul is perfectly able to protect British commerce, and to collect information of passing events in any subordinate town in Germany.   The real diplomatic business must always be transacted at Berlin, and our embassy in the Prussian capital cannot be made too efficient in its *personnel,* or in the means placed at the ambassador's disposal.   Here, indeed, frugality would be ill-placed ; for it is of real importance to the British nation to be worthily represented at the seat of the federal government, and to stand on a footing of friendship and confidence with the German empire.

I was myself for some years a member of the diplomatic body, and I have had intercourse with many diplomatic persons, both British and foreign, in all ranks of the service. My experience has not tended to raise my estimation of the profession in general.   There is a great deal of smooth talk about trifles, much running about to hear what is passing and to hunt up secrets, and many long-winded despatches without any point.   The activity of the smaller diplomatists, called the *mouches,* is amusing enough.   They cater for the ambassadors and envoys of the greater powers, and are rewarded by their patronage and invitations.   But all this bustle usually comes to nothing.   What is wanted is more reflection and political sagacity.   It is easy enough to talk and write, but to think well is another matter, and without much thought it is not possible to hazard a prediction of coming events.   Prince Bismarck, it would seem, is by no means disposed to appreciate the diplomatic profession beyond its worth.   In a letter to a friend, dated from Frankfort in 1851, that great statesman is made by his biographer to say [1] :—

' Frankfort is wretchedly wearisome.   Even the coolness of fellow countrymen and party associates I had in Berlin is an intimate connection compared with the relations one makes here, being in fact nothing more than mutually suspicious *espionnage.*   As if one had anything to detect or to conceal !

[1] See Hesekiel's Life of Bismarck (translated by Mackenzie), p. 211.

The people here wrong themselves about the merest trifles ; and these diplomatists with their important nothings already appear more ridiculous to me even than a deputy of the second chamber in his full-blown dignity. Unless outward events take place,—and those we clever members of the Germanic diet can neither guide nor predetermine,—I now know accurately what we shall have done in one, two, or five years, and could bring it about in twenty-four hours if the others would for a single day be reasonable and truthful. I am making enormous progress in the art of saying nothing in a great many words. I write reports of many sheets which read as tersely and roundly as leading articles ; and if Manteuffel can say what there is in them after having read them, he does more than I can. Each of us pretends to believe of his neighbour that he is full of thoughts and plans, if he would only tell ; and at the same time we none of us know an atom more of what is going to happen to Germany than of the next year's snow. Nobody, not even the most malicious sceptic of a democrat, believes what quackery and self-importance there is in this diplomatizing.'

If such were the occupations of the diplomatic body at Frankfort, where, during the existence of the Germanic diet, there was really some little business to be done, it may be inferred what is the value of their actual labours at the residences of the petty German princes, where there is not, nor ever can be, any pretence of negotiations, or of any business beyond matters of compliment, or court ceremonial. Even the British mission to the Hanse-towns had a peculiar importance in a commercial point of view ; but as this has been abolished on account of its political insignificance, I conceive that the same principle ought to be rigorously applied to every one of the German states which has merged its sovereignty in that of the new Germanic confederation.

The envoys of Great Britain in foreign states are justly accounted honourable and generous-minded men. They are gentlemen in the best sense of the word. Here and there an experienced statesman is to be found among them. But, upon the whole, British diplomacy has not been successful in gaining the confidence of foreign governments. For a number of years past England has almost withdrawn herself from continental affairs, and the notion, whether right or wrong, prevails, that we are indifferent to the fate of foreign nations, except in so far as our commercial interests are involved in their well-

being. This is the reason why important political secrets are
withheld from the knowledge of the British representatives
abroad. It explains why the inimical relations between
Prussia and France which led to the late war were not fully
communicated to our ambassador at Berlin, and why he was
left in ignorance of the dangerous overtures which had been
made to Prince Bismarck on the part of the ruler of France
for their mutual aggrandizement at the expense of independent states. If the British cabinet had been properly fore-
warned of the gravity of the situation, it might possibly have
found the means of admonishing the French Emperor against
beginning the fatal enterprise which led to his downfall. At
the best, the fact that the governments of the neutral powers
were completely taken by surprise at the breaking out of the
war reflects no great credit upon the political sagacity of the
diplomatic agents maintained by those powers at the French
and Prussian courts. It was once suggested by Archbishop
Whately that a prophecy-office should be established by the
crown ; that candidates for employment should be invited to
deposit prophecies of events to happen at periods to be specified by them, and that those whose predictions had been the
most exactly fulfilled should be placed in high posts in the
state service. Tried by such a test, I fear there are not many
members of our diplomatic body who would be entitled to
claim advancement, however striking may be their literary
accomplishments, or their qualifications in a social point of
view.

It is the earnest desire of the national liberal party in Germany, that the small courts should be placed on the footing
determined by the Frankfort constitution of 1849, which pre-
cludes them from sending, or receiving, diplomatic agents.
Prince Bismarck has hitherto been indifferent about the
matter, or has been reluctant to act precipitately in it against
the feelings of the petty princes. But the French intrigues
in the secondary states have already proved prejudicial to the
national interests, and the working of the agents of Russia is
not likely to hasten the accomplishment of German unity.
The probability, therefore, is that the German parliament will
not be disposed to tolerate much longer the existing state of
things, and will insist that the foreign affairs of the nation
shall belong exclusively to the federal administration. As
regards the British government, its true policy in this, and in
all questions affecting Germany, appears to me to be to sympathize with the true interests of that great and intelligent

people, and to do what in it lies to promote the constitutional freedom and national unity of the large portion of the Teutonic race which has at last been able to re-establish itself as the German empire. The Germans are eminently worthy of political liberty, and the more of it they come to enjoy, the more they will be disposed to cultivate the friendship and alliance of their free and sturdy neighbours of the British isles.